NEW DIRECTIONS BOOKS

Fall 2010

ROBERTO BOLAÑO

The Insufferable Gaucho. Tr. by Andrews. Five stories and two essays. "Electrifying" —*Time.* "A spellbinder" —*Newsweek.* $22.95 cloth

SIR THOMAS BROWNE

Urn Burial. Intro. by W. G. Sebald. One of the most influential essays in Western literature. "I love him" —Borges. *An ND Pearl.* $9.95 pbk.

JENNY ERPENBECK

Visitation. Tr. by Bernofsky. A house outside Berlin lies at the heart of this darkly sensual, elegiac novel. "Wonderful" —*Playboy.* $14.95 pbk. orig.

QURRATULAIN HYDER

Fireflies in the Mist. Novel. A Bangladeshi love story. Hyder is one of the "must reads" of Indian literature (Salman Rushdie). $15.95 pbk. orig.

ABDELFATTAH KILITO

The Clash of Images. Tr. by Creswell. Winner of a PEN Trans. Fund Award. Stories. "A marvelous book" —Elias Khoury. $12.95 pbk. orig.

JAVIER MARÍAS

While the Women Are Sleeping. Tr. by Jull Costa. Short stories by "one of the most original writers at work today" (Wyatt Mason). $21.95 cloth

EZRA POUND

(Celebrating Ezra Pound's 125th Birthday)

ABC of Reading. New intro. by Michael Dirda. "Incredibly alive and intelligent and first-rate" —*N. Y. Times.* $14.95 pbk. **New Selected Poems and Translations.** Ed. and annotated by Richard Sieburth. Greatly expanded and annotated. Indispensable. $15.95 pbk.

AHARON SHABTAI

War & Love, Love & War: New and Selected Poems. Tr. by Cole. "Shabtai ha the red coal on his tongue" —*N.Y. Times.* $15.95 pbk. orig.

ROSMARIE WALDROP

Driven to Abstraction. New work. "One of the leading voices in contemporary American poetry" —*Boston Review.* $14.95 pbk. orig.

COMING UP IN THE SPRING

Conjunctions:56
TERRA INCOGNITA:
THE VOYAGE ISSUE

Edited by Bradford Morrow

Voyages are as old as literature itself, tales of migration across continents or seas. Unknown worlds, be they inscribed in true or imaginary accounts, are as ripe for literary exploration as ever. In the spirit of the ancient mythographer Euhemerus and of Sir John Mandeville, whose mendacious travelogue was believed by many, including Columbus, to be based on fact—and in tribute to such voyagers as Cervantes, Swift, Sterne, Twain, Calvino, Sorel, Naipaul, Matthiessen, Chatwin—*Terra Incognita: The Voyage Issue* will gather the testaments and peripatetic observations of contemporary writers who have set out for Elsewhere.

Through poems from afar, travel diaries, immigrant narratives, postcards, new ancient legends, epic quests, mind trips, manipulated histories, and dispatches from a wide range of innovative authors, readers will travel to places they have never visited before. This special issue will offer a whole *orbis tertius* of unexperienced locales and unmapped lands, along with journeys into the deeper recesses of consciousness itself. Robert Coover, Charles Bernstein, Elizabeth Hand, Peter Gizzi, James Morrow, and many other writers in *Conjunctions:56, Terra Incognita: The Voyage Issue* will bring to life what they discovered out there in the land of wind and ghosts.

CONJUNCTIONS

Bi-Annual Volumes of New Writing

Edited by
Bradford Morrow

published by Bard College

CONJUNCTIONS is published in the Spring and Fall of each year by Bard College, Annandale-on-Hudson, NY 12504. This issue is made possible in part with the generous funding of the National Endowment for the Arts, and with public funds from the New York State Council on the Arts, a State Agency.

SUBSCRIPTIONS: Send subscription orders to CONJUNCTIONS, Bard College, Annandale-on-Hudson, NY 12504. Single year (two volumes): $18.00 for individuals; $40.00 for institutions and overseas. Two years (four volumes): $32.00 for individuals; $80.00 for institutions and overseas. Patron subscription (lifetime): $500.00. Overseas subscribers please make payment by International Money Order. For information about subscriptions, back issues, and advertising, contact us at (845) 752-4933 or conjunctions@bard.edu.

Editorial communications should be sent to Bradford Morrow, *Conjunctions,* 21 East 10th Street, New York, NY 10003. Unsolicited manuscripts cannot be returned unless accompanied by a stamped, self-addressed envelope. Electronic and simultaneous submissions will not be considered.

Conjunctions is listed and indexed in Humanities International Complete.

Visit the *Conjunctions* Web site at www.conjunctions.com and follow us on Facebook and Twitter.

Cover design by Jerry Kelly, New York. Cover painting by Stephen Hicks: *Catherine & Henry*, oil on panels, 47 x 47 inches, 2007. Reproduced by permission of the George Billis Gallery, New York.

Available through D.A.P./Distributed Art Publishers, Inc., 155 Sixth Avenue, New York, NY 10013. Telephone: (212) 627-1999. Fax: (212) 627-9484.

Printers: Edwards Brothers

Typesetter: Bill White, Typeworks

ISSN 0278-2324

ISBN 978-0-941964-71-5

Manufactured in the United States of America.

TABLE OF CONTENTS

URBAN ARIAS

Edited by Bradford Morrow

EDITOR'S NOTE

THEY ARE AMONG the oldest of human experiments in habitation, these living collectives known as cities. From the days of Mesopotamia and beyond, countless multitudes have chosen to leave behind valleys, plains, and mountains to gather in vigorous beehives of commerce and culture. City life is not for everyone. The lack of privacy, the noise, the sheer overstimulation, the great degree of severance from the natural world—these and so many other factors make cities anathema to many. Others couldn't imagine living anywhere else. The diversity, the access to goods and services, the architectural splendor, the museums, parks, zoos. Yet some, such as the inimitable Thomas Bernhard, whose extended interview here continues *Conjunctions'* longstanding effort to help bring his work into English, are comfortable neither in the city nor the country, and travel back and forth between the two poles of urban and rural, in search of community on one hand and solitude on the other.

In *Urban Arias* the reader may visit—while sitting quietly in the country, or suburb, or town, or even some metropolitan megalopolis—any number of cities from Paris to Tokyo, London to Los Angeles, Varanasi to Berlin, Miami to Rome, San Jose to Las Vegas, Havana to Chicago, Lincoln to New Orleans to the city that initially inspired the issue you hold in your hands, New York. Here, too, are cities of the unfettered imagination, curious places like Altobello and Anthem, where Jellyheads and Scarecrows respectively reside. Wander down the avenues of *Urban Arias* and you will even discover a city made of meat and gingerbread. Cities we know. Cities we imagine. Cities we imagine we know.

Of course, one cannot help but think of the cities that hum along outside these pages. The Caracases, Pragues, Moscows, Beijings, Lagoses, Rio de Janeiros of the world. This atlas, call it, of fictive and poetic works is not meant to be comprehensive but rather a portrait of the very idea of urban existence.

—Bradford Morrow
October 2010
New York City

The Count of Monte Cristo's Daughter

Paul La Farge

THERE WAS A PROBLEM with Justin's flight from New York City to San Jose, California: Just when the cabin doors were closing, three security persons came in and walked back to a kid dressed like a snowboarder, in a middle seat a few rows behind Justin. "Excuse me, sir." The kid took his earphones off. "Sir, can you please come with us?" They were not friendly or its opposite, tense or its opposite. They waited for the kid to get up and walked him out. Then there was a delay as the ground crew opened the cargo doors, took out all the luggage, and heaped it on the tarmac in the middle of a July rain. One of the security personnel was still on the plane, searching the area where the kid had been sitting. After a few minutes, Justin twisted around and asked nervously, "What is it? A terrorist?" The security person, a man in his fifties, with steel gray hair and a saggy gut, looked up. "Sir," he said, "please return to your seat." "I'm not *out* of my seat," Justin said. "I'm just asking you." "Please sit down, sir," said the security person loudly. Soon the whole plane was watching them. It was as if Justin had become dangerous, when all he wanted to know was what they suspected the kid of doing. What was wrong with wanting to know? He settled back in his seat and closed his eyes as if the exchange had made him tired, which, in a way, it had. What was worse, by the time the ground crew got the rain-soaked bags back on the plane, they'd lost their takeoff slot. They lurched into the air two hours late and banked over a country almost entirely covered with cloud. All the way across the Midwest, Justin fumed about the incident. The disaster he had possibly avoided, being blown up in midair, hurtling into some monument, bothered him less than the humiliation of being rebuked for asking a simple question. Finally mountains veered out of the cloud like brown trucks; the plane sank; in a moment Justin was skimming over a lattice of blue-green lights strung out around the black bay. He folded his tray table, bit his lip, and felt his stomach rise as everything else went down.

They were supposed to arrive in the afternoon; now it was night.

Justin wheeled his bag along the curb wearily, looking for the shuttle to his hotel. He came to a pretty Asian woman in a T-shirt. "Excuse me," he said, "do you know which bus is the Sheraton?" "We're waiting for it," the woman said. We? An older man in a rumpled suit, a cart of suitcases. "Where are you coming from?" Justin asked. "Guangzhou," said the woman. "Business trip?" The woman nodded. What else would bring anyone to San Jose? Although Justin had his own reasons for coming here tonight. He'd once been in love with a woman named Gillian, who lived in San Francisco. His love never went anywhere—she lived with an architect named Andrew, who watched over her jealously—but Justin hadn't been able to stop being in love with her. Eventually he moved to New York, and went on with his life. He thought he'd put Gillian out of his mind, but when his boss sent him to San Jose to make a presentation to a new client, he flew out two days early in the hope of seeing her again. "Me, too," he said.

The shuttle came and Justin helped the Asian couple to load their bags onto it. Their bags were incredibly heavy; Justin wondered what was in them. Commercial samples? Statuary? Anyway, he'd broken the ice; the woman told him that her name was Aurea. The older man was her father, as Justin might have guessed. Aurea spoke English with no accent whatsoever: She'd grown up in Mountain View, and gone to college at Berkeley. She and her father had moved to China ten years ago. She liked it OK, but she missed the Bay Area, her friends. Guangzhou was crowded and lonely. As she chatted, Justin felt himself unwinding. He told her the story of the police and the snowboarding kid. "That's so scary," said Aurea. "A terrorist on your plane!" "He didn't look like a terrorist," Justin said. "What do they look like?" asked Aurea. Good point. Still, Justin wanted to talk about what had happened, and Aurea seemed like a sympathetic listener. He described the incident with the security person, his anger and shame. "That's a bummer, for sure," Aurea said. Her father looked at Justin but said nothing. The shuttle drove down a six-lane street void of traffic, past businesses that offered indistinct services. Hair, nails, maybe eyes and teeth. Cars.

Then they were at the hotel, and Justin realized it wasn't his hotel. This might be *a* Sheraton, but it certainly wasn't *the* Sheraton, or even one of the more important ones. Three white stories made a halfhearted L around a scrap of pool, dark for the night. Aurea and her father descended from the van; Justin hesitated. He ought to say something to the driver, to be taken to *his* hotel, which, although he had never seen it, was surely bigger than this one, and more decent. On the other hand there was Aurea, struggling with a bag that probably weighed more than she did. It wasn't like one hotel was really different from another, Justin thought, and helped Aurea with her luggage. He took down his own suitcase and followed her, his bag squeaking along behind him like an indicator, a sign to all who cared to read it that a human being was on the move. "Well," Aurea said, turning to Justin when they entered the lobby, "maybe we'll see you tomorrow!" Justin smiled and nodded. It seemed as if their conversation was over, but in fact they were going to the same place, the reception desk. To Justin's misfortune, there were two clerks on duty. He had to explain to the second clerk, a friendly woman named Vivian, that he did not have a reservation. "No problem," Vivian said, smiling. "How many nights will you be staying with us?" "Three." "King-sized bed OK?" "Yes," said Justin, a little embarrassed. Aurea chose that moment to lean over and say, "Have a good night!" Then she and her father took their room keys and wheeled their bags to the elevator, and Justin turned back to Vivian and arranged his mode of payment.

Up in his room, Justin thought about calling Gillian. It was ten o'clock on Saturday night; she'd be awake. She was a night owl; once they'd sat on the balcony of her apartment, smoking cigarettes and talking about German philosophy, until dawn. Gillian was one of those people who seemed to have shoehorned herself into a life that was a size too small for her: She ought to have been a bohemian, but in fact she lived in the marina with an architect, wore silk scarves, got up early to run by the water. He'd asked her why she did it that night on the balcony; this was before he'd given up on seducing her away from Andrew. "Don't you worry that you'll get tired of living a double life?" he'd asked. "You don't understand," Gillian had said. "It's not a double life." She took a long drag on her cigarette. "It's all me, just like the inside and the outside of this house are all the same house." "I *don't* understand," Justin said. "Which is the inside and which is the outside?" Gillian stubbed out her cigarette and smiled at no one in particular. "Look," she said, "you can see the moon." That was the end of that part of their conversation. Justin wanted very badly to call Gillian now but he hadn't told her he was coming, hadn't talked to her in almost a year. He didn't want to scare her away with his need. He went down to the hotel restaurant, thinking he might have a drink. Aurea's father was there, sitting by himself at the bar, his fingers curled around a Coke, looking vacantly at a football game on TV. *Poor guy's probably jet-lagged out of his mind,* Justin thought. *What's the time difference between here and China?* Justin thought of joining him, but decided against it. Something about Aurea's father put him off, his silence, maybe, or the way he sat straight up at his bar stool, not moving at all. Besides, Justin was more tired than he had thought.

It was nine thirty in the morning when Justin woke up. He went downstairs, hoping for breakfast, and ran into Aurea and her father in the lobby. Aurea was wearing a white sundress and big black sunglasses pushed up on her head; her father was dressed as he had been the night before, in a wrinkled green cotton sports coat, khaki slacks, a white button-down oxford. Justin wondered if he'd slept at all. "We're on our way to the museum," Aurea said. She looked at her father, and hesitated. Then she said, "Would you like to come along?" "Sure," Justin said, "why not?" He'd kept the day free, hoping he might spend all or part of it with Gillian, but it was too early to call her—his whole plan had been thrown off by the snowboarding terrorist kid. He certainly didn't want to spend the day alone at this strange forlorn hotel. Justin followed Aurea and her father outside. It was brilliant blue daytime; the sun seemed to be coming from everywhere in the sky, lighting the deserted street like a movie set. Aurea pushed her sunglasses down over her eyes. The three of them stood there awkwardly at the curb, not speaking. Then Justin said to Aurea's father, "So, you live in China?" It was an idiotic thing to say. The father didn't answer. Maybe he didn't speak English. Justin wished he hadn't accepted Aurea's invitation; probably she had only asked him to be polite. Now she was wondering what he was doing, tagging along. He was about to make an excuse—he'd forgotten something in his room; he had to make a call—when a cab pulled up and they all got in. Aurea gave the driver an address and almost at once they were on a freeway, rushing past other cars that were rushing past a landscape of muddy tans and greens, hills and sheds and towers built from metal struts, everything preternaturally distinct in the sunlight. Now for the first time Aurea's father spoke: "How much do you know about the Rosicrucians?" *Uh oh,* thought Justin. He knew a little about them, from an occult-section-of-the-bookstore phase in junior high. A secret society, founded in the Middle Ages. Something to do with the Freemasons. Freemasons plus magic, maybe: alchemy, eternal life. Cowls. *Da Vinci Code* stuff. Was Aurea's father recruiting Justin into a secret society? This seemed like an awfully haphazard way of going about it. "Nothing, really," he said.

Aurea's father explained that Rosicrucianism was a combined and perfected metaphysical system developed by philosophers over the ages. He made it sound like a new model of toothbrush. "It is the science of self-mastery," he said. "You may ask, what exactly does self-mastery mean? It means learning how to chart your own course through life. How to find the means to make the right choices and decisions. It means seeing your present circumstances as unlimited opportunities for growth because you have the ability to change your situation. It means being able to take charge of your life and help those around you to achieve a happier and healthier existence." Did Aurea's father think Justin was in need of self-mastery? Was this somehow about what he had been saying the night before, about what happened on the plane—and did Aurea's father know that Justin had allowed himself to be driven to the wrong hotel? "Achieving mastery of the self is the first step to attaining mastery of fate," Aurea's father said. Aurea looked embarrassed for both of them. Then the cab stopped and they got out, opposite a high white stucco wall, interrupted by a gate in the Egyptian style.

What was this place? It wasn't Egyptian; it was barely "Egyptian." It looked like someone had taken some Egyptian scenes from Bible comics and rendered them haphazardly in concrete and white stucco. A replica sphinx crouched on a pediment; a replica obelisk climbed out of a blue California fountain, dry, its basin littered with oblong dark leaves. Suddenly Aurea's father had his camera out and he was taking pictures of everything, nodding to himself, like he'd been here before, not as a living person, but in a dream. He was nodding as if to confirm, yes, these were the things he had seen in his dream. He took hold of Aurea's arm and stationed her next to a bronze bust of some bald man from the 1940s; he pulled her down a flight of steps and made her stand in a kind of basin. Justin, abandoned, looked around on his own. A big building attracted his attention; he read a notice that informed him that it was a lecture hall for Rosicrucian initiates. Everyone else please keep out. But the gates were chained; no one was clamoring to get in.

When they went inside the museum proper, it was even worse. The display cases were sparsely stocked with late-period Egyptian odds and ends, punctuated with crude dioramas and relief maps of the Nile delta that lit up uselessly when you pushed a button. Aurea's father spoke knowledgeably, now gesturing at the exhibits, now pointing at himself, as though he were an ancient Egyptian, there to offer them a valuable firsthand perspective on the artifacts. They came to a mummified child, like a big bandaged hot dog with a head: "First the brains are drawn out through the nose with a hook," Aurea's father said, "then an incision is made along the side with a sharp Ethiopian stone." It was creepy. Aurea's father sounded like a recording played back through a human being's body, his voice hollow and somehow distant. Not to mention his use of the present tense: An incision *is* made? After a while, Justin drifted away from them. He went down into a life-sized replica of a tomb, then up again into a room where the civil life of the ancient Egyptians was on display. Why all this Egyptian stuff, Justin wondered, and where were the exhibits in which the secrets of the Rosicrucian order were revealed? Or was that the point: Was the museum intended not to educate its visitors, but to keep them in the dark? He imagined secret rooms behind the ones he saw, where Rosicrucians in black cowled robes watched his vain progress and chuckled to themselves.

Eventually he found himself in a cul-de-sac, where a scale model of a building was preserved in a Plexiglas box: ONLY MODEL OF ITS KIND IN THE UNITED STATES! Justin looked at it vacantly. White plaster, stepped pyramid, tiny stairs. Tiny people in the courtyard for scale. Justin felt that way himself: as if he existed only *for scale*, to make it apparent to some outside observer just how big the world really was. He leaned against the wall, then sank to the floor. He rested his head on his arms and closed his eyes. After a while, he heard footsteps approaching, and Aurea called his name. She sounded worried. "Over here," Justin said. He was touched that she should worry about him. To Justin's further surprise, Aurea sat down beside him. "I came to apologize for my father," she said. "He gets really excited when he talks about this stuff." "No need to apologize," said Justin. "I'm just tagging along. You two should do your thing." "He's so boring," Aurea said. "He thinks everyone is interested in exactly the same stuff as him. The Egyptians this, the Egyptians that. I mean, who cares?" "I was wondering," Justin said, "shouldn't there be something about the Rosicrucians?" Aurea seemed not to hear him. "The thing is," she said, "he's had a really hard life." Suddenly, without Justin's having done anything either to encourage or to prevent her, Aurea was talking about her father's childhood. His parents had been poor farmers; he'd come to the U.S. on his own and won a scholarship to MIT. He'd invented a kind of computer switch, and started a company, but then he got into trouble. "Trouble?" said

Justin. "Yes," Aurea said, "he was double-crossed by his business partners." Justin was going to say, *How dramatic,* but just then Aurea's father appeared. He looked displeased at finding them seated on the ground, but all he said was, "Come on. It's time for lunch."

They went to an Italian restaurant across the street from the museum. The restaurant was practically empty, but it seemed to inspire a kind of awe in Aurea's father. "Many important people have come here," he said. "Raymund Andrea himself has come here." "Who's Raymund Andrea?" Justin asked. It was the right question. For the first half of the meal—linguine with clams for Justin, spaghetti Bolognese for Aurea and her father, Cokes all around—Aurea's father talked about the life of the great Raymund Andrea, a British Rosicrucian, the author of many learned books, and also, it seemed, a combatant in the Second World War. "Can you imagine," Aurea's father said, "when he was forty years old, Raymund Andrea volunteered for the British Special Boat Service? He fought alongside men half his age. They traveled up and down the Aegean in special folding boats, strangling German sentries with their bare hands." This sounded like fable to Justin but he was too polite to say anything. Aurea's father was flushed; a dot of red sauce danced on the roof of his chin. "What is even more impressive is that his eyesight was very poor," Aurea's father said, "not unlike my own." Aurea smiled apologetically, as if to say, *I'm sorry my father is boring you again.* But Justin had no chance to be bored. Without transition, Aurea's father said, "It was in the prison library that I discovered Raymund Andrea's great work, *The Technique of the Disciple.*" "Prison?" Justin involuntarily gawked. "Yes," Aurea's father said. "I committed the entire book to memory. It begins with these lines: *A master said to his pupil, But you have to remember that you are at a hard school and dealing now with a world entirely different from your own.* When I read these words, I felt that I had at last encountered a mind capable of understanding my despair. What I had taken for the end of my life was in reality a school, and my work there was to learn." Aurea's father had spent six years in prison, and he had studied the Rosicrucian literature with unimaginable attentiveness. "You may ask me literally anything about the teachings," Aurea's father said. "I know them all by heart. With this knowledge came, by slow degrees, the power of self-mastery." It was a story straight out of *The Count of Monte Cristo,* Justin thought. Next, Aurea's father would describe how he had dug his way out of prison with a spoon, and the years he had spent plotting his revenge. He looked at Aurea again. Where had *she* been while he was in prison? She was expressionless, picking at her green salad. "Very interesting," said Justin. "It is an enormous power," Aurea's father said. He looked at his watch. "We had better go, or we will be late for the planetarium show." He asked for the check and Justin reached for his wallet. "No need," said Aurea's father. He put down a credit card without looking at the bill. Aurea still hadn't looked up from her salad.

They went out into the too-bright light. "Come, we'll see the planetarium," said Aurea's father, but Justin didn't feel like seeing the planetarium. There was something too strange about Aurea and her father; their fate, whatever it might be, was not his own. "I'm tired," Justin said. "I think I'll go back to the hotel." "Sleep later," Aurea's father said. He grabbed Justin's wrist. It was ridiculous: Justin barely knew these people, and they were leading him around like a child. "Let go of me!" he said, louder than he had intended. Aurea's father let go of his wrist. "Sorry," Justin said, not to him but to Aurea. "It's OK," Aurea said. Her father just stood there, not even deigning to look offended. Justin walked angrily away from them both. For someone who valued self-mastery so highly, Aurea's father seemed pretty comfortable telling other people what to do. Maybe he didn't care what anyone else thought; maybe his time in prison had made him indifferent to the desires of mere mortals. Justin felt sorry for Aurea. It couldn't be easy to be the daughter of the Count of Monte Cristo, to have a father with superhuman powers and an inflexible will. He imagined Aurea dropping something on the floor, a scarf, say, and the Count of Monte Cristo staring at her icily until she picked it up. Fat chance she had of attaining self-mastery, so long as she stuck with him.

Having reached this conclusion, he looked around, and realized that he had no idea where he was: an anonymous street of identical houses. Worse, he'd left his phone at the hotel. But where was the hotel? How could he get there? Justin kept going in the direction he was going, but came to nothing, only more streets and houses. The sun was relentless, it was even worse than Aurea's father, shining and shining and shining, robbing the world of rest and depth. He wandered through a city of bright, flat squares, a city that seemed at once completely unreal and in some not yet articulated way completely threatening. Only by concentrating his anger at Aurea's father, the security guard on the plane, the history that had led his country to fear teenagers in headphones, was he able to keep moving forward. He imagined himself speaking to Gillian: *It isn't right,* he said. *You can't assume you know what's best for other people. You have to let them make their own decisions, otherwise it's . . .* but he didn't know what it was. *It's totalitarianism,* he finished lamely. *Don't be paranoid,* Gillian said. *Why do you always think life is so sinister?* Why indeed? Justin had only begun to answer that question when he came to a main street, a bus stop, and threw up. *Bad clams,* he thought miserably, *I ate bad clams.* He stood there with his hands on his knees, reading a stencil on the curb, FLOWS TO BAY.

Back at the hotel, Justin lay on his made bed. Now that he had cooled down, Aurea's father seemed harmless, and even comical. Mummies! Rosicrucians! The Special Boat Service! He was a kind of joke, a bizarre joke. Justin dozed for an hour, then brushed his teeth and called Gillian. He got her voice mail. "Hi, it's Justin," he said. "I know it's been a long time, but I'm in the Bay Area on business and I'd really love to see you. I'm free tonight, maybe give me a call?" Then he put on his bathing suit and went down to the pool. Justin swam laps, dodging a pair of overweight children who were trying to climb onto one another's shoulders while a Komodo dragon of a mother looked on. He lay in a beach chair, warmed pleasantly by the sun, which was lower and weaker than it had been before. He went upstairs to change; Gillian hadn't called. He ate dinner in the restaurant and sat at the bar, looking out at the dark pool and the traffic moving sparsely past. Aurea and her father did not appear.

Justin went over the materials for the presentation he'd be giving the next morning. He wondered whether Gillian had decided not to call him back. He remembered the last conversation he'd had with her, the night before he moved to New York. They'd gone out for Vietnamese food, at a fancy restaurant in her neighborhood, and Justin had implied, sullenly, that if Gillian hadn't been so coupled with Andrew, he, Justin, might not be leaving. "That's not fair," Gillian had said. "You can't blame me for your decisions. Anyway, I wish you were staying. I like having you here." Justin had apologized. It was just that he felt like he was on the outside, he said. All his life he'd been trying to get to the inside of something, some *structure,* and yet despite all his efforts he remained on the outside of it. It wasn't just Gillian who wouldn't let him in, it was the whole city that made him feel as if he were looking at it from the outside. With admiration, with love even, but always from the outside, never from within. Gillian smiled at that. "The outside and the inside are the same thing," she said. "Maybe for you," said Justin, "but you have Andrew." The rest of the evening had been awkward. Not a big deal. Still, Justin wondered who was right—he or Gillian. Were the outside and the inside really the same? If so, why did he feel so external?

Justin gave his presentation the next morning. It went well; if the client didn't bite it wouldn't be Justin's fault. He went out to lunch with their team, a jovial, youthful group, then returned to the hotel. Gillian still hadn't called. Justin asked the clerk if he could leave a message for the Asian couple. He wanted to apologize for running away; he wanted to talk to Aurea again. But the clerk told Justin that they had checked out that morning. It seemed like a long way to travel for two days in San Jose, but that was none of Justin's business. He told himself that it didn't matter. He was still the same person he had been two days ago. His timing was off, that was the worst you could say: He'd wanted to talk to Gillian but she wasn't around. As for Aurea and her father, they were pure mystery, a chance for something that Justin had not taken. He was old enough to know that life was full of mysteries like that. You didn't need to believe in any kind of secret truth to see it. Every conversation that broke off midway was a mystery; every person you met was a hidden order into which you would never be initiated.

Stupefied by sadness, Justin sat on his bed and switched on the TV. The local programming had been interrupted by a special bulletin: Emergency vehicles in great numbers surrounded a one-story building in an office park on the other side of the city. HOSTAGE SITUATION, read the news ticker. Slowly, through the pall of his thoughts, Justin understood that a gunman had gone into an office building and taken the employees hostage. An Asian man in his thirties, possibly a former employee of the company he was now threatening to blow up with a suicide vest. He wasn't talking to the police, but a hostage specialist was on his way down from San Francisco. Meanwhile sharpshooters had taken up positions on the roofs of buildings nearby. God, Justin thought, the world is full of fucked-up people. First the snowboarder, now this guy. He packed his bag, and as he was putting his toothbrush back in its plastic travel case, he thought, oh, holy fuck, what if it's the Count of Monte Cristo? He stood in front of the television, his heart pounding. An Asian man in his thirties. Possibly a former employee. *Double-crossed.* Fuck, fuck, Justin thought. They got the age wrong but it's him! He must have taken a cab to the office park, lingered outside, futzing with his weapons. How the hell did he get weapons, Justin wondered, but maybe he had special powers, unlimited wealth, the skills to make a suicide vest out of household chemicals in a hotel bathroom. Then his mouth went dry. Where was his daughter, where was Aurea?

Justin didn't even think about it. He deduced the address almost miraculously from the Internet, and took a cab as close as he could to the office park. He told his story to a young, bored cop whose job it was to keep the public at a distance. The cop radioed his commander, and grudgingly admitted that Justin's information might be useful. In fact, the commander wanted to see Justin in person. *I'm right,* Justin thought, *I'm right I'm right!* He could hardly stand it. On the other side of the police cordon, what had seemed like organized human activity revealed itself as dizzying chaos. Police officers shouted at each other, ran back and forth carrying spotlights, cables, rifles with telescopic sights. It was like they were making a movie that had already flopped. They had to keep making it, but really they were just going through the motions, thinking about how to shift the blame. The young cop led Justin to a group of men in civilian clothes, who were drinking coffee. "Who's this?" one of them asked. "Friend of the nut," said the young cop. The other man looked at Justin piercingly. "You know this guy?" "Yes." "Is he going to do it?" "I don't know," Justin said. "Thanks a lot," said the other man, and turned away. Justin was crushed. Didn't they want to know anything about Aurea's father? The young cop was already leading him away, but the other one told him to stay. "Don't move, don't talk to anyone, don't touch anything," the young cop said.

Justin followed his instructions; there was nothing else to do. All around him, men with rifles watched the office building. The sun set; the sky turned pink, blue, green. Spotlights illuminated the office building from every direction, as if it were a monument. For some reason Justin found himself thinking about the tomb in the Rosicrucian museum. Would a future civilization build replicas of American offices circa 2008? He imagined himself as an explorer of the office building in the distant future, trying to figure out what everything had been for. *First the brains are drawn out with a hook.* His reverie was interrupted by the arrival of the hostage negotiator, who looked like a plump Warren Beatty in a sweater vest and thick black glasses. His arrival seemed to calm people down. "So," he said after a long, soothing silence, "where do you want to begin?" One of the plainclothes cops told the negotiator what they knew, which was next to nothing. No car, no photos, no positive ID. "Fucker won't even say what he wants," said the cop. "Interesting," said the negotiator. "Could someone please bring me a marker and a sketch pad? And a coffee?" An assistant was sent back behind the lines. "I know him," Justin said plaintively. "I met him at the airport." "What's his name?" the negotiator asked. "I don't know," said Justin. "He has a daughter named Aurea." "Is she with him?" "She must be," Justin said. "She goes everywhere with him." There was a conference; no one knew anything about a daughter. "You know how to reach her?" Justin shrugged helplessly. The assistant came back with a cup of coffee, a bulletproof vest, a Magic Marker, and a big pad of white paper. The negotiator drank some coffee and looked at the blank paper. Then he looked at Justin. "Can you think of anything that might be helpful?" he asked. "He's a Rosicrucian," said Justin. "He spent some time in prison. He came all the way from China to take revenge on his business partners. His daughter went to Berkeley. She's very nice. Her problem is, she doesn't know how to say no to her father." The negotiator put the end of the Magic Marker between his teeth. After a while, he knelt on the ground, uncapped the marker, and wrote, CAN WE TALK? He turned the page and wrote, WHAT DO YOU WANT? On a third page, he wrote, THINK CAREFULLY.

A cop helped the negotiator into the bulletproof vest. He walked between the line of vans, past the policemen who lay prone, their guns trained on the office building. When he was about twenty feet from the front window, he stopped and held up his sign. Justin admired the negotiator, standing there all alone, spotlit, armed with only a few words written in block capitals on a sheet of construction paper. Justin wondered if he would ever do anything so brave. Had one of the blinds moved an inch? Everyone was looking at the office's front window, then back to the negotiator, whose face projected benevolent nonjudgment. If Justin had been in the building he would surely have come out by now. Even standing where he was, he found himself wanting to confess his own shortcomings, his cowardice, his selfishness, and indecision. *I am a failure,* he wanted to say. *A long time ago I had a dream of knowing how the world works but now I see that although the world may be knowable I will never know it. I will always be on the outside of it because I am afraid.* Then his phone rang.

"Hello?" Justin said. "Hi," said Gillian, "are you still in San Francisco?" The plainclothes cops stared at him. "Yes, I am," Justin said. "I'm sorry I didn't call sooner," said Gillian. The negotiator turned back from the window. He tapped at the page that read CAN

WE TALK? "Andrew and I broke up," Gillian said. "I mean, we broke up over the weekend." "I'm so sorry," said Justin. "It had been in the air for a long time," Gillian said. "Which you probably knew, right?" "Can I ask what happened?" Justin said. The negotiator was nodding. "It wasn't anything," said Gillian. "We got into a fight about a Crock-Pot he'd been storing in the pantry. I wanted him to throw it out, and he didn't want to, and one thing led to another." Gillian coughed. "Actually, I threw all his stuff in the Dumpster." "Whoa," said Justin. "That's intense." The negotiator turned the pages anxiously and tapped at the one that read WHAT DO YOU WANT? "I know!" said Gillian. "I wasn't planning on it, but once I got started, it felt so good I didn't want to stop. Now that it's over, I wish I hadn't done it." "Maybe he had it coming," said Justin. The negotiator looked alarmed. The cops were rooting urgently through their gear. "Possibly," said Gillian. "I'll tell you the whole sordid story over a drink. When are you free?" "I can be free now," Justin said. "Great," said Gillian. "Let's meet at the Galaxy Room in an hour." "OK," said Justin. "See you." He hung up. It would take him at least an hour to get to San Francisco, but he made no move to go. Everyone was silent. Everyone was looking at him. It was an incredible feeling, like flying in a dream. The negotiator was holding up the third sign, THINK CAREFULLY. The plainclothes cop asked, "Did he say what he wants?" "Yes," Justin said after a while. "He wants me to come in."

City Under Sun

Lyn Hejinian

Despite confusing display, unyielding surfaces, the city is not inhospitable to a competent culinary shopper, an expert at gathering groceries. She is impervious to ploys, indifferent to novelty. There is no longer anything new, nothing new happens anymore. This is the conclusion Nietzsche reaches with his aperçu "God is dead." As Walter Benjamin points out, since then humans have had "to face with heroic composure" the eternal return of the same. But even that heroism is lost to us now. Everything is new and that is what's no longer new—the lack of novelty in the endless iterations of newness. Nothing old occurs anymore, either, except novelty's old news. History, in that sense, is dead too. Everything is the same. It is all hum and grid. Rhubarb is rote; edamame has entered Standard English. There are two large supermarkets equidistant from the building in which I live, one ten blocks south, one ten blocks northwest. I am entirely familiar with the way they are laid out. Produce to the right as one enters the door, against the wall. Citrus first. Nonetheless, shocks proliferate; what returns is perpetually unfamiliar—every commodity is unprecedented, though unsurprising. Within every story another story is hidden, autonomous and unfolding though scarcely noticed except now and then, inadvertently, when, just as with a slip of the tongue a woman exposes a bit of the turbulent life under way in her unconscious mind, a rat scurries through an open window with a doll's head in its mouth, or a man shouts a couplet from a passing bus ("o queens of urbanity, kings of the crush / let's sing of convenience, importance, and plush"). Feral children come off the fire escapes. A highly educated mother masturbates triumphantly. Her name may be Alice Milligan Webster, but that name is significant only to those for whom it names her—it has only that, local, significance, if any. The city has 101,377 names, around 9,800 per square mile. Tio Levette, Nina Lee, Ludmilla Kaipa, etc. The sun emits a continuous roar, but from such a distance that it doesn't seem it can possibly be addressing any of us. With the death of the ahistorical or prehistorical God, history should have been born; sense perceptions should be able to discern something of the past, which bears the meanings and functions of the things that come before them. But history has no face. The shoppers flock to kiss the gleaming lemons. The city rumbles with unsubdued composure; its buildings betray little of what goes on inside them. The city players and planners all keep a low profile and work fast. They are left to their proliferating tasks. And, like Don Quixote, the literary scholar sets forth to do her work. Why like Quixote? Because what she engages with doesn't exist. There was no Emma Bovary to dream Madame Bovary's dreams. And if the literary scholar asks if the nameless narrator of Henry James's *Turn of the Screw* has really seen a ghost, the answer is that there was no nameless narrator but only the narration, with its ambiguous progress. Entering the supermarket with an empty cart pulled from the chain of carts standing ready by the door, I turn sharply to the right, past the avocados to the melons, in front of which I park my cart out of the flow of other shoppers. I move like an unregulated chess piece across the large checkerboard pattern formed by the floor's square tiles. *Madame Bovary* was Flaubert's "book about nothing," a test of "the axiom that there is no such thing as subject—style in itself being an absolute manner of seeing things." Flaubert took on Guy de Maupassant as a student of sorts. "He forced me to describe, in a few phrases, a creature or an object so that it was clearly distinguishable from all other creatures or objects of the same race or species. . . . Homework consisted of a practical exercise: Observe a grocer on his doorstep, a concierge smoking his pipe, or a cab-horse in a row of cabs, and then, 'with a single word,' show how that particular grocer, concierge, or cab-horse resembles no other." I tear off a plastic bag and reach over a display of parsley; I select a single head of butter lettuce from the dewy, green display. The tips of its outer, darker leaves are imperfect—they are slightly torn and rust stained, travel worn. But the inner leaves are a pale, variegated green, tender without being limp. This is the most succulent of lettuces. I've now added a cucumber, a head of endive, and a rubber-banded bunch of scallions to the shopping cart. I'm letting myself go. *Little* Lyn is in the produce section of a grocery store eating raw peas from the pod; *big* Lyn can remember the pods, the peas, the bin, the wood floor, the handsome, genial grocer: Roy of Roy's Market whom little Lyn carefully conflated with Roy Rogers, whom interim Lyns have had little occasion to remember, and whom big Lyn recognizes to have been very like an expensive animated porcelain (and later plastic) doll. A commodity. The radio cowboy offered one of the "aberrant or bizarre solutions to the question of where or how to live" in mid-twentieth-century America. Who offered him? To whom? Why? Everyday city life is a macrosystem, naturalized into invisibility, sometimes oppressive and sometimes so transparent as to seem to leave living unimpeded, nothing but green lights and a clear conscience and prospects or detritus: a black lacquer vase in an antique shop window; property lines; the drift of history; radiators; Venice; a small dish of potato chips; a photo of a dead man; reading glasses; College Avenue; the pungent smell of a tomato plant; a college education; a citywide strike; anxiety: "[T]he true object of anxiety is precisely the (over)proximity of the Other's desire." Is the problem that the Other will impose his or her desire on one, that one will be forced to satisfy the Other's desire, rather than one's own, leaving one's own desires unsatisfied? Or is the problem that the Other's desire, when seen too closely, is repulsive (this is what Slavoj Žižek suggests, but it seems equally likely that, when forced by the confrontation with the Other's desire to look too closely at one's own, one will find one's own repulsive). I develop a few animosities as I gather groceries, and here and there a fleeting sense of camaraderie. Like Michel de Certeau, I "dream of countless combinations of existences." A novelist is in many ways like a ringmaster and a sociologist. He or she announces, and thereby calls, people into view, where they are fated to perform and to fare (poorly or well). An essayist is, however, a performer—an athletic bareback rider or juggler or high-wire walker or trapeze artist, or one of the clowns: whapping or being whapped by other clowns, wig flying into the ether on a string, shoes flapping, pants dragging, jumping into a barrel over which a lion leaps while elephants trumpet and a monkey plays a drum. The clowns are variously criminals or detectives or victims of life. The public pays to play its part, that of being the public. Fredo is discerning, Freddy is demanding, Helen is devouring, Quindlan is disdaining, Askari Nate Martin is detecting, and Sue is dismayed. Sid stays away.

The site is beautiful, a city with a "Mediterranean feel" and hills. Leo follows Sid, they go from one circus to the next. Dropping a Baggie of sunflower seeds and a Baggie of oats into his cart, and leaving it where it stands, Minnie Jones backtracks a bit and goes down aisle one to get a jar of marmalade, which is among the jellies and jams just past the peanut butter and honey and across from the candy near the front of the store. She never drives her cart into the aisles and feels a twinge of approval as she overhears Montgomery say to Helen, "You don't need the cart if you're just going halfway down aisle three for a box of sugar." Minnie Jones is a person who accepts her fate and believes it is never the function of family life to subtract members; family life is all about addition and flow. Life is subject to "false halts" more than to "false starts." The revolutionary task before us is to create conditions in which the old and the new can occur again. History is to be resuscitated, though the disaster of monotheism should be avoided. With private ownership of land, myth-enchanted social culture along with its myth-suffused, story-bearing spaces came to an end. Monotheism is the religious principle closest to the sensibility of the home owner. The heavens ceased to be social. Our identities are no longer bolstered, we have to reconfigure the world in such a way as to admit all that gives evidence of existing along with us. It is from kernels of impersonality—the fruits of the public sphere, where events and incidents that are not of one's doing, fragments of other people's existence, are encountered by chance—that one becomes a person in the city. I find myself watching a tall, shabbily dressed man wheeling a grocery cart south along Seventh Street in which a fat woman in an overcoat is crouched, holding a paper bag. The rules that establish a relationship between them, and between them and me, and between me and the intrusive friendliness of the tellers at the bank I enter after noticing them, are derived from the game called Napkin and Knife. As Peggotty remarks in *David Copperfield*, "I don't know how it is, unless it's on account of being stupid, but my head never can pick and choose its people. They come and they go, and they don't come and they don't go, just as they like." Everyday life is perpetually erupting into space and withdrawing from it. But to call it "erupting" suggests something abrupt. Public urban space, even the smallest, is analogous to a pause, however long prolonged, but it bears affinities with rest too, and with patience, however sorely tested. Visitors may walk through it, residents may inhabit it, cars and buildings and pedestrians and noise may crowd it, and animals may traverse it or scuttle along its margins. It is available and accessible for cohabitation and communication, for acts of sharing, interacting, play, public displays of affection, flaunting, vying, acknowledging. People are out, strolling, hurrying, socializing, lining up, blocking the sidewalk, nodding to panhandlers, taking a break from their unshared and unshareable anxieties, fears, problems (or pleasures). Within the city's buildings, the immediate is under perpetual translation and transmission. Its "talk of communication actually refers only to solitudes." To escape the barrage of media, we go out, away from our media-occupied private spaces (which the media renders strangely anonymous) and into public spaces: city streets, perpetually charged with anxiety and desire, and public parks, refuges for eccentricity and unproductivity. Everyday life seeps from the city's interstices. I swipe the credit card and wait for the receipt to print out. The sun is coming through the doors. My arms straight, head up, pushing the bagged groceries in the cart in front of me, I make it to the car in nineteen strides. Kiddies, kiddies, follow me / The streets, the trees, the feast, the sea. It's a city with 36,485 "actively managed street and park trees," which is to say *public trees*. They are unevenly distributed, abundant in the hills, and more sparse in the more densely urban "flats." The same salient reason can be attributed to the fact that the poor live on the hillsides above some cities (for example, Rio de Janeiro and Mexico City) and the rich on the hillsides above some others (e.g., Berkeley and Oakland): difficulty of access. It is among the labors of the poor to return home in the former and among the privileges of the rich to do so in the latter. Fragments of street music circulate—a bicyclist's bell, a siren, a vagrant with a guitar. Her beagle straining at the leash, a woman turns a corner and disappears. This isn't a city that "never sleeps." There's no bus service between 1:00 and 5:00 a.m. The city plot is knotted. It is composed of knots of conditions, situations, circumstances, terms that are not synonymous, by the way. The stronger the knots, the more vivid the plot. As morning returns, the sun recovers the city. Properly speaking, political struggle is not about ends but about beginnings. Political struggle seeks to open new possibilities for happiness—ordinary happiness, the happiness of ordinary lives. Thousands of people march through the city, chanting and brandishing signs and banners. They swarm through the streets approaching City Hall, they fill the Civic Center plaza with speeches and music. Protesting cuts to the budget for public education, students from Joaquin Miller Middle School are flying banners saying "Know All, Be All," "Don't Dumb Us Down," "Knowledge Is Power," etc. "So we appeal to you, sun, on this broad day. / You were ever a helpmate in times of great churning, and fatigue."

NOTES.

"to face with heroic composure": Walter Benjamin, *The Arcades Project*, trs. Howard Eiland and Kevin McLaughlin (Cambridge, MA: Belknap/Harvard University Press, 1999), 337.

"the axiom that there is no such thing . . .": *Letters of Gustave Flaubert 1830–1857*, ed., Francis Steegmuller (Cambridge, MA: Harvard University Press, 1980), 154.

"He forced me to describe . . .": Quoted in Graham Robb, "Cruising With Genius," in *The New York Review of Books*, Feb. 26, 2009, 33–34.

"aberrant or bizarre solutions . . .": Michael Sheringham, *Everyday Life: Theories and Practices from Surrealism to the Present* (Oxford, UK: Oxford University Press, 2006), 2.

"[T]he true object of anxiety . . .": Slavoj Žižek, *Welcome to the Desert of the Real* (London and NY: Verso, 2002), 22.

"dream of countless combinations of existences": Michel de Certeau, *The Practice of Everyday Life*, tr. Steven F. Rendall (Berkeley, CA: University of California Press, 1984), 21.

"I don't know how it is, unless it's on account of being stupid . . .": Charles Dickens, *David Copperfield*, Chapter VIII: "My Holidays, Especially One Happy Afternoon."

"talk of communication actually refers only to solitudes": Henri Lefebvre, *The Production of Space*, tr. Donald Nicholson-Smith (Oxford, UK: Blackwell, 1991), 389.

"So we appeal to you, sun . . .": John Ashbery, *Girls on the Run* (New York: Farrar, Straus and Giroux, 1999), 9.

'Til There Was You

Stephen O'Connor

JACK'S SINGULAR DISCOVERY was that things are, in fact, as they seem. Keys that get lost, for example, especially those that turn up in what would appear to be in plain sight—on a desktop, a counter, or the middle of a made bed—actually do cease to exist until the instant they are found. Likewise, the sky is, in fact, a bowl placed over the earth—a pale blue bowl, matte surfaced, lighter near its rim, darker near its crown, or, at night: a sort of colander, randomly punctured by buckshot, light shining through. The sky will, of course, sometimes seem vast and immaterial. Often this is only an illusion, the inevitable consequence of the fact that things (airplanes, birds) really do grow smaller as they move away. But if you are walking across a field one night, and the sky should look to you like nothing so much as the eternity of nonbeing in which isolate and innumerable instances of being scintillate in varieties of pink, green, and brilliant white—well then, you can be reasonably assured that's exactly what it is.

Most people have difficulty accepting Jack's discovery until they come to understand that there is nothing fixed or absolute about truth and falsehood, reality and fantasy, good and evil, etc., etc. All such dichotomies are purely a function of human emotion—of fear and desire, especially. When we are content, everything is real and true and good. That's obvious, isn't it? You're canoeing on a lake with the one you love. You're laughing delightedly at each other's jokes, trading nibbling kisses that promise much more profound satisfactions when you return to your cabin. The sun is an oblong of radiant orange melting into its rippling reflection. Peepers are peeping, crickets are loosing their nets of song in distant fields—who but a lunatic would question the authenticity or legitimacy of such a moment?

It is only when we want incompatible things simultaneously or when our desires smack against our fears that we become obsessed with distinguishing the true from the false, reality from fantasy, evil from good. Think of those countless grinding 4:00 a.m.s that human beings have had to endure in the service of this obsession. Think of all the lives made boring, shameful, and bleak by one or another white-knuckled vision of good, and of all the nations and peoples slaughtered because of some truth proclaimed from a mountaintop. The beauty of Jack's discovery is that it reduces such hair splitting, chest thumping, soul starving, and savagery to pantomime. But that is not at all to say that Jack's discovery elevates or purifies human nature in any way. Alas, it does nothing whatsoever to relieve us of the burden of who we actually are.

This is Jack on the night he made his discovery. You will notice that he is not in possession of the average good looks, intelligence, emotional stability, and sense of humor that heretofore had been his lot in life. His eyes: bulging, asymmetrical; the larger one vein laced, scarlet, oozing a yellowish fluid. His mouth: also asymmetrical, more ragged gash than biological organ. Posture: hunched. Shoulders: barely wider than his neck. That sinus-withering pong wafting about him: an emanation of the greasy secretion glossing his nose and lips, streaming down his ribs and thighs.

Jack's transformation took place over a couple of weeks, and started slowly, with what appeared to be (and was, of course) mild conjunctivitis. He and Grace were lazing in bed one sunny midsummer Sunday, as they had on countless other Sundays over the last seventeen years. She loved to waken in a sun-filled room, so slid from under the covers and went to the window, allowing Jack a moment in which to admire her long and fluent oscillations, her sandy pink, her hazelnut brown, and her gold: here tufty and tarnish dark, there lanky and flaxen bright.

Grace was not, in fact, an especially beautiful woman. The various parts of her body didn't always add up, and then there was her chin: a mere bump along the road between her lower lip and Adam's apple. Jack knew that Grace was not beautiful and didn't know it at the same time. In his eyes, she constantly shuttled between out of this world and so-so. The truth is that what most attracted him to her was her capacity to ache. Inside Grace there was a field of sodden ash under a weighty gray sky. The only birds there were harsh-voiced winter birds: crows and jays. But this field was where she felt most herself, and where she could be found walking during almost any idle moment. Often Jack would be right at her side, his chilled, red fingers interlaced with hers, his clothing penetrated by the same dank breeze as hers, his hair mist pearled and his cheeks stippled with the same tiny, trembling drops. It moved and excited Jack to think that the woman he loved could walk this field and pedal a bike through city traffic simultaneously. Jack found deep poignancy in this fact, minor key harmony, truth as a form of beauty. And now, pulling back the curtains, Grace had just gilded her front half in morning sun—what could be more wonderful!

But for some reason, as he and Grace both luxuriated in the effects of morning sunlight on her bare skin, Jack's thoughts drifted back to the previous night, and in particular to something strange she had done with her tongue. At the time, it had seemed surprising and delicious, but now—all at once—it seemed ominously unprecedented, like nothing she could ever have improvised on her own. "My eye feels funny," he said, as she made her way back to bed. "Itchy," he said. "Does it look bloodshot?" She crinkled the bridge of her nose and peered at one eye, then the other. "Nope," she said, and kissed him on a cheekbone.

A few days later, he came home early from work and found her sitting on the floor in a corner of the kitchen, talking on her cell phone, the fingertips of her free hand pressed in a clump against the middle of her forehead. As soon as he entered the room, she snapped her phone shut and smiled at him broadly. "Who was that?" he said. "No one," she replied, her eyes glittery with tears. In that instant, his shoulders slumped, though not so much that anyone would have noticed, and his conjunctivitis, which had been improving, spread to the other eye.

A day later, while driving Jack to the Commodity Spot, Grace began to talk about a movie she had seen, and seemed, at first, to think he had seen it too. A look of panic crossed her face. "That must have been someone else," she said. "Some other movie, I mean." And then she seemed to lose the ability to speak. For a moment, Jack was tempted to ask her what she had been meaning to say about the movie, but he didn't. And by the time they pulled into the mile-wide parking lot, his lips had gone bloody and one corner of his mouth was slightly higher than the other.

At dinner the following Friday, Jack exclaimed incredulously, "But you've always hated brussels sprouts!"

"No, I don't. I love them."

"Human flesh in the form of a tiny cabbage," he said. "That's what you always called them."

"Well, I've changed my mind. Can't I change my mind? Why won't you let me evolve? Why do you insist that I always stay the same?"

Thence commenced the first hint of Jack's ocular asymmetricality. Thence the first faint waft of his sinus-withering pong.

Jack actually laughed when Grace told him it was Buddy.

Buddy: his college roommate—befuddled, endearing, loyal, and permanently childlike, the perfect fat-guy sidekick to an action-movie hero. Buddy actually was a fat guy, but he could sing like Neil Young, and played a mean slap bass. In college, everyone had assumed he was headed for rock stardom, but in the twenty-three years since, he had supported himself first as a clerk in a vintage-record store, and then—once the Internet drove the store under—as a receptionist in a vet's office. Jack too had wanted to be a rock musician, but his hands were too small. "Hold up your hand," his grandfather, a dentist, had told him one Christmas, then pressed his own hand against Jack's. "Perfect match!" his grandfather said, and then he said, "You may be a lousy guitarist, but with dinky hands like these, you could be a million-dollar dentist!" So Jack went to dental school, and now he owned a duplex loft on Carbolic Avenue, a two-hundred-year-old farmhouse in the Uplands, and a pied-à-terre in Paris. And, of course, he had also met (cracked molar, exposed nerve, eye-stabbing pain) and fallen in love with Grace.

Buddy's romantic life—or so Jack had heretofore believed—had been confined to his one "great love," the high school girlfriend who had dumped him for the math genius–sports bookie who, after nearly a quarter-century, still kept her well supplied with BMWs, designer gowns, Xanax, and cocaine. Whenever Buddy mentioned her name, his eyes would go moony, his forehead dark with tortured hope, and he would speak in a breathy, sentimental singsong. Jack loved Buddy. "What a sweet guy," he always said. But then he would heave a heavy sigh. He couldn't help it. And Grace was the same. "Poor Buddy," she said whenever Buddy's name came up. Then she'd shake her head and lower her voice: "Poor, poor Buddy."

And so Jack had laughed when Grace told him.

Her face went parrot red; the skin between her eyebrows suffered tectonic dislocation. "What kind of a response is that?!" she said.

"You can't be serious!" said Jack.

"How did you get to be such a fucking weirdo?" Grace said. "What the fuck did I ever see in you?!"

With that, she was gone.

Jack stood staring at the slammed loft door, its echo coming back to him off half an acre of hardwood flooring, industrial detail work (wood-beam ceiling, cast-iron staircase), six potted palms, a

Jacuzzi, a hulking, twelve-burner stove, four TVs.

Grace had been carrying a suitcase when she slammed the door, and had had her gooseneck lamp clipped under one arm. That lamp had stood at her bedside ever since she was a little girl, in every place she had ever lived—house, dorm, apartment—and had been the solitary furnishing she had brought along when she moved into Jack's loft.

A codicil to Jack's discovery is the principle that all appearances are interconnected and that no seeming can occur in isolation. Thus it is true that, although Jack's transformation began to accelerate as he stood staring at that door, it might never have gotten so extreme had Grace and Buddy not also begun to change.

Before Grace even reached the bottom of the staircase, she had gained at least a couple of inches in height, and become distinctly modelesque. As she strode out onto Carbolic Avenue, her oscillations attained that degree of grandeur normally reserved for surges at sea or enormous trees in a strong wind. And then there was her chin! What could Jack have been thinking? Could a chin possibly have been more perfectly proportioned? More chuckable? More deserving of tender adoration? How could he ever have brought his mouth to Grace's without first adorning her chin in butterfly nips and lip caresses?

And Buddy too! How was it Jack had never noticed Buddy's rock jaw and hawklike gaze? Far from moony or forlorn, Buddy's habitual expression was classic nineteenth-century American: upright, self-reliant, ruggedly individualistic. He radiated exactly that fortitude and steadiness of purpose that women found irresistible. How could Jack have been so blind?

These and many other seeming revelations preconditioned Jack's transformation. And as they crashed sickeningly into his self-esteem, he grew ever more stench enclouded, gash mouthed, boogly eyed, and asymmetrical. His complexion flourished with moles. He slumped. His head became indistinguishable from his shoulders. His arms bowed and shrank to quasivestigial proportions, and so on and so on . . . until, in the end, he seemed to have been retooled as a toad by a psycho with a machete. Repulsive, in other words. Unlovable—*totally*. Fated for solitude. No wonder Grace had run from him! Who wouldn't?

*

After an extended session of misery and self-condemnation, Jack fled his loft in quest of the solace of alcohol. But no sooner had he pushed through the swinging doors of Stripetown Local than he had to contend with the glances cast his way by the other patrons, even by the regulars, with whom he'd traded weather and sports commentary for decades. Steely glances. Contemptuous. Glances that said, "What makes you think you belong here?"

And, in fact, he didn't belong. So again he fled. But it was the same at the next bar. And the next. He fled and he fled and he fled, and eventually found himself down in the Rumination District, at one of those joints whose denizens seem to have accreted to their barstools out of a miasma born of disappointment, illness, and urinal deodorizing tablets, where every lightbulb is dust encrusted and the illumination it sheds at least a hundred years old. But here too: the sideways glances, the mutterings, the contemptuous turnings away. He took a seat at the bar and, within a minute, the stools on either side of him were vacant. He picked up his glass, moved to a table in the corner, and that whole side of the room went silent. One by one, the tables near his were abandoned. Even an ancient drunk, asleep on a ripped vinyl banquet, lifted his head, squinted in affront, and staggered to the far side of the room.

Discovery is the process by which the unnoticed passes through impossibility into obviousness. The final stages of this process generally transpire within split seconds, but the earliest can seem to occur—retrospectively, at least—with geological lassitude, or to be manifestations of such monumental stupidity and incuriousness that the historian of ideas may feel moved to take his subjects by their shoulders and shout into their dull visages: "You stupid, dimwit fuck-ups! Can't you see what's right before your eyes?!"

It is important to remember that, at this particular moment of the night, Jack was not able to see what was right before his eyes, because he had not yet been able to lift his head far enough above the welter of assaults, disillusionments, shocking revelations, and the actualization of long-denied home truths to recognize their secret structure and true significance.

It would have been easier for you. Had you been walking beside Jack as he left the bar that night, you would have had the distinct advantage of being able to observe how averagely oblivious passers-by morphed into leering mockers at the touch of his eye beams. You could have watched empty doorways and parked cars become inhabited by deliriously passionate couples the instant Jack glanced their way, and seen how all of the women were heartbreakingly reminiscent of Grace, with one shaking gold and flaxen-bright tresses as she pulled her lover's mouth to her own, another covering her lover's face with greedy kisses just as Grace had once covered Jack's, and yet another—incomprehensible as this may be—rocking back her head and touching the tip of her nose with the tip of her pointy tongue just exactly as Grace had done the first time Jack took her pelvis in both hands and pushed into her.

This was more than Jack could stand.

"Fuck you, Gracie!" he shouted at the oblivious lovers, and then he began to run.

And for a while he was able to lose himself in the running, the sweating, the panting, the burning throat, in the way the night broke down into its constituent parts: spotlit bank towers drifting beyond a weed-ruptured parking lot. Lunar moth aflutter in pink streetlight. Beer keg on tailgate and no one in sight. Street led to street led to street—like corridors with their roofs ripped off—and the city altered, unfolded, showed him neighborhoods he'd never known existed—Ardtown, Electrodia, Gap Station—street names he'd never heard of—Cream Row, Kix Alley, Hostage Avenue. Street after street with every window black. Gleaming piles of windshield glass. Speedboat on sidewalk. Vacant bank offices like movie sets for purgatory. His footfalls slapped back at him off factory facades. His panting went metallic whenever he ran through a tunnel.

But in the end: futility. In the end: no escape. Every song drifting out a bodega doorway or Dopplerizing behind a passing convertible told a story of lost love, barroom loneliness, *that night we danced beneath the stars*. Around every corner (no matter that he'd never been there before): the mailbox Grace had leaned against the first time he told her he loved her; the stoop they'd sat on, talking about their childhoods until the sky above the rooftops went rose; the fire hydrant he'd run over the day they'd had their first fight. And always those lovers in their doorways and parked cars. And always those gasps coming down from third-floor windows, those high, quavering, elongated cries—they were Grace's. Always. They had to be.

And so it was that Jack found himself he knew not where, breathing creosote and motor oil, dangling his feet over dimly radiant shards of plastic and Styrofoam that bobbed on invisible water. Rat talons clickity-clicked over splintered wood. A gunshot was followed by the sound of breaking glass. Then a long silence. A silence so long that sound itself seemed to have been extracted from the realm of possibility. And a new quality came into the darkness, a sort of solidity, as if darkness were no longer an absence of light, but a thing in itself, permanent, implacable, filling the empty spaces between every other thing. The world shrank. The world grew ever more still, ever more incapable of change, like a locked attic room, where the solitary window had been shuttered against the light, and an empty chair sat before an empty table and nothing more significant would ever happen.

After a while Jack realized that if he reached out his arm he could touch the night sky. And when he did so, he found that the stars were a sort of ash that rubbed off on his fingertips, and that the Milky Way was a trail of cinders mounting toward what he could only conclude was ultimate oblivion—which is to say, toward the only state he was, at that moment, capable of desiring. As he walked along this trail, he found himself passing near the moon, a yellowish sphere anchored to the sky by a rude assemblage of girders, along the top of which was a narrow wooden catwalk. Jack's legs still hurt from running. His lungs still burned. He made his way across the catwalk and took a seat on the moon's north pole.

The surface of the moon turned out to be much smoother than he would have thought, and warm, like a globe lamp with a lightbulb inside. The horizon was not more than eight feet away. And it was just possible for Jack to peer through the fog of the moon's yellow radiance, and make out the city, spreading off in every direction like one hundred billion glowing cigarette tips, like a disco-ball planet lit by an orange sun, like the earth's bright, pulsing heart.

Then something happened.

Something in the winking and wavering of orange lights in black night. Something in all those lights that was an incalculable multiplication of a single light being turned on or off in accordance with the whims, needs, and destiny of the individual whose hand was on the switch, or whose foot shifted between brake pedal and gas. And something, too, in the way the black night was a dome containing all that was, and in the way the city was reflected in that dome, and in the way the city and its reflection extended endlessly in opposite directions on every side. Something in all of this that seemed beautiful and poignant and too good to be true, and that, in the end, made Jack wonder how it was possible he could be sitting on the moon, and how it was that the moon should be so warm and so smooth, and whether it was safe to be sitting on a glass globe so high in the sky, and whether it was possible for him to get off the moon before it cracked, which it wasn't and it did.

And so it was that Jack made his discovery among a million tumbling moon shards. And so it was that likelihood drained from all the facts of his life, and that he understood how nothing that was had, actually, to be. And he was finally able to lift his head above the welter of his misfortune, and recognize the secret structure and true significance of all those sidewalk and barroom glances, that business with Grace's chin and Buddy's jaw, with his own toadish deformity, and the mystifying disintegration of his happiness with Grace. And he was able, in fact, to zip back through each page of his memory's flipbook all the way to his first wince, first cry, first postuterine surprise.

So many triangulated cogitations. So many unremembered instants coming back in baroque complexity, amid a countryside of possibilities. So many mysteries shooting straight through revelation and back out into mystery. How was it possible in the hair-whipping wind, in the constant reorganization of up and down, in the hurtling expansion of the glowing cityscape for one brain to process all this information? The answer was: It wasn't. And so time had to become more capacious, split seconds had to take on the qualities of hours and days. And, since time is a form of space, its enlargement was a form of slowing down, which meant that when, at last, Jack came to be reunited with the street, he settled as gently as a dust mote reaching the bottom of a light beam.

The moon was gone. Jack had destroyed it—scattering it across rooftops, sidewalks, and car hoods all over the city. But that was of little consequence, because consequence itself had been degraded by his discovery. Every instant had just been disconnected from every other, and freedom had been injected into the universe. The door to that attic room blew open. Its shutters flew back. Light poured through the window, and people poured through the door. Music was playing. Someone was dancing with the empty chair. The table itself was dancing on its four spindly legs.

Jack rolled onto his hands and knees and stood up, already noticeably less stunted, his mouth less gashlike, his eyes symmetrical again, and no longer oozing. As street opened onto street, as avenues rotated past like the long beams of lighthouses, as he climbed steps, crossed canals, and made his way along endless shadow-strewn sidewalks, he felt something like resolution, something like peace. The songs spilling out of windows and doors and hissy-whispering out of earbuds had lost their capacity to trouble him. He was living in a world where nothing was determined, where every instant of being was a manifestation of faith—and so he had hope.

Back through Gap Station, Electrodia, Ardtown, back through the hundred new neighborhoods that had been added to his city, back through the Rumination District, back and back until he was seeing Grace again, in every doorway and parked car, down every alley and through every partially opened bedroom blind. And he could never glance away fast enough to avoid that plunging pain, that weakness, that feeling of being so helpless, unwanted, and deeply alone. But he kept going because he could not believe that Grace could have turned away from him so suddenly and completely, that however much in love she might have been with Buddy, a part of her would always still be in love with Jack, a part of her would remember bicycling with him across Italy, how they had woken together in the plangent sunshine of a Nova Scotia dawn, and had looked into each other's eyes, grinning and sighing; a part of her would still gasp at the memory of the first time he took her pelvis in both hands and pushed into her. And that part, inevitably, at some point or another, would drive her out onto the street so that she could be alone, so that she could think, so that she could find a way to undo the terrible mistake she had made with Buddy.

In the end it happened exactly as Jack had imagined. Grace was leaning her forehead against the window of an Italian restaurant just off Rosenberg Square, the one they had gone to on their third date, the first restaurant they had thought of as "our place." It was dawn. The restaurant was dark, the chairs upside down on the tables. Grace rolled her head against the glass and looked at Jack with tear-rimmed eyes before he had even called her name. "Oh God!" she said, in equal parts grief and joy. "I can't believe you're here!"

They ate breakfast in a diner amid cabbies and cops. Clattering crockery. The clicks and clinks of knives and forks. Flapjacks drowned in sweet brown syrup. Muffins oozing butter. Bottomless cup of coffee following bottomless cup.

Every now and then, simultaneously, they would stop talking, stop eating. They would grasp hands across the tabletop. "I'm so happy!" one of them would say, and the other one would say, "Me too!" grin warmly, and say it again, "Me too!"

After breakfast, they walked along Eloise Avenue and into the park, where they stretched out on a grassy hilltop, kissed, professed their love, kissed again, apologized, and forgave each other. "I can't believe it!" they took turns exclaiming. "I just can't believe it!" And then they would kiss again, and apologize and forgive each other, over and over.

The city had never looked more beautiful. The buildings mounted into a perfect sky like the crystallized exaltations of angels, platinum sunbeams gleaming off their western flanks, their eastern flanks purple and blue. Clouds coasted over cornices and spires like fantastically white water lilies. Advertising dirigibles drifted like sleeping fish. A gentle breeze shivered the tree leaves, and the trees seemed larger and lusher than they had ever been, and more densely laced with birdsong.

Jack and Grace were also more beautiful than they had ever been, but not movie-star beautiful. Theirs was the sort of beauty that leaves its possessors free to be sincere, free to seem just exactly the sort of people whose love could be passionate, humble, and true. There was no longer anything toadlike about Jack's mouth, eyes, or stature. He was wiry, tousle headed, good natured, and a well-preserved forty-five. Grace's mild chinlessness was back, but only as the perfect corrective to her modelesque oscillations and her gold and flax-bright tresses. It was the locus of her vulnerability, the attribute that made her endearing, desirable, real.

But every now and then, even in the midst of their happiest of moments, Jack would feel a tremor of uncertainty, and Grace would give him a funny look. Then he could see the recognitions mounting, one after another. And, gradually, her expression would grow cloudy and still.

"Oh, Jack!" she would say. "I'm so afraid!"

"Hush." He would put his finger against her lips. "Hush."

And then he would murmur, "You're *so* beautiful." He would smile and look into her eyes. "I love you," he would say, kiss her, and say it again: "I love you, I love you, I love you." And she would tell him she loved him too, that she had always loved him, that she always would. And after that, for a while, everything would be fine.

The City in the Light of Moths

Tim Horvath

THE PROJECTIONIST'S HEART BROKE as the spool of the film he was screening snapped, sending a thousand frames rocketing through the room. But we have elided crucial moments: the groping for scissors; the hands, known for steadiness, atremble; and a last look through the thick glass before the lunge. The first cut missed but the second connected, and then he'd watched the life exit slowly, like some enemy combatant dying in his arms, so close he could taste its breath, watch last prayers sputter on its lips.

He'd imagined innumerable iterations of this, foiling terrorists and rescuing his block, no, the whole city. In his imaginings they charged in in ski masks and released the radioactive xenon that glowed inside his projector, or forced him at gunpoint to put on their radical film, or one where the screen would go blindingly bright at some point, scorching every retina in the room as if they were all standing at White Sands, unprotected, followed by a sonic boom that would shred their tympana. His fantasies expanded and contracted but inevitably wound up with him as the guest of honor at some gala, Inez's thin fingers entwined with his own under the table, "*Wesssss . . .*" engulfed in applause.

Now he gazed down into the theater that stretched out below, "the canyon," they called it, as if it had been shaped by wind and water and time, the backs of heads anthropomorphic rocks. The rocks were looking back up at him. Instead of irate cries, an eerie silence welled up, a thin veneer over a thousand sighs. He could win them back, he thought. Some down there knew him, some loved him, maybe not in the way he loved Inez, but still, the word suited. It would take, though, a move as boldly restorative as this was destructive, and as he glanced down he could see the film was even now tumbling into the room like floodwater.

Wes was required by law and by the powers vested in him as a projectionist to get another film flung up there as soon as possible. An audience in the lurch, *in cinemus interruptus*, would grow restless quickly. Uncountable other films commanded the sides of buildings for twenty miles. If he was lucky they'd pick themselves up and march out, grumbling and shaking their heads, some to return never, none happy. His wall might get its first mark, and Hatcher would rail at him: "Wes, what were you thinking, this ain't the boondocks. The Historic District. Diplomats, power players. At a debut, no less."

But darker possibilities loomed. The rowdy, the addicts—all it took was one or two, plus swirl in a couple of drinks—who might come right to the door, and let's say they began pounding and yelling about tearing him apart limb from limb? He gripped the scissors tight. It wouldn't be the first time a projectionist had been treated to vigilante justice. Technically outlawed, such violence was, but judges tended to look the other way, as if they themselves were watching a film on the wall opposite. Case in point: that dude over in District 4.1.5.E who'd twisted the lens so that the film was flipped on its side, but still, these things happen, except that out of spite or obstinacy or simple boneheadedness, he'd refused to right it, sinking deeper into his lip's curl when the boos and hisses reached fever pitch, and then when they'd yanked the bench slats out of the pavement and torn off the iron rests for battering, he'd still refused to right the film or even admit any wrongdoing. When they'd finished with him he'd been rearranged so that it was said that from that point on he would look at the world ever sideways.

Wes had always blamed the projectionist, but now he felt a shudder of empathy. Things happened fast. He thought of the opening of *The Wild Bunch*—lazy western town, women and children parading and singing down the dusty street. You knew it was about to be bad, but not how sudden and thick the blood would spurt. He reviewed his options. Under normal conditions he could change a flat in under a minute. Its seal broken, the emergency reel would hold him till he could get to the archives, and he had another film to change down the block, but he still had thirty-eight minutes to get to that.

But he stood paralyzed, stunned, not even sure whether he'd just seen what he thought he'd seen. Maybe he'd conjured the whole thing? Had that even been Inez up there?

Inez came home exhausted every evening these days, eyes bloated and hair mussed as she slipped past him into the tight apartment and made for the couch. Her stockinged feet pointed at where some ottoman ought to sit as she swigged her cognac and coke down to the ice in the imitation snifter, while he sipped coffee and geared up for his own shift. No, she didn't really want to talk about her day. No, nothing was different, nothing she could pinpoint. They were putting her on more projects, true. She was competent, had proved herself, and now they had her editing like three or four things at a time. She had to work through lunch and mind her crumbs at the console. She stayed late. This was how things happened, how you got shunted up the ladder. It was happening. At once she was editing a documentary about people obsessed with hats, a murder mystery about a surgeon whose twin brother has slain him and taken over his office, and a comedy with indie leanings about anarchists in love.

Such gear switching was inseparable from what she loved about the job, what she loved about Palamoa. Why they stayed—born there, they'd been suckled alike on celluloid, barely blinked a blink without a film in their peripheries. (*Film*, went the song, *you long, blinking train.*) Till he was three, Wes had fallen asleep each night with *Mothlight* flickering against his ceiling: semitranslucent red-pink wings that burst into petals and veiny leaves and ramifying shapes that then broke apart into a red-pink snow, all of it fluttering above him gentle as a blanket. *Brakhage*, the incantatory name of the filmmaker he'd later learn from his mom, just as he'd learn that she always knew he was asleep when his cries faded and she could still make out the faint crackle of silent film wending its way.

Hard to picture Inez as "Julia" then, hard to picture her milking and bailing, sidestepping shit amidst the grunters and lowers on her family farm in what were then Palamoa's outskirts. She still rose early. Everything else had shifted: Now where her farm was were the cineburbs, and Inez turned heads (human, not livestock) in stunning strapless things and camisoles you had to study closely to tell if you were seeing through them, while the handsome barn, a five o'clock shadow of paint peel, had itself made an appearance in several films. As kids do, she'd plotted escapes—New York, Ganzoneer, any elsewhere—and somehow gotten sucked right into the city's center.

Once Palamoa had drawn ships and sailors eager to reverse scurvy and celibacy, rushing headlong for the inland markets, for memories and paid oblivion. While they got off their sails got replaced: The Palamoans redid ships from top to bottom, but it was sails that built her, giant factories attiring ships in blaring new canvas. Today's waterfront shimmered, lobster boats sharp hued, whitecaps whispering of depth, but for the cameras, really. Wes and Inez, like many young couples, lived out by the factories, taking advantage of the laughable rents and cheap eats. As they walked past the old buildings they could hear the outsized machinery churning out screens, and a figure of speech had it that you could still cross an ocean with a Palamoan sail.

Inez must have seen things as malleable to infinity. Why scrub plates and ruin skin, when, with a slight rearrangement, you could put their dirt-bedeviled state at the front of the reel and their squeaky virginity at the end? Something like this must have been her thinking. How else could she justify such blatant neglect, like she couldn't see the piles she was leaving, the clogs she caused?

Wes cleaned up after her in those early days, not begrudgingly—it was *her* he was cleaning up for. And it was a novelty to him—he'd always prided himself on his disheveledness, his clothes creases that blurred into rumples, scornful of those who cared about such things. He was gawky and had to duck under low-hanging doorways; his glasses were scratchy, and he projected for parties and knew where to score if he didn't already have the substances you wanted. He was a hipster. His tattoo was unique. It ran up his right arm, like something in Sharpie, a hunter done in a few strokes, sneaking up on a bright red bison. When he showed it to Inez, she traced it as if she might feel the pigments.

"Is it static?"

Wes had smiled. It looked static, all right. The renderer, a friend from the art school Wes had dropped out of, had done it seamlessly; even Wes couldn't tell where skin became screen. He twitched and she gave a little gasp as it activated, and the hunter pursued the bison, who snorted comically twice and then ran into a cave. The skin blacked out until, with a blast from the hunter's torch, light returned. The punch line was the bison posed against the wall of the cave, holding preternaturally still, blending in perfectly with the paintings of animals already there. It was gorgeous, actually, this last scene, worthy of the Lascaux artist him or herself.

"Wow," she said. "Play it again, Wes."

After he did, she pulled up her own shirt to reveal hers, not animation but black and white on the center of her back, her family's farm somewhere off in the country done as a home movie, retrochromed to look older than it was, her grandfather holding up a fish, languorous cattle in a field. It was tasteful, and the bump of her spine, jutting in the middle and stretching the screen in odd places, only added to the charm. It made his feel like an amateur sketch. Everyone had heard the stories about tattoos jarred into motion in the act of lovemaking, the lover helpless to turn them off, and he wanted this, now, to be the case for them, and, reaching out to caress the bump, could see her tattoo refract onto his fingers, felt himself connect to her then, something that could still happen, then.

And now he took deep breaths and strategized as to how to buy himself some time. Stress he was used to . . . they'd cut back—the economy, everyone hurting, probably inevitable if you could play reality backward as he did sometimes just messing around in the booth, but regardless, positions had been cut, and now Wes often did the work of, by his calculations, his gripe-boasts to Inez, two or three men—he says *men* even fully cognizant that there are fantastic women projectionists, Daniella Riordan, need he say more, though it wasn't all that common, convention no doubt instead of anything deep down in the helices. Say "projectionist" and, as with "doctor," the synapses summon up a male.

He's no doctor, of course, neither the prestige nor the pay nor, indeed, the malpractice, though they treated him and the MDs and the shrinks as equals at the mandated trainings on cinaddiction. He still wasn't sure where he stood on the controversy. Nervous systems so enmeshed with films that they were *needed*? Ask him before that party and you might've gotten a different answer. Some artsy guy whose name he can no longer call up goes to a film-free party and gets stuck in the bathroom, don't ask how, and in there he just goes haywire, hyperventilating and rolling on the floor. When they pry open the door, his eyes are husks of glass, face flaring red, and his fists—these he'll never forget—clenched so that his nails leave indentations in his palms. Random frat boy makes the mistake of suggesting he just have a drink and chill out. It takes six to pull the addict off him, face bloodied, and to drag him out to the quad where something is showing. In minutes, he's calmer than a monk. Before that Wes'd been one hundred percent sure it was all mind, but the single incident brought matter neck and neck. It was a weird thing culturally. You could still joke about it but a growing number got classified and wore the wrist chains and took offense if you made light. Still, that's what the emergency reel was for. By law and as a precaution, he needed to get something up there, and so, for the first time in his career, he reached for the bright red wheel.

*

Wes and Inez stayed in spite of what the world had to say about them, how it typecast them, the Palamoans—gluttonous image ingesters, perpetual dupes, back floaters in a lotus sea. Get a few drinks in her and Inez fired back, a side of her that drew him originally. He loved to sit back and listen: *Yeah, navel gazers and deadheads, like you're not going to find those everywhere? Come on, could we possibly be any more* disillusioned*? We gaze at more navels—see more, experience more. Innies? Outies?* (She'd lift up her own shirt at this point to reveal her own adorable outie.) *Tonight if I want to I can see a film about gay Indians or the sex lives of Mongolian sheepherders. I mean, everywhere people eat, shit, fuck, and live their little lives, but we . . . we live across history. We know elsewheres.* He dug that she really did want to learn about all of those things, then, at least.

In soberer states, she'd extemporize about how Palamoans knew exactly where the cogs of illusion meshed and where the seams flickered by undetected, how life could be adjusted with the efficiency a tailor takes to a suit: a few seconds trimmed here, an inversion or two, a telling juxtaposition, voilà. Other cities may have known the wrath of monsoon and hurricane, but in Palamoa it was film, film coming down in torrents and pouring onto cutting-room floors, and it could unleash as much havoc as a force of nature, could sweep you away if you weren't careful, leave you stunned and shell-shocked on your porch, wondering what had hit you. If anything, the Palamoans were consummate realists: none of that romantic crap for them, no waiting for rescue, no delusions of being on some grand hero's journey. Their only deity was the mise-en-scène, the frame—the smudgy/hyperlucid/eclipsed/doub/led/fickle frame—that ushered in and closed out, made for happening and nonhappening. The line between abject cowardice and awe-inspiring courage might have everything to do with the frame and nothing at all with your heart. But, Gunther might have posed, what if you were outside the frame? Did you even exist then?

Inez could talk a streak, but for a while she shared her innermost thoughts only with Mervich, Henry H., who'd attained some celebrity with Reintegration Therapy, taking the splintered, shattered heap that contemporary life foisted on you and making you whole, gluing you back together. *Guy's all the king's horses*, Wes had thought. The treatments, from what he could gather, involved cooking and consuming a steady supply of veggie burgers sold by Mervich himself (they looked like Martian rocks) and taking long, hot baths. Mervich was a millionaire and was seeing Inez thanks to one of her work connections. But she swore by him. That went on for several months, and then one day his fees shot up inexplicably. From that day forward Mervich's name was non grata around the apartment, and Wes wondered but didn't pry, sure she would share when she was ready, but that was never to make it into the frame.

"Into the frame"—yes, metaphors froth in his consciousness up there in the booth. Things can get slow; once he's seen the feature for the fifth time, even at a remove—muffled audio, twice reflected in the double-paned glass—his mind does some odd turns. So, for instance, the give-out reel and the take-up reel move at the same time, but never at the same speed or in the same direction. When the film is starting out, the front wheel spins rapidly backward, and the lower one advances slowly forward. As the film progresses, they switch roles, so that by the end the lower reel is zipping along and the top one has slowed down. But there's that moment—an instant, technically—the absolute midpoint, when the reels, spooling in opposite directions, must be, laws of physics, rotating at the exact same speed. As that instant is perceived it is already gone. The screen betrays nothing; only the one in the booth could know.

And isn't this he and Inez? In mind and body, they occupy almost separate realities. When she is working, he is sleeping in or running his errands, and when she gets home he's headed out the door to project. Hours later he'll stagger in, hopped up on cola and movie candy, or maybe his late-night perambulations have brought him to a peaceful place and he can simply steal under their sheets and listen to her breathe. Only at extremely rare moments are they precisely synchronized. And even then, opposites in so many ways.

Who, he wonders on occasion, is the one in the booth?

The projectionist's nightmare: *He is not in the booth.* Well, then, the booth—who's manning it? The film running, the booth empty. Where is he? Mired in vague dream coordinates. And the film is hurtling toward its end, which he senses, viscerally as you might intuit the imminent death of a loved one many miles distant. Shit, shit. Running and running, he can't get there, anywhere. The booth stays empty.

In a snap, he was no longer in the booth, the emergency reel up and doing its job. He'd already lost part of his audience, but a sizable number were sticking it out. He'd always wondered what the red reel held, secretly hoping it would be *Mothlight*. It wasn't—it appeared to be a history of film and the city: scene from *Cinema Paradiso* where old Alfredo rotates the projector's beam out into the square. Voice-over: "*. . . which some would call Palamoa's moment of conception.*" Cut to: workers hammering sail on a mast. Scratchy jazz, herky-jerky motion. The stilted quality of a flipbook, its charm. Talk flanked by quaint quotation marks. Pleats, dames.

"Thanks for your patience!" he called out, stepping onto the floor. "A first time for everything! Please enjoy the show while we work out the technical difficulties upstairs!" Should've been wittier, he thought, should've been Wes-ser, called the backup reel *the reserve grapes*, thrown in some innuendo about the busted sex scene. He was still way out of sorts, though. Anyhow, he could already see them sinking back into their benches, settling into a story that they could never get too much of.

But instead of returning upstairs he slipped away, crossed the street, and ducked into a hidden alleyway. He felt the liberation of a kid playing hooky. On the next block, something epic, Russian, wintry was showing, and beyond that? It was a funhouse, only a funhouse asked of you a single mind state, that peculiar to funhouses, whereas Palamoa demanded a continuous pivot, a peering into the pockets of life as they turned themselves inside out one by one. The films were free, of course, to Palamoans. It had been written into the city charter at the Dimming: They'd never charge their citizens—what next, tax their moonlight, nickel-dime them for the evening breeze?

The breeze, faintly briny, buffeted him along now as he walked. As a teenager he must've covered every block at least once. Ever revising his route, its logic. He'd do this time-travel thing, careful not to repeat any era, meandering through history decade by decade. Chaplin bumbling around inside the house teetering at the edge of a cliff in *The Gold Rush* → the dank, misty tunnels below LA in *He Walked by Night* → the binocular dance of voyeurism of *Rear*

Window → *The Apartment*'s sadlovely rows of corporate futility → the stills at the peerless opening credits of *The Wild Bunch* → the purple ambush at the close of *Vagabond* → *Pulp Fiction*, any scene, really, but most of all the car, the car, the car → *City of God*'s featureless roof rows, sizzling tempers—he could gallivant over a century, cover the planet in a single swoop. If he timed it right he could hit most of his favorite scenes. It felt like being on a jet plane and watching a continent pass underwing—desert, mountains, lake, city, coast. Going in reverse had its own pleasures, and if you picked your route wisely you could find your way back to the Lumière brothers and Muybridge's horse levitations, which felt akin to catching a glimpse of the Big Bang from the Hubble.

Usually there was no method to his travels beyond serendipity and his nose, free-floating in the zero gravity of visual possibility until something caught him and held him in thrall and denuded him of time and place. Sometimes hormones overcame him and he'd find himself down by the river amid the blocks of warehouses no one had bothered tamping up the paint job on. X-town, where the moans and grunts, feigned and surely some genuine, of couples and threesomes and beyond, would've carried for miles, but were mercifully drowned out by the sweeping sound tracks of less prurient walls. The streets here, darker, cloaked the pedestrian in anonymity, but once he'd spotted one of his teachers there, a Mr. Youngman. Youngman had nodded but said nothing, as if to suggest some shared understanding, some masculine code, though from that day on they averted eyes in the halls.

Past X-town sprawled the Memorial District, a veritable city unto itself. Here they showed solely home movies of the dead, and it was transfixing simply to stand here, taking in snippets of life, candid moments—a steaming blueberry pie outheld, a frilly bikini making its beach debut, gentle ribbing about an old clunker. Only the wealthy got their own walls; for most, an hour if they were lucky, and you learned to time your paying of respects, developed a fondness for the spirits who shared that brick space with your loves. Visiting his own dad's four-minute, thirty-seven-second wall, he'd been struck at various times by:

—his dad's gangliness as he held Wes aloft at the beach and did voice-overs of some encounter between Wes and a dauntless gull

—how even in this joy his expression was sad, as if he knew

—though they never spoke, the mourner who came after him, a woman whose age he could never place, who'd lift her black veil only in the blank seconds before her own father or husband came on, then lower it immediately after, like a curtain

—the awareness that the moths who'd brought him such comfort as an infant had been dead, allowed to live again only as long as the film played

—the notion that one day the Memorial District would run out of walls.

Now he crossed in front of some fire-spitting cyborg that appeared to be taking on a meteor shower with its fists, and he was filled with a surge of pity for the genre junkies, strung out on one block, the ones who OD'd on these sci-fi films nightly, or who dieted on a steady intake of chick flicks, or those who pitched camp on Lynch Row, imbibing *Mulholland Drive* for time umpteen (by sheer repetition it would come to make sense and ordinary vision go bent and surreal). Even now he would cross midstreet if he got too close to the horror-mongers, their eyes fat with blood like sated ticks, their ears echo chambers of screams, their skin scabrous. They looked like they'd come right off the screen and would keep coming at you. A bit wiser than his teenage self, he realized that many of them scraped by as extras by day and just didn't bother stripping off their makeup.

That you could live here and know only your own kind, rarely venturing beyond your own neighborhood . . . it amazed him, peripatetic who assumed that the city was sprawled out for him, a thousand gifts waiting for his tearing hand. Nowadays, he shuttled mainly between two booths, but at his core he was promiscuous, wanting it all. With films, that is; no such temptation with women, eyes for Inez alone, minus the occasional glance at a union meeting toward Daniella Riordan.

No question this walkout would cost him. His job was probably history. Maybe he could plead with Hatcher, but likely not. At the intersection he paused at the "Don't Walk" clip with renewed appreciation for the footage of the guy waiting at a corner, his comical watch consultation and eye roll. More than a minor celebrity, "Don't Walk Guy" was an existential hero. His "Walk" counterpart, who burst blithely into the intersection, was tougher to find abiding human connection with. When his clip came on, Wes simply crossed.

No, there was no going back. The very thought should have been terrifying, maybe a little exhilarating, but all he could feel was numbness. No longer was he that teenager. He wanted the allure of what beckoned around the corner, but could only feel Inez's image behind, before, around him, her pale body, expansive, folded over edges, rooftops, fire escapes, exposed from angles that only he and a couple of others had ever laid eyes on, till now.

He rehearsed what he might say, tried out lines. "If you'd only told me . . ." "One nude scene, no big . . ." "So I'm a stepping stone . . ." "I *feel* . . ." "Fuck . . ." Outrage felt warranted but pointless. Saintly understanding rang hollow. Blood pounded in his skull. Maybe what cinaddicts felt, withdrawing. He felt his mental screen fracturing: It split, splintered—quadrants, ninths, shards. In one corner he had her by the wrist, in another stared her down, insouciant in the face of her confession; in one they were *figuring things out*. In one scene he entered, drew, and fired three bullets into her chest and watched the sheets absorb her blood, and in another he let her discover him screwing Daniella Riordan in his booth; in one he was loading his stuff onto a moving truck and in another he had her hauling hers up and in another she was weeping and begging forgiveness and in another she was even now with *him*, the other one—another begging—he who'd been visible mere moments ago on his own screen, a place as intimate in its way as his bed, and Wes recognized him at last, some producer she'd introduced him to once. Now he replayed the scene, foreign shadows slithering across her body's dunes, but this time his own entered and intervened, and she clutched at the sheets in the universal gesture of the caught, and the film went on with him in it but he couldn't see what happened next.

He needed a blank wall. A wall without image was a wall wanting image was a wall potentially anything. A wall was a screen was naked was stripped down was calling, calling for colored ions to dance up and down it, lick it caress it make love to it. Behold the naked wall. The wall without image, rare enough in Palamoa that it bore an element of eros, like women's flesh in Muslim countries. A wall was a wrist, an ankle, a filament of flesh, an object of longing and craving, something with which one might have a brush but never possess.

*

The rain felt well timed, bracing. Maybe he'd been dozing through the relationship of late. Dots were there for the connecting. All along, he should have foreseen her betrayal. Clues peppered everything down to their jokes, obvious jokes, obvious clues. He, she claimed, was the stereotype of a projectionist: aloof, holding himself at a distance, never *taking action*, never revealing anything significant about himself and projecting—of course—onto others: accusations, quibbles, warts—able to see himself only via others. And he played into it, too—"Or maybe I'm just projecting here," he would say, rolling his eyes at the lameness even while conceding its likelihood.

No kid dreamed of becoming a projectionist. It was akin to dreaming of becoming the person who cleans the space suits. Nah, the kid wants to be the astronaut, free-floating from a tether, waving to the marble world, next in peril, oxygen dwindling, some critical part burned to a crisp and the world holding its breath. The kid wants to be *aboard* the *Apollo 13*, second wants to be the actor, third to direct it, fourth do the makeup, fifth to hold the lights, tied with fifth to screen the film, tied with fetching water for the actors.

Always, she'd assumed she'd wake up next to a filmmaker someday, thought this whole projecting gig was one long temp job. And for a while he'd talked about going back to school. But it hadn't happened. Over time he'd come to embody projectionism, fused with his projectors in a sort of Buddhist oneness. Some might have been ashamed of the job, but not Wes. He embraced it, went as far with it as you could go. Not just anyone could land a job at 1.2.1, right smack downtown against the smooth side of an old granary with the antiquated equipment, antiquated except that it was the only stuff that could really do the job, which he'd tell you about if you had an hour and nowhere to be. Did you know there were anywhere between three and nine (nine!) reels that had to be loaded on to get through the film? Did you know those things weighed ten pounds, that he had to carry six at once sometimes; who needed a gym? Or that Wes had two blocks and had worked five once when some exotic flu was going around? Anyone could operate the digital stuff, be a robot like the automated system they tried to replace them with every few years, but it took a special breed to do what Wes did. He mixed films into one another like a DJ, blending them together, running closing credits into opening ones, dissolving like his hands were acid. One night he took a nature documentary and draped it, like sheer fabric, over a thriller about investment bankers. The sharks, gray apparitions too long deprived of sun, wended their way through cubicles as if the office had just that day filled with water. Was that *plankton* in the vending machines? Marvelous.

Word got around—Wesley was *one to watch*. He fancied himself a grandmaster with chessboards lined up and down, snot-nosed prodigies from all nations put in their places as he slid his retinue of warriors and church officials around the board. Or a Vassilonian chef who juggled several complex dishes at once, undaunted by the dozens of burners. His mom boasted about him to her bridge club, that he had a girlfriend and a lease, and assured him that his father would've been "busting his buttons." The only ones he couldn't seem to dazzle were the only two he wanted to, Inez and Gunther. Dissolve into

Gunther. They are kids, still, on the tracks. They are, what, nine? Ten? In his memory it is a single, long take, the day endless, tracks extending through industrial complexes and abandoned fields and farmland, the ties never letting you settle into an exact rhythm, the boys hatching schemes for derailings, robberies, and kidnappings of secretly willing ladies.

Gunther grabs his shoulder. "Stop."

Between ties, they pause, listening. Wes hears nothing. In the distance, the blocky yellow lights of warehouses and streets, not the single white one growing closer.

They walk on, Gunther chanting some hip-hop tune of his own devising.

Wes knows even then that Gunther wants the actual train, the giant projectile of steel bearing down on them. He knows Gunther will bail from the rails but wants the blowback of air, his clothes billowing outward, his hair splaying, intimations of death and danger. Wes wants these things but does not. He wants Gunther to like and respect him and hang out with him. He wants to go to movies with Gunther, but Gunther does not like to go to movies. Gunther likes girls, real ones.

Flash forward to full-grown Gunther, an avowed, unabashed anticinemite. "Just wait," Wes's mother had insisted, "he'll come around," which he'd always believed, but lately he'd begun to concede it might never happen. Gunther was staunch.

It was something of a cliché: You'd go anticinemitic in college and then become some industry clone a year after graduation. There were, too, the older ones who predated the Dimming and still spoke nostalgically of before, right up to the citywide debates that trialed their tongues and brought forth arguments of such verve and eloquence they were sure they'd triumph. But the darkness had gone forward. Some had had the wherewithal to leave, but for others where would they go; how would they relearn the topos of sidewalk and curb, find an edible knish, decent shoes, and so they stayed on, their grumbling a steady soundtrack even as film lashed at their laundry lines, and it was fortunate that many were hard of hearing and kept to their apartments.

Gunther was old at heart, Wes's mom said, but Inez begged to differ, saying rather that he'd never grown up. Like Wes, he'd been steeped in film from the womb, his mother one of the balloon-bellied who spent hours of her pregnancy under the endlessly looping sonogram in 2.5.6. Just being there, the scientists told them, brought the unborn bliss, for they would sense always a womb that limned the world.

Gunther and Wes had played on streets that were studios and sets and theaters. How, then, to account for his demurral, his stoic resistance? Some wanted the zoning laws to be stricter, wanted to preserve some streets as oases of contemplation (as if there weren't contemplative films. See *Fog Line*, see Tarkovsky *passim*). But Gunther wanted it gone, all of it.

Of course he and Inez butted heads. He'd stare into his plate when Wes tried to bring them together; "Dinner with the Dim," Gunther had dubbed it. He'd held his tongue, at least, refraining from accusing her of "nocturnocidal tendencies," part of his larger rant about how the whole *city* was an anthill of cinaddicts, not just those with the wrist chains.

"It was like I wasn't even there for your asshole friend," Inez told him that night. "Your nut case, paranoid recluse of a friend. I don't get it. I don't understand the basis of your friendship. You're going in opposite directions in life. I hope."

"It's largely racquetball based these days," Wes told her, which bore some truth. Play they did, though ball whacks were interspersed with confidences and discussion of Deleuze.

She shook her head. "This boy loyalty, I don't get it. If you were brothers it would be one thing. Tell him to grow the fuck up."

He had the sudden urge to see Gunther, wanted his ear, wanted to talk to someone who'd known him since they were measured in inches. Maybe Gunther could offer something, make it go away. He changed course, ducked into another alleyway, little more than a crevice. Gunther's neighborhood was riddled with these narrow old-city vestiges, too close quartered to squeeze films into. They were sanctuary for the Gunthers and, if you believed certain newspapers, terrorist breeding grounds. It was the most ethnically mixed part of Palamoa, neighborhoods that huddled close and went dark early. He hadn't memorized the way but remembered a temple and a botanica, and if he could find one of these he knew he could find Gunther's.

Oh but the darkness was a balm. At that moment he would've stepped straight into another one of Gunther's meetings. The pitchest black he'd ever been in. Literally they'd led him underground, blindfolded, far enough down that street noise receded entirely. Somewhere in the city's guts. It was cold, and even when his eyes adjusted there was nothing upon which to anchor his vision. That was the idea: light purge. They sat in silence for a while. He heard his own breath, no other, and felt attuned to the slightest twitchings of his brain. An ululation arose, followed by something hornlike, and then, one by one, like surfacing orcas, the voices broke:

". . . out of a hundred . . . maybe twelve to pursue further, two of whom said they might come not sure if they're among us right now."

"One is."

". . . helped a seventy-two-year-old move to New York."

". . . alongside scientists on studies of lungs and particulate matter."

". . . book, *Palamoaization and the Posthuman* due out next year from . . . University Press . . . academic respectability . . . infiltrate the higher institutions of learning . . . the classrooms."

Drawn originally by curiosity, Wes knew Gunther wanted to win him over to the whole shebang, including the orgy at the end, nakedness, and exploration of touch that shrugged off gender or orientation or background or number involved. Thankfully Gunther had warned him; Wes pictured Gunther himself reaching for him, or returning to daylight not knowing, and so he had opted out of this part of the night, which was fine. Plus he'd just started dating Inez at this point and had no intention of cheating on her.

"It's not even sexual, really," Gunther had insisted. "It's a bracketing out of everything that Palamoa stands for and embracing all that it rejects."

"Sure, not sexual." Wes wondered whether Gunther had really deluded himself so thoroughly in the name of disillusionment.

*

Maybe he and Inez just needed to get away more. Inez had accompanied the higher-ups to a couple of festivals as part of her job, but the only trips they'd taken together were to Colorado, where Inez's parents had retired after the farm sold. They'd flown into Denver a year into their relationship, made a vacation of it. Altitude or psychosomatic reaction, the first couple of days for Wes were a continuous migraine, everything too sharp, vertiginous. The third evening he strode into a moment as incontrovertible as déjà vu. They were on some street in Lodo closed to traffic, and after dinner and drinks they strode by a Cuban place where a live band out front blared a sweet old mambo, trumpets darting around a sultry crooner. A few feet ahead of Wes, a woman sashayed in a tight black dress, the correspondence between her movement and the sound track so exact he was spellbound, and he wanted to point it out to Inez, who, to his delight when he turned, herself looked like a screen star. She'd been watching with him and declared, "You want her," and he'd tried to convey what he'd experienced but she wouldn't hear of it. "You're human," she said. "It's OK." Then, suggestively, "Make it up to me later."

As they'd gone on arm in arm by the light of the closed shops, headed back toward their hotel, the windows arranged and decorated to snare attention, lit to magic, he had the sense that he was watching a film slowed down, frame by frame, and a further epiphany came on, something that couldn't be confused with sexual desire as easily as a woman's swaying. It was something like: Every city desired to be Palamoa, to be at once frame and light and motion. Palamoa itself, possessing all of these, was yet unsatisfied, for it in turn desired to be a single film that encompassed all, an ideal one that ran through all projectors at once, infinite, one that you would clip at intervals only so that you could splice more, newer footage into the old. He felt that if he could've only expressed this he would've endeared himself to Inez forever.

Maybe he should've called first, was his thought as he rapped Gunther's knocker. Gunther opened the door enrobed, like someone just awakened. For a bachelor he lived well. His unshaven face and the extra pounds, Wes supposed, would not be liabilities in the dark. Gunther always had some blue-haired chick on his arm, some girl who'd quiver, electrified by his "opiate of the masses" talk. Usually the relationship lasted till the girl wanted him to move away from Palamoa, and Gunther steadfastly refused, citing Socrates-like noblesse oblige.

"Shouldn't you be at work?" Gunther asked. Wes caught alcohol on his breath mingled with something from the kitchen that had once been in the sea.

He explained it to Gunther—what he'd seen, how he'd killed the film.

"You're sure it was her?"

"Positive. I doubted it at first. I made sure."

"A telltale birthmark? A chipped tooth?"

"It was her."

"Come in."

Within, sure enough, was the girl du jour, her hair not blue but the ripped T-shirt and spiderweb stockings and the Che button and one with a red slash through a film icon.

"My oldest pal," Gunther introduced him, and then, shaking his head as if he couldn't believe it, "a pro*jectioneer*."

"Hey, man, I don't judge," said the girl, whose name turned out to be Aurora. "You're just the hands of the system, anyway, not even like the kidneys, much less the brains."

"No offense."

"Sorry," she said. "You've had a rough night. Let me kick you when you're down."

Gunther spooned him some grilled scallops over salad and poured him wine, then launched into his spiel. Of *course* Inez had cheated on him. She was cheating on herself, living in a world of simulacra piled atop simulacra, nothing underneath, no foundation but for her makeup, sleeping her way to the top, but, as in an Escher, the top was the bottom, she was just a product of her society, her episteme, etc., etc., etc. Wes knew he should feel grateful but the rhetoric felt canned—he wanted something about Inez and only Inez, something that would make him hate her and leave the rest of the world unaffected.

"Frankly, no woman's worth losing your job over." It was Aurora.

Gunther nodded in agreement. This took him aback. He'd been sure Gunther was going to seize the opportunity to recruit him for the cause. And he was on the brink of signing on for the anticinematic resistance himself, ready to plaster a wall, to disrupt a screening, to grope and be groped in the dark.

Aurora went on. "How long ago did you leave? How quickly can you get back?"

"I don't know. . . ." He, always vigilant about time, having lost it. Had it been an hour?

"This 'backup reel' is still . . . backing you up?"

"Maybe," said Wes, on his feet now.

Gunther sounded righteously aggrieved now. "Are you going to allow her to ruin your life, take away your means of production?"

At once he felt lucid, poised, coiled. To have allowed her betrayal to steer him astray, how foolish.

"I should go back, shouldn't I?"

"Can you?"

"It may be too late. They may have shut me down."

"OK," said Gunther, pursing his lips. "Look. Here's what we do. *You* cut the film, right? No, the film was already cut. A small-scale civil disruption. Our ensemble, we'll own up to it. I'll make the call. We do that, you know. Monkey wrenches in the works. Switched reels, power outages . . . hasn't happened to you yet, has it?"

In Gunther's eyes he could see that all this time he'd protected, spared. "No, it hasn't," he said as Gunther and Aurora stood there and waved him, parentally, off into the downpour.

He had braced himself for almost any eventuality, but not the one he found: both films still going—*as if he'd never left*. Methodically he switched the other film on the next block, then headed for the booth where he'd done the deed. He threw his full weight against the door to jar it open. Within was bedlam, since the first projector, never shut down, had been unspooling film all the while, hemorrhaging it onto the floor and the counters and every available inch—tentacles and tendrils of film curling and extending from floor to ceiling, a morass he could wade through, feeling it shudder beneath him. Like a drunk who stumbles across a highway unharmed, the film seemed to have avoided passing in front of the second projector's lens. Thus it hadn't eclipsed the other, had in some mysterious fashion altered nothing, and the crowd—the seats were still mostly full—watched on, blissfully ignorant. He tugged at random strands, knots, pulling on them and holding them up to the light. None yielded Inez. He could make out a house, some establishing shot, a strange beauty in its sheer repetition.

Releasing it, he flicked the switches, and both projectors fell silent.

Soon enough this would become a crime scene. Maybe Gunther had already called, the authorities on their way. His time was waning. He flipped on the streetlights and could see their faces—*Again?*—and, film trailing behind him, he hoisted the giant reel and carried it down the stairs into the canyon.

"Ladies and gentlemen," he announced, "we're all the victims of a minor disaster tonight." He urged them not to panic. The anti-cinemites, it would appear, had struck. He searched their eyes for fear, rage, but found none, so, emboldened, he went on. Maybe they could help him find the spot where the film had been torn asunder. Together they could salvage it, reconstruct it. Maybe, he heard a new intensity infuse his voice, they could stand up to whoever had done this, show the film, damn it, through to its end. Wordlessly, then, they began to rise to their feet, some quicker than others, and reach out, tentatively at first, then with growing resolve, for the film, each of them taking a small strand, positioning their fingers carefully, pinching at the edges. To disentangle it they had to spread out, and the line that began to form went in both directions, up the stairs, down the block. He could envision a whole new way of watching a film, walking beside it, even zooming along at twenty-four frames per second—what a ride that would be! Their arms were outstretched: matronly women, businessmen with sleeves rolled up, a woman in a wheelchair, familiar faces and new ones, arms with wrist chains and bare ones. Even Gunther, it struck him, could get behind this. In the lamplight, they resembled nothing more than mourners bearing aloft a long, winding casket. All films, he thought—everyone—should be held like this once. Eventually they'd locate the end, the fatal wound, and remembering as much, he made himself slow in his movements, as if he might prolong this forever, might never find Inez, might instead slip inside one of the intervening frames and dwell there indefinitely, unknowing.

Four Poems

John Ashbery

THE ART OF STUPIDITY

Those who died did not remember it.
The living were as before.

How do you address that ooze?
For supposedly doing things when the light was ripe
like the song we inherited
that wants to join other people.

Beard and homeland trashed, tetched,
ashtray gone astray.
He yells monstrance, iconostasis
leaning in to sag ominously
after the pussycats have left.

I was a Wampas baby.
That he would do it
seemed fairly likely.
Rest, rest, rest city.

John Ashbery

SILENT AUCTION

A sundial in the *jardin des supplices*
indicates a convenient, if makeshift, hideaway,

just what we were looking for
in the time of our engagement.

Grosgrain flutters from a corncrib.
The sheep are all past.

When I went for a walk it seemed
as though the whole city was there,

confined in trombone-like tubes.
One salesman asked me to please hold thy neighbor,

another, if brightness was indeed falling.
I answered as best I knew, telling him

to look it up in an old phone directory.
Not twenty pages later I passed the woman

who knew this was a lie, but bravely
took it on the chin for me. Some women are great!

My first is a lanky stuffed gorilla.
I did all these things in the past.

Whole embassies have crashed, and now, thank you,
the measurable pain is coming due.

We who segued on the sidelines,
unfelt-up and driven, know how it aches

and keep our peace. Wow, kitty, that sure
looked real, you've got to admit, and I in my wrapper

and mama in her cap put out stories about the new
mood that slurped above the horizon,

the *Tannhauser* lost in the local *mer des glaces,*
for once unsung, though thoroughly inebriated.

OR THAT OLD IDENTITY

The angel is just starting to tick.
Word of the setback seeps under doors
in the city's sex district. The police
have warned against just this sort of punk setback
for ages. How will the long-faced peers react?

Can such things be?

About a half mile down the road
an acceptance speech sputters and unwinds.
Better the dark card and the igloo
than the unfashionable turn of events.
Summer gloves against hills turned to dark
in winter. I was as a little child one day
and the markers came, spoiling for a drift.

Let thine awful trigonometry
fade,
others bruise past, soaring.

It doesn't occur that he shout
because you have a lot of gangsters,
(mustn't feel pressured)

and he says he speaks with the

John Ashbery

THE ECONOMY

In all my years as a pedestrian
serving juice to guests, it never occurred to me
thoughtfully to imagine how a radish feels.
She merely arrived. Half turning
in the demented twilight, one feels a
sour empathy with all that went before.
That, needless to say, was how we elaborated
ourselves staggering across tracts:
Somewhere in America there is a naked person.

Somewhere in America adoring legions blush
in the sunset, crimson madder, and madder still.
Somewhere in America someone is trying to figure out
how to pay for this, bouncing a ball
off a wooden strut. Somewhere
in America the lonely enchanted eye each other
on a bus. It goes down Woodrow Wilson Avenue.
Somewhere in America it says you must die, you know too much.

City/Body: Fragments

Susan McCarty

CORNER OF A AND FOURTH/EYE

IN NEW YORK, there is an important distinction to make between where you live and where you sleep. You sleep in your apartment. You live in the city.

It is a dripping August, which you know by the smell of it: dried urine, rotting garbage, and the unleaded smell of cabs burning off fuel as they idle in the shimmering heat, each a mirage, a promise of something better on the other side. You can't get into a cab today because the ten dollars in cash and change sitting on the desk in your apartment is all you have until payday, which is Friday. Today is Sunday. You don't have a bank account because the check-cashing place is convenient to your apartment. Also, you don't trust yourself with a bank account; the margin of error is always, always so small. Instead, you like to watch the stack of cash dwindle in front of you. It causes you anxiety, but it also makes you feel as though you are in control of something here, in New York. You are in control of nothing, of course, but the illusion helps.

Because you sleep in the East Village, in a studio apartment in an old tenement that you share with a roommate, you walk the streets for entertainment. On paydays, you allow yourself a Cuban sandwich from the take-out counter on Avenue A. Today, however, you simply stand in front of the door for a few minutes, because smelling something is almost as good as eating it, and smelling something other than urine and garbage makes you happy. The smells are engrossing, in fact, which is why you don't notice what has been going on behind you until there is the sound of something whining through the air, not very far from your head, and then the noise of the bystanders, who must have been there all along, suddenly rushes in and you turn in time to see two men grappling with each other, in the street, just feet away. One of them has a hammer. In the moment it has taken you to notice the scene and become confused by it, the man with the hammer bounces it off the side of the other man's head and there is a sound that would, under other circumstances, be a satisfying sound—the sound of a job being completed, of something being forced into its proper place. You actually see the eye of the struck man wobble in its socket, as if it has just been dropped there to settle. And they are both screaming—one in anger and the other in pain, but the sidewalkers are screaming too and so the scene takes on a kind of miserable white noise wherein no one person's distress can be sorted from another's.

The police sirens are what finally cut through and break the cord that had knotted around you, anchoring you to this place to watch a man maybe get killed. This is true for everyone, and when the cop car screeches up, the men have already run off together, like wild elopers, one with his hand over his eye and a trail of blood down his shirt, the other just behind him, brandishing the hammer like a cartoon wife with a rolling pin after a mouse.

ST. VINCENT'S/LOWER LEFT QUADRANT

David Beckham has broken the second metatarsal in his left foot. You do not care very much except that the picture of him in the sporting publication open on your lap—he sits on the ground, one hand over an eye, one hand on the foot, worried and in pain—is the only thing distracting you from your own pain (back, lower left quadrant), which is unlike any pain you've had before. It is also distracting you from the St. Vincent's ER, which is the least comforting place you've ever been. Everything is a shade of grayish green. There are no plants or tissue boxes. There are spots of dried blood on the floor in front of you. You sit facing the windows and feel like you're in prison. You are trying not to pay attention to the couple seated to your left. You try to focus instead on the lesser pain of Becks, but your neighbors are difficult not to overhear.

It's the meth, the boyfriend says, he's been doing it all weekend. The ER attendant asks the man who is not the boyfriend how much meth he has done this weekend. The man is weeping quietly. He sits straight up in the green vinyl chair, one hand gripping the chair arm, the other twisting his boyfriend's hand, which has gone white and slightly blue from the pressure. His eyes don't look anywhere. I don't know, all of it? says the boyfriend, grimacing at his twisted hand, but content to bruise, to share. The expressionless attendant makes a note on a clipboard. And when did he do the, uh, procedure? she asks.

I don't know, says the boyfriend. I just woke up and went to the bathroom and he was sitting on the toilet like that. Like what? asks the attendant just because she wants to hear it again. With his . . . the boyfriend whispers but can't talk too quietly because his man has started to make a low whining sound in his throat. With his testicles stapled to his thigh, he finishes and puts a hand on the head of the whining man, who is wearing loose, dry-weave exercise shorts.

You have glanced up from Becks to catch this glimpse and you'd almost forgotten yourself but here is the breathless punch again. You jerk in your seat and pant. Your vision tunnels, momentarily, the periphery dark and fogged out. You seem to pulse in empathy with your neighbor. Later, you will learn that a UTI has crawled up your urinary tract to your kidneys, which are infected, which can be life threatening but is also easily treatable.

The man with the staples in his balls lets out a thin howl, which is unlike a dog howl. It is not rounded and full and conclusive. It's the sound of pure pain. The bemused ER attendant has come back out of the triage station and even she looks concerned now. You look back down at the photo because you feel very strongly that you would also like to howl, that you would like to hold this man's hand and go a little hysterical with him.

There is a bustling—the attendant and the boyfriend are trying to coax the patient into a wheelchair. You can't imagine how he got here, how he walked at all, down the stairs of his apartment building, to the curb to hail a cab. It must have taken tremendous reserves of strength. He must be exhausted. There is a yelp and a moan followed by some rustling, and the squeak of rubber tires on sanitized linoleum.

David Beckham looks very tired and perhaps as if he is about to cry or has just finished crying. Probably just about to cry—there is something like disbelief in his face. It is 2002 and his foot is worth several million pounds. Something knocks at you from the wrong side, from the inside. You close your eyes, and Beckham's gleaming shin guards stay with you, ghost your retinas for a moment, then dissolve.

WORLD TRADE CENTER/HEAD

You meet a friend for dinner at Molly's, which is full of the usual regulars—undocumented Irish construction workers and investment bank lackeys: the administrative assistants and data enterers and mailroomies. You are eating a medium-rare burger with one hand and decadently smoking with the other. It is almost as if you intuit that this won't be possible for very much longer. You haven't been following it, but the bill will be passed in December; the bars and restaurants smoke free by spring.

You are on your second Guinness, which makes you want to put on music. You like Molly's juke because it has the most Pogues albums in the city, plus it's been one of those days—frequent lately, it seems. You feel funny but you don't know why. You don't even know what you mean by funny. Which is what you say when your friend, who is having the shepherd's pie and also smoking, asks. Tomorrow's the anniversary, he reminds you. How have you worked in an office all day, printing letters and time-stamping materials to be copyedited and proofed, penciling dates in your boss's calendar even, without seeing?

I walked, he says without prompting, seven miles home to Brooklyn. I drank an entire bottle of whiskey that night. When I woke up the next morning I thought it had all been a nightmare. Really? you ask. No, he says, not really. I spent the night throwing up in my bathroom, completely sober.

So you didn't drink an entire bottle of whiskey?

No, I did that. But I didn't forget. That part's wishful thinking.

You weren't living here then so it's not your memory to share, but you listen to him talk a little more about the dust and the fear and the posters, some of which still hang in gray swelled strips on the lampposts and scaffolds around town. They are unreadable now, but no one will take them down. As you listen, something uneasy shifts inside you. The room darkens a bit and the sound of the other patrons is suddenly deafening. You stand up, unsure of where you are going, until he puts a dollar in your hand and requests "Fairytale of New York."

The jukebox swims in front of you—you can't make out the numbers next to the track listings and you seem to be having trouble drawing a full breath. The door is two feet away and you leave the jukebox queued with money to get some fresh air, to get out of this cave for just a minute.

The street is empty, and in the deepening dark of the night, you see that the blue lights are on. There is no cloud cover tonight, so they rise up from Ground Zero as far into the sky as you can see. You wonder if there are astronauts out there right now and if they can see these other twin towers, these ghosts. You have never looked at them for very long because, even though you have no religion, and the thought is frankly stupid, you are afraid that if you look at the lights long enough, you will see the spirits of the dead being sucked up in them, like some tractor beam to heaven, a pneumatic salvation. Like jumping off a building in reverse. You try to take a deep breath but your breath won't come. The lights go out.

When you come to, you see the upside-down faces of strangers and between two of their heads, the blue lights. You are extremely confused. If someone asked you your name, you would not be able to say. There is no sound but a soft ringing. Then your friend's head juts into view and his voice cuts through the white noise: What happened? Where'd you go? Jesus Christ, you're bleeding.

You decide not to say anything until someone tells you what's going on. Your friend sets you up and cradles you and puts a napkin—where did he get the napkin?—to your chin and if you are glad for something it's that the tower lights have left your field of vision. You sit on the sidewalk while concerned people bird-walk around you and make noise on their cell phones and then there is an ambulance and then you are inside it and your friend holds your hand and your hair when you throw up into a white bag, but until you turn to go crosstown to Bellevue, to stitches and the diagnosis of a concussion, and some half-baked hypotheses about undercooked meat and low blood sugar, you make yourself look at those two lights through the portholes in the back of the ambulance doors, as if your looking could mean anything at all.

EMPIRE STATE BUILDING/PHALLUS

You have been inside twice now and up to the top once, but you can't remember much of the trip except that the lobby ceilings seemed too low, too gray, and the elevator went so fast your ears popped. When you think of the Empire State Building it is always an exterior view, jutting beyond the tops of the Village brownstones, a guiding beacon at night, when the streets creep together and the city rearranges itself. When the grid seems to disappear, there is always that great glowing pyramid tip. They change the lights on it according to the seasons or holidays, but in your mind, it always glows red, white, and blue—a sign of American optimism, a great anchor of capitalism, that directional daddy, standing guard.

You look at it now, reassured you're headed north. This part of the city feels friendly. The old tenements crouch close. The shop windows are lit and full of the kinds of businesses you never have need for—a stationery shop, a designer pet-clothing boutique, a restaurant that serves $30 macaroni and cheese. It is not even late, only freshly dark, which is why you are not scared, but merely surprised, when the passenger door of a semicab parked on the street opens as you come parallel to it and a man in a gray hoodie, eyes wide but expressionless, yells to you from the depths of the truck. He looks you straight in the eye and asks a simple question.

How does it look? he says. And you, stopped now, the Empire State eclipsed by the massive brow of the cab, can only ask, What? Your voice hangs in the air for a frozen moment and in that moment you see that the man has his cock in his hand, is yanking on it violently. You can't help but be transfixed by the head of it, squeezing past his white-knuckled hand. You realize that he is about to pull his own dick off in front of you.

Then the man is talking again, and automatically your eyes move back to his face. His own eyes are still wide, but now they are worried too. I'm going to see my girl, he says. But I been driving on minithins all night. Is it hard enough?

Your legs have realized, before your brain, that it is best to leave quickly, that the ladies selling French paper twenty feet away will not be able to help you should this man decide to drag you into his cab and make material his question. But really, no, that is not what you think. That is what you should have thought. On some level your brain has responded mechanically to the danger, but consciously, the only situation you know that resembles this one is a joke. And so you laugh. You turn around and trip away nearly screaming with it. Later, you spend your last five dollars on a cab ride home.

RIDGE AND RIVINGTON/MOUTH

Your first mistake is that you are wearing headphones. You try to remember to take them off on the subway platforms and at night, on the street, but there are so many rules to remember. This one sometimes escapes you, especially when you are listening to very good music, which occasionally makes you feel as if you are starring in a movie and the movie is your life, which is one of the more pleasant feelings New York inspires in you. Occasionally, New York makes your life feel much bigger and more interesting and possible than it is. This makes it easy to forget.

You are also wearing heels—the tall and tottering kind. You can't run in them—you can barely even walk. But you are walking, alone, from a bar in SoHo to your boyfriend's apartment on the Lower East Side because it is faster to walk across this part of town, even in tippy shoes, than to take a cab.

You see him first as you turn onto Delancey. He is walking alone. He wears a white T-shirt and a green stocking cap and looks like everyone else on the sidewalk tonight, which is why you forget him almost as soon as you see him. He drops back and you stutter-step on to your mix CD. It is only when you turn again onto Clinton that you sense someone behind you and stop to pretend to look at a menu in a restaurant window. Your Discman is in your coat pocket and you turn it off. Out of the corner of your eye, you see the man, the white T-shirt. He has turned the corner too, and he is walking slowly. You don't know if he slowed his walk when you stopped to read the menu or if he has been walking that way this whole time and you are just being paranoid. But your paranoia is not unfounded—lately, more than usual, dead girls have been in the news.

In fact, you realize, as you read the description of a rosemary-lemon lamb risotto for the third time, that the bar you have just left is very near the Falls, where just a couple weeks ago that grad student was abducted and later found raped and strangled, bound with packing tape and dropped off near the Belt Parkway like a gift. And the actress, last year, not two blocks from your boyfriend's apartment, one block from where you stand right now. You were out that night too, doing what you can't recall. You remember her last words from the newspaper, though. What are you going to do, shoot me? she asked them. They did. This is how you remember to be good.

You should go into the restaurant. You should go into the restaurant and order a drink and call your boyfriend and tell him to meet you here. But when you look around again, the man is gone. You begin to get mad. This fucking city, you think. You tell yourself a joke. A girl walks into a bar . . . there is a punch line. Something to do with putting out, with being put out. The punch line is she didn't keep her mouth shut, of mouths taped shut, a bullet in the lung. You'll be goddamned if you'll slink into that restaurant. You turn and begin to walk determinedly up the street. You find your keys in your pocket and poke them like claws through your clenched fist. You clench your jaw to match your fist. Soon there are footsteps behind you again. You barely turn your head and get a glimpse of white cotton. The city thickens its breath.

Here's something funny you know: The Falls is owned by the Dorrian family. They also own Dorrian's Red Hand, which is where Robert Chambers met Jennifer Levin the night he walked her to Central Park, raped and bit her, then strangled her to death. Once, a man you were seeing took you to Dorrian's and you walked back to his place through the park, past where she was killed. He wanted to spook you. Just a bit of fun.

You are running unsteadily now, really more of a lope than a run; certainly this lead-assed shamble will not save your life. You can't hear him behind you over your own breath and the shod clop of your heels. Somehow, you manage to dial your boyfriend with your free hand. Open the door right now, you say as you round Rivington, his door half a block away. There is something in your voice because he doesn't say a word over the phone, but in a few more seconds you see him emerge onto the lit stoop. He is waving, but not smiling. You rush up the steps and pull him into the hallway and push the locked door shut behind you. There is no one on the sidewalk or the street, just your own reflection in the glass door, your pale, translucent face laid over the night, eyes like drill holes, lips parted and mute.

MANHATTAN/HANDS

An Australian tourist has brought you here, has attached himself to you in the cold gray moments before dawn. You shiver in your down parka after so many hours in the club, and that after-hours dive, and when he grips you closer, the feathers in your coat puff from the sudden pressure. You smell of sweat and whiskey and his cologne, something cheap and strong and chemical, but somehow not unpleasant. His hand twists softly in yours in a way that means he is about to say something.

Here's a spot, he says and stops walking and you both look around. Here? you ask. You are standing at Twenty-third and Eighth, a monotonous Chelsea corner without charm or color. Your tongue is sore from the hours you've spent twisting it into improbable shapes in his mouth. You'd gone to Centro-Fly with some friends late last night, dressed to get the cover waived—something artfully shredded, glittering webs of fabric.

It happens every so often that you crave the kind of release you can find in a place like Centro-Fly, with all those beautiful strangers, each one a possibility, it doesn't even matter of what. What matters is by the end of the night you are abandoned to it all: the low lights and the bass pulse of the music, a sweaty flirtation in every corner, the anonymous press of curious limbs.

You don't know his name because he told you, but you couldn't hear, and so you asked him to repeat it and you still couldn't hear, but you nodded as if you had. This is probably why he calls you "Love" instead of your own name and you don't mind. He'd started a conversation by asking if you were French—the best pickup line you'd ever heard, worthy of reward. You'd tried on a Parisienne pout in response, allowed him to buy you a drink and become quickly entangled in a misty corner of the club, all legs and mouths and fingers. Tomorrow, he will leave with his friends and return to Sydney and you will never see him again and this is the way it should be—his presence now perfect because of the totality of his absence later.

He has brought you here to witness. There's this thing he'd read about in the paper yesterday, this thing that happens twice a year, once at dawn, once at sunset, where the sun aligns perfectly with the cross streets of the city, the grid, and . . . here he frowns.

And what? you ask, but he doesn't know. It's a thing you're supposed to see at least once in your life, he says, the sun barreling down the streets of Manhattan like a huge, spectral taxi.

Of course, you say. And there is nothing more important to you right now than to stand on this corner, next to this dark Baskin-Robbins, and look down the barrel of the cross street for the dawn. Sometimes things are that simple. You smile as he puts his nose in your neck and sighs.

The streets are nearly empty this early on a Sunday morning and this makes the city seem like a wilderness. As you watch, the sun begins its crawl over the top of the edge of that wilderness the East River. It angles through the tall muddy buildings thrown up around it like canyons, as if they had always been there and always would be. The buildings on either side of the street seem to cup the sun, but cannot hold it, begin to disappear behind its needle-thin spikes, which creep toward you until they engulf you too and you feel yourself begin to disappear. But when you look behind you, your shadows belong to giants. Your Australian smiles at you and for a moment you're in love, entranced, held by him, by the city, kept safe in these palms and, looking back down Twenty-third Street, you think how the city proffers so many kinds of darkness, but here, on this corner, just now, a new kind of light.

Dada Capital of Exiles

Norman Manea

I AM LOOKING DOWN on Central Park and recall from half a century ago in a small town in Northern Romania a tall, white-haired man proclaiming his poem, "The Colors Red and Black." Gazing over the park, I remember those Stalinist-era verses:

> In New York, everything is beautiful.
> Heroes come, heroes go.
> Children, born for Sing Sing,
> Cover the streets like pellagra.
> Yellow karate-blood
> Pulses through each building.
> In the harbor the Statue of Liberty!
> Behind her elevated falsehood
> Yankee ghosts howl at the moon
> Tormented as if from pellagra
> By the colors red and black.

The red of the Revolution, of course, and the black of the oppressed race. Cliché was the common currency of all Communist dictatorships, but they had the opposite effect of what the regime intended, for they cast an aura of forbidden fruit around the slandered New World metropolis, making it seem a glowing Olympus of modernity, an urban Everest of adventure.

The few trips I was allowed to take as a citizen of Socialist Romania did, of course, have moments of rapture for me, novice that I was. Yet New York remained a dream, so foreign and distant that I never imagined I would have the chance to compare illusion with reality. My eventual escape to New York had nothing to do with tourism. Sudden terror before this omnipresent, all-devouring monster was soon overtaken by fascination.

The critic Irving Howe, a New Yorker of long standing, tried to temper my enthusiasm. "To enjoy this city you need a good apartment and a certain salary." I was living in a miserable hotel in a rundown neighborhood, consumed with a newcomer's neurotic insecurity. Yet I found everything irresistible, the city's rhythms and colors, its contrasts and surprises. That Walt Whitman and Mark Twain, Herman Melville, Henry James, and John Dos Passos had lived here, that Enescu, Brancusi, or Eugene Ionesco had been successful here in no way raised my hopes.

Life in and with this city was as hypnotic as a drug. Over the last seventeen years this addiction was established through daily negotiations with life's routine. New York's metabolism filled me with its energy and its toxins.

Although I felt that I, an exile in the land of exiles, belonged ever more to a world to which no one can really be said to belong, on September 11, 2001, I was finally able to proclaim, "I am a New Yorker," just as President Kennedy had declared himself a Berliner when that former National Socialist capital was in danger of becoming a Communist capital.

The Old Testament tells how work on the tower in Shinar, in ancient Babylon, was disrupted because man aspired to reach the heavens and divinity. Suddenly the builders could no longer understand each other. Different languages divided them. In present-day Babylon in Chinatown, in Little Italy, in Russian Brighton Beach, and in the alleys and byways of New York, all the world's languages are spoken. The builders of the twin towers, whatever their native tongues, wanted to be Americans, citizens of the New World, the towers they built symbolizing the stature of freedom.

The attack on the towers of Babel was unexpected but not unpredictable insofar as it represented the hatred of Allah's fanatical followers for the symbols of modernity. In the World Trade Center, human creativity and collaboration were universally codified. Of course, the building lacked poetry. Yet the towers could have been a symbol of worldwide poetry, not commerce. As the Surrealist poet André Breton said, "It is above all our differences that unite us."

Surprisingly, for such an extensive, cynically efficient cluster of humanity, the city displayed surprising civility and solidarity during and after the attacks. It immediately regained its strength, its sense of humor, and its industriousness. After September 11, 2001, skyscrapers, clubs, and restaurants of all kinds sprang up like mushrooms, with almost more vitality than before. Moreover, the city refused to give its votes to a president who exploited its disaster for political gain.

Romania is often called the Land of Dada, not because one of its sons, Tristan Tzara, was a founder of Surrealism, but because of the absurdity and paradoxes of its daily life, particularly in its politics. In exile, I immediately identified with another capital of Dada, the "cosmic republic, that speaks all languages in a universal dialect," as Johannes Baader put it. Here, the old and the new are accomplices in celebrating life "in all its incomprehensibility"—exactly the subversiveness that the Dadaists loved.

A famous map painted by my friend and compatriot Saul Steinberg depicts the global village as seen from Manhattan: The distance from the Hudson River to the Pacific Ocean is the same as the distance from Ninth to Tenth Avenue on the Upper West Side, and somewhere beyond the calm ocean float Russia, China, and Japan. Saul's other maps evoke his past: Milan, the city of his youth; Zurich, where Dada got its explosive start; and the Romanian city Buzău, where he was born.

A map of my own fate would encompass Bukovina as my native land, the Transdnistrian concentration camp of my childhood, the Communist labor camp Periprava, where my father's identity was altered, the Bucharest of my student years and my adulthood, Berlin, my exile's starting point, and finally New York, where my exile found its residence. This fate is its own "Babel," a confused mixture of memories and places.

Here on the Upper West Side, in the middle of a triangle formed by Central Park, Lincoln Center, and the Hudson River, I was once in the habit of beginning each day with an exotic act of devotion, a ritual of humility. I now had a good apartment and a certain salary, so Irving Howe's conditions for life in the city were fulfilled. From my window, I watched the Rubbish Gangster: shaven head, bull neck, and swollen nose, from which dangled mucus-encrusted strands of hair, his short arms bursting with criminal power. Every day, at the same hour, he appeared with his metal trunk stuffed with all that he had collected from street-corner garbage cans; it was as if he wanted to ensnare me with his street sorcery so that I could see the city's unfathomable contrasts.

The writer, caught up in the shelter of solitude, does not have much time to wander about. His neighborhood is his world, the geography of his calendar. Luckily, the streets of New York offer extraordinary spectacles wherever one is. In the Bronx or in Soho, in Washington Square or Times Square, in front of the New York Public Library or near a hot-dog stand, across all the planets' races, the banal vies with the exceptional for one's attention. All faces, ages, and events, sooner or later, can be found here.

Routine increases banality and thoughtlessness; the personal disappears. You pursue your business here as only New Yorkers can, but every once in a while you look up and wonder, "How did I get here?" Or, rather, "How on earth did mankind come so far?"

I often look at New York's architecture as if looking at an art book. On my way home from Bard College, in Annandale, where I teach, I am greeted by the George Washington Bridge majestically suspended over the Hudson River. It is a glorious welcome, even in fog.

The same is true of the skyline. Approach the city and you see the urban center of the world—a hard and harried place, marked by social contrasts as dizzying as its skyscrapers and with a sense of transience as elevated as its buildings. Its workforce labors round the clock and its inventiveness, energy, and diversity counter provincialism with scorn. Like America itself, although so utterly different, New York can only be comprehended "synthetically." This festively incoherent capital of Dada is a spectacular fusion of freedom and pragmatism. Misery and magnificence, seduction and neurosis create and recreate the dynamic, unmistakable spectrum of New York life.

In this city you learn to limit yourself. It is impossible to take in at once all of the innumerable symphonic or jazz concerts, or parades celebrating ethnic or sexual minorities. You can't attend all the lectures, panel discussions, and auctions where everyday dramas and dreams are bartered. You can't sit in all the taxis driven by these loquacious ambassadors from India and Russia and Haiti, from Pakistan and Ghana and Guatemala. At best you can grab a mere crumb of this frenetic global kaleidoscope. In the end, in New York you own nothing more than the instant, the now, the right now.

Again I look over Central Park. "Dada covers things with an artificial tenderness," wrote Tzara. "It is snowing butterflies that have escaped from a prophet's head."

From Breathtaken
Text by C. D. Wright
Photographs by Deborah Luster

I.

napping in her car with her 19-week fetus

at the tattoo parlor behind the barber shop

in a coffee-colored shotgun, 7th Ward a triple,
one of the men wore women's clothes

in the chest by a neighbor

under a cell tower

during a concert at Hush

next to a snowball stand

in a trash bin facedown

in the shadow of the Superdome

facedown she brought a flower to the spot

in the driver's seat

fleeing into Sleepy's Lounge

while walking down Chippewa, 8:20 p.m. she had on the dress he bought her

facedown

bringing back stuff to make gumbo

lying on his back on Willow   watching the dark torsos of clouds

shots sprayed from a green van

working on a house   he loved his mother's pies

by his idling car

faceup   watching the clouds bulk up and blow over

in the passenger seat on Sister Street

walking home, 5:25 p.m.   carrying a bottle of whole milk

in a room at the Travelodge   pending identification

in the family living room   watching his program

parked in his pickup   half a muffuletta in his lap

beneath a tree   looking up through a canopy of speckled light

in a pile of debris   outside a blighted house

faceup

after being carjacked the night before

after they raped her they shot her

one spoke

inside his apartment

from a black Acura

felled on Constance

while changing a flat on I-10 eastbound

the sun severed by rebar

his girlfriend

Hush

through a slot in his stockinet

in his favorite shirt

in the stairwell   of an Algiers complex

on Josephine on Christmas night   a double

on the sidewalk on St. Ann   wearing counterfeit Nikes

facedown   he tried to avoid the cracks in the walk

beside a bicycle   a thin chevron of hair above the lip

side entrance of St. Luke's

last seen leaving a club   in the Sugar District

inside his water-damaged apartment

inside a blue Volkswagon on Ursuline   a witness

to a murder trial postponed

[first the killer had to drop off his kids]

II.

corner of Hollygrove and Palm

over the Industrial Canal on Chef Menteur

lying on Olive Street   looking at the moon

swollen, urinous

inside a silver Isuzu

corner of Touro and N. Roman

at the former Sugar Bowl Lanes   decomposed

near Elysian Fields overpass

in the backyard   watching the rags of cloud float over

driving north

driving a black Buick Regal

driving on Felicity

on the sidewalk about noon   clouds

pushing past the lenses of his Ray-Bans

in the courtyard of the housing complex

N. Roman again   hushed

inside a red Chevy Lumina

in the Community Care   Psychiatric Hospital

after being stomped and beaten   and forsaken

facing   a mud nest under a gallery

on Dauphine

in the backyard   wearing counterfeit True Religion jeans

in the front yard

Calyisse, 19 and Fitzgerald, 19   in an abandoned house near Fig Street

in Gert Town   home of Blue Plate Mayonnaise Factory

near Fig Street   elevation 0

III.

[*Fabulous*, that was her byword]

inside a black Toyota Scion

inside her ransacked house

inside Happy Jack Social and Pleasure Club

lying in the street facing

a deflated basketball under a parked car

IV.

N. Prieur again

in his FEMA trailer asleep with the TV on

in the Tallowtree neighborhood

inside his home with his throat slit

in his house on Terpsichore   [by gunshot unless otherwise noted]

on Claiborne at the line   between Pigeon Town and Hollygrove

New Year's Day   in front of his grandmother's house, 6th Ward

shot 14 times   [courtesy of NOPD]

at a graduation party in the backyard   a girl totally in love with poetry

mother of a 30-month-old   the father ambushed in his car

a few days after she learned she was pregnant

he never even knew   [her cycle was off]

by men in black   coming out from the trees shooting

in a car chase

sprawled   out of a black Chevrolet Monte Carlo

twins   on Telemachus and Baudin

under a vehicle   from a beating

intersection of Conti and Treme

in the Holy Cross neighborhood

in Le Petit Motel   an unidentified woman

in the 8200 block of Chef Menteur

at Cooper public housing

downed next to an abandoned complex in St. Roch   [found by a dog] at Cooper public housing again

his mama is going to miss him

something awful

on Elysian Fields

on Touro again

found in her pickup

former NOPD

near Downman Rd. ramp

in a baby blue Volkswagon

talking

through the car window

smoke gushing out of her nostrils

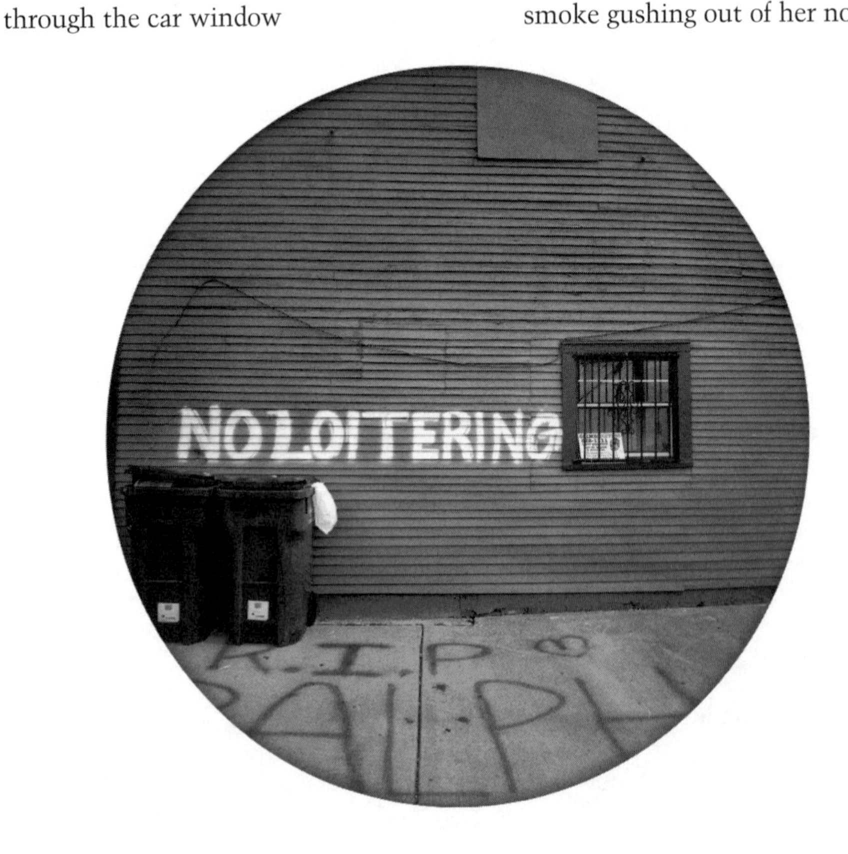

at Iberville again

in the back of the head near the Commons Bar

homeless, stabbed in torso

homeless, stabbed in back

on Loyola

on Danziger Bridge, a boy, 17 in the back [NOPD]

on Danziger Bridge, a man, mentally challenged in the back [NOPD again]

behind the wheel of his new car

by a peer, 14

on Babylon Street, 17, by peers

in Gert Town elevation 0

home to Blue Plate Mayonnaise Factory

playing dice on the porch a triple

three more still breathing Lower Ninth

Jack's Bus Stop

near the Super Sunday parades

in town to visit relatives for Memorial Day when he stayed in Houston

he was out of the woods so his mama thought

in Terrytown named for the developer's first girlchild, a triple

near intersection of Old Gentilly Rd. and Michoud, found beside the road

Brittany, 17 [who never met a stranger]

the baby would not stop crying multiple fractures and tears in the anus

in the Ninth Ward, a double

in St. Roch near intersection of Johnson and Music

N. Claiborne and Frenchmen

Wendy a bartender at Aunt Tiki's and Starlight by the Park

corner of Governor Nicholls and Dauphin by 3 teens

[turned in by the parents]

his shredded heart feeling death upon him

the evidence voluminous

I put her body in water I'm willing to give you that the prisoner replied

that other, that's a gray area

he got off watching their eyes roll to the back of their heads

a fellow inmate testified

a preponderance of evidence requires a lower standard than proof

beyond a reasonable doubt

once you start talking about more than more murder

and the defendant is ugly to look at or ugly acting or has an ugly history

in water evidence such as semen

can wash away be ruined by marine life

the Handcuff Muzzle™ is an effective and versatile restraint device

the Handcuff Muzzle™ is made of vented mesh nylon

[this material has a long life expectancy]

this material is washable and comes in a variety of colors

the Grommet guarantees a snug fit

in two main sizes one is for securing females or males

with your smaller hands

the other size is for your general population

an X-large bag by special order

the Wrap is the ultimate immobilization system

never think upward unless downward first

it's police blotter time did you lock the side door

well, I said, hell to yes

V.

inside a white Chevy Impala

in the rear of Fischer public complex

on the side of abandoned Kennedy High

lying in an alley next to an abandoned house faceup

dreaming of electric sheep

The Graveless Doll of Eric Mutis

Karen Russell

THE SCARECROW THAT WE FOUND lashed to the pin oak in Friendship Park, New Jersey, was thousands of miles away from the yellow atolls of corn where you might expect to find a farmer's doll. Scarecrow country was the actual *country*, everybody knew that. Scarecrows belonged to country men and women. They lived in hick states, the "I" states, exotic to us: Iowa, Indiana. Scarecrows made fools of the birds, and smiled with lifeless humor. Their smiles were fakes, threads. (This idea appealed to me—I was a quiet kid myself, branded "mean," and I liked the idea of a mouth that nobody expected anything from, a mouth that was just red sewing.) Scarecrows got planted into the same soil as their crops; they worked around the clock, like charms, to keep the hungry birds at bay. That was how it worked in TV movies, at least: horror-struck, the birds turned shrieking circles around the far-below peak of the scarecrow's hat, afraid to land. They haloed him. Underneath a hundred starving crows, the TV scarecrow seemed pretty sanguine, grinning his tickled, brainwashed grin at the camera. He was a sort of pitiable character, I thought, a jester in the corn, imitating the farmer—the *real* king. All day and all night, the scarecrow had to stand watch over his quilty hills of wheat and flax, of rye and barley and three other brown grains that I couldn't remember (my brain stole this image from the seven-grain Quilty Hills Muffins bag—at school I cheated shamelessly and I guess my imagination must have been a plagiarist too, copying its homework).

This mission had nothing to do with us or with our city of Anthem, New Jersey. Anthem had no crops, no silos, no crows—it had turquoise Port-o-Pottys and neon alleys, construction pits, dogs in purses, bag ladies with powerful smells and opinions, garbage dumps haunted by the wraith white pigeons; it had our school, the facade of which was currently covered with a glorious psychedelic phallus mosaic, a series of interlocking dicks spray painted to the scale of Picasso's *Guernica* by Anthem's tenth-grade graffiti kings; it had policemen, bus drivers, crossing guards; dolls were sold in stores.

And we were city boys. We lived in projects that were farm antonyms, these truly shitbox apartments. If flowers bloomed on our sooty sills, it must have been because of some plant Stockholm syndrome, a love our sun did not deserve. Our familiarity with the figure of the scarecrow came exclusively from watered-down L. Frank Baum cartoons, and from the corny yet frightening "Autumn's Bounty!" display in the Food Lion grocery store, where every year a scarecrow got propped a little awkwardly between a pilgrim, a cornucopia, and a scrotally wrinkled turkey. The Food Lion scarecrow looked like a broom in a Bermuda shirt, a broom with acne, ogling the ladies' butts as they bent to buy their diet yogurts—once I'd heard a bag boy joke that it was there to spook the divorcees. What we found in Friendship Park in no way resembled the Food Lion scarecrow. At first I was sure the thing tied to the oak was dead, or alive. Real, I mean.

"Hey, you guys," I swallowed. "Look—" And pointed to the pin oak, where a boy our age was belted to the trunk. Somebody in blue jeans and a T-shirt that had faded to the same earthworm color as his hair, a white boy, doubled over the rope. His hair clung tight as a cap to his scalp, as if painted on, and his face looked like a brick of sweating cheese.

Gus got to the kid first. "You retards." His voice was high with relief. "It's just a doll." He punched its stomach. "It's got straw inside it."

"It's a *scarecrow*!" shrieked Mondo.

And he kicked at a glistening bulb of what did appear to be straw beneath the doll's slumping face. A little hill. It regarded its own innards expressionlessly, its glass eyes twinkling. Mondo shrieked again.

I followed the scarecrow's gaze down to its lost straw: dark gold and chlorophyll green strands were blowing loose, like cut hair on a barbershop floor. Some of the straw had a jellied black look. How long had this stuff been outside of him, I wondered—how long had it been *inside* of him? I looked up, searching the boy scarecrow for a rip. A cold eel-like feeling was thrashing in my belly. That same morning, while eating my Popple breakfast tart, I'd seen a news shot of a U.S. soldier calmly watching blood spill from his head. Calm came pouring over him, at pace with the blood. In the next room, I could hear my ma getting ready for work, singing an old pop song, rattling hangers. On TV, one of the soldier's eyes was lost behind the sticky pink sheet. The camera closed in; a second later the footage switched to the trees of a new country under an ammonia blue sky.

I couldn't understand this—where was the cameraman or the camerawoman? Who was letting his face dissolve into calm?

"Let's cut it down!" screamed Mondo. I nodded.

"Nah, we better not." Juan Carlos looked around the woods sharply; he looked up, as if there might be a sniper hidden in the pin oak. "What if this"—he pushed at the doll—"belongs to somebody? What if somebody is watching us, right now? *Laughing* at us. . . ."

It was late September, a cool red season. The scarecrow was hung up on the sunless side of the oak. The tree was a shaggy pyramid, sixty or seventy feet tall, one of the "famous" landmarks of Friendship Park; it overlooked a ravine—a split in the seam of the bedrock, very narrow and deep—that we called "the Cone." Way down at the bottom you could see a wet blue dirt with radishy pink streaks along it, as exotic looking to us as a sea floor. Condoms and needles (not ours) and the silver shreds of Dodo Potato Chip bags and beer bottles (mostly ours) had turned the Cone into a sort of sylvan garbage can. The tree spread above it like a girl playing at suicide, quailing its many fiery leaves.

Years ago, before we started loitering here in a dedicated way, the pin oak had been planted to commemorate an Event—there was an opal plaque nestled in its roots. We knew this much but we didn't know more—some delinquent, teenaged forefather of ours had scratched out everything but the date, "1957." The plaque looked like a lost little moon in the grip of the tree's arachnid roots. I always felt a little cheated by the plaque; it was a confusing kind of resentment; I didn't really care about the "why" of the tree at all but I didn't like how this plaque was an open secret either, a mystery that was always itching at us. It bothered me that we were so poorly informed about the oak's first purpose that we did not even have the option of forgetting it, using our patented June 1 method, whereby we expulsed a year of school facts from our brains in spasms of summer amnesia. (Harriet Tubman—did he invent something? The War of 1812—why did we fight that one? For tea? Against Mexico or Sicily?) Forgetting was one of my favorite things to do at Camp Dark; I felt like a squid, sending jets of inky thoughts into the Cone.

The plaque was illegible, but the oak's glossy trunk was covered in gougings that you could easily read: V hearts K; Death 2 Asshole Jimmy Dingo; Jesus Saves; I Wuz Here!!! We'd added ourselves:

MONDO + GUS + LARRY + J.C. = CAMP DARK

The "deep end" of Friendship Park we called Camp Dark. Camp Dark was Anthem's lame try at an urban arboretum, a sort of surprise woods bordered by gas and fire stations and a condemned pizza buffet. THE PIZZA PARTY IS CANCELED read a sign above a bulldozer. These central acres of Friendship Park were filled with young deciduous trees and naive-seeming bluish squirrels. They chittered some charming bullshit at you too, up on their hind legs begging for a handout. They lived in the trash cans and had the wide-eyed innocent look and threadbare fur of child junkies. Had they wised up, our squirrels might have mugged us and used our wallets to buy train tickets to the true woods, which were about an hour north of Anthem's depressed downtown, according to Juan Carlos—only Juan Carlos had been out there. ("There was a river with a purple fish shitting in it," was all we got out of him.)

Recently, the Anthem City Parks & Recreation had received a big grant, and now the playground looked like a madhouse. Padded swings, padded slides, padded gyms, padded seesaws and go-wheelies: All the once-fun equipment had gotten upholstered by the city in this red loony-bin foam. To absorb the risk of a lawsuit, said Juan Carlos; one night, at Juan Carlos's suggestion, we all took turns pissing hooch onto the harm-preventing pillows. Our park had a poop-strewn dog run and an orange baseball diamond; a creepy pond that, like certain towns in Florida, had at one time been a very popular winter destination for geese and ducks but which had for some reason fallen out of fashion in the waterfowl society; and a Conestoga-looking covered picnic area. Gus claimed to have had sex there last Valentine's Day, on the cement tables—"pussy sex," he said, authoritatively, horrifying us, "not just the mouth kind." Our feeling was, if Gus really had tricked a girl into coming to our park in late February, they most likely talked about noncontroversial subjects, like the coldness of snow and the excellence of Gus's weed, while wearing sex-thwarting parkas.

We'd started hanging at Friendship Park four years ago, when we were ten years old. Back then we played actual games. We hid and we sought. We did benign stuff in trees. We amassed a stupidly huge plastic weapons cache in the hollow of the pin oak, including a Sounds of Warfare Blazer that as I recall required something like sixteen triple-A batteries to make a noise like a female guinea pig putting a brave face on her tuberculosis. Those were innocent times. Then we got shunted into Anthem's combo middle-and-high school, and now we came here to drink beers and antagonize one another. Biweekly we shoplifted liquor and snacks, in a surprisingly orderly way, rotating this duty ("We are Communists!" shrieked Mondo once, pumping a fistful of red-hot peanuts into the sky, and Juan Carlos, who did homework, snorted, "You are quite confused, my bro").

Participation levels varied, but usually it was the core four of us at Camp Dark: Juan Carlos Diaz, Gus Ainsworth, Mondo Chu, and me, Larry Rubio. Pronounced "Rubby-oh" by me, like a rubber ducky toy, my own surname. My dad left when I turned two and I don't speak any Spanish unless you count the words that everybody knows, like "hablo" and "no." My ma came from a vast hick family in Pensacola, pontoon loads of uncle-brothers and red-haired aunts and firecrotch cousins from some *nth* degree of cousindom, hordes of blood kin whom she renounced, I guess, to marry and then divorce my dad. We never saw any of them. We were long alone, me and my ma.

Juan Carlos had tried to tutor me once: "*Rooo*-bio. Fucker, you have to coo the 'u'!"

My ma couldn't pronounce my last name either, making for some awkward times in Vice Principal Derry's office. She'd reverted to her maiden name, which sounded like an elf municipality: Dourif. "Why can't I be a Dourif, like you?" I asked her once when I was very small, and she poured her drink onto the carpet, shocking me—this was my own kindergarten trick to express a violent unhappiness. She left the room and my shock deepened when she didn't come back to clean up the mess. I watched the stain set on the carpet, the sun cutting through the curtain blades. Later, I wrote LARRY RUBIO on all of my folders. I answered to RUBIO, just like the stranger my father must be doing somewhere. What my ma seemed to want me to do—to hold onto the name without the man—felt very silly to me, like the cartoon where Wile E. Coyote holds on to the handle (just the handle) of an exploded suitcase. Latching into pure space.

The scarecrow boy was my same height, five foot five. He had pale glass eyes and a molded wax or plastic face; under his faded brown shirt his "skin" was machine-sewn sackcloth, straw stuffed. So: He had a scarecrow's body but a boy's head. I took a step forward and punched his torso, which was solid as a bale of hay; I half expected a scream to roll out of his mouth. I looked down—I was standing on a snarl of his guts. Would a scarecrow's organs look like this? I wondered. Like birds' nests. A grass kidney, a flammable heart. Now I understood Mondo's earlier wail—when the scarecrow didn't cry out, I wanted to scream for him.

"Who stuck those on its face?" Mondo asked. "Those eyes?"

"Whoever *put* him here in the first place, jackass."

"Well, what weirdo does that? Puts eyes and clothes on a giant doll of a kid and ropes him to a tree?"

"A German, probably," said Gus knowingly. "Or a Japanese. One of those sicko sex freaks."

Mondo rolled his eyes. "Maybe *you* put it here then, Ainsworth."

"Maybe he's a theater prop? Like, from our school?"

"He's wearing some *nasty* clothes."

"Hey! He's got a belt like yours, Rubby!"

"Shut up."

"Wait—you're going to steal the scarecrow's *belt*? That ain't bad luck?"

"Oh my God! He's got on *underwear*!" Mondo snapped the elastic, giggling.

"He has a hole," Juan Carlos said quietly. He'd slid his hand between the doll's sagging shoulders and the tree. "Down here, in his back. Look. He's spilling straw."

Juan Carlos was jerking stuffing out of the scarecrow and then, in the same panicky motion, trying to cram it back inside the hole; all this he did with a sly, aghast look, as if he were a surgeon who had fatally bungled an operation and was now trying to disguise that fact from his staff. This straw, I recognized with a chill, was fresh and green.

"You got your 'oh shit!' face on, J.C.!" Gus laughed. I managed a laugh too, but I was scared, scared. The straw was scary to me, its pale colors and its smell. A terrible sweetness lifted out of the doll, that stench you are supposed to associate with innocent things—zoos and pet stores, pony rides. He was stuffed to the springs of his eyeballs. *Put it all back, Juan,* I thought hopefully, *and we'll be OK.*

"Uh. You dudes? Do scarecrows have fingers?" Mondo held the scarecrow's left hand, very formally, as if he were suddenly in a cummerbund accompanying the scarecrow to the world's scariest prom.

"I mean, usually," he added lamely, as if this were a normal topic to solicit our opinions on, the prevalence of scarecrow fingers.

"His body is soft." Gus demonstrated this for us, punching it. "But his face is, like, a wax? Not-straw. Some other shit. Plastic."

Only it wasn't generic, like a mall mannequin. Even the dark blue eye color looked particular, familiar. His features were weird and specific, like the face of a wax actress in a museum. Someone you were *supposed* to recognize.

"What the hell?" Gus whispered, twisting the scarecrow's face by its plastic chin. The chin was pocked with a fiery braille of blemishes and cuts, so convincingly nasty that you half expected them to ooze. The longer I stared at him, the less real I myself felt. Was I really the only one who remembered his name?

"Weird. His face is *cold*." Juan Carlos ran a long finger down the scarecrow's crooked nose.

"He's not wearing his glasses," I mumbled. Now that I knew who this was I was afraid to touch his face, as if the humid wand of my finger might bring him to life.

"His face is hard," Mondo confirmed, knocking on the scarecrow's forehead. "His eyes are . . . uh-oh. Oops."

Mondo turned to us, grinning.

"Oh shit!" Gus shook his head. "Put them back in."

"I *can't*. The little threads broke." Mondo held out the eyes: two grape-sized balls, an amethyst glass soaked blue by the last light of day. "Any of you bitches know how to sew?" Intense pinks were filtering through the autumn mesh of the oak. It was dusk, sunset; the park was now officially closed. "Seriously?" Mondo asked, sounding a little panicky now. "Anybody got glue or something?"

I stared at the sprigs of thread where the scarecrow's eyes had been. Now his face was putty white from the "T" of his nose to his forehead. A little firefly was lighting up the airless caves of the doll's nostrils, undetected by the doll. *You're even blinder now,* I thought, and a heavy feeling draped over me.

Then I heard the question I'd been dreading: "Don't we know this kid?"

Now Mondo stood on his toes and peered into the scarecrow's eyes with a shrewdness that you did not ordinarily expect from Mondo Chu—his mind was lost inside one of those baby-fat faces that he couldn't seem to age out of, with big slabby cheeks that squeezed his eyes into a narcoleptic squint, although outside of school Mondo could get pretty annoyingly energetic. There was some evidence that Mondo did not have the happiest home life. Mondo was half Chinese, half *something*. We'd all forgotten, assuming we'd ever known.

In fact, as a "we," Camp Dark was pretty fiercely uninterested in the details of its members' lives outside of school or beyond the fenced urban woods of Friendship Park. Silence policed the shady meeting point under our oak. I didn't know, for example, if Juan Carlos's big sister was pregnant or just getting large on Hershey's Kisses, or how Mondo got the yellowish bruises that covered his flabby upper arms. Inside of our "we," nobody would ask you about your ma's cancer or your alcoholic aunt, your moon-eyed half sister, your family's debts, nobody commented on the emotions that might fly across your face and raise your fists and nobody demanded a bullshit weather report from you either, a reason for your anger—not like the teachers, who were always demanding that sort of phony meteorology from us. We cracked jokes together in Camp Dark, but I think it was the silence, all those unasked questions, that bound us. At school we beat down kids as a foursome and this too we did in an animal silence. We'd drag a hysterical kid behind the red-brick Science Building—this march could look a little medieval, like some Gallows Day parade, each of us taking up an arm or a leg—and then we would hammer and piston our fists into his clawing, shrilling body until the kid went slack as rags. For us, this process was a necessary evil. We were like four factory guys, manufacturing the quiet, a calm that was not available to us naturally anywhere in Anthem. We'd kneel there, panting together, and let the good quiet bubble around our fists like glue.

It was Mondo who cracked the mystery. He didn't *solve* it, I don't mean that—in fact he made the mystery much worse. That's what I pictured anyhow, when Mondo tapped the mystery with his little eureka! hammer—hairline cracks appearing in a round, solid shell. Yolk came oozing out of the mystery, covering all of our hands, so that we became *involved*.

"Oh!" Mondo fell back on his heels and let out a bee-stung cry. "It's *Eric*."

"Oh." I took a step away from the tree.

Juan Carlos paused with one hand lost in the doll's back, still wearing a doctor's distant, guileful expression.

"Who the fuck is *Eric*?" Gus snarled.

Then Mondo, grinning loonily like a Jeopardy! champ, grabbed the scarecrow's left arm by the wrist and made it shake hands with the cold air between us. "Don't you assholes remember him? Eric Mutis."

Sure, we remembered him now: Eric Mutis. Eric Mutant, Eric Mucus, Eric the Mute. Paler than a cauliflower, a friendless kid who had once or twice had seizures in our class. "Eric Mutis is an epileptic," our teacher had explained a little uncertainly, after Mutant got carried by Coach Leyshon from the room. Eric Mutis had joined our eighth-grade class in October of the previous year, a transfer kid. One day Mutant was sitting in the back row of our homeroom; the teacher never introduced him. Kids rarely moved to Anthem, New Jersey, and generally the teachers made the New Boy or the New Girl parade their strangeness for us; but Eric Mutis, who seemed genuinely otherworldly, much weirder even than the Guatemalan New Boy, Eric Mutis arrived in exile. He sank like a stone to the bottom of our homeroom. One day, several weeks before the official end of our school term, he vanished, and I honestly had not spoken his name since. Nobody had.

In the school halls, Eric Mutis had been as familiar as air; at the same time we never thought about him. Not unless he was right in front of our noses. Then you couldn't ignore him—there was something provocative about Eric Mutis's ugliness, something about his oblivion, his froggy lashes and his worse-than-dumb expression, that filled your eyes and closed your throat. He could metamorphose Jilly Lucio, the top of the cheer pyramid, a dog lover and the sweetest girl in our grade, into a harpy. "What *smells*?" she'd whisper, little unicorn-pendant Jilly, thrilling us with her acid tone, and only Eric Mutis would blink his large, bovine eyes at her and say, "I don't smell it, Jilly," in that voice like thin blue milk. Congenitally, he really did seem like a mutant, incapable of shame. Even then, at age twelve, before our glands made us all swell into monsters, I felt allergic to the kid. His ugliness panned into a weird calm, and this combination was like a bully allergen. A teacher's allergen, too—the poor get poorer, I guess, because many of our teachers were openly hostile to Eric Mutis; by December, Coach Leyshon was sneering, "Pick it up, Mutant!" on the courts.

The courts, the grass behind them—that was where Camp Dark came to order. We did what you might call these "alterations" on the blacktop. At recess we'd descend on Eric Mutis like deranged tailors, trailing these little threads of Eric's spittle and Eric's blood. But his costume—the smoggy yellow cloud of his hair, his sickly bus-terminal complexion—it was his skin. We could not free him, we could not torch the costume off him. He wouldn't change, no matter how often we encouraged him to do so with our insults and the instruction of our "pranks" and fists. We stole his Hoops sneakers, hung them up on the flagpole, we smashed his gray Medicaid glasses three times that year, his hideous glasses, with frames the width of my TV set; and then he'd come to school in a new pair of the same eyesore frames, the same nine-dollar Hoops sneakers, fresh from the Starmart box. How many pairs of Hoops did we force him to buy—or, most likely, since Eric Mutis queued up with us for the free lunch program, to steal?

"Why are you so stubborn, Mutant?" I hissed at him once, when his face was inches away from mine, lying prone on the blacktop—closer to my face than any girl's had ever been. Closer than I'd let my ma's face get to me, now that I'd turned thirteen. I could smell his blue bubblegum, and what we called "Anthem cologne"—like my own clothes, Mutant's rags stunk of diesel and fried doughnut grease and the sweet, fecal waft off manhole covers.

"Why don't you *learn*?" And I Goliath crushed the Medicaid glasses in my hand, feeling sick.

"Your palms, Larry." Eric the Mute had shocked me that time, calling me by name. "They're bleeding."

"Are you retarded?" I marveled. "*You* are the one bleeding! This is *your* blood!" It was our blood actually, but his voice and his monotone blue eyes made me furious. "WAKE UP!" I backed away to give Gus space to deliver an encore kick. "Listen, Mutant: DO . . . NOT . . . WEAR THAT UGLY SHIT TO SCHOOL!"

And Monday came, and guess what Mutant wore?

Was he wearing this stuff out of rebellion? A kind of nerd insurrection? I didn't think so; that might have relieved us a little bit, if the kid had the spine and the mind to rebel. But Eric Mutant seemed terribly oblivious of his own appearance—that was the problem—he wore that stuff witlessly, shamelessly. We couldn't teach him how to be ashamed of it. ("Who did this? Who did this?" our upstairs neighbor, Miss Zeke from 3C, used to holler, grinding her cross-eyed dachshund's nose into a lake of urine on the stairwell, while the dog, a true lost cause, jetted another weak stream onto the floor.) When we took Eric Mutis around behind the red-brick Science Building, he never seemed to understand what his crime had been, or what was happening, or even—his blue eyes drifting, unplugged—that it was happening to *him*.

In fact, I think Eric Mutis would have been hard-pressed to identify himself in a police lineup. In the school bathroom he always avoided mirrors. The school bathroom was tiled, naval blue for boys, which made the act of pissing into a bowl feel weirdly perilous, as if at any moment you might get plowed under by an Atlantic City wave. Teachers used a separate faculty john; I'd cracked younger kids' skulls on those tiles before. Eric the Mute knew this much about me—that was the one lesson he took.

"Well, hallo there, Mutant," I'd whistle at him.

More than once I watched him drop his dick and zip up and sprint past the bank of sinks when I entered the bathroom, his homely face pursuing him blurrily and hopelessly in the mirrors. This used to make me happy, when kids like Eric Mucus were afraid of me. (Really, I don't know who I could have been then either.)

"Well," Gus sighed, dragging down his dark earlobes, which was his baseball signal to the rest of us that he'd *lost* it, his patience with our dithering voices, his faith in debate fertilizing an action. "We could do an experiment, like. Seems pretty simple. One way to find out what old Eric Mutant here—"

"The *scarecrow*," Mondo hissed, as if he regretted ever naming it.

Gus rolled his eyes. "What the *scarecrow* is doing in the park? One way to learn what he is supposedly protecting us from? Would be to cut him down."

"But, Gus." I swallowed. "What if something does come to Anthem?"

"Well, Rubby . . ." Gus shrugged. "Then we'll have some fascinating new information about this scarecrow, won't we?"

We had been riffing on this: What threat, exactly, was this scarecrow keeping away from Friendship Park? Not crows, that was for sure; but what was the Anthem equivalent, the urban crow? Rabid cats? A flock of mob gunmen, or sewer rats? Those poor Canada geese that kept getting sucked into the engines of jet planes at the Anthem airport? (That one was my idea.) What could a doll of a child scare away, a freak like Mutant?

The oak shivered above us; it was almost nine o'clock. Police, if they came upon us now, would write us up for trespassing. *Come upon us, officers.* Maybe the police would know the protocol here, what you should do if you found a scarecrow of your classmate strung up in the woods.

"I'm with Larry. I don't think that's a good idea anymore, either," said Mondo. "To cut him down. What if something really bad happens? It would be our fault."

Juan Carlos nodded. "Look, whoever put this up is one sick fuck. I don't want to mess with the property of a lunatic. . . ."

Juan was still enumerating his understandable concerns when Gus, who had fallen quiet, walking around the tree and finishing everybody's brews, stood up. A knife sprang out of Gus's pocket, a four-inch knife that nobody had known Gus carried with him, one of the kitchen tools we'd seen used by Gus's pretty mom, Mrs. Ainsworth, to butterfly and debone chickens. Down went Eric.

"GUS!"

We stood up just as the scarecrow shucked the oak permanently, and plummeted into the sky. Watching him go over, I felt dread without a drop of surprise—it felt like we were watching a horror movie that we'd seen a thousand times before, *The Scarecrow of Eric Mutis Dives Into the Cone*! I can still see the stars swarming around the pin oak and Gus sawing at the rope, Gus giving Eric Mutis's doll a little push—joylessly, dutifully, like a big brother behind a swingset—the plaque catching at him like a stumbling stone, illegibly flashing, the doll launching over the roots, headfirst, into a night that shrank him, into the Cone's collapsing sky, the doll falling and falling and then, *not*. He landed on the rocks with a baseball crack. I don't know how to describe the optical weirdness of the pace of this event—because the doll fell *fast*—but the doll's descent felt unnaturally long to me, as if the forest floor were, just as quickly, lunging away from Eric Mutis. Somebody almost laughed. Mondo was already on his knees, peering over the edge, and I joined him: The scarecrow looked like a broke-neck kid at the bottom of a well. Facedown, his limbs all scrambled on an oily soak of black and maroon leaves and strata of our glass. Had it lost more straw? Black plants waved down there and I couldn't tell which weeds might have belonged to the scarecrow. One of his white hands had gotten twisted all the way around. He waved at us, palm up, spearing the air with his long, unlikely fingers.

"OK," Gus said, sitting back down next to where he'd dug his red beer can into the leaves, as if we were at the beach. "You're all welcome. Everybody needs to shut up now. Let's start the clock on this experiment."

We emerged from the park at Gowen Street and Forty-eighth Avenue. A doorman waved at us from a fancy apartment building. Awnings sprouted above all of the windows like golden claws. When the streetlights clicked on without warning, I think we all stifled a scream. We stood on the dirty tarmac of the sidewalk, bathed in a deep-sea light. Even on a nonscarecrow day I dreaded this, the summative pressure of the good-bye moment—but now it turned out there was nothing to say. We split off in a slow way, a slow ballet—a moth, watching the four of us from above, would have seen us as a knot dissolving over many moth centuries underneath the green air. It occurred to me that, given the lifespan of a moth, one kid's twitch would occupy a year of insect time. The scarecrow of Eric Mutis would have twirled down for moth aeons.

"What the hell is so funny, kid?" the doorman shouted. I had been spawning a slow smile on my face, imagining the decades of moth time going by as my smile grew: *Merry Christmas, Happy New Year, sleigh bells ring, Mr. Moth, here comes spring. . . .*

That night marked a funny turning point for me; I started thinking about Time in a new way, Time with a capital "T," this substance that underwent mysterious conversions. On the walk home I watched moths go flitting above the stalled lanes of cars. I called Mondo on the phone, something I never did—I was surprised I even had his number. We didn't talk about Eric Mutis, but the effort of not talking about him made our actual words feel like fizz, just a lot of speedy emptiness. You know, I never tried to force Eric Mutis from my mind—I never had to. Courteously, the kid had disappeared from my brain entirely, about the same time he vanished from our school rolls. Were it not for the return of his scarecrow in Camp Dark, I doubt I would have given him a second thought.

I am in the shower, Eric Mutis is where? I tied myself to mental train tracks, juxtaposing my activities against Eric Mutis's imaginary ones—was he blowing out twisty red and white birthday candles, doing homework? What hour of what day was it, wherever Eric Mutis had moved? I pictured him in Cincinnati squiggling mustard on a ballpark frank, in France with an arty beret (I pictured him dead too, in a dreamy, compulsive way, the concrete result of which was that I no longer ate breakfast). "You don't want your *Popple*, Larry?" my ma screamed. "It's a Blamberry Popple!" The Blamberry Popple looked like a pastry nosebleed to me. What was Eric eating? How soundly was he sleeping? ("Did we break Mutant's nose?" I asked Gus in homeroom. "At least once," Gus confirmed.) Now each of my minutes cast an hourglass shadow and I divided into two.

But inside the Cone, as it turned out, the scarecrow of Eric Mutis was subdividing even faster.

Every day for a week, we went back to stare at the facedown scarecrow of Eric Mutis in Friendship Park. It lay there in the sun, sleeping it off. Nothing much happened. There was a mugging at the Burger Burger; the robber got a debit card and a quart of milkshake. Citywide, bus fare went up five cents. A drunk driver in the Puerto Rican day parade draped a Puerto Rican flag over his windshield like a patriotic blindfold and crashed through a beautiful float of the island of Puerto Rico. Nothing occurred on the crime blotter that seemed connected to Eric Mutis, or Eric Mutis's absence. No strange birds flew out of exile, no new shapes came to roost in the oaks of Friendship Park now that the scarecrow's guard was down. Downed by us, I thought angrily, like a cut power line. Drowned in air, like the world's stupidest experiment.

Had Eric Mutis's scarecrow been babysitting a crop? Some Jersey version of the Amish seven grains? Years of city trash and plastic guns, that was Camp Dark's harvest. I thought of the slippery weeds crushed underneath his face, the rocks and cans glowing like blind fish in the ravine.

"Did Eric have a dad? A mom?"

"Wasn't he a foster kid?"

"Where did he move to again?"

"Old Mucusoid never said—did he? He just disappeared."

At school, the new guidance counselor could not help us find our "little pal"—the district computers, she said, had been wiped by a virus. Mutis, Eric: no record. His yearbook slot was an empty navy egg between the school-mandated grimaces of Omar Mowad and Valerie Night. ABSENT, it read in red letters. We consulted with Coach Leyshon, whom we found face deep in a vending-machine cheeseburger behind the dugout.

"Mutant?" he barked. "That dipshit didn't come back?" We broke into Vice Principal Derry's file cabinet and made depressing, irrelevant discoveries about the psychology of Vice Principal Derry—his top drawer contained about five million pointless green pencils, a Note to Moi! memo, in pen, that read BUY PENCIL SHARPENER, and a radiant mélange of glues.

Next we consulted the yellow pages at the city library, Ma Bell's anthology of false alarms—we thought we found Mutant in Lebanon Valley, Pennsylvania. Voloun River, Tennessee. Jump City, Oregon. Jix, Alaska, a place that sounded like a breakfast cereal or an attack dog, had four Mutis families listed. We called. Many dozens of Mutises across America hung up on us, after apologizing for their households' dearth of Erics. America felt vast and void of him.

Gus whammed the phone into its receiver, disgusted. "It's like that kid hatched out of an egg. What I want to know is: Who made him into a scarecrow?"

Again the yellow pages got consulted. This time we weren't even sure what sort of listing to scout for. Who made a doll of a boy—some modern Mary Shelley? An artist, a child taxidermist? We looked for ridiculous things: SCARECROW REPAIR, WAX KIDS.

I found an address for a puppeteer who had a workshop in Anthem's garment district. Gus biked out there and did reconnaissance, weaving around the bankers' spires of downtown Anthem and risking the shortcut under the overpass, where large, insane men brayed at you and haunted shopping carts rolled windlessly forward. He spent an hour circling the puppeteer's studio, trying to catch him in the act of Dark Arts—because what if he was making scarecrows of *us*? But the puppeteer turned out to be a small, bald man in a daffodil-print shirt; the puppet on his table was a hippopotamus, or perhaps some kind of lion. This Gus learned on his twentieth revolution around the workshop, at which time the puppeteer lifted the window, gave a friendly wave, and told Gus that he had just telephoned the police.

"*Great*," sighed Juan Carlos. "So we still have no clue who made that doll."

"But how the fuck you going to confuse a hippo and a *lion*, bro!" Mondo grumbled. Often Mondo's reactions would miss the mark entirely and slam into a non sequitur, as if his rage were a fierce and stupid bird that kept landing on the wrong tree, whole woods away from the rest of us.

"Chu, you have a brain defect." Gus stared at him. "Something that cannot be helped."

"Maybe Mutant did it," I said, almost hopefully. I wanted Eric to be safe and alive. "Did he know that we hang out in the park? Maybe he roped the scarecrow there to screw with us."

"Maybe it was Vice Principal Derry," said Juan Carlos. "One time, I'm walking to the bus, and I see Mutant in Vice Principal Derry's office. Through that window that faces the parking lot, right? And I sort of thought, 'Oh, good, he's getting some help.' But then Derry catches me looking, right? And he stands up, he's fucking *pissed*, he shuts the blinds. It was so weird. And I saw the Mute's mug—" I could see it too, Mutant's leech white face behind the glass, I *had* seen it framed in Derry's office window, Eric Mutis swallowed in Derry's leather chair, wearing his queer gray glasses. "And he looked . . . bad," he finished. "Like, scared? Worse than he did when we messed with him."

"Why was he in Derry's office?" I asked, but nobody knew.

"I saw him get picked up from school," Mondo volunteered. "After second period, you know, cause he had one of his twitch fests? The, uh, the seizures? And this dude in the car looked so old! I was like, Mutant, is Darth Vader there your dad?"

This too was something we all suddenly remembered seeing: a cadaverous man, a liver-spotted hand on the steering wheel of a snouty green Cadillac, tapping a cigar, and then Mutant climbing into the backseat, the rear window as foggy as aquarium glass and the Mute's head now etched dimly behind it. He always climbed into the back-seat, never used the passenger door, we agreed on that. We all remembered the cigar.

Gus hadn't stopped frowning—it had been days since he'd told a truly funny joke. "Where did Mutis live in Anthem? Does anybody remember him saying?"

"East Olmsted," said Mondo. "Right? With a crazy aunt." Mondo's eyes widened, as if his memory were coming into focus. "I think the aunt was black!"

"Chu," Juan Carlos sighed. "That is not your memory. You are thinking of a Whoopi Goldberg movie. Nah, Mutant's parents were rich."

"Oh my God!" Mondo clapped a hand to his face. "You're *right*! That was a great movie!"

Juan Carlos directed his appeal to Gus and me. "Kid was loaded. I just remembered. I'm, like, ninety percent sure. That's why the Mute pissed us off so bad . . . wasn't it? Dressing like he was on welfare and shit. I think they lived in the Pagoda. Serious."

I almost laughed at that—the Pagoda was an antislum, a castle of light. Eric Mutis had never lived in the Pagoda's zip code. In fact, I had visited the house where Eric lived. Just one time. This knowledge was like a wild thumper of a rabbit inside me. I was amazed that no one else could hear it.

Wednesday morning, I went to Friendship Park on an empty stomach, alone. The sun came with me; I was already an hour late for songs with Miss Verazain in Music I, a class that I was certainly failing, since I stood in the back with Gus and made a Clint Eastwood seam with my lips and sang only in my mind. It was the class I loved.

That day we were set to sing some classical stuff, words floating uselessly on the surge of one of those "B" or "C" composers, Bach or maybe Chopin, these dead men whose songs sawed through time with violins and uncorked a forest to let a soft green light flood out, and into the voices of my friends—back then I would have said that Music I calmed me down better than pot and I didn't like to miss it. But I had my own business with the scarecrow of Eric Mutis. I'd been having dreams about both Erics, the real one and the doll. I twisted on my pillow and imagined it loaded with straw. In one dream, I got Coach Leyshon's permission to sub myself in for him, lashing my body to the pin oak and eating horsey fistfuls of a bloodred straw; in another, I watched the doll of Eric Mutis go plunging into the Cone again, only this time when his scarecrow hit the rocks, a thousand rabbits came bursting out of it. Baby rabbits: squeamish, furless thumbs of pink in the night, racing lemming quick under the oaks of Camp Dark.

"Eric?" I called softly, well in advance of the oak. And then, almost inaudibly: "Honey?" in a voice that was not unlike my own ma's when she opened my bedroom door at night and called my name but clearly didn't want to wake me, wanted instead who-knows-what? A squirrel watched me with an aggravating fearlessness as I entered Camp Dark, scratching its chest fur like a man in a soiled little shirt. I kicked it away and got on my knees and held on to the oak's roots like my bike's handlebars, peering down into the Cone.

"Oh my God."

Whatever had attacked the scarecrow in the night had been big enough to tear his arm off at the root. Green and beige straw spewed out of the hole. *You're next, you're next, you're next,* my heart screamed. I straightened and ran and I didn't slow down until I passed under the stone arch of Friendship Park and saw the violet-gray speck at the bottom of the hill that became the glass umbrella of the #22 bus stop. I did not stop until I burst into Music I, where all of my friends were doing their *do re mi* work. I pushed in next to Gus and collapsed against our wall.

"You're very late, Señor Rubio," said Miss Verazain disgustedly, and I nodded hard, my eyes still stinging from the cold. "You're too late to be assigned a role."

"I am," I agreed with her, hugging my arm.

There was one day last December, right before the Christmas break, where we got him behind the Science Building for a game that Mondo had named Freeze Tag. The game was pretty short and unsophisticated—we made a kid "It," the way you'd identify an animal as a trophy kill, if you were a hunter, or declare a red spot "the bull's-eye," so that you could shoot it:

"Not it!"

"Not it!"

"Not it!"

"Not it!"

We'd grinned and our four bodies in our white gym shirts made a grin too, where we'd gathered in the witchy grass of the back-lot ball field. We were up to our knees in the grass, advancing. Two halves of a circle. We didn't corner the kid, Mutis, we made actual lips around him. From above we would have looked like a mouth, closing. The rules were simple and yet Eric Mutis stared at us with his opaque blue eyes, staked to the field, and gave no sign of understanding it.

"You're *it*," I'd explained to Eric.

Everybody followed me toward Camp Dark in a line.

"Here comes the army!" cackled a bum with whom we sometimes shared beers, one of a rotating cast of lost men whom Gus called the Bench Goblins. He had a long stirrup-shaped face that grinned and grinned at us when we told him about the scarecrow of Eric Mutis. Long fingers brushed at the oatmeal of wet newspapers that covered his cheeks.

"No," he said, "I don't see nobody come this way with no *doll*."

"One week ago," I prodded, but you could tell that this unit didn't mean much to the guy. He had amassed a slippery skin of newspapers on his legs with headlines from early August.

All last night it had rained; the leaves were shining, the red playground foam looked like a giant's dental equipment. We marched forward. I wasn't the oldest or the tallest but I was the leader now, and why? Just because I knew the bad scene waiting for us behind the treeline. And, in fact, I knew a little more about the real Eric Mutis than I was letting on. I had some brewing theories, nothing I was ready to voice, about why the scarecrow had arrived in our city. *It is a very good thing that we elect our presidents in America,* I thought, because this had to be the wrong basis for picking a leader—if I was at this particular moment the best informed about the danger we were heading toward, I was also the worst scared.

"So what do you think did it, Rubby?" Gus asked.

"Yeah. An animal, like?" Mondo's eyes were gleeful. "Is it all clawed up?"

"You'll see. I dunno, guys," I mumbled. "I dunno. I dunno." Each word crawled like a gray mouse up the bars of my ribs to my throat. Mice dug their pink claws into my belly and my heart. (Could mice have done that to the scarecrow of Eric Mutis? Chewed off and carried away a whole arm? Could ants? Maybe the threat was multiple, pestilential, and smaller than I'd thought.)

Hypothesis 1: A human is doing this.

Hypothesis 2: An animal, or several animals, are doing this. Smart animals. Surgical animals. Animals with claws. Scavengers—opossums or something, the waddlesome undertakers of the park.

Hypothesis 3: This is being done by . . . Something Else.

But when we reached the Cone and they peered over the edge—I hung back, leaning on the oak—everybody started to laugh. Hysterically, a belly-clutching laugh, like three hyenas, Gus first and then the other two.

"Good one, Rubby!" they called.

I was shocked. "Why are you *laughing*?"

"Oh, shit, that is a *good one*, Rubby-oh. This is a classic."

"This is your best yet," Juan Carlos confirmed with a gloomy jealousy.

"Dang! *Larry.* You're like a goddamn acrobat! How did you get *down* there?"

Eyes were rolling at me in a semicircle. I found myself thinking of Eric the Mute, Eric the Mutant, and what we must have looked like to him.

"Wait—" I rolled my wet eyes back at them. "You think *I* did that?" Everybody nodded at me with a strange solemnity, so that for a disorienting second I wondered if they might be right. How did they think I had managed the amputation? I tried to see myself as they must be imagining me: swinging down into the Cone on a stolen phys ed rope, a knife in my back jeans pocket, the moon hanging over Anthem in a crescent, its light washing over the Cone's rock walls and making the place feel even more like an unlidded casket; I watched myself approach the doll in the reeds, the doll that had been waiting for my attack with a patience rivaled only by the real Eric Mutis's; I heard the doll's right arm ripping away as I grunted the knife into the fabric, the moon shining on, the world watching us out of one slit eye, like a cat, a cracked Anthem stray. And then what? Did my friends think I'd swung the arm back to the surface, à la Tarzan? Carried the arm out of the park in my book bag?

"I didn't do it!" I gasped. "This is not a joke, you assholes. . . ."

I got up and vomited orange Gatorade into the bushes. It was all liquid—I hadn't been eating. Days of emptiness rose in me and I dry-retched again, listening to my friends' peals of laughter echo around Camp Dark. Then I surprised myself by laughing with them, so uncontrollably and with such relief that it felt like a continuation of the retching—like disgorging my claims of innocence and crawling on my hands and knees back inside our "we." My lungs filled with and expelled this relief, which I knew would only last as long as we could loft the joke. After a while the laughter didn't sound connected to any of us. It was like a thunderhead, a stampede—sound poured all over us. We blinked at each other, under the laughter, our mouths open.

"And the Oscar for puking goes to . . . Larry Rubio!" said Juan Carlos, still doubled over.

A bird floated softly over the park. Somewhere just beyond the treeline, city buses were wheezing a cargoload of citizens to and from work. Some of these were our parents. I felt a little stab, picturing my ma eating her yellow apple on the train and reading some self-improvement book, on a two-hour commute to her job at a day nursery for rich infants in Anthem's far richer sister county. I realized that I had zero clue what my ma did there; I pictured her rolling a big striped ball, at extremely slow speeds, toward babies in little sultan hats and fat, bejeweled diapers.

"My ma's name is Jessica," I heard myself say. I could not stop talking now, it was like chattering teeth. "Jessica Dourif. Gus, you met her once, you remember." I glared at Gus and dared him to say he'd forgotten her.

"Rubio? Why . . . ," Juan Carlos said slowly, picking around my body like an Inquisitor, ". . . the hell . . . are you telling us this?"

I was staring down at the scarecrow's shredded body. A gash down his back had hemorrhaged a dirty-looking straw. A golden bird was hopping around down there, pecking and pecking. *Now YOU need a scarecrow,* I thought, watching the bird savagely tease out straw from the old hole.

"I've never met my father," I blurted. "I can't even say my own fucking last name."

"Larry," Juan Carlos said sternly, standing over me. "Nobody cares. Now you pull yourself together."

*

What followed over the course of the next eight days progressed with the logic of a frightening nursery rhyme:

On Tuesday morning, the scarecrow's hands were gone. Both of them. I pictured the white fingers crawling through the park, hailing a cab, starting a new and incognito life somewhere, perhaps with a family of unwitting tarantulas in New Mexico. Eric Mutis, the real Eric, he too could be living in a painted desert now, with a new father or a new guardian. Or in a mountain town, maybe. Living at a ludicrous altitude, his body half eaten by the charcoal clouds of Aspen. By the sea. In Salamanca, Spain. In a cold cottage on the moon.

By Wednesday, the scarecrow was missing both coruscating Hoops sneakers and both feet. Everybody but me snickered about that one. We'd stolen Eric Mutis's Hoops maybe a dozen times last year, we stole Hoops from any kid stupid enough to wear them—Hoops were imitation Nikes, glittered with an insulting ersatz gold, and just the sight of a pair enraged me. The "H" logo was a flamboyant way to announce to your class: Hey, I'm poor! Once Gus and I had gotten a three-day suspension for jerking off the Mute's Hoops sneakers and his crusty socks and holding an "America the Great" sparkler to his bare feet—just to mess with him.

"Larry!" Gus said, clapping my back. "How did you get out of the Cone with two *shoes* in your hands? This is some Cirque du Soleil bullshit! You got to try out for the Olympics." He checked the backs of my arms for fresh nets of scrapes. "What, are you flying down there?"

"I am not doing this," I said quietly. I was getting hoarse from saying that. I realized with a grim shock that I was leaning against the oak in exactly the spot where we'd found Mutis's scarecrow.

"Maybe," I said in a whisper, "we can fish him up . . . ? Hook him out? Maybe we can get down there and, and bury it."

"Are you *crying*, bro?"

Everybody complimented me on my "acting." But they were the actors—believing their easy suspicion, pretending that I was the guy to blame. Only Mondo would let me see his smile tremble, and I felt a little better, thinking hard at him: *Mondo, whatever's happening down there, I am not behind it, OK?*

On Thursday, his second arm was gone. Ripped whole, presumably, from the cloth shoulder, so that you got an unsettling glimpse of the gray straw coiled inside the scarecrow. *Not-it, not-it, not-it,* I'd been thinking all week, a thorny little crown of thoughts.

"What's next, Rubby? You going to carry a guillotine down there?"

Not it! I worried I was about to ralph again.

"You bet," I said. "How well you all know me. Next up, I'm going to climb down there and behead Eric Mutis with an ax."

"Right." Gus grinned. "We should follow you home. We're gonna find Mutant's arm under your pillow. The fake one, and probably the real one too, you psycho."

And they did. Follow me home. On a Saturday, after we discovered that the doll's legs had disappeared—the scarecrow was starting to look like a disintegrating jack-o-lantern, pulpy and crushed, with a sallow vegetable pallor. I was "It." I was the only suspect. Under a dreary sky we left the scarecrow where it was, everybody but me laughing about how they'd been fucked with, faked out, punked, and gotten.

"You rotten, Rubby-Oh," grinned Gus.

"*Something's* rotten," agreed Mondo, catching my eye.

Afterward we walked very slowly across the park toward my ma's apartment on First and Stuckey, where we lived in ear-splitting proximity to the hospital; from my bedroom window I could see the red and white carnival lights of the ambulances. Awake, I was totally inured to the sirens, a whine that we'd been hearing throughout Anthem since birth—that urgent song drilled into us until our own heartbeats must have synced with it, which made it an easy howl to ignore; but I had dreams where the vehicular screams in the URGENT CARE parking lot became the cries of a gigantic, abandoned baby behind my apartment. All I wanted to do in these dreams was *sleep* but this baby wouldn't shut up! Now I think this must be a special kind of poverty, low-rent city sleep, where even in your dreams you are an insomniac and your unconscious is shrill and starless.

When we got to my place, the apartment was dark and there was no obvious sustenance waiting for us—my ma was not one to prepare a meal. Some deep-fridge spelunking produced a pack of spicy jerky and Velveeta slices. This was beau food, suitor food, a relic from my ma's last live-in boyfriend—was it Curtis Black? Manny Somebody? Which one had been the jerky lover? As the son, I got to be on a first-name basis with all of these adult men, all of her boyfriends, but I never knew them well enough to hate them in a personal way. We folded thirty-two cheese slices into cold taco shells and ate them in front of the TV. Later I'd remember this event as a sort of wake for the scarecrow of Eric Mutis, although I had never in my life been to a funeral.

They searched my apartment, found nothing. No white hands clapping in my closet or anything. No legs propped next to the brooms in the kitchen.

"He's clean," shrugged Gus, talking over me. "He probably buried the evidence."

"I *do* think we need to go down into the Cone," I started babbling again, "and bury him. What's left of him. Please, you guys. I really, really think we need to do that."

"No way. We are not falling for that," said Juan Carlos quickly, as if wary of falling into the Cone himself.

Accusing me, I saw, served a real utility for the group—suddenly nobody was interested in researching scarecrows at the library with me, or trying to figure out where the real Eric Mutis had gone, or deciphering who was behind his doppelgänger doll. They already had a good answer: I was behind it. This satisfied some scarecrow logic for my friends. They slept, they didn't wonder anymore. That's where my friends had staked me: behind the doll.

"Let's go there one night, and just see who comes to shred and tear at him like that. We'll be the scarecrow's scarecrow, haha . . . ," I gulped, staring at them. "And then we'll know *exactly* . . ."

Mondo winced and snapped the TV on.

"Nice try, Rubby!" Gus crunched through a taco shell. The pepper specks that covered the yellow shell looked exactly like the blackheads on Gus's broad nose. "Oh, I bet you'd *love* that. Nighttime. Phase Two of your prank. Get us all good in Camp Dark. I can't wait to see how this all turns out, kid—what sort of Friday the Thirteenth ending you got planned for us. But we are not just going to walk *into* it, Rubby."

It felt like we sat there for hours before somebody asked: "What the hell are we watching?" Nobody had noticed or commented when the station switched to pure static. My ma had an ancient, crappy RCA TV, with oven dials for controls and little rabbit ears; I always thought it looked more authentically futuristic to me than my friends' modern Toshiba sets. Spazzy rainbows moved up and down, imbuing the screen with an insectoid life of its own. Here was the secret mind of the machine, I thought with a sudden ache, what you couldn't see when the news anchors were staring soulfully at their teleprompters and the sitcom comedy families were making eggs and jokes in their fake houses.

Eric's face—the face of scarecrow Eric—swam up in my mind. I realized that the random, relentless lightning inside the TV screen was how I pictured the interior of the doll—void, yet also, in a way that I did not understand and found I could not even think about head-on, much less explain to my friends, *alive*. My apartment was as silent as the rainbowed screen; with the TV on mute you could hear a hard clock tick.

"Hey! Rubio! What the *fuck* we watching?"

"Nothing," I snapped back; a wise lie, I thought. "Obviously."

For three days, little pieces of the doll of Eric Mutis continued to disappear. Once the major appendages were gone, the increments of Eric's scarecrow that went missing became more difficult to track. Patches of hair vanished. Bites and chews of his shoulders. By Monday, two weeks after we'd found it, over half of the scarecrow was gone; with a sickening lurch I understood that it was too late now, that we were never going to tell anyone about him. Nobody who saw the wreck in the Cone would believe that it had been a doll of Eric Mutis.

"Well, that's that," said Juan Carlos in a funny voice, gazing down at the quartered scarecrow. In the Cone, his light spring-and-autumn straw was blowing everywhere now. All that bodiless straw gave me a nervous feeling, like watching a thought that I couldn't collect. His naked head was still attached to the sack of his torso, both of these elements of Eric Mutis intact and ghoulishly white.

"That's all, folks," echoed Gus. "Going once, going twice! Nice work, Rubby."

I shook my head, feeling nauseated. I'm still not sure how that silence overtook us. How did we know that we'd missed our window to tell an outsider about the scarecrow? Why didn't we at least discuss it—bringing the police to Friendship Park, or even V.P. Derry? This might have been an option last week but now, as mysteriously as the parts themselves had disappeared, it wasn't; we all felt it; we hadn't acted, and now the secret was returning to the ground. Eric Mutis was escaping us again in this terrible, original way.

That Friday, the scarecrow's head was gone. Now I thought I detected a little ripple of open fear in the others' eyes. It was me, I realized, that they were afraid of. All of the laughter at my "prank" had fizzled out. I was afraid of my friends—terrified that they might actually be onto something.

"Where did you put it?" Mondo whispered.
"When are you going to stop?" said Juan Carlos.
"Larry," Gus said sincerely, "that is really sick."

Hypothesis 4.

I think this knowledge sat on the top of my mind for days and days. But it must have been unswallowed, undigested, like a little white bolus of food on a tongue—because I didn't exactly *know* it. Not yet.

"I think we made him," I told Mondo that night on the phone. I don't know how, I don't mean that we, like, stitched him up or anything, but I think that we must be the reason . . ."

"Quit acting nuts. I know you're faking, Larry. Gus says *you* probably made him. My dinner's ready—" He hung up.

About the static—sometimes that was all you could see in Eric Mutis's eyes. Just a random light tracking your fists back and forth, two blue-alive-voids. When we laid him flat in the weeds behind the Science Building, it was that emptiness that made us wild. The overriding feeling I had at these times was that I couldn't stop hitting him—*OK, I shouldn't be hitting him at all,* I'd think, *but if I stop I'll make things worse.* The right light would return to his eyes and he would know what I had been doing. Stopping the punishing rhythm, without any warning, I'd risk waking him from a dream. Me too, I'd wake up breathless. Somehow I swear it really did feel like that, like I had to keep right on hitting him, to protect him, and me, from what was happening. Out of the red corner of one eye I could see my own wet fist flying. The slickness on it was our snot and our blood.

Only one time did anybody stop us.

"Leave him alone," said a voice approaching from the awning of the Science Building. We all turned. Eric Mutant, breathing quietly in the weeds below us, rolled his eyes toward the voice.

"You heard me," the voice repeated, and, miraculously, we had. We stopped. The four of us followed Mutis's example, and froze. This voice belonged to our librarian, Mrs. Kauder, a woman whose red-lipped face and white hair made her shockingly attractive to us. Here she came like a leopardess, flaunting all her bones.

Somebody wiped Eric's blood onto his own sleeve, a decoy swipe.

Now we could credibly asseverate, to the librarian or to Coach Leyshon or to Vice Principal Derry, that our assault on Eric Mutis had been a fight. The librarian fixed her green eyes on each one of us—every one of us except for Eric she had known in elementary school.

"Now you go back to your homerooms," she said, in this funny rehearsed way, as if she were reading our lives to us from a book. "Now *you* go to Math, Gus Ainsworth—" She pronounced our real names so gently, as if she were breaking a spell. "Now *you* go to Computers, Larry Rubio. . . ." Her voice was as nasally as Eric's but with an old person's polished tremble. It was a terribly embarrassing voice—a weak white grasshopper species that we would have tried to kill, had it belonged to a fellow child.

"Remember, boys," the librarian called after us. "That is a *no*-no! We do not treat each other that way. . . ." She finished with a liquidy rattle, so that you could almost see the half-sunk moon of her optimism bobbing up and down inside the sentence (this librarian was a forty-year veteran of her carrels and I think that light was going out).

"Now *you*, Eric Mutis," the librarian said softly. "You come with me."

And here's the thing: That was just a Wednesday. That was nowhere near the worst of what we did to this kid, Mutis. I think we needed the librarian to keep reading us her story of our lives, her good script of who we were and our activities, for every minute of every day—but of course she couldn't do this, and we did get lost.

"Do you think Eric is alive?" I asked Mondo. We were alone in Camp Dark; Juan Carlos had improbably gotten a job as a Food Lion bag boy and Gus was out with some chick.

Mondo looked up from his Choco-Slurpo, shocked. Even the junior size of the Choco-Slurpo contained a swimming pool of pudding. The junior was like the idiot adult son of the gargantuan "jumbo."

"Of course he is! He changed schools, Rubby—he's not *dead*." He sucked furiously at chocolate sludge, his eyes goggling out.

"Well, what if he died? What if he was dying all last year? What if he got kidnapped, or ran away? How would we know?"

"Maybe he still lives right around the corner! Maybe he helped you to put the scarecrow up! Is that it, Larry?" he asked, offering me the fudgy backwaters of the Choco-Slurpo. When Gus wasn't around, Mondo became smarter, kinder, and more afraid. "Are you guys doing this together? You and Eric?"

"No," I said sadly. "Mutant, he moved. I checked his old house."

"Huh? You what?" Out of habit, Mondo heaved up to chuck the junior cup into the Cone, our trash can of yore, momentarily forgetting that the Cone was now a sort of open grave for Eric Mutis; with the freakishness of blind coincidence, Mondo happened to look up and notice an inscription on the sunless side of the oak; not new, judging from its scarred and etiolated look, but new to us:

ERIC MUTIS

&

SATURDAY

The letters oozed beneath an apple green sap and were childishly shaped; the kid had pierced the heart with a little arrow. When I saw this epitaph—because that is how they always read to me, this type of love graffiti on trees and urinals, as epitaphs for ancient couples—my throat tightened and my heart raced in such a way that my own death seemed a likely possibility. *Mayday, God! O God,* I prayed: *Please, if I am going to die, may it happen before Mondo Chu attempts CPR.*

"Look!" Mondo was screaming. For a moment he'd forgotten that I was supposed to be the culprit, the engineer of this psychotic joke. "Mutant was here! Mutant had a *girlfriend*!"

So then I filled in some blanks for Mondo. I offered Mondo the parts of Eric Mutis that I had indeed been hoarding.

Something was alive in the corner. That was the first thing I noticed when I set foot in Mutant's bedroom: a stripe of motion in the brown shadows near the shuttered window. It was a rabbit. A pet, you could tell from the water bottle wired to its cage bars. A pet was not just some animal, it was yours, it was loved and fed by you. Everybody knows this, of course, but for some reason the plastic water bottle looked shockingly bright to me; the clean good smell of the straw was an exotic perfume in the Mute's bedroom.

"You think this will fit you, Larry?"

Eric held out a shrunken, wrinkled sweater that I recognized.

"Uh-huh."

"You better now, Larry?"

"Terrific. Extra super." I was, in fact, almost out of my mind with embarrassment—I had been riding my bicycle on the suburban side of Anthem, on my way to see a West Olmsted kid who owed me money, when I felt a fierce pain in my side and I went flying over the handlebars—I landed a little way from my bicycle, where I sat in the street watching the front bicycle tire spinning maniacally with a pebble in my fist that turned out to be my tooth. I knew the car—it was the green Cadillac. It was that gargoyle from the school parking lot who had almost killed me. I was still sitting in the road, hypnotized by the blue sea glare on the asphalt, when I watched a pair of Hoops sneakers come jogging toward me.

"Hi, Larry," he'd said. "You all right? Sorry. He didn't see you there."

I had been planning to say: "Is that maniac your dad? Mr. Hit and Run? Your caretaker or whatever? Because I could sue, you know."

Instead I watched my hand slide inside of Mutant's hand and form a complicated red-and-white mitt. It was a slippery handshake, my palm bleeding into it, my bike stigmata—I waited for Mutant to say something about that time I smashed his specs. But his ugly, big-eared face lowered to me and then I was on my feet, following him through a scarred wooden door, number 52, the knocker of which was a brass pineapple with filth-encrusted tropical checkers. Tackiness and incoherence, that's what awaited me in Casa Mutis, as augured by that fruity knocker—the living room was a zombie zone of grime and confusion. Chaos. The furniture was arranged in a way that made it look like a family of illegal squatters, the plaid sofa rearing on its side, even the appliances crouched. Mutant made no apologies but hustled me into a bedroom, his, I guessed; here he was, going through drawers, looking for a change of clothes to lend me. If I went home covered in blood and toting the twisted blue octopus of my bicycle, I explained, my ma, terrified by how close I'd swerved toward death, would murder me. I pulled Mutis's sweater on. I knew I should thank him.

"That's a rabbit?" I asked like some idiot.

"Yeah." Now Eric Mutis smiled with a brilliance that I had never seen before. "That's my rabbit."

I crossed the room, in Eric Mutis's boat-striped sweater, to acquaint myself with Eric Mutis's caged pet, feeling my afternoon curve weirdly. It was sitting on a little mountain of food, the rabbit. It had piled that food so high that its tall ears had pushed flat against its skull, which I thought made this rabbit look like a European swimmer.

"I think you are spoiling that rabbit, dude."

Big fifty-pound bags of straw and food pellets filled all the corners of the room, sharing space with less bucolic stuff: a shitty purple tape deck and a vat of roach-zapping spray, grimy cartoon-print pajama pants and underwear that looked like free-range laundry to me, no hamper in sight. Mutis had stocked this place for the apocalypse, turned his room into a bunny stronghold. (Where did Mutis get his rabbit funds from? I wondered. He got the free lunch at school and dressed like a hobo.) Pine straw. Timothy, orchard, meadow. Alfalfa—plus calcium! said one bag below a humongous Swiss cheese–colored rabbit with what must have been, for a rabbit, a bodybuilder's physique. The rabbit smiled gloatingly at me, flexing muscles you would never suspect a rabbit possessed.

"My Christ, do they put steroids in that alfalfa?" I peeled off the price sticker, feeling like a city bumpkin. "Twenty bucks! You got ripped off!" I grinned. "You need to buy your grass from *Jamaica*, dude."

But he had turned away from me, bending to whisper something to the trembling rabbit. Seeing this made me uncomfortable; his whisper was already a million times too loud. I felt a flare-up of my school-day rage—for a second I hated Eric Mutant again, and I hated the oblivious rabbit even more, so smugly itself inside the cage, sucking like an infant at its water nozzle. Did Mutant know what kind of ammo he was giving me? Did he honestly believe that I was going to keep his lovenest a secret from my friends?

I strummed my fingernails along the tiny cage bars. They felt like petrified guitar strings. "What's his name?"

"Her name is Saturday," said Eric happily, and suddenly I wanted to cry. Who knows why? Because Eric Mutis had a girl's pet; because Eric Mutis had named his dingy rabbit after the best day of the week? I'd never seen Eric Mutis say one word to a human girl, I'd never thought of Eric Mutis as a lover before. But he was kicking game to this rabbit like an old pro. Just whispering a love music to her, calling down to her, "Saturday, Saturday." Behind the cage bars his whole face was changing. Mutant kept changing until he wasn't ugly anymore. What had we found so repulsive about him in the first place? His finger was making the gentlest circle between the rabbit's crushed ears, a spot that looked really soft to me, like a baby's head. The rabbit's irises were fiery and dust dry, I noted, swiping hard at my own with Eric's sleeve.

Inside the cage, the rabbit twitched phlegmatically, breathing underneath waves of Eric Mutis's love. The rabbit didn't change at all. Not one whisker trembled. This struck me as pretty rude behavior, on the part of the rabbit. I was just a bystander to their little feeding here, and I could feel my heartbeat getting steadily faster. Behind the bars, Saturday was wrinkling her nose into a joyless, princessy expression, as if breathing air were an onerous obligation that she wished she could give up. What was the big attraction here? I wondered. This pet rabbit had all the charm and verve of a pillow with eyes.

"Want to pet her?" Mutant asked, not looking at me.

"No."

But then I realized that I *could* do this; nobody was watching me but Mutant and his voiceless rabbit. Some hard pressure flew away from me like air out of a zigzagging balloon. I let Mutant guide my hand through the door of the cage and brushed the green straw off her fur. Still I thought this pet was pretty stupid, until I petted her hide in the same direction that Mutant was going and felt actually electrified—under my palm, a cache of white life hummed.

"Can I tell you a secret?"

"Whatever. Sure." At that moment, it was my belief that he safely could.

Eric Mutis opened a drawer; there was so much dust on the bureau that his elbow left a big tiger stripe on the wood. There was so much dust everywhere in that room that the clean gleam of Saturday's cage made it look like Incan treasure.

"Here." The poster he thrust at me read LOST: MY PET BUNNY, MISS MOLLY MOUSE. PLEASE CALL ###-#####! The albino rabbit in the photograph was unmistakably Saturday, wearing a sparkly Barbie top hat someone had bobby-pinned to her ear, the owner's joking reference, I guessed, to the usual, magical algorithm of rabbits coming out of hats—a joke that was apparently lost on Saturday, whose red eyes bored into the camera with all the warmth and personality of the planet Mars. Even "found," hugged inside the photograph, the creature was escaping its owner. The owner's name, according to this poster, was Sara Jo. "I am nine," the poster declared plaintively. The date on the poster said "Lost on August 22." The address listed was 49 Delmar, just around the corner.

"I never returned her." His voice seemed to tremble at the exact same tempo as the rabbit's shuddering haunches. "I saw these posters everywhere." He paused. "I pulled them all down." He stepped aside to show me the bureau drawer, which was filled with every color of the Miss Molly poster. "I saw the girl who put them up. She has red hair. Two of those, what are they called . . ." He frowned. "Pigtails!"

"OK." I grinned. "That's bad."

Suddenly we were laughing, *hard*, even Saturday, with her rump-shaking tremors, appeared to be laughing along with us.

Eric stopped first. Before I heard the hinge squeak, Eric was on his feet, hustling across the room on ballerina toes to shut the bedroom door. Just before it closed I watched a hunched shape flow past and enter the maple cavity of their bathroom. It was the same old guy who had almost mowed me down in the snouty green Cadillac on Delmar Street not thirty minutes ago. Relationship to Eric: unclear.

"Is that your father?"

Eric's face was bright red.

"Your, ah, your grandfather? Your uncle? Your mom's boyfriend?"

Eric Mutis, whom we could not embarrass at school, did not answer me now or meet my eyes.

"That's fine, whatever," I said. "You don't have to tell me shit about your situation. Honey, I can't even say my own last name."

I barked with laughter, because what the hell? Where the hell had that come from, my calling him "honey"?

Eric smiled. "Peaches," he said, "that's just fine."

For a second we stared at each other. Then we roared. It was the first and last joke I ever heard him try to make. We clutched our stomachs and stumbled around, knocking into one another.

"Shh!" Eric said between gasps, pointing wildly at the bedroom door. "Shhh, Larry!"

And then we got quiet, me and Eric Mutis. The rabbit stood on her haunches and drank water, making a white comma between us; the whole world got quieter and quieter, until that kissy sound of a mouth getting water was all you could hear. For a minute or two, catching our breath, we got to be humans together.

I never returned Mutant's sweater, and the following Monday I did not speak to him. I hid the cuts on my palms in two fists. It took me another week to find a poster for Saturday. I figured they'd all be long gone—Eric said he'd torn them all down—but I found one on the Food Lion message board, buried under a thousand kitty calendars and yoga and LEARN TO BONGO! fliers: a very poorly reproduced Saturday glaring out at me under the Barbie hat and the words LOST! MY PET BUNNY. I dialed the number. Sure enough, a girl's voice answered, all pipsqueaky and polite.

"I have news that might be of some interest to you."

She knew right away.

"Molly Mouse! You found her!" Which, what an identity crisis for a rabbit. What kind of name is that? Worse than Rubby-oh. Kids should be stopped from naming anything, I thought angrily, they are too dumb to guess the true and correct names for things. Parents too.

"Yes. That is correct. Something has come to light, ma'am."

I swayed a little with the phone in my hand, feeling powerful and evil. For some reason I was putting on my one-hundred-year-old voice, the gruff one I used when I ordered pizzas on the phone and requested the Golden Years senior discount. I heard myself reciting in this false, ancient voice the address of the house where Saturday and Eric slept.

At school, I breathed easier—I had extricated myself from a tight spot. I had been in real danger, but the moment had passed. Eric Mutis was not ever going to be my friend. Twice I called Sara Jo to ask how Molly Mouse was doing; her dad had gone to the Mutis house and via some exchange of threats or dollars gotten her back. "Oh," the girl squealed, "she's doing *beautiful*, she loves being *home*!"

Eric Mutis's eyes, locked inside the gray corrals of his Medicaid frames, now became a second, dewless glass. Whenever anybody called him Mucus or Mutant, and also when our teacher called him, simply, "Eric M.," his face showed the pruny strain of a weight lifter, puckering inward and then collapsing, as if he were too weak to hoist up his own name off the mat. When we hit him behind the Science Building, his eyes were true blanks. When we finished with him they had looked like a doll's eyes—open, staring, but packed solid with frost, like the blue Antarctic. Permafrost around each pupil. Two telescopes fixed on a lifeless planet. Nobody had understood Eric Mutis when he arrived late in October and then by springtime my friends and I had made him much less scrutable.

"Larry—," he started to say to me once in the bathroom, several weeks after they'd come for Saturday, but I wrung my hands in the sink disgustedly and walked out, following Mutant's example and avoiding our faces in the mirror. We never looked at each other again, and then one day he was gone.

Mondo and I crossed the playground in a slow processional. "Jesus H., are we graduating from something?" I grumbled. "Mondo, are we getting married? Dude, let's pick up the pace. Mondo?"

Mondo had stopped walking in the middle of the playground. One of the few pieces of playground equipment that had survived the city pogrom and the red foaming were the zoo pogos, the little giraffe and the donkey on a stick. Mondo sat on it; the pogo groaned beneath his weight. He turned and looked at me with the world's most miserable face.

"I am not going."

I said nothing.

"I am changing my mind," he said, the little pogo donkey listing east and west beneath him. He leaned a fat hand on its head and broke its left ear off. "God*damn* it!" He stood up, as if some switch inside him had broken off. I was glad that I wouldn't have to convince him of anything. I was glad, even, that he was afraid—I hadn't known that you could feel so grateful to a friend, for living in fear with you. Fear was otherwise a very lonely place. We kept walking toward the scarecrow.

"This is stupid," he mumbled. "This is crazy. No way did we make the scarecrow."

"Let's just get this done."

An idea had come to me last night, after telling Mondo the story of Saturday. An offering to make, a way to satisfy whatever force was feeding on the doll of Eric. It wasn't a good one, but the other option was to leave the scarecrow untouched down there until it disappeared.

"Get *what* done?" Mondo was muttering. "You won't even tell me why you're going down there. . . ."

"Do you want to go home? Do you want to wait until he's totally gone?"

Mondo shook his head. His chubby face looked tumescent and red, not unlike the playground foam, as if his cheeks were swelling preemptively to protect him. Far away a plane roared over Anthem, dismissing our whole city in twenty seconds.

"Shut up, Larry!" Mondo yelped near the duck pond, when a car backfired and I jumped and brushed the flabby skin of his arm. "Watch where you're going!"

Our flashlight beams crossed and blinded one another. After this we did not talk. Night had fallen hours ago—I didn't want to be interrupted by anyone. Nobody was around, not even the regular bums, but the traffic on I-12 roared reassuringly just behind the treeline, a constant reminder of the asphalt rivers and the lattice of lights and signs that led to our homes. Friendship Park looked one hundred percent different than it did in daylight. Now the clouds were blue and silver, and where the full moon shone, new colors seemed to float up around us everywhere—the rusty weeds on the duck pond looked tangerine, the pin oak bulged with purple veins.

"How's it going tonight, Mutant?" Mondo asked in a nervous voice when we reached the oak. He chucked something into the Cone—the plaster donkey's ear. It landed squarely on Eric's back. This was all that was left of the doll of Eric Mutis, his last solid part. Something had drawn its delicate claws down the scarecrow's back, and now there was no mistaking what the straw inside it actually was, where it had come from—it was rabbit bedding, I thought. Timothy, meadow, orchard. Pine straw. The same golden stuff I'd seen bagged that day in the Mute's dark bedroom. I took a big breath; I wished that I could imitate the scarecrow and leap into the Cone, swim down to him, instead of crawling along the rock wall like a bug.

"It's moving!" Mondo screamed. "It's getting away."

I almost screamed too, thinking he meant the doll. But he was pointing at my black knapsack, which I'd slouched against the oak: a little tumor bubble was percolating inside the canvas, pushing outward at the fabric. As we watched, the bag fell onto its side and began to slide away, inch by inch, the zipper twinkling in the moonlight as the pouch pushed over the roots.

"Oh, shit!" I grabbed the bag and slung it over my shoulders. "Don't worry about that. I'll explain later. You just hold the rope, bro. Please, Mondo?"

So Mondo, staring at me with real fear as if we'd never met, as if I'd only been impersonating his good friend Larry Rubio for all these years, helped me to tie the eighteen-meter phys ed rope to the oak and loop one end around my waist. It took almost forty minutes to lower myself into the Cone, but in fact my friends' suspicions had prepared me for this descent—I had already imagined myself backing into the ravine. I stumbled once and let go of the rock wall, swinging out, but Mondo called down that it was OK, I was OK (and I don't think it's possible to overstate the love I felt in that moment for Mondo Chu)—and then I was crouching, miraculously, on the mineral blue bottom of the Cone. The view above me I will never forget: the great oak sprawling over the ravine, fireflies dotting the lacunae between its frozen roots like tiny underworld lights. Much farther away, in the real sky, snakes of clouds wound ball round and came loose.

I crouched over the scarecrow's torso, which at this moment could not have looked less like a scarecrow's anything—if you didn't notice the seam of straw, you might have thought it was a battered sofa cushion. Featureless and beige. I plucked up a green straw and felt a lurching sadness. Anybody with a mirror in his house knows the strangeness of meeting himself, his flaws, in light. This doll was almost gone, the boy original, Eric Mutis, was nowhere we could discover, and somehow this made me feel as if I had broken a mirror, missed my one chance to really know myself. I tried to resurrect Eric Mutis in my mind's eye—the first Eric, the kid we'd almost killed—and failed. A face started to stutter together, shattered whitely away.

"You made it, Rubby!" Mondo called. But I hadn't, yet. I unzipped my backpack. A little nose peeked out, a starburst of whiskers, followed by a white face, a white body. I dumped it sort of less ceremoniously than I had intended onto the relic of the scarecrow, where she landed and bounced with her front legs out. It wasn't Saturday—I couldn't steal Saturday back, I'd figured that would appease or solve nothing, but then this doll wasn't the real Eric Mutis either. I'd bought this nameless dwarf rabbit for nineteen bucks at the mall pet store, where the Dijon-vested clerk had ogled me with true horror—"You do not want to buy a *hutch* for the animal, sir?" Many of the products that this pet-store clerk sold seemed pretty antiliberation, cages and syringes, so I did not mention to him that I was going to free the rabbit.

Mondo was screaming something at me from the near sky, but I did not turn—I didn't want to let my guard down now. I kept my feet planted but sometimes I'd move my arms crazily, as if in imitation of the huge oak dancing its branches far above me. When I thought a bird was coming our way, I hollered it away. Shapes caught at the corner of my eye. Would the thing that had carried off the doll of Eric Mutis come for me now? I wondered. But I wasn't afraid. I felt ready, strangely, for whatever was coming. The substitute rabbit, I saw with wonderment, was rooting its little head into the pale fibers sprouting out of the scarecrow; it went swimming into the straw, a reversal of its birth from my black book bag—first went with its furry ears, its bunching back, the big, velour skis of its feet. I was there, so no birds dove for it or anything. I was standing right there the whole time. I stood with my arms stretched wide and trembling and I felt as if the black sky was my body and I felt as if the white moon, far above me, unwrinkled and shining, was my mind.

"La-arry!" I was aware of Mondo calling me faintly from the twinkling roots of the oak, lit up all wild by the underworld flies, but I knew I couldn't turn or come up yet. Owls, I worried, city hawks. The rabbit bubbled serenely through the straw at my feet. Somewhere I think I must still be standing, just like that.

Paris Burns

Y*van* Goll

—Translated from German by Jed Rasula

Cinnabar ship *PARIS*
Mariner of town hall heraldry and tramways
In the mistral of prisons a swinging signboard

LIBERTÉ ÉGALITÉ FRATERNITÉ

From the towers of St. Sulpice
Angels fly up
In invisible lifts
Pianolas sing in the veils
Angelus
5 in the morning
Apocalyptic freight trains
Slowly enter the station in the rain
Bringing the golden oranges of dawn
You catch the first bus
To Châtelet

The white crows of the press
Squabble over the night carrion
Quickie last judgment in three lines
Scriptures for the subway:

"A hairdresser
Hangs himself
With wife's hair

12 Negroes
On board the Goethe
Shot for blasphemy

General strike
At the Vatican
Pope has stomachache

A comet
Over New York
Revives three million dead

He loved her
She loved him
Ten years in penitentiary"

But on republican boulevards
Morning cafés blink
Houses with sleepy bags under window-eyes
Thriving businesses
Charming founts in colorful urinals
As though sweet thyme grew there
And the last widows of the night
Draw veils of mist to their bosoms

A statue
Is raised in the night
Guillotine on Boulevard Arago
On which a blue blackbird perches
A murderer
Chuckles
Teases his hair
On the front page of the morning papers
With all the milk deliveries
And suburban trains mourn Europe
Already rolling
The golf ball rolls in golden
Sawdust
No: rises
Behind mankind sneaking up
Round
Red

SUN!

You should not kill!

But the sun is no death's head
It's a dandelion bloom
It's the hairstyle of a typewriter girl
First window in Montmartre
Diamond in my necktie!
In Paris
It's in all the bakeries
Smelling of cornflower fields
Three-kilo
Bread

Behind the bedpost
Good wives tuck away a bottle of spirits
For when the postman brings
Perpetual destiny

Reception rooms are well heated of course
The dermatologist writes a death certificate
In the green plush of the waiting room
Smiling nuns
Play with tiny red germs
Manicurists
Get a discount
At each bus stop
I wait for my great unknown
How much longing the bus conveys!
At first she smiles, and later
You have to dose her heart with raspberry ice cream

Three hundred times she was called Isabel
But now it's Bad Zuzu
Birdie fallen into a few hotel rooms
Her heart's a puppet
That closes its eyes when you tilt her
But when she cries
You already see the wrinkled mouth of an old dame
Her eyelids flutter with fear like maple leaves in fall
Together we discover nature
Little puffs cavorting in St. Cloud

Real primroses around the gas factory!
And green moss in the bosom of the ancient goddess
Proves that even the rain has character
But nothing ages as quickly as a morning landscape
All at once the tree is dust
The stream comes back with a dirge
Of mint! We don't have time to be Greek!

Turnabout, globespun
Circuses
Copper Pantheon
With pink garters quickly whipped!
On the iron fountain of the Eiffel Tower
The driving belt from moon to moon
Spans the planetary velodrome
On a rattling unicycle rides the SUN
Winning the handicap
Noon
ZENITH
Sweating in its yellow sweater
The world race is nothing less
Than motorbikes mounting the Milky Way
And at Longchamps on besotted steeds
The lemon jersey jockeys shout
HURRAH!

The man summons the divine world champion
All the hairdressers of Europe
Hurl themselves into *Soul or Else*

NOON

High tension
700,000 volts
Twirl the nerve battery
The platinum needle of the Eiffel Tower punctures the ulcer of a cloud
Fever
Typhus ward
Blast furnaces
Snow trains
Incandescence 44 degrees plus or minus

Yvan Goll

Fir forests burn like paper
Icebergs slide down the equator
Comet's tail curled
Aluminum eagle
Collapsing
Oh crazy turn of the century
Taking the measure of the gold standard sun
And I fear for my heart
Going off suddenly like a pistol!

But the brickwork
Sphinx
Barks: WORK WORK
In the factories pimped sirens snort
Puddle push cut solder turn dredge plow heat sweep embroider tap lift die
Oh socialist: Sebastian in the burning fiery red
Worked up into a lantern
Hoarse prophet
Pointing to the new Tuileries
Vaillant-Couturier
From Belleville dark clouds buzz closer
Red torches ignite the prisons

LIBERTÉ ÉGALITÉ FRATERNITÉ

But the sower has put her
Phrygian cap on askew
The pensioners' whores
On all the 2-franc pieces
Dance tangos

Smiling maidens of the Folies-Bergère
I know what oregano means
Through Senegal
Then Canada
The dreadnoughts go crazy in your ports
Your blue-white-red hair
Lights victory torches
All over Europe
Yet I know your humility, young lady
Alone in a bleak hotel

Haggling over secondhand blouses
And at noon over a petrol burner
Two soft-boiled eggs
Postcards from Nice on the broken mirror

But next to the revamped hotel
Is the fortune-teller
Modern Pythias
On a piano stool
Pumped on cheap Ceylon tea
Selling poor girls
Some lucky star
Three nines speedy marriage
Queen of spades in play
And behind the Japanese screen
The KING OF HEARTS is smoking
Marxlandia

Oh Place de la Concorde
What does the obelisk
Of wisdom
Reveal?
At the Admiralty
In a moldy office is a portrait of Madagascar
Cornflower blue admirals
With goatees
Dish out
With their magnetic pencils
Ironclad crosses on Gibraltar
Alphonso XIII clutches his top hat
Presidents of the Republic in all the windows
But the Crown Prince Hirohito
With a cynical smile
Executes the diplomatic corps

VIVE LA FRANCE!

Accident
Rumors
One-second film
One head

One hat
One head out of fifty thousand heads
Fashioned in good commoner style
One head
Falls
Rolls
Oh pitiless car treads
Blood
Stone—oh!
Oh head with paternal beard
Maybe it was Jochanaan
Just risen from the subway
Any head
My head maybe . . .

All the reporters' blue ink fades
The photograph bows to world history
The rotary machines
Spit out gray reptiles
And in all the news bureaus
I open Pandora's boxes
Over the stock exchanges of London and Brussels
A white
Fleshy
Greasy
Hand
With mother-of-pearl cuff links
Symbol of cursed creation mounting mounting to a cramp
All the gramophones know the price of Royal Dutch
La Marseillaise

ALLONS ENFANTS DE LA PATRIE

On the Boulevards
One recites the litany of the holy numbers of the age:
Oracle
420
606
66
75
The poker of CULTURE!

In Chicago a famous tile falls into the street
In Greenland a seal expires
In Shantung the Finance Minister bursts into song:

I have a crown
On my tooth

I have a hundred shares
In Olympia Mines

I have a family vault
For twenty centuries

I have
I have

Even as the day grows old
On my tooth I've got gold

And he tenders his resignation
Moscow telegraphs Gomorrah:

REVOLUTION!

Workers in blue tramway tank attack the Louvre
On all the café terraces bloom the May cockades
"Singer sewing machine guns"
The railway workers are on strike
The express trains rest in the pinewoods
For four days
The radio-telegrams buzz
Bees around the Eiffel Tower
From afar the Mont-Blanc station transmits
Diamond signals
"Comrades, get your special edition!"

Ideal of ideals
Boxing bout in Jersey City
The new century's law of the fist
The Butchers' Association sends a delegation over the ocean

Yvan Goll

*

Attention! Round one!
Europe shakes hands with Negro Zeus
Blue-white-red shorts
The male breast bulges pink steel
Morse in a fever
Four fists crank the world's honor
Time stands still in America
Munitions factories shut down
All over the Atlantic steamers halt
Round four
Mountains roll
Banks robbed
77 suicides
300 coronaries
Knockout!

The STATUE OF LIBERTY smiles

In despair a war breaks out
Skeletons beat the drums
The price of sugar rises
Free burials
From cattle cars beribboned heroes bawl
A dried-up heart's pasted into a stamp album
Express trains with coffins
Link Rome to Stockholm

Now for the first time
At an empty café table
A GENIUS discovers
A love of mankind!

Café SOUL center of the world!
Brothers and sisters exchange cigarettes

CAFÉ DES WESTENS CAFÉ DE LA ROTONDE
CAFÉ TERRASSE CAFÉ PRAGUE CAFÉ STEFANIE
CAFÉ

Swimming in the iced coffees are undiscovered stars
The whirling blades of thinking brains
Plunge deep into placid mirrors
Die, young poet, of skeptical truth
Painters vault ultramarine balconies in the sky
Political will clenches its head like a fist
Oh epoch of the people!
Fernand Léger's cinnabar dynamos
Burst the plaster walls
Lipchitz sings new sphinxes
The burial ground of the Louvre collapses
Grass grows in the ears of Gothic apostles

Meanwhile
Even the waiters
In tails
Sell contraband
Brotherhood
à 50 centimes

Locomotives
Centaurs
Ride gleefully howling along the boulevards
Sea wind and birds of prey on their shaggy chests
But in tender arms
The blue sources of night meadows
Go home lightly bearing
Iron rainbows

Paris
Diamond on Europe's throat
Made iridescent by a million arc and oil lamps
On the Arc de Triomphe a jazz band plays
Pantheon cymbals
Trocadéro organ
Oh Paris foxtrot!
In the breeze the flute of the Eiffel Tower softly sings

On the first platform of his Tower
Mr. Eiffel, magician in sports cap,
Personally receives the poets of Europe for dinner

Yvan Goll

Symphony concert of clouds
Acoustics of the cosmos
And after the third course: Lightning-grilled stars
Recite

BLAISE CENDRARS

O Tour Eiffel
Feu d'artifice géant de l'Exposition Universelle

Sur le Gange
A Bénarès
Tu te penches, palmier géant

Et au Pôle-Nord
Tu resplendis avec toute la magnificence de l'aurore
boréale de ta télégraphie sans fil

En Europe tu es comme le gibet

Au cœur de l'Afrique c'est toi qui cours
Girafe

Tu es tout
Tour
Dieu antique
Bête moderne
Spectre solaire
Sujet de mon poème
Tour
Tour du monde
Tour en mouvement

VALENTIN PARNAKH

Пресс гидравлическій в ночи меднобетонной
800 тонн
16 рычагов орудуёт колонной
И ребр уклон
Скрещенья скрениты и скреб

Тормазов стрђней и стропил
Скрип крутьев стрђл решеток ребр
Шмыг рђзь и грыз когтей и пил

VICENTE HUIDOBRO

Los hombras de mañana
Vendrán a descrifrar los jeroglificos
Que dejamos ahora
Escritos al revés
Entre los hierros, de la Torre Eiffel

This poetry festival lasted all night
Monsieur Eiffel made a gift to each of three shares in his Company
Patron Prometheus
Paris keeps on burning
The bracelets of the Grand Boulevards were platinum
And the war widow Seine wore her black pearl lanterns
All the jewelers got the Nobel Prize
The Opera House
Undermined with Maggi dice
Guarded by ballerinas

Berlitz School: Academy of the Fifth International

At the Musée Grévin Marat asked 3 francs for an interview
Café de Madrid: congress of traveling piano salesmen
And all the adulterers marry their detective

Oh Queen of Romania sell me your love
I'm called Ivan
Like a good European I'll shoot you tomorrow!
I'll seek my final despair in the cinema
Protected by the Swiss of Notre-Dame
On the posters Charlotte Corday
Laughs at her humanitarian award
And flaming airships
Project the photo of Lenin
Onto Saturn

Stop!
There you are, violet Zuzu,
Soft blossom on Printemps paper display
Will you sell me a ream for this heavenly poem?
Because the larks died for us
I'll toss rosy bank drafts in the air

Jacob's ladders and elevators
Ascend
In our poor Eden Hotel!
Crazy telephone
Stained menus with funereal borders
And the porter is only an anxious patriarch
Where is Australia?
When do the steamboats leave for Saint-Cloud?
The police drive a sky blue car
On a distant meadow bobs the wagtail
Freight trains
Alarmed with their cargo of rotting oranges
Tomorrow's sunrise is canceled

Last
Red light
At the tram stop
My heart
Gives out

What time is it?

—for Carl Einstein

Destroy All Monsters

Greg Hrbek

HARUO NAKAJIMA/MONSTER ZERO

MONSTER ZERO SWEPT, swooped, as if on wires suspended from the roof of the cosmos, over the dead horizon of Planet X. Fuck these aliens in their shiny jumpsuits, whoever the fuck they were, out here on the blind side of Jupiter. Made no difference who had been here first. What was *first*?—indigenous was one thing, but *first*—and even indigenous (now that his middle head, the most cerebral of the three, came to think of it) had a spurious ring to it, because there was always something before, always something earlier than the now, before humanoids, even before *kaiju* like himself, who'd been lurking in oceanic trenches or nesting inside dormant volcanoes or trapped in hurtling meteors for millennia unknown, who knew how long, but a hell of a lot longer than there'd been any anthropoids stumbling toward pathetic notions of spiritual and technological fruition. Now he felt the fire in his fangs, now tasted the sweetness of it on his forked tongues, and a moment later a triad of gravity beams, crackling threads of electromagnetism, bolted from his three maws. No gravity beams, of course (beams later, animation department), but as he swooped over the sound stage, Nakajima couldn't help but notice: no pyrotechnics either. What the fuck. Plastic explosives were supposed to be going off in three separate directions (corresponding to the distinct angles of his heads) along the surface of the miniature planet, throwing up great clouds of plaster dust and jolting the underground tunnels and command centers of slit-eyed space invaders—but Nakajima, inside Monster Zero, in the triple-digit heat of the synthetic rubber suit, could not hear any moon rock blowing sky-high; only the boss blowing his top. Cut! Cut! Just like that, the take, the attack, was over. Someone had screwed up down there. Some puny assistant too incompetent to light a goddamn fuse. I'll electromagnetize him, thought Monster Zero. It was the kind of idea that always originated in the head that was right of center: the angry head, the head that was never happy unless anthropoids were being terrorized and famous landmarks were being smashed to smithereens and so-called civilization was generally going up in flames; and even then, even when it all finally came together in postproduction, even as the effects departments inked the gravity beams and synched the demoniacal shrieks, already Monster Zero would be feeling the return of a rage that could only be slaked by another surprise attack. Sometimes the middle head had to wonder. As for the other one, the left one: Strange waves came from the brain in that head. A Toho Company–American International Pictures Production. Hiroshima. Nagasaki. And the nominees for Best Actor in a Supporting Role are. Nick Adams, *Twilight of Honor*. 1964.

MIRIAM SCHUMANN

Nick Adams. Nick Adams. Miriam had tried to think. The name did not ring a bell. The headshots—of a man with blond hair slicked back in a wave, not handsome exactly, but attractive, a wholesome face, an amiable smile, a boy in a man's body—had not looked familiar. The director, Ishiro Honda, had told her the American had been nominated the year prior for an Academy Award. She had not heard of the film. The day he arrived, in a Hawaiian print shirt and sunglasses, she met him at the airport. The chauffeur took Mr. Adams's suitcase and Mr. Adams took Miriam's arm. Call me Nick. She had been told to impress the honored guest with a tour of the metropolis. So they drove on the new Expressway Number 4 and saw Tokyo Tower and wound up trapped in the madness of downtown at midday. An entanglement of automobiles and trolley cars and pedestrians; highway overpasses and elevated tracks, air hammers slamming rivets, jet planes on approach and departure. At Sukiyabashi, the electronic billboard read 83 decibels, then 84 . . .

Mr. Adams—

Nick.

All right. Nick. Is Los Angeles very busy too?

He gave her that winning smile and said: Miriam, L.A. is Sleepville compared to this cuckoo place.

Greg Hrbek

NICK ADAMS/ASTRONAUT GLENN

Tokyo.

Never in his life—thirty-four years and counting—had Nick imagined he'd find himself here. He had sworn, in fact, in more than one interview with more than one hack columnist, that he'd never make a picture overseas. But here he was, in Japan, of all places. To pilot the flagship rocket ship of the United Space Nations, the United Nations of Space, something like that, to a strange new planet. Of which he knew next to nothing. Because he had not read the script. "You're an astronaut," his agent had told him a year earlier, over gin martinis at Romanoff's. "There's giant monsters in the picture too. One has three heads." A giant three-headed monster, Nick had thought, surveying the joint, eyes smarting just a little. He had to take a leak, and set down on the bar his stemmed glass and set sail for the men's room, and that's where he was, streaming piss into a pure white porcelain basin, when Marlon Brando appeared beside him, unzipping, unpacking the penis of a thoroughbred horse.

Who are you? Brando said.

Nick Adams.

Don't wink at another man when he's urinating.

I don't.

Only Maoists and repressed homosexuals wink at urinating men.

Oh, I'm not queer, Nick said.

Brando didn't seem to hear. He had tilted his head up, closed his eyes as if to begin a heavenly ascent. Nick stole another glance before tamping his own average member into his trousers. Brando pissed: a torrent of piss, like hydroelectric outflow. Nick flushed and went to the sink. Washed his hands. Put the wave of his blond hair back in place. Now what? Keep talking. Ask him if he saw the picture. Courtroom drama, poor sap on trial. That was me. Maybe you saw the ads in the trades. Maybe you were at the Oscars. But Nick didn't say anything else to Brando that day. He fled. Fled to the bar. Willson, still there. Pinching a toothpick between thumb and forefinger, sucking Tanqueray off an impaled green olive. Nick wanted to clock him. Right there in the middle of Romanoff's. Three punches in his fag nose, one for each head of the goddamn monster who was out there in the shadows of the solar system, hiding, waiting for Astronaut Glenn.

*

Willson had told him where to go. The Shinjuku District. A neighborhood called Nicho. But Nick was beat, jet-lagged, and, in the morning, he had to meet Honda at Toho. He went to the hotel lounge and discovered the bartender was American. Grew up in Newark. No kidding, Nick said. I'm from Jersey City. Audubon Park. He drank highballs and confessed. He was in Tokyo to do a monster picture. Finally, around midnight, the concierge came looking for him. Telephone, Adams-san. She pointed him in the direction of the house phone. What time was it in the States? He couldn't do the math. Probably Saperstein. Maybe Willson. Wondering if he'd found the baths. Nick picked up the phone.

Hello.

Guess what I'm doing, said his wife after an awkward long-distance delay.

What are you doing.

Fucking.

He hung up and placed a twenty on the bar and wandered the floors of the hotel, trying to find his suite. Finally, he recalled the key in his pocket with the number printed on it. He scheduled a wake-up for seven and took a Promazine and fell asleep in the same clothes he'd worn for the crossing.

MIRIAM SCHUMANN

In the morning, Miriam was fifteen minutes early and Nick was half an hour late. She sat by the big window of Mr. Honda's office that looked out over the back lot of Toho, reading the English translation of the shooting script. *The Great Monster War*. She had never seen one of these movies. *Kaiju eiga.* She knew about them, of course. They were very popular here. But she had never felt the slightest urge to buy a ticket and watch one. Not that she wasn't interested in cinema. She saw every Kurosawa film. Sometimes she even went to American movies. John Wayne, Grace Kelly, Marlon Brando speaking in *hyōjungo*. She knew other expats who found the effect humorous. Miriam couldn't stand it. Given a choice, however, she would take the phoniness of dubbed dialogue over the total inanity of giant monsters fighting a war in outer space.

Honda-san, Adams-san has arrived. Mr. Honda flipped a switch on the intercom and instructed the secretary to show the American in immediately. The heavy door opened and as soon as Nick appeared on the threshold, Miriam could feel color coming into her cheeks. How maddening. Blushing over what? Mr. Honda stood up. Miriam braced for the usual confusion. The Easterner would bow and the Westerner would almost poke his eyes out trying to shake hands. But the two men walked right up to one another and successfully introduced themselves.

Konnichiwa, Honda-san.

Konnichiwa, Adams-san.

Morning, Miriam.

Good morning, Mr. Adams. I mean Nick.

Next came questions and answers about the trip, the accommodations. Each time one man spoke, the other looked to Miriam for the translation. Then Mr. Honda invited Nick to join him at the conference table on the other side of the office and again, as he had yesterday at the airport, Nick took Miriam by the arm. And he pulled out a chair for her. Smelling very strongly. Of soap.

EIJI TSUBURAYA/VISUAL EFFECTS

Tsuburaya Eiji, towering over the Chiyoda Ward in his suit jacket, dark glasses, and fedora, forgot for a moment about Monster Zero and remembered how, on that March night in 1945 (a year after Hajime had been born and a few months shy of Hiroshima and Nagasaki and, at long last, after too long, the end)—how he, Eiji, with all the might of his forty-four years, had prayed silently to his wife's god, praying, even as he told his elder son in a voice strong and sure the tale about Sir Old-Man-Who-Makes-Trees-Blossom, that the American bombs would miss them; or that they, his family, would pass somehow unburned through the fire. Kami-sama, Kami-sama! Honda-san is on his way with the American! Tsuburaya calmly removed cigarettes from the lining of his jacket. He knew very well that Honda was on his way with the American. The time was 10:25. They were to arrive at half past. Why must production assistants constantly state the obvious? And call him by that ridiculous honorific? He continued his inspection of the set. Everything looked good. Then he noticed the automobiles across from the Diet Building. Not arranged realistically. He put a cigarette in his mouth. Held it ready between his lips while he went to one knee and disturbed the uniform order of the automobiles by shifting one a few millimeters this way, another a few millimeters that way.

There.

Now his Tokyo was ready to be brought down. Tsuburaya stepped off the set and lit his cigarette. Pacing while the cameramen took their light readings and the wire operators checked their knots and Nakajima changed into Monster Zero. They had done this before, he and Nakajima. The first time, Nakajima had attacked as the fire-breathing sea creature; the second, as the supersonic pteranodon. Today, he would attack as the three-headed space dragon. And the American would be watching. Nick Adams. Tsuburaya had not heard of him. Of course, he had seen *Rebel Without a Cause*. A film that had moved and disturbed him. But Adams's part as a teenage villain had been very small. If the young actor had made any impression, it had not been a deep one. Recently, Adams had come close to a high honor in the States. An Academy Award. He had not won. But Tsuburaya fully expected him to behave as if he had, as if a single brush with acclaim conferred godhood. And what will the man know of me? Of any of us? Nothing. Of that Tsuburaya was quite certain. No matter. The American would be Honda's headache. Tsuburaya had his own concerns. Eight wires, four operators, three cameras shooting in tandem. Nakajima from the northeast, wings flapping, heads lashing. Signal Kobori to trip detonator one and your lovingly created world will come apart, buildings bursting, plaster dust rising, kerosene-soaked rags catching fire so Tokyo might burn again as it did that night when the B-29s came from the South Seas and for six hours Masano held and nursed the panicking infant and you told Akira one tale after another, secretly praying, outwardly gagging on the wind-borne flatus of burning gasoline and poison gas and what you knew to be the char of human bodies, your mind insisting all the while on one word: monsters, monsters. Tsuburaya had finished the cigarette. Kami-sama, Kami-sama! Look, the American is here!

NICK ADAMS/ASTRONAUT GLENN

Willson's directions: Get into a cab and say Shinjuku. And just as Willson had foretold, the driver grinned at Nick and delivered him to a nexus of streets ablaze with sex: with neon and girls, black haired, pale skinned, calling out from curtained doorways. It had been raining. The streets were wet. Each car, in passing, sounded to Nick like a wave on a beach, heard through lidded eyes under the narcosis of summer sun, as in those days—1946, 1947, the Jersey Shore: Point

Pleasant, Avalon, Ocean City—days when there were only girls. Places he'd not been back to, and to which he knew he would never return. He belonged to a different ocean now, to the coastline of the saints: Santa Monica, San Buenaventura, Santa Barbara. He belonged to Henry Willson. The prick. As he walked past exotic dancers and peep shows, under foreign signage and the reflections of it in darkened windows, Nick wondered who was more contemptible: his prick of an agent or his slut of a wife.

Hello.

Guess what I'm doing, she'd said.

Fucking.

No. Filing for divorce. I've got the papers right here in front of me. I get the house, Nick. I'm going to live here with Ally and Jeb. And don't you dare try to do a goddamn thing about it.

Carol. Hey. Hello.

She had hung up, or they'd been disconnected. Either way, Nick had stood there, in the hinterlands of the hotel lobby, holding the phone, as if the call were not over, though he knew perfectly well it was over. Midnight now. In the sleazy groin of a weird city. Trying to find someone. But where? Nick felt dizzy. Shouldn't have had that second drink, shouldn't have taken a pill in the taxi. The way he found the place was the way you find places in dreams. Suddenly: tiled floors, pools of water, welcoming steam. Nick had been to all the ones in Los Angeles. Pico, Gemini, the Palace. That's where he'd gotten his break. A balding, chinless man with a pickle for a cock. Henry Willson. He looked like a child molester. He was actually a talent agent.

Konbanwa.

It sounded like a greeting. Certainly, the boy's eyes were friendly. Body perfectly hairless, an abdomen like the membrane of a drum. Nick took his hand and walked deeper into the warm mist.

MIRIAM SCHUMANN

The next morning, Miriam was the late one. She had taken too long dressing, cursing her dowdy clothes, the drab sweaters and skirts interred in the antique wardrobe that had been her mother's in the old house in Denenchofu. Then it was too late for a trolley. She would have to take the subway. At the Shibuya stop, she allowed herself to be pressed by a white-gloved attendant into the hot crush of an overcrowded car and no sooner did the train move than a hand began to feel her breasts. Miriam could not see the man. Didn't want to. Try to think of something else. Of Kyoto. The mountains in autumn. A temple overarched by the changed leaves of maples. From Yurakucho station she ran to Toho. Not watching as she crossed the lobby of the studio (rather, looking in her briefcase for the shooting script, for the day's xerographed scenes), she walked into him: a custodian in a gray jumpsuit, grotesquely scarred on his face, scalp, and neck. She had knocked the broom from his hands. *Sumimasen,* she said, bowing; the accident had been her fault alone. But the poor man would not stop apologizing in the most formal manner. He'd seemed very old at first, but now, as he snatched up his gray cap and covered his head, bowing and bowing again, Miriam could see that he wasn't much older than she and that the scars, red and crustaceous, were those of a burn victim, a bomb victim. *Sumimasen,* she repeated, moving away now. To the gate. Onto the lot. Breathing heavily. From the run. And from the shock of seeing the man, and colliding with him. A *hibakusha*. Yoshiko had taught her that word, a word for those who had been in Hiroshima and Nagasaki—and lived. The custodian was one of them.

Up ahead: the wardrobe department. Costumed actors clustered outside, laughing and gesticulating. Nick was at the center of the group in an orange astronaut flight suit, a huge smile on his face.

Miriam, he said, waving to her.

I'm late.

Don't sweat it. I'd like you to meet some people. Astronaut Fuji, the king of Planet X, and Miss Namikama.

The first man was dressed just like Nick. The other man and the woman, whom Miriam understood to be playing the parts of alien invaders, wore silver uniforms that gave them the look of futuristic fencers. They introduced themselves, but Miriam didn't seem to hear the names. Her mind still on the accident in the lobby, her mind working like a counting machine, estimating the man to be thirty, thirty-five, making him ten or fifteen in August of 1945, when she, a girl of eleven, had come from the wet heat of a New England summer into the shade-drawn afternoon of the parlor to find her mother sobbing over the armchair radio from which a voice was announcing that the war was over, finally over. Six months later: New York to California, California to Hawaii, Hawaii to Tokyo. Her father, a man from a dream in a khaki uniform, waiting for them on the tarmac, embracing her desperately—and then, on the way to the house, forewarning her: Boys and girls, Miri, orphans, some younger than you, living on the streets, and men, soldiers turned beggars, missing parts. . . . In the coming months, when walking to the market with Yoshiko, Miriam would bring candies for the children and coins for the men, though Yoshiko disapproved of the practice. No, Miri-chan. But why *not*, Yoshi? For a long time, for months, there was one boy in particular, always begging in the same place: on a street corner near the market, by a pole with *kanji* characters painted upon it and appended with a sign that read, in Roman letters: TIMES SQUARE. Every time she saw the boy, Miri couldn't look, yet couldn't look away. His skin, the scars. What had happened to him? Yoshiko refused to explain. Then, one day, she finally explained, and then, one day, the boy was gone. Now, they were all laughing, whoever they really were. Astronaut Fuji and the king of Planet X and Miss Namikama. Nick was doing an impression of someone, a famous American actor. It was spot-on, but Miriam couldn't think of the name.

ISHIRO HONDA/DIRECTION

That evening, Honda met up with Kurosawa. A few blocks from the studio, at an *izakaya* that Kurosawa said made the best skewered chicken in the city. Honda did not agree. But then he was not an expert on skewered chicken. It was spring, the cherry trees blooming, a sweetness in the air when the petals stirred on the trees and fell to earth, making Honda think of corny songs from the war. Up and down the street, hanging lanterns glowed in the dusk like the hives of radioactive bees.

Ino-chan.

Kurosawa had already ordered the sake and consumed more than his share of the bottle. Now, he poured out a cup for Honda.

Cheers, Ino-chan.

Cheers, said Honda, sitting down and taking a sip. Kurosawa drained his own cup and poured himself another. Honda's old friend was drinking again. In the old days, before the war, it was beer near Shibuya Station, sake with dinner, then on to the Ginza bars for whiskey. Back then, they were boys, getting drunk to speak in tongues about movies, projecting onto a screen of shared imagination all the films of their dreams—and not in the wildest of them did Honda see monsters coming from the sea and air to raze and burn. It was never his dream. He came back from the war and made a war picture. The *kaiju*: That was Tsuburaya's idea. Now, after nine movies going on ten, the monsters were like Honda's adopted children. Kurosawa finished the first bottle of sake and ordered a second with the food and started complaining about his shoot, a bit player named Sada whom the master had found it necessary to scold to the verge of tears. Kuro-chan didn't get along with any actor but Mifune, which recalled for Honda how well he'd gotten on all day with the American. Admittedly, Honda had been apprehensive at first: A coproduction with a foreign actor he'd never met, much less auditioned—never in a million years would Kuro-chan agree to such an arrangement. But Adams had been easy to direct. Moreover, everyone had taken an immediate liking to him.

Incidentally, Kurosawa said, I saw your American today.

Adams.

He waved at me. He was waving at everyone on the lot in that absurd costume, as if he really had just returned from the moon.

You mean Planet X. You see, Kuro-chan, there is a mysterious planet on the far side of Jupiter—

Ino-chan . . .

And the space dragon with three heads—

Ino-chan, spare me. Your story lines aggravate my ulcers.

Honda smiled and chewed his soybeans. Once upon a time, that twist of derision in Kuro-chan's voice could hurt his feelings. But as every passing year took him a little deeper into his fifties, Honda felt an ease, a contentment he'd thought would always evade him. Strange now, to think of the heartache and the harpings of that inner voice. Why can't you be Kurosawa? The answer turned out to be simple. Because you are Honda. Not a visionary, not a master. Merely the friend of one.

NICK ADAMS/ASTRONAUT GLENN

The divorce papers arrived by airmail. All that day, Nick had been beneath the surface of Planet X, shooting scenes with the alien controller, a hell of a good guy named Tsuchiya, who had been in every Kurosawa picture since *Rashomon* and cracked everyone up with impersonations of Marlon Brando. Around five, they wrapped for the day. As Nick walked across the lot, cherry trees in flower made him think of the boy from the baths, and a spike of feeling nearly doubled him over. Needed a pill. Was he taking too many? One upon waking and another upon going to sleep; one to get into and another to get out of character. Starting to lose count. He opened the door of his dressing room. The envelope had been slipped underneath. NICK ADAMS C/O TOHO STUDIOS. Though it was the middle of the night in Los Angeles, he placed the call. United States, Oleander-653.

Hello?

Carol. Listen.

Nick?

There's a movie in London. Right after this one. You could go over with Ally and Jeb. I'll take you to Paris on the weekends. Then after the shoot . . .

He couldn't understand his own self. Even Honda, Tsuchiya, all these strange kind people, made more sense to Nick than Nick Adams, who was wearing an orange astronaut costume on a movie studio in Tokyo asking his harpy wife to join him in England while he did another B-list picture for that shylock Saperstein. Horror picture with Karloff. Spooky mansion. Some sort of curse. Monsters in the greenhouse. Nick must have fallen asleep. Holding the divorce papers and the telephone. Now he was dreaming. Of darkness. And suffocating heat. Buried alive, he guessed. Closed up in a coffin that felt like a second skin. He could hear people on the outside. Astronaut Fuji, Tsuchiya. All gibberish. But another voice, too—female and comforting. Translating. He's in there. Get him out. Don't let him die like this. But Nick knew it was already too late. He had passed on a long time ago, when that loopy son of a bitch, a veteran of the Pacific War, had picked him up in Las Vegas and driven him to Los Angeles through Death Valley in the high noon of summer 1948. Nick could not remember the man's face, but the voice was undying, unchangeable, like narration from a great beyond. You think this is hell. Believe me, kid. This is not hell.

MIRIAM SCHUMANN

Miriam couldn't make sense of the story. Every day, she received new pages of the script—Nick's scenes for the following day—but not in proper order. First, they did pages 25–35 on a set at Toho. Then they caravanned to Hokkaido to shoot the final scene on a cliff above the Sea of Japan (Glenn and Fuji in civilian clothes, reacting to a climactic brawl of monsters yet to be staged in miniature by the effects director), then back to Tokyo and the astronaut costumes, back to the very beginning, the rocket ship and the strange planet in the shadow of Jupiter. She wasn't sure how it would all coherently fit together. How *could* the sum be coherent when each part was so nonsensical? One night, at a cocktail party at Mr. Honda's country house, Miriam had a little too much sake and she said to Nick: Isn't it funny.

What?

The movie. The dialogue and the plot. Everything . . .

He flinched at her words. Alone in the garden, cherry trees arching over them, a full moon, her view of things afloat on gentle swells. Miriam Schumann kept, and would always keep, one memento from the war. A girl's tea set stamped OCCUPIED JAPAN. Expressions of surrender. For years, she had read them on the faces of orphaned children, maimed soldiers, drivers and maids, even in the eyes of officials who'd entered the house as honored guests. Somehow, that night in the garden, she failed to see that Nick had been defeated too. She thought he felt insulted. To make amends, she said very brightly: Oh, I've been talking with a fan of yours.

She pretty?

Not a girl. A man. He knows you from a Western. American Westerns were very big here—he says yours was the best.

That's nice to know.

He works at the studio. As a custodian . . .

Miriam wanted to tell Nick the whole story. How she'd collided with the man in the lobby and then a few days later, saw him again, same gray jumpsuit and cap, broom and dustpan, again her throat clogging with guilt, and when he called—*misu, misu*—she pretended not to hear. What could he possibly want from her? What could she ever say? *Misu,* he repeated. This belongs to you. Holding something between two burned and palsied fingers. A brooch, a piece of costume jewelry.

What's his name? Nick asked.

Mikio.

Miriam watched Nick turning a cherry blossom over in his hand, the flower glowing faintly in the moonlight, the garden embowered with flowers and faintly glowing. He's a *hibakusha,* she finally said—and then explained the meaning of the word.

Greg Hrbek

MIKIO TANAKA/HIBAKUSHA

The season ended. Now white petals lay all around, like ashfall. Not near his tenement home under the gray-green smog of the port, but in the parks of different wards and in the back lot of the studio. Mikio swept the dead flowers from the walkways and remembered the ash of Nagasaki. For him, a clear blue sky would always be the sky of that morning. Any plane overhead, that plane. Yes, he had heard it. On an errand by bicycle, and while returning, the river flowing at his right side, he heard the sound. Like a fly in a bottle. Must be very high up. He looked, bicycle swerving on the dirt road. Clear blue day, morning sun crowning Mount Kompira. For some reason, he rang the bell on his handlebars, as if to say, "Here I am." Then the entire city fainted—

Mikio-san.

He looked up from the heap of petals. Miriam-san, of course. The only one here who calls me by my given name. And with her: the American. How many actors had Mikio seen in his years as a *kozukai*? It was only natural that none of them should say good morning or wave hello to a man like himself. More monster than man. But twice in these weeks had the American star waved to him from a distance, and now here he was walking toward Mikio, looking at him directly, looking at him. So ashamed Mikio felt, like a gray ghost of himself about to fall into white silence, as the city had that day—fainting, falling—and yet even when the atomic wind reached him and blew him and his bicycle off the ground, even as he somersaulted backward through the air like a circus acrobat, and the bicycle left his hands and feet, still his legs turned invisible gears as in a dream of bicycling, and seemed still, even now, as the American offered his hand, to be turning them. *Konnichiwa,* the American said. *To moushimasu* Nick Adams.

A.D. 1968

Hurtling back to earth in the future year 1999, Monster Zero remembers the American. There is a photograph of the three of them—Adams, the woman translator whose name Monster Zero cannot recall, and himself—taken back in 1964 on Planet X. In the photo (still displayed in Nakajima's dressing room at Toho), the American looks very happy with his boyish smile and his arm around the long, rubbery neck of Monster Zero's middle head. The middle head remembers Adams fondly. Sad now to hear of his death.

Only thirty-six.

How frail and short the lives of humans. How final their ends. But the space dragon has more pressing concerns than the accidental suicide of one puny anthropoid. On earth, the century is turning and the shitstorm is on. The radioactive *kaiju* are loose. The lizard and the pteranodon and the pupal moth and etcetera. All of them. And closed up in the hot sarcophagus of the monster, swooping through the cosmos like a puppet on piano wire (no cosmos, of course; cosmos later, effects department), the man feels a terror spreading through him, equal parts remembrance and premonition: a memory of things to come.

Lincoln

Peter Orner

THAT YEAR WE LIVED on Holbrege in a small one-story house with a patch of dirt in the back Sheila always talked about making a garden out of. Everybody else on the block lived in similar houses and during the long summer we all spent weekend days on the small concrete slabs that were the best anybody could do for porches. I don't remember any of our neighbors' names, only that we sometimes drank a few beers together and talked about how could it be this hot already and not even June. I was an adjunct in the English Department. Sheila was a poet who didn't believe universities and poetry had anything to do with each other. She got a job waiting tables at the Golden Wok and it was there that she met someone, another waiter. Before she got the job there we used to eat there sometimes. The Golden Wok was cheap and open late, a big sprawling place that even when it was filled with people had a way of looking empty. I left Lincoln the following year and have not been back to Nebraska since, except for a few times driving across it on I-80. I never stop in Lincoln for gas. When I lived there I was told that it had once been a beautiful city. This was before, apparently, they ruined it by building too many highways, and for a smallish town, even if a state capital, Lincoln did seem to me to have an inordinate amount of highways. Still there was the Sunken Gardens with all the flowers in a kind of bowl and also the houses on Sheridan Boulevard. Sheila and I would drive up and down Sheridan Boulevard and look at those houses. Once she pointed to one of them and said, in all seriousness, "Who would we be if we lived there?" Her bare feet were on the dash. I remember that particular house. It was big and white with what she had called a porte cochere. Sheila was from the South and she said such stupid little outdoor garages were common there. Another time she said, "Hang the rich by their own petards. My father used to say that—and he was rich. It means by their own umbilical cords, or something like that."

I remember hearing that at one time Lincoln was the licorice capital of the world. Maybe it still is. Near our house was a little park with a couple of netless tennis courts and I used to sit at a picnic table and read for class. I remember reading *To the Lighthouse* out there and coming to that moment where Mr. Ramsey, in the dark of the morning corridor, reaches out for Mrs. Ramsey not knowing that she's already dead. It happened, like most things, offstage.

Model City

Donna Stonecipher

1.

It was like trying to imagine the existence of a city in which no more building is possible, a city that is already perfectly, completely, sparklingly, imperviously built.

*

It was like imagining living in that city, in which the citizens are content with the already built, in which architects do not exist, and the very word "architect" has an old-fashioned ring to it, like "apparatchik" or "castellan."

*

It was like living in that city as an architect, and being unable to move to another city for sheer fascination, spending all day looking out the window at the perfectly built city, its perfect skyscrapers and airports and churches.

*

It was like being the architect and knowing that all cities everywhere are all already built, as he sits at his window all day, fascinated, looking out at all of it all already perfectly built.

2.

It was like slowly becoming aware one winter that there are new buildings going up all over your city, and then noticing that every one of them is a hotel.

*

It was like thinking about all those empty rooms at night, all those empty rooms being built to hold an absence, as you lie in your bed at night, unable to sleep.

*

It was like the feeling of falling through the "o" in "hotel" as you almost fall asleep in your own bed, the bed that you own, caught at the last minute by ownership, the ownership of your wide-awake self.

*

It was like giving in to your ownership of yourself and going to the window, looking out at all the softly illuminated versions of the word "hotel" announcing their shifting absences all over the city.

3.

It was like reading *The Arcades Project* and thinking about how amazing it would be to go shopping in the past, when every store was an antiques store, and any antique could be had for a song.

*

It was like reading *The Arcades Project* and thinking about how time adds or subtracts value to objects and people, how some objects come to us as savants out of the past, embossed with knowledge.

*

It was like putting down *The Arcades Project*, switching off the light and lying in the dark badly wanting a first edition of *Les Fleurs du mal*, badly wanting an original Atget.

*

It was like lying in the dark wondering if one would have known back then what one knows now, or if one can recognize value only after history has recognized it, if one merely apes the intelligence of time.

4.

It was like bringing a picnic lunch on a Sunday to the converted industrial park, built over a closed mine, or an old quarry filled with lake water, repurposed.

*

It was like setting out the grapes and the French cheese and the wine on the blue-checked tablecloth, spread over the innocuous-seeming earth, seeded with secrets.

*

It was like suddenly, green grape in mouth, understanding the tenacity of landscape to seem, and your own tenacity to the seemliness of the landscape, to the rigor of the picnic.

*

It was like swimming in the man-made lake flooding the quarry, dynamite blasts as rumored as the stocked fish possibly nibbling speculatively at your ankles.

5.

It was like the Socialist dream of the palace of culture, to place all culture together in one marble building in the very center of the city, like a big marble filing cabinet where culture can be filed away.

*

It was like requisitioning the idea of the palace and bequeathing it to the people, who would come and become kings and queens in the *royaume* of the filing cabinet of culture.

*

It was like entering the palace of culture and walking down the endless yellow marble hallways leading to rooms, lecture halls, stages for culture—and feeling filed away oneself, a curious tourist queen.

*

It was like the dream of writing poems lined with endless yellow marble hallways, interrupted from time to time by the crystal orgasms of chandeliers, it was like the desire to write in Socialist Baroque.

6.

It was like seeing a fox one day right in the middle of the city—a real fox, not a taxidermied fox, nor a fox logo, nor a foxy person that one might want to sleep with.

*

It was like stopping and staring at the fox, along with all the other people walking down the street, all stopped in their tracks and staring in astonishment at the fox.

*

It was like watching the real, soft, cinnamon-colored fox, the only object moving in the landscape, moving silkily along the overgrown median, darting glances over at the people standing on the sidewalk, staring.

*

It was like the concentrated attention placed on the fox's perplexing appearance deflected by the fox, who keeps moving down the street, headed to a fox den known only to the fox—dark, liquid, insolvent.

7.

It was like coming out of an unfamiliar subway station headed for a destination and noticing a sign that says "Sugar Museum, 500 m" and suddenly changing your plans for the day, your destination.

*

It was like walking along the "500 m" announced by the sign for the Sugar Museum and thinking, only five hundred meters to the unending sweetness I deserve, your original destination forgotten under a cascade of sugar crystals.

*

It was like riding dutifully on the subway to a destination and knowing nothing of the Sugar Museum, knowing only destination, knowing nothing of the Sugar Museum and how it can alter plans.

*

It was like walking two hundred meters and then suddenly understanding the nature of the Sugar Museum, and turning around to set out again for the original destination. For its nature is seduction. Seduction and renunciation.

8.

It was like going to an exhibition where all the artworks are about melancholy, and falling into fits of uncontrollable laughter, especially before a case of little ivory skeletons "intended for private reflection."

*

It was like looking at the faces on those skeletons and asking yourself why skulls are always grinning like that, what they have to grin about, and then realizing we are all always grinning like that, under our faces.

*

It was like feeling that grin under your face at all times, even when you are sobbing, or expressionless, reading a thick book late at night next to a dark window: There you are grinning, despite yourself, down at the book.

*

It was like leaving the melancholy exhibition nearly sobbing with laughter, picturing the memento mori, the tiny skeletons in some noblewoman's gloved hand, as she privately reflects, secretly grinning.

9.

It was like watching the city slowly powdered over with snow from your bedroom window, the molecular makeup of the city slowly altered through the powdery intimations of ossification, the symbolic.

*

It was like watching the snow slowly powder over the construction site across the street, which will one day be a hotel, the snow filling in the space temporarily where one day there will be permanent temporariness.

*

It was like slowly coming to think of the snow as permanent, the construction site as permanent, the grand opening of the hotel permanently postponed, the spring postponed, the grand opening of the crocuses.

*

It was like feeling powdered over with snow oneself, as one is part of the city; apart from it, watching it from the window, to be sure; but a part of it, a powdered-over temporary part.

10.

It was like wandering through the ersatz medieval town and wondering how many centuries it would take to turn into a real town, or even if it ever could, since its origins were ersatz.

*

It was like marveling at the precision of detail in the ersatz town, in its illuminations and crenellations, and marveling also at the mistakes, the well-meaning mistakes in execution, in executing the real ersatz.

*

It was like wondering about the viability of the ersatz medieval town, peopled only by tourists and stocked with expensive ersatz Heimat cafés—just like real medieval towns, the continent over.

*

It was like wandering through the ersatz town and wondering about the origin of ersatz, about the authenticity of authenticity, about the sorrows of patina, the magnificent duplicities of age.

The Horror
Michael Sheehan

> *It's completely unscientific, absolutely absurd, violates every rule of common sense, and it's completely contrary to the rules of logic and intelligence.*
>
> —The Professor

WHEN THE HORROR STRUCK LAS VEGAS—as was given ample play on CNN and every other news channel—it wasn't so bad really, for the first three days, because there were so many other channels. Most important, TBS was showing a special marathon broadcast of *Gilligan's Island*. The reception was not affected by the Horror and all was as it had been the day before for Dombie Laughler, who sat stoically throughout the first three days of the Horror as he had been sitting, watching the marathon of good old Gilligan's Isle, which, to Dombie's pleasure and stupefaction, was a full replaying of all three seasons of the show.[1]

On the fourth day everything changed.

Outside, looters who remained in the city despite the emergency evac notice that had gone out and the sirens wailing from hidden locations like a thousand unseen minarets had taken over the Strip, which now teemed with debris and garbage, the shattered remains of a hundred roulette wheels mingling in the street with tattered tumbleweeds of felt torn from low-stakes poker tables, and, in the midst of it all, along with the small fires that now raged and now died down in the canalicular Venetian, the pyramidal Luxor, and escaped (the flames did) in wisps like flicking tongues from the windows of the mock Empire State Building that still presided (in its attenuated and charred prestige) over the ruinous Carthage of the faux New York skyline, the Eiffel Tower lay in the street, its iron rungs twisted, its sides coated with scraps of cheap booklets soliciting sex and half-price day-of tickets to the comic Louie Anderson,

[1]*Gilligan's Island* ran on CBS Saturdays at eight thirty from 9.26.1964 to 4.17.1967, comprising ninety-eight episodes, not counting the pilot, in total.

among others. The looters had torn the Strip apart, working for hours to tear the slots and tables from each casino, throwing bedding and furniture out of twentieth-story windows, stealing food and souvenirs and later setting them aflame in the streets.

Dombie had not been outside since the beginning of the *Gilligan's Island* marathon, or for the thirty days prior, and so he was unaware of the Horror's aftereffects on his city. He knew, in some way, of the Horror, since, of course, TV programming is very intrusive, and messages crawled across the bottom of the screen—beginning during the final fifteen minutes of 2.22, "Forward March,"[2] which really is the best part—detailing the call for Las Vegans to evacuate the city immediately but peaceably, related to the "toxic event," which was quickly dubbed the Horror by the local FOX News syndicate, though by that time Dombie had stopped looking for answers about the sirens that continued all day from somewhere outside—forcing him to raise the volume to a probably pretty unsafe level—and had checked that his doors were locked and settled in for 2.26, "Will the Real Mr. Howell Please Stand Up."[3]

Dombie was closing in on *Gilligan's Island*'s unexpected finale, 3.30, "Gilligan, the Goddess" (he was actually right in the middle of 3.25, "The Secret of Gilligan's Island," when it still seems possible the castaways will discover a way off the island), when the screen suddenly blacked out, and then presently was restored by the red-blue-green emergency broadcast, which, since the TV volume was turned loud enough to ensure dialogue and canned laughter could be heard above the keening wails coming through the window, caused Dombie to jump and in the process throw the remote (which he hadn't used since adjusting the volume up, but which was his only immediate hope of turning the volume down) and so he stumbled from the sofa and crawled to the TV set, clicking it off in his panic.

The TV had not been off for thirty-three days.

Dombie's CNS registered the enervation of days without movement (barring the occasional flexion of a thumb or finger sufficient to raise the level of the volume and switch channels during commercial breaks on TBS when Gilligan (the Skipper, too) disappeared

[2]A gorilla on the island discovers a cave with a hidden cache of WWII weapons and besieges the castaways, hurling hand grenades from behind a bush (original air date [OAD] 2.17.1966).

[3]In which the castaways discover an impostor Howell (played by Jim Backus [Mr. Magoo]), who is swindling the millionaire's fortune back home on the mainland, but then washes ashore on the island. Hilarity ensues.

for an almost unendurable period (until the Horror filled all the other channels with terrible pronouncements of the catastasis coming and calls to arms and the trumpet of Azrael blaring from the mouthpieces of a faceless, nameless mass depicted decamping from the city over and over in slow motion), as well as days without nourishment, which altogether produced a sensation of nausea, urtication, and utter discomfort like nothing Dombie had ever felt—and, for a brief period, he blacked out.

Prior to his awakening, and while still in fact unconscious, Dombie experienced what some might call an out-of-body experience, which is to say he dreamt he was lost on *Gilligan's Island*, mired in the plot of 1.14, "Water, Water Everywhere,"[4] as the frog, desperately wishing to make love to Ginger, but in order to do so (of course) he must first be turned into a man, which for whatever reason can only be effected by the receipt of a kiss from Gilligan, who has gotten himself stuck (improbably) in an eagle's nest one hundred feet up in the air, in which the giant mother eagle has mistaken him, Gilligan, for her own hatchling, and so is trying to regurgitate into his mouth, and you can see where that will lead, but meanwhile, as Dombie the frog tries to court Ginger, Mary Anne[5] has become infatuated with the talking/singing frog (*brekekekex ko-ax ko-ax*) and Ginger is clearly starting to make advances (as yet undetected by their intended target) toward Mary Anne, sexual advances, as it were, prompting a little and amphibious love triangle, and Dombie realizes he is trapped in a reality TV show based on *Gilligan's Island*, in which the survivors are intentionally "cast away" in order to come to blows over the expectable tensions arising from a small ship's worth of strangers being thrown together and forced to live codependently in close quarters.[6] This oneiric interlude was (albeit stressful in its thwarted sexual desires and sophomoric pleasure derived from petty

---

[4]Potable water is becoming scarce, until a frog arrives (voiced by Mel Blanc) and saves the day.

[5]Played by Dawn Wells, born in Reno, NV, and accused of being Bob Denver (Gilligan)'s marijuana supplier during his 1998 arrest.

[6]Much like the plot (from which, really, this "paranormal" experience is likely a derivative, born of hours and hours of *Gilligan's Island* saturating his mind) of 1.02, "Home Sweet Hut," in which the castaways build a communal hut, which only causes conflict until the point at which no one can stand it anymore and so all the castaways decide to build their own huts, a tidy solution, irrespective of the incredible proximity of the huts (of necessity), and of course the show lets the matter rest, as though these seven people lost at sea would get along any better in separate huts set a few feet apart than they did in one hut, even taking as a given that the individuated huts were improbably modern and well outfitted.

and tiresome altercations) actually a nice reprieve from the reality of the scene at just that moment—with an oddly orange aureole of light outlining the bulky figure of Dombie crumpled crudely against the faux-wood feet of the coffee table, breathing as though in pain, with the occasional gasp common to those afflicted with apnea.

Dombie, awaking finally on Day Four to the dirty vista of his red gilded rug into which his face was pressed heavily, knew nothing of the world outside.

He managed to calm himself and turn the TV back on, and get the volume quickly under control. All the stations were showing the same emergency broadcast signal. Dombie sat back on the dusty red gilded rug, despondent. The emergency broadcast continued to blare at a quieter level, its ominous B-flat minor mingling with that of the sirens coming from wherever outside. Had Dombie been counting, he would have understood that this marked Hour Fifty-two of the Horror, the afternoon of Day Four. The pixelated image[7] on the screen dumbly told him what had happened and repeated the need for any remaining residents to immediately evacuate the area, emergency quarantine stations having been established in the following places, etcetera, and any remaining "victims" should "immediately proceed to the nearest."

Dombie understood it was time he faced his phobias and went out to find exactly why *Gilligan's Island* had been taken from him (hoping still against hope to see the ending to the show). A panic set in as Dombie began moving his limbs in the slow machinations of

[7]When Dombie was seven, and watching the initial broadcast of 3.18, "The Hunter" (in which a big-game hunter washes ashore and promises to rescue the castaways if only Gilligan can survive the Most Dangerous Game: twenty-four hours with hunter Kincaid at his heels [OAD 1.16.1967]), he sat more or less as he was sitting right now, his body resting approximately eighteen inches away from the TV screen, the static clipping off its convex surface every so often, leaning (he was) forward from his cross-legged position at an angle of roughly sixty degrees, his hands placed on either side of the screen, his face leaning closer and closer (12 inches, 8.5 inches) to the screen, feeling its static energy and the heat it generated and beginning to lose himself in the images as they blurred and distended and surrounded him, seeming to come right out of the TV screen as though it were he, himself, running from Kincaid, or tracking Gilligan, as though in a moment more he could perhaps feel the island's gentle breeze on his forehead, his mother cried, "Don't sit so goddamned close," hitting him on the back of the neck with the spatula she was holding—using it to scrape the frosting that clung to the sides of her KitchenAid mixing bowl (it was Dombie's sister Arla's eleventh birthday)—which then left a thick, sticky streak of whipped chocolate, tangling with his hair and staining his shirt, for which (the dirty shirt collar) he would later be punished, the dry martinis obliterating her role in the incident, "It's bad for your eyes. Plus the radiation."

standing: the understanding that the island was lost to him; he would have to navigate the world outside again.[8]

What had happened to Dombie was unnameable.[9] He thought of it as inertia, the slow leaking away of energy from a life system. Eventually everything comes to a stop. For some reason, for Dombie, this seemed to have happened early.

To say that he took joy in *Gilligan's Island* is itself a complicated concept, since half the time the show would bore deep down into him, and he would weep, the whole world of the show suddenly having become profoundly sad.

Before he was able to lock himself in for the thirty-three days (initially having told his supervisor simply that he would be out of town for two weeks—which required renting a space at the airport for his car, putting a special message on his answering machine, and shuttering his house; he even went so far as to have his mail held for him [like anyone would ever check up on any of this]), Dombie spent what remained of his savings on toilet paper and canned goods, Ramen noodles, and Rice-A-Roni, and settled himself in for, he figured, "as long as it would take." What Dombie had failed to realize was how long it would take. Once he had locked himself away from it all, it only became harder and harder to return to normal, to change his answering-machine message, to retrieve his car. Since he was technically not around, he could not leave the house for fear someone would see him and had to avoid windows, even though they were heavily draped. Then just moving through the house became too much, mementos and even rooms themselves causing him to think

---

[8]In a TV movie (*Rescue from Gilligan's Island*, 10.14–21.1978) rejoining the cast of *Gilligan's Island* (except Tina Louise, replaced by Judith Baldwin, as Ginger), the survivors are rescued and reunite in Hawaii one year later and decide to celebrate their unfortunate three-hour catastrophe with a short cruise, and you can already guess what happens. That they would get shipwrecked a second time is bad enough, but that they would ever step foot on a cruise ship after their experience is simply faulty logic. The (already rather precarious) structure of the world within the show is damaged by this premise, insofar as the viewer no longer finds the characters' motivations plausible. Their other actions on the show are grounded by being in response to something outside the characters' control, viz. a tropical storm ("*The weather started getting rough, the tiny ship was tossed; if not for the courage of the fearless crew, the* Minnow *would be lost*"), leaving them shipwrecked on an uncharted, uninhabited island somewhere in the Pacific.

[9]Although etiologically more clear, the Skipper was likewise haunted throughout the show by his time serving in the navy in WWII. Among other instances, particularly affecting is 1.30, "Forget Me Not," in which the Skipper has amnesia and confuses the other castaways with Japanese soldiers during hypnosis, administered as a cure by The Professor.

about the life he had locked outside, and within several days he was closing off parts of the house, remaindering the safe zones. Since his intention was simply to watch TV (i.e., *Gilligan's Island*, as described, but also [as he decided on the second day of the stranding] all the TV shows that had occurred in his lifetime, a telic mission without real means of completion, recreating his past by rewatching shows that seemed now like moments of his own experience, like memories), only the least necessary parts of the house for this enterprise were left to him. (This caused an obvious problem with regard to going to the bathroom, which issue created levels and levels of anxiety and obsessive thinking on Dombie's part, but suffice it to say a solution was reached, however uncomfortable.) Because of the increasing disconnect from the world, and the panic attendant upon stepping outside, as the days locked in and the ability to return grew in inverse proportion, the hour-long process of moving a few strides to the door was mentally, internally excruciating.

Dombie had not seen daylight since shutting himself in, and had not thought to expect such a stark contrast. The effect was almost precisely that achieved by the cut between Dorothy's black-and-white Kansas home and the land of Oz outside her door (or between the first and second seasons of *Gilligan's Island*, the former being black-and-white, the latter Technicolor)—a fluorescent, photonic, putrid orange light poured in, created by the refraction of the city's thousands of electric lights (from casinos, street lamps, abandoned car headlights, homes, etcetera) in the luminous cloud cover that wafted thickly just above the rooftops.

What most people failed to register about the Horror was this cloud-cover effect, created by the chemical mixing in situ of the materials dumped on U.S. Highway 93 and the natural components of air, perhaps including the carbon monoxide created by the cars that attempted to flee the event. The materials were, the government later acknowledged, en route to Yucca Mountain and the underground nuclear-waste storage facility there, which was not supposed to be in operation for many years to come (despite having initially been on line for 2001 at the latest). The truck carrying the materials (estimated to be seventeen tons) lost control coming down a steep grade, jackknifed in an attempt to regain control and decelerate, and then rolled onto its side, emptying the contents of its tarpaulin-covered bed onto the highway, where tightly sealed containers of nuclear waste materials were damaged and even forced open by the impact created by the speed at which the truck had been traveling.

Twenty-three cars coming down the highway behind and/or driving along in front of the truck were involved in the initial accident, which resulted in the deaths of seven, the youngest of whom was four (Elaine Meyers, who was allowed, despite precautions on the vehicle, to ride in the front passenger seat of her mother's sedan, without a seat belt), the oldest of whom was ninety-one (Reginald Anderson, of San Joaquin, California, a longtime gambler), and included (the deaths did) the driver of the truck. The obvious details—number of cars and persons involved, time, location, collateral damage—of the incident were reported by police who arrived on the scene and later died of radiation sickness. A two-mile section of the highway was shut down within an hour, and as the chemical cloud began to form from the spilled substance and the air, the call for the city to evacuate from the path of the oncoming toxic event went out. Such a toxic event could perhaps have been expected to happen, from some basic probability regarding the number of trucks coming through the area, the personnel hired to drive the trucks (nothing against them, just noting they were not highly trained specialists, in this instance, as much as commercial truckers [and, hey, *quandoque bonus dormitat Homerus*]), and the highly toxic composition of the materials being transmitted, along with a rough statistical analysis of accidents occurring on that particular stretch of highway. However, the event was unexpected or even seen as impossible when it was discovered, due to the fact that the U.S. has transported over three thousand shipments of spent nuclear fuel without incident, and worldwide over seventy thousand tons have been transported for safe storage since 1970, without a single incident, and the government further spread this confusion by refusing to admit they themselves could have expected it, or at least knew hazardous waste materials were being moved by truck across that stretch of highway to their ultimate resting place deep in the bowels of the Yucca Mountain ridge (despite the public's belief that such was not in fact happening), to the west of the historic Nevada Test Site (where nuclear weapons ranging up to five megatons were tested between 1951 and 1962, when the ban on atmospheric testing was signed by President Kennedy; testing continued underground until 9.23.1992), which thus prompted (the governmental silence did) a lot of public speculation during the first three days that this was a terrorist incident.[10]

[10]Along with parody of present-day social and political issues, certain stripes of paranoia and conspiracy run through the castaways' ninety-eight episodes on the island. This makes sense, given the timing of the show's creation, and the world the island

An anthelion was projected across the face of the roiling parti-colored cloud bank as if it were God's own sign, though, of course, it was (arguably) quite the opposite. The whole scene, when looking up, was so beautiful as to almost completely invert the viewer, though once the viewer's gaze was lowered, the littered streets were gray (except where rogue fires still burned brightly), and the orange light gave everything an unreal aura, like walking in daylight while wearing 3-D glasses.

Dombie crawled on all fours out into the street, and did not look up. The men who had only just begun (on Day Four) to roam the city in hazmat suits were a long way from Dombie, where he crawled. A card under his right hand showed a woman spreading her posterior, boasting Convenient Access for only $69. Sounds came from somewhere, perhaps the echoes of the sirens that still blared, even though the assumption was that all had left the city, or had died. (Mistakenly, it was believed the toxic event would kill much more quickly than in fact it did. This should have been better anticipated, the slow rate of decline, since during the decade of atmospheric tests begun in the 1950s, in this same and nearby areas, the fallout from nuclear tests at the Nevada Test Site birthed various types of cancer in hundreds of thousands of people, many of whose families are still tied up in litigations trying to claim the government's proffered reparations for this "oversight.") Or would die, and, callous though it sounds, there is only so much anyone can do for the drowning, the irradiated, the burned. At some point, it's just collection, and these men knew it, and had also (more importantly) to contain the spread of the toxic event by releasing particulate matter that (it was hoped) would force the cloud back into precipitate form and only contaminate the already-contaminated area of Las Vegas and environs, which would be pretty much uninhabitable for fifty thousand years thereafter, roughly.

Mirroring Dombie's own posture, a mangy dog waddled tumorously down the same street, maintaining at all points a radius of at least thirty feet from Dombie, where he crawled, which was not out of pain or even really Horror-specific terror so much as a nascent

---

was supposed to be separate from. Interestingly, in a bit of *Gilligan's Island* trivia, the pilot ("Marooned"), which was unaired until 10.16.92, was filmed in November 1963, with filming continuing on 11.22.63, shortly after the shocking news of President Kennedy's assassination. This is why, when the *Minnow* launches on its ill-fated three-hour tour (shot on 11.26.63), flags in the background can be seen flying at half-staff.

anxiety attack that was right on the verge of his consciousness and could only be (was then being) talked down by moving slowly, close to the earth, refusing to look up and register the scene before him for more time than was required to ascertain his approximate whereabouts, and also of course mumbling repeatedly to himself, offering realistic assurances to counter his obsessive panic, like "Nothing bad is happening, you will be fine, there is nothing ahead of you in the street, you can walk down the street, normal people walk down streets all the time, every day, you can walk down the street, you are a normal, adult person, you are fine," etcetera, which all related specifically to Dombie's own personal issues about leaving the house and moving through the real world, rather than having anything at all to do with the Horror, which would naturally have prompted the opposite mantra, as was sensible, the world in which he crawled being so severely contaminated as to kill living things whose genesis would so far outdate Dombie's demise as to make a consideration of the time lapse silly.[11]

The dog, Rusty, had not been without owners for long, but long enough. At one time Rusty had been a faithful and lovable watchdog, a beloved member of a family of four, the Hendricksons, but since early on in Day One, Rusty had been abandoned to the riot-torn streets and the noxious clouds hovering just above street level. An old black-lab-mix mutt, Rusty had bad hips, and during the past days had quickly acquired a variation of the sickness that would kill so many thousands, but in Rusty's case simply expanded his body in a sequence of asymmetric excrescences. Rusty had a tougher time of the Horror than his human counterparts, crawling Dombie included, and knew (or had the basic instinctual sensibility) to treat all other animals, living things, as enemies, hostiles. Where Dombie—had he been thinking not about *Gilligan's Island* but about the greater hazard at hand (the Horror)—should have looked upon any other being as a possible source of his salvation, Rusty saw the crawling man as nothing other than (1) curious, and (2) possibly threatening. So, Rusty growled, arched his back slightly, allowing his hackles to suggest a greater height, and moved cautiously, distantly, angrily along, following Dombie's path. Rusty's hips moved outward, as though his back legs were built without connective tissue binding the joints, his knees wobbling, his legs splaying left and right, his thick, lumpy belly

[11]When in 2.23, "Ship Ahoax," the castaways all start suffering from their island isolation, it is only through the expedient of a crystal ball that Ginger can console the castaways, stilling their stir-craziness by giving them each something to hope for.

almost touching the ground as he stepped awkwardly (and it seemed painfully) forward.

Dombie moved slowly along, realizing with each hand thrust forward and each knee slide ahead that he would never make it.[12] The reality all around him was gaining (finally) hold, the ashen city streets, the abandoned world in which he now struggled even to move, and Dombie (the panic attack moving much more quickly than he was) began to put together the whole scene: The city was filled with a really weird orange light; no one else was around, the world seemed completely emptied; he was still clinging to *Gilligan's Island*; the sky roiled and glowed; the city smelled chemical, a bit like urine, and with the acrid tinge of burnt human hair; the TV's messages about evacuating had referred to "any remaining survivors" and had used the term "nuclear," suggesting in all probability he had survived (improbably) a nuclear holocaust, and was now the last man alive, adrift here (on his knees) in the tundra of nuclear winter; Gilligan wanted to stay on the island, had in fact sabotaged all attempts to leave it.[13]

Lost in the above set of realizations about his place in this scene, and struck by the sudden clarity of hopelessness, Dombie lay flat down, and stopped moving altogether.

Seeing Dombie lie down, Rusty began barking at him.

It was not until Rusty barked that Dombie registered that another living being was there with him.[14]

Dombie had to raise himself onto his elbows to see the dog, its back almost a perfect arch, more like a cat, really, its matted fur in

---

[12]When, one by one, the others start disappearing on 3.13, "And Then There Were None," the terror of his aloneness overtakes him and Gilligan believes it is his fault they're all gone, and he dreams he is Dr. Jekyll, who mutates into Hyde whenever food is mentioned and is on trial, with the other castaways dream-morphed into a judge, a witness, a bailiff, and attorneys.

[13]This was, of course, because even as a bumbling goof on the island, Gilligan preferred the fantastical world of being shipwrecked (as do we, the viewers) to the real world. Had the castaways gotten off the island and been sent back to the mainland, there would have been no more show. The reunions prove this, by resituating the characters in improbable scenarios rather than putting Gilligan, The Professor, et al back into everyday life.

[14]On *Gilligan's Island*, something as simple as a dog would appear on the island, but it would bear unreal importance. A frog, a monkey, a parrot impersonating gangsters, a lion washed ashore in its cage, a gorilla, a pigeon, a giant spider, a duck. In the context of being shipwrecked and lost on the island, everything took on a new and absurd meaning. Whether the dog talked or didn't didn't even really matter. Where did a dog come from? What could it mean? Was there some special significance to this animal's appearance here?

clumps and tangles, visible dirt and debris contrasting with the black of its body, barking and shifting awkwardly on those lame legs back and forth within a short arc of the circumference of the circle that had Dombie as its center. Dombie had never owned a pet, and was not particularly fond of animals, especially dogs, but then this dog was barking loudly and nonstop, and it almost sounded as if the dog were trying to communicate something, glottal sounds snapping curtly through its spittle- and foam-lined gums, showing bright pink with each sound it made. Dombie sat himself all the way up, the dog having snapped him out of the panic attack, or at least distracted him from everything else going on, and he whistled once, through the dog's ongoing chorus, and called, "Here dog, good dog." The dog didn't move, and when Dombie shifted toward it, positioning himself to crawl its way, the dog barked louder and bared its teeth, moving more aggressively around the invisible boundary it had created surrounding Dombie.

"Here dog, good dog," Dombie repeated.

Rusty had been barking at Dombie as though to alert him, but now was clearly barking at him as a threat, warning him not to move any closer. Dombie was shaken a bit by the dog's obviously unfriendly response, but he was not so much afraid as just disappointed. He stood for the first time since leaving the safe confines of his house, and—glancing cautiously behind him at the dog every couple of steps—began moving through the abandoned and littered street. Rusty followed faithfully, barking whenever Dombie looked back at him, or paused in his progress.

Dombie's street was a fifteen- or twenty-minute drive from the Strip, and was lined with homes that looked more or less identical from the outside. Barring the scraps of paper that ominously fluttered past, and the unreal sky and the smell and the distant sound of the sirens still blaring, the emptied street was quite nice. The looters now gone, having left behind one house splintered and the next pristine, the untouched condos stood empty of occupants but preserved within as though they showed the fashions of the time in a to-scale museum. Everything was as it had been the week before, excepting very minor signs of the flurried exodus undertaken by the owners on Day One.

Although it was now early evening and the sun had set, the sky remained luminous and bright, a tumult of cloud mass seething above everywhere he looked. The city lights that had not been extinguished shone off the thick underside of the cloud and the sickening semidaylight would continue to reign for another three minutes.

For a moment, as Dombie looked both ways—up and down this deserted street, across the portion of his city (which included the Stratosphere) he could see—it seemed it was all his. That he could live here, alone, forever, as he had perhaps wanted to all along.[15] Moving in and out of other people's homes, immersing himself in their lives for just that long—their successes, everything left behind wholly intact—and when he grew tired of any given home, any given life, he could move on, switch to the next, a lawyer, an architect, a stripper, a professor, a blackjack dealer. It was a paradise, this abandoned city, filled perfectly with all he needed, with the molds of any life he wished to imagine were his.

Dombie walked out to the center of the street, Rusty arched and growling thirty feet away, and looked up at the improbably radiant sky, the orange and red and pink and coral and carnation and cerise and fuchsia and tangerine and gamboge and goldenrod and lemon and carmine and mustard and ocher and sienna and pear and pumpkin and peach and saffron and tawny and vermilion and terra-cotta and wheat and zinnwaldite and wisteria and thistle and ruby and russet and puce and persimmon and orchid and heliotrope and old rose and chestnut and denim and ecru and emerald and eggplant and gold and lavender and lilac and chiffon and cinnabar and cyan and carrot and olivine and tea rose and buff and tan and fawn and mahogany and hazel and tangelo sky, and a single flake appeared above him, not fifteen feet above his head, falling slowly, a tiny colorless flake, and he watched it as it fell, coming closer and closer, until it landed softly on his cheek.

All around him now, as he lowered his gaze, these flakes of seemingly supernal snow were falling, and the street began to disappear under their almost pearlescent cover. Rusty's pelt, where he stood, growling and shuffling side to side in his awkward gait, showed the shimmering traces of the precipitate. The sky was shedding its colors

[15]Over and over again on *Gilligan's Island*, someone would wash ashore intentionally trying to escape society, civilization, the everyday rest of the world. A long-lost aviator whom the castaways helped return to civilization after thirty years but who longs for his old solitude in 1.24, "The Return of Wrongway Feldman"; the reclusive artist, Dubov, in 1.34, "Good-Bye, Old Paint"; a band of teenybopper heartthrobs (Bingo, Bango, Bongo, and Irving) in 2.12, "Don't Bug the Mosquitoes"; the movie producer Harold Hecuba in 3.04, "The Producer"; an unprepossessing woman (who, after a makeover, becomes Ginger's doppelgänger, and tries to take Ginger's place) in 3.14, "All About Eva." Each time the castaways have to try convincing this would-be social escapist that the world is worth returning to. But, in the eyes of those bent only on escaping the real world, why would the castaways ever want to return?

now, turning ashen and wan and gray as the flakes fell more steadily, showering down blizzardlike, thickly coating the Vegas streets and Dombie himself, his arms now down at his sides, his feet ankle-deep in the accumulate.

Rusty began moving closer, barking as he did, until he was within three feet of Dombie. He continued to bark as he moved even closer, his sense of potential threat overcome by his confusion about the falling flakes filling the world around him.

Dombie could no longer see through the precipitate falling everywhere, and he found himself sinking to his knees.

Rusty shifted from barking to whimpering, and edged closer to Dombie, pressing his nose against the man's side, pushing his disfigured body tight against the lumpy form of the now nearly seated man, as though for warmth. Though his back legs barely supported him in the effort, and the convex curve of his spine essentially made the act impossible, Rusty wrapped his front paws around Dombie's left arm and began thrusting, pumping the air while stepping side to side, his awkward legs and fetal curl denying him all but the fantasy of the act, if dogs could fantasize, and the pleasure of physical canine love.

Flakes fell like paint peeling off the celestial palimpsest, revealing what had been there all along. The colorful, unreal sky was moving atavistically back to black and white, back to the origins of things, the world that once was.

His efforts at taking action had come to naught. Dombie realized he'd never see the castaways leave the island.[16] For a moment he had the strange sense of having left something behind, and yet—out here, he was also newly full of importance. He was acutely aware of himself, aware that this was him here. He'd managed the shift from inertia to action, after all, hadn't he? *Gilligan's Island* had gone from his primary reason for being to something somewhere in the background. This moment, this was his. Something about this struck Dombie as beautiful. Slowly sinking in the ashy matter while the dog humped the air between them, Dombie continued to look up.

[16]What is the island, really, if not the catalyst for action? Though the castaways are intent only on leaving it, isn't the island that which gives meaning to their efforts? Being stranded on an uncharted, uninhabited island somewhere in the Pacific is the first principle for their whole philosophy. Does it matter how absurd or improbable it is? Does it matter what their actions are, or if they ever do get anywhere?

Two Stories

Etgar Keret

SEPTEMBER FOR GOOD

—Translated from Hebrew by Sondra Silverston

WHEN THE CRASH CAME, NiceDay was the first to go. They'd always been a luxury brand, but after the Chicago riots even the wealthiest clients cut off their service. Some did it because of the unstable economic situation, but most of them just couldn't face the neighbors. The shares lay on the world trading floors, bleeding point after point. And so NiceDay became a cautionary tale of the depression. *The Wall Street Journal* headline ran "September Gone Bad." This, of course, was a play on their "September for Good" campaign, in which a swimwear-clad family stood around on a sunny fall day . . . decorating a Christmas tree! The ad had worked, big-time. One week postlaunch they were moving three thousand units per day. Affluent Americans bought. So did the less affluent, if they could fake it. NiceDay became a status symbol. The official stamp of a millionaire. What executive jets were to the nineties, and into 2000, NiceDay was to now. NiceDay: weather for the wealthy. Say you're based in Greenland, say all the snow and gloom is driving you batshit, one swipe of your credit card and, with a satellite or two, they'd set you up with a perfect fall day in Cannes, delivered direct to your own balcony, every day of the year.

Yakov "Yaki" Brayk was one of NiceDay's earliest adopters. He truly loved his money and had a hard time parting with it, but even more than he loved the millions he made selling weapons and drugs to Zimbabwe, he loathed those humid New York summers and that gross feeling you get when your sweaty undershirt sticks to your back. He bought a system, not just for himself, but for the whole block. Some people mistook this for generosity, but the truth is he did it just to keep the great weather with him all the way to the bodega on the corner. That bodega wasn't just where he got the unfiltered Noblesses they imported from Israel especially for him. No, more than anything, it marked for Yaki the boundary of his personal space. And the minute Yaki signed the check, that block turned into a weather paradise. No more gray rain, no more dog days. Just September, twelve months a year. And not, God forbid, one of those off-and-on, partly-sunny, partly-cloudy New York Septembers, but the dependable kind, the kind he grew up with in Haifa. And then, out of the blue, came the Chicago riots and suddenly here were the neighbors telling him to cease and desist with the gorgeous fall posthaste. At first he didn't give them the time of day, but then came those lawyers' letters and someone left a slaughtered peacock on his windshield. That's when his wife asked him to turn it off. It was January. Yaki turned off the fall and instantly the day turned short and sad. All because of one dead peacock and an anorexic wife with an anxiety disorder who, as always, was able to control him through her weakness.

The recession went from bad to worse. On Wall Street, NiceDay hit rock bottom. So did shares in Yaki's company. Then after they hit rock bottom, they drilled a hole in the rock and went down a little farther. It's funny, you'd think weapons and drugs would be strong during a worldwide recession, but that's not how it worked out. People were too broke to buy medicine, and they very quickly rediscovered an old forgotten truth: that weapons with chips are a luxury, just like electric car windows, and that sometimes all you need is a stone you found in the yard if you want to smash in somebody's skull. They very quickly learned to manage without Yaki's rifles, much more quickly than Yaki could get used to the unseasonably cold and wet mid-March. And Yaki Brayk, or Lucky Brayk, as the tabloids liked to call him, lost his shirt.

He kept the apartment, the company accountant managed to retroactively put it in the anorexic wife's name, but all the rest was gone. They even took the furniture. Four days later, a NiceDay technician came to disconnect the system. When Yaki opened the door, he was standing there drenched with rain. Yaki made a pot of coffee and they talked for a while. He told the technician how, not long after the riots, he'd turned the system off. The technician said a lot of customers had done the same. They talked about the riots, when a furious mob from the slums had stormed the Indian-summery homes of the city's wealthier residents. "All that sun of theirs, it was driving us crazy," one of the rioters said on a news commentary show a few days later. "Here you are freezing your ass off, just trying to make your next gas bill, while those bastards, those bastards . . ." At that point, he burst into tears. The camera blurred his face to hide his identity, so you couldn't actually see the tears, but you could hear him wailing like an animal hit by a car. The technician, who was black, said he was born in that same neighborhood in Chicago, but today he was ashamed to admit it. "That money," he said, "all that fucking money fucked up the whole fucking world."

After they'd finished their coffee, when the technician was about to disconnect the system, Yaki asked if he could turn it on just one last time. The technician shrugged and Yaki took that as a yes. He pushed a couple of buttons on the remote and out came the sun from behind a cloud.

"That's not real sun, you know," the technician said proudly. "What they do is image it, with lasers."

Yaki winked and said, "Don't spoil it. For me, it's *the* sun."

The technician nodded. "A great sun. Too bad you can't keep it out till I get back to the car. I'm sick of this rain."

Yaki didn't answer. He just closed his eyes and let the sun wash over his face.

MY BROTHER'S DEPRESSED

—Translated from Hebrew by Miriam Shlesinger

It isn't like just anyone walked up to you in the street and told you he's depressed. It's my brother, and he wants to kill himself. And of all the people in the world, he had to tell it to me. Because I'm the person he loves the most, and I love him too, I really do, but that's a biggie. I mean like wow.

Me and my little brother are standing there together in the Shenkin Playground, and my dog, Hendrix, is tugging away at the leash, trying to bite this little kid in overalls in the face. And me, I'm fighting with Hendrix with one hand, and searching my pockets for a lighter with the other. "Don't do it," I tell my brother. The lighter isn't there, in either pocket. "Why not?" my little brother asks. "My girlfriend's left me for a fireman. I hate university. Here's a light. And my parents are the most pitiful people in the world." He throws me his Cricket. I catch it. Hendrix runs away. He pounces on the kid in the overalls, pushes him flat on the lawn, and his scary rottweiler jaw clamps down on the kid's face. Me and my brother try to pry Hendrix off the kid, but he won't budge. The overalls' mother screams. The kid himself is suspiciously subdued. I kick Hendrix as hard as I can, but he couldn't care less. My brother finds a metal bar on the lawn, and whams it down on the dog's head. There's a sickening sound of something cracking, and Hendrix collapses. The mother is screaming. Hendrix has bitten off her kid's nose, but completely. And now Hendrix is dead. My brother killed him. And besides, he wants to kill himself too. Because to him having his girlfriend double-cross him with a fireman seems like the most humiliating thing in the world. I think a fireman is pretty impressive actually, rescuing people and all that. But as far as he's concerned she could just as well fuck a garbage truck. Now the kid's mother is attacking me. She's trying to gouge out my eyes with her long fingernails, which are painted with repulsive white polish. My brother picks up the metal bar and bangs her one on the head too. He's allowed to, he's depressed.

Four Poems

Marjorie Welish

IN THE FUTURITY LOUNGE
IN THE FUTURITY LOUNGE

1.

No depth meant. Stealth attributed

as silhouetted against orange shadows: orange shadows officiated

incline, slope, ramp, and crevice into which habitués

sat or sit, might have

styled themselves, typing in the vicinity of an idea whose technologies have
    extruded a pause.

The zone voted. An object works. Walk-in signage is suffused with

the floor plan planted in the floor-through floor not unlike

paper. YOU ARE HERE, with the plan, the plan's countryside

coexisting with the plan's latitudes. DESCRIBE TWO MOMENTS.

And having departed from the typewriter,

no chair

is to be found.

2.

And having departed from the typewriter

the song stylist has timed out.
But here's the

walk-in signage, where architecture had been;
orange code for each function: entrance/exit, computer station, lavatory, hearth, other? 1
floor plan, a diagram, embedded in floor at entrance, giving symbolic orientation to . . .
postmodernism for which the visitor is keyed to meaning as the guide was not. Meaning, or metalanguage?
differential in floor plane: slope, incline, ramp, terrace, crevice, niche; fluidity of functional structure;
noise: human clutter underestimated, semiotic rheostat dimming; 2
alterations: made to improve convenience and safety but expressed as interference; 3
writing: verbal model presupposed in conceptual art. 4

1. color is intelligible here as signage only insofar as one realizes that color is information.
2. people and their stuff not entirely factored in; and was the gift shop anticipated?
3. barrier set "temporarily" on rim of slightly terraced ramp, for instance.
4. key terms for functional aids meant to substitute for structural self-evidence in a postanalytic theory of architecture.

3.

X *cannot come today but will come tomorrow*
always
keeping the promise
on ramp or ramparts.

Grave inscription: ENTER
SAME grave
inscription

on ramp or ramparts—no, I take it back—size and shape are to be found only
there
where all proclamations descry screens
below grade
step on stepping-stones, winding stairs together with at least two exits, and
ramp conforming

to the building code, send subject on a quest for
orange wariness, hunted bird
with wire
boar with covered pit
rabbit with children's book
SAME contract
on ramp or ramparts—no, I take it back—size and shape are to be found only
there
where all proclamations descry screens

on which to type themselves—
the forces of

orange are at work! Hearth and lavatory glow as they rotate
at a speed of one revolution
per day

in velocities velo cities, as Velamir is a fast-moving person
so futurity tailgates the past, peels rubber. V. disbelieved acceleration
as relative
and so
was pulled down by it
rose-tinted.

4.

Nocturnal typewriter extruded. With chair throughout, air underneath—
creating a dispute,
in shadow, encountering
you intercepted, a chair typed
and paper swollen with amphitheater's engorged shadow
in the vicinity of an idea.
Steal away.

Marjorie Welish

The zone voted. An object works. Walk-in signage aflame with proclivities
not unlike an incline deferred
or a pause that inherits a stop.
View radiator. YOU ARE HERE, with the heat, the heart's launch
coexisting with health's per diem. DESCRIBE TWO MOMENTS.
And having departed from
the typewriter (Smith Corona declares bankruptcy in 1995) the documentary
meant other future perfect

maths (28,000 BCE, Europeans notch and tally)

Early (in 1938 the Bíró brothers put out the first ballpoint) remainder

Earlier firm evidence that

Earliest the first the first-known knowable fire

View radiator: YOU, a milieu for which HERE is a launch, poster, placard
my standard
territory *even when they tear up their own posters*. Tear up their future
perfect
fire. PLEASE
[POST

Earliest known future perfect

—Prompted by Rem Koolhaas/OMA, IIT McCormick Tribune Campus Center, Chicago

Marjorie Welish

IN THE FUTURITY LOUNGE (DETAIL)

Earlier firm evidence that

In the event that

A fact ignited our perfected enthusiasm, roseate guesses and graphics through
which we exited

First fact

Advent of fact

meets problematic, foliage for an underground set beneath a provident blaze of
corrugated
space-time HERE premature,
preliminary to a nice onset of popularity
and neo-vague agog.

Prior to eclipse:
advent of the new vague (human) agog and (avian) silence

YOU
facial
fall salient

Earliest the first the first-known knowable fire

Earlier than today

Early green

—Prompted by Rem Koolhaas/OMA, IIT McCormick Tribune Campus Center, Chicago

Marjorie Welish

TO BE CONT.

A turnstile for . . .

an incision

a LION

a folie (mindful of that elevated Parc de la Villette), derives its altitude from the tracks: interleaved with overgrowth, a concrete walk that ramifies now and then in spots and at edges to allow for plants to remain interleaved with pedestrian path even as transplanted locales and some trees create flanking borders the length of the line; some narrow slatted benches rising from cantilevered concrete also express the line, split and ramified, to install all social and natural structural function.

A LION

. . . insofar as they solved the problem of retaining the sense of wildness while accommodating the pedestrian traffic, traffic that would obviously have ruined the growth if . . .

Laying bare the rail

laying bare the rain

Pointing to the traffic, the frame; meanwhile the lion rescues the pedestrian (the LION rescues the liar) and dead end where a spur now allows idling above traffic. Please Be Seated. PLEASE BE SEATED. Extrude bench from floor, render verisimilitude of platform for Standing Walking Sitting and of Lying laid bare in said versatility of bench to raise flooring to beach language now locked into position. Versatility of referring . . .

WILDERNESS. He wrote LOOK but DO NOT TOUCH concerning this. Since pedestrians would kill . . .

the grassy WATERFRONT

already deviating from space as it accommodates the preexisting nonidentity of . . .

. . . avenue through the constructed fraying of walk, and transition is constant is a constant path is not as straight as the rail line itself but "weaves" interweaves its functions WALK DON'T WALK

immobilizing incision?

The gift of no destination is. Strolling is as was an urban substitute for walking to and from.

And yet he was sent to the gulag for looking up from under . . .

Scripted space did/did not affront you, Beauty locked/unlocked Truth locked/unlocked and intimated floor that is the spur for seating the sun meanwhile unlocks.

Walk but not seamlessly. You are not pretending to be nature the garden pretends but this garden professes textual strategy of a poststructural repetition following the . . . the railroad itself transposed the avenue. Constructed fraying of walk and WALK AND DON'T WALK, BUILT as a constant.

Lying on the bare flooring locked/unlocked SUN; intimated from floor was Beauty unlocked and extruded. Beauty extruded a spur for seating; the SUN meanwhile goes languorous now that it is disused—no, it goes as it went aggregating patches of grid . . . ng the preexisting nonidentity of . . .

Occluded folie. Occluded folie temporarily.

A turnstile

was railroad then undergrowth, then overgrowth revealed a prospect. TO BE CONTINUED. Plot from dereliction: a garden. Create scenic spot from derelict zone. Create beauty free/not free of modest/immodest free/determinate but modest when compared with . . .

not poor in referring.

—In response to Diller Scofidio + Renfro, High Line, New York

Marjorie Welish

SPASM, FOR WALL

Supported by a stolid scythe bearer, a gamin dressed in seismic shocks and tics conveys the relevance of modern dance as sign.

As against experience.

Leaning against experience appearing to lean against the sign of wall

The scythe-bearing sign unperturbed by tics and shocks breathing the air.

Ionisation by Edgard Varèse shall have been traffic by now.

Apron or no apron, apron (black) shifted to the hip of the skirt (red) of the scythe-bearer's counterpart.

The pair paced itself to synchronized counters such as arms admitting left and right to go abroad

Out into the traffic paces the scythe bearer.

Annul wall with prompt.

Peering or peeping she fingers the differential of wall-within-wall then explicates this slide as divergent bed for rewarding the body.

In spasm, the full extent of the cross-section.

—Noted at Steven Holl Architects: Holl/Acconci, Storefront for Art and Architecture, New York

Some Varieties of Being and Other Non Sequiturs

John Madera

VARANASI, GARRULOUS CITY swathed in fog, dusty streets teeming with saffroned Sadhus smoking hashish; sun-dried women carrying babies and bundles and the weight of age and memory and beauty and rot; barefoot children—their threadbare clothes windows on their whittled bodies—selling postcards of the ghats and temples to privilege-insulated tourists; and a virtual menagerie composed of pugnacious monkeys, lumbering cows, immovable buffaloes, scatter-brained chickens, and countless chirping birds carving arcs in the air; city whose filigreed temples are flanked by shacks and rubbish heaps; grunting city that mocks my practiced sincerity; city whose talons grip the nape of my neck; recombinant city entered through a multiplicity of openings: doors, windows, gateways, dreams; recursive city: it mumbles: breath to death; it mumbles: birth to earth; sepulchral city: it rasps: dust in the shadows, dust in the wall cracks, dust in the air, dust on the windows, dust in the whitewashed sky.

It was Sunday. In four days, the name Lashkar-e-Kahar would sound and eddy out, and cleave an abyss between before and after, yield blackened cries and inmost sobs.

Having ridden a rickety rickshaw from the train station at Mughalsarai with a driver snake-charming serpentine streets, imperiously passing other auto-rickshaws, pedal cabs, unhelmeted motorcyclists, and pedestrians slaloming around; and negotiating the opposing traffic full of their lookalikes—the air punctuated with crisp carillons, accusatory honks, and my own rickshaw's apartment-buzzer chirp, and its fluttering engine: tut-tut-tut-tut-tut-tut-tut-tut-tut-tut-tut-tut-tut-tut—I was anxious to set my belongings down, and though I had more weight than I could handle, belongings were not what I wanted unloaded from my body, nor was it my sense of belonging since I had long since lost that in my bright-eyed and hammered years; nevertheless, it was with this buckled-knees feeling that I immediately searched for a guesthouse rather than follow my original plan to become invisible, that is, to lose myself in the city; for I had set out to get away from the nagging of this follows that, to escape this fumbling-for-a-foothold feeling, but instead what replaced, no, predominated over that like river sediment cementing over a plain was this feeling that I was an outline, a contour, the borders of whatever it was I was widening out, losing form; and peering through a palimpsest of memories I was not sure were even my own anymore, not mine because if it is true that we are irrevocably altered by whatever or whoever touches us, then, as a result, those experiences we thought were our own must belong to someone else; I wondered, then, who was this person, transformed, yes, but still composed of these layers of memory? Did this mean that the only appropriate end for a life lived in perpetual blankness was an unmarked grave?

Walking up the cracked steps and through the door of what would be my home for the coming days—a sleepy sandalwood scent in the air—I scanned the paint-chapped walls, cracked floor tiles, and the worn furniture's stringy upholstery, and an eager clerk who smiled, splattered me with pleasantries, softened me with "sirs," and beckoned a boy to help me with my bags. And lazing on the counter before the clerk, a cat, framed by a wedge of light, knowingly eyed me, sussed me out as the luftmensch that I was: an impractical amalgam of flesh and air, contemplative and useless: a drifter living off the remains of his already meager savings. Glowing behind the clerk was a large largely unreflective mirror that still made the room seem larger. The man, splaying open a thick mildewed book—a chained pen flopping out like a fish out of water—asked how long I was planning to stay with them, fingered a line for me to sign in time with the airy music he had playing from a box. Until the day I leave, I said, and from his smile I gathered that he understood what I meant. I asked him what we were listening to. "Summun, Bukmun, Umyun"—do you know Pharoah Sanders? he said. He was asking if I was aware of him, of his music, but I said, Yes, we are old friends. I was doing this a lot: interpreting questions to mean something different than what they were intended to mean. You like jazz, I said. It was a small world, after all, he said and laughed, his laughter wet through, as if it had been bathed in something clear. I did not correct his misremembering of the phrase. I asked him what it meant. Music means whatever you want it to mean, sir, he said. I tried to mirror his inscrutable, beatific smile. Oh, it means Deaf, Dumb, Blind, sir. My life in 3-Ds, I said, rapping my knuckles on the counter. There were funnier responses, of course, but I had been tired of the game long before we had even begun. He laughed again. Sometimes we put it on infinite repeat, he said, that and the next song, "Let Us Go into the House of the Lord." I liked what he said about the music, about putting it on infinite repeat. I took it to mean something more than the programmed repetition he was talking about. I was doing this a lot, too: investing more meaning into what people said, into what happened around and to me. He told me he had once worked in a hotel where the managers had played jazz to attract Westerners, and he laughed recalling how customers would complain, how they had wanted to hear Indian music, even filmi, those odd ebullient sound tracks, which he could never bear to listen to. But jazz had "taken hold" of him, he said. He told me more about jazz—and the names flew by. After more prodding from him, I shared that I was here to walk along the shores of the Ganges. He told me that John Coltrane's wife, Alice, a devotee of Sathya Sai Baba, an Indian guru, had sprinkled the saxophonist's ashes into the holy river. I had nothing to say and so I just listened, followed the rise and fall of his words more than the actual meaning. Seeing me zone away, the clerk apologized and pointed to the stairs where the boy waited for me. As I followed him toward my room, the cat, a sandy-colored thing, pounced to the floor, and, before slinking into a shadowy corridor, slowly swiveled its head and blinked at me.

From my room's balcony, ginger smeared by the sun, I eyed the locals like a god (how my mind was still stuck in a mundane monotheism amidst India's poly-everything was a mystery to me) gazing upon his witless creation—so unlike chess, where the figurines with their unchanging features, roles, and gestures perform precisely on a Euclidean battlefield—and the narrow winding streets, streets as labyrinthal as consciousness, as full of uncertainty as they were of wonder, and just as filthy. Wildstyle geometries: riverbank stairs on top of stairs overlapping stairs colliding into stairs leading up to temples and palaces and guesthouses. Five bare-chested men sat cross-legged facing the river. A fleet of old boats floated at the ramparts, long bamboo steering poles jutting out from them like locusts' antennae. A group of boys wrestled each other into the water. A whimsically mustachioed man spoke into a rockabilly-type microphone, glancing intermittently at a tome on his lap. Two men carried an enwrapped and garlanded body atop a makeshift bamboo stretcher and rested it on four big blocks of ice. A tatterdemalion of a man, a Harijan, one of Gandhi's so-called children of god, tended the flame of a pyre. I watched a torso bubble and drip and blacken, and then husks of it fall away, exposing a rib cage the fire, too, slowly consumed, but the spine, while charred black, remained intact, irresolute as if still fulfilling its duty to prop some body up, and a river-facing skull, flesh even now around its mouth, seemed about to laugh, its teeth, then, spilling out of its maw, before the lighter of the pyre crushed its dome with a bamboo pole, finally freeing its soul, releasing it from the circle of birth and death. Nearby, an oblivious emaciated goat munched on a garland of marigolds. Eyes sweeping back to the Ganges, I saw two men on a boat weigh down the body of a leper with stones and then heave it into the river; the sound of it, from where I was, perfunctory, curt. But I could not possibly know all of this. Things were escaping from me now much like air from a tired and deflating windbag.

Later, after a plate of koftahs: balls of minced beef that effervesced in my stomach, and an assortment of fried and baked breads, all washed down with a mango lassi, I sat at a table thinking about how I was thinking, and I thought about how hard it was to move, how I was trapped in one of Xeno's paradoxical ideas, trapped thinking about the impossibility of motion: I had to get halfway there before I could get the whole way, but before that, I would have to get a quarter of the way before I could get halfway, and . . . well, then, I was trapped in an infinite regress—there could be no first step; if I cannot start it, how, then, can I ever complete it? This thinking paradoxically propelled my body—my energy, no, my will unraveling like one of those balsawood windup rubber band–powered airplanes set aloft—and emptied my head in order to sail straight over the other heads bobbing around me, and toward something else, something higher, something less concrete but somehow more real, something like air, maybe; something that waited for me, no, something that followed me, ran away from me, and waited for me, something that was both a shadow and whatever was its opposite (do the shadows we cast even have an opposite?): something impossible like that. Instead, I was sucked through litter-strewn streets like the lumpy bolus searing through my intestines, through an alleyway of arches where a gallery of birdcages hung from walls, where translucent canopies billowed like sails; through another alley where piles of potatoes, brainy cauliflowers, unraveling cabbages, nosy carrots, phallic cucumbers, woody bulbous turnips, gold papery onions, Christmasy red and green chilies, itsy-bitsy pebbly peas and beans, chunks of okra, bitter bottle pointed and ridge gourds, globular radishes, lugubrious pumpkins, and cairns of tomatoes all sat on winsome wicker bowls. Streams of people—sometimes sidling against me and matching my stride, sometimes allowing me to move ahead and then running to catch up with me in a kind of peripatetic polyrhythm—plied me with promises of marble-floored former palaces, air-conditioned guesthouses with the best view of the holy river; enticed me with doughy dumplings soaked in rosy syrup; frozen custards and fried funnel cake–like confections dusted with cloves, cardamom, and saffron; and warm puddings loaded with nuts and dried apples, mangos, bananas, guava, papaya, or pineapples; beguiled me with intimations of relaxing massages, with the mention of ganja, a sure physic for stress, anomie, and angst; or simply solicited me for rupees; and so I felt as if I had metamorphosed into a living automatic-teller machine. It did not help that I still wore a cuffed button-down long-sleeved shirt and dark slacks, albeit both very much rumpled, and lace-up oxfords, the stitched details across the rounded toes lost beneath three weeks' worth of caked-on dirt. Though certainly less than charitable, I was just about ready to give up everything.

I had come to know Varanasi as I had come to know what I knew, which was little, about India—well, no, not even as little as the tittle of its "i"—first through my feet, and then through my eyes and ears; and what I had learned was that Varanasi was a concatenation of contradictions and that instead of sorting them out or reconciling them somehow I should simply revel within this old city's darkness and light, its chaos and stillness, its abundance and scarcity, its silence and noise. But nothing could really prepare me for the ghats. Decrepit and funereal, there was still a kind of magic to them, but no, saying it was magical was—well, how can magic be possible in a disenchanted world? Call it strange and beautiful then, an atmosphere where every measure of intimacy was performed center stage: people bathing, laundering, eating, brushing their teeth—sometimes using just a finger—shaving, sleeping, and praying, and pissing and shitting; everything but sex; and vendors hawking food, saris, incense, and trinkets; and cows, goats, and dogs roaming around everywhere. Ritual ablutions in a dirty river, it was total immersion here: flowers and food and bottles of water, juice, and tea and statues from the Hindu pantheon and religious books and saris and shirts and pots and pans and cutlery. If this city were holy, it was because of its seeming unconcern with appearances, its flagrant disregard for order.

It was dusk when I came to the Harishchandra ghat where I dipped my hands at the river's edge, and watched little flowery candle floats drifting languidly; coracles, budgerows, and canoes floating slowly by; cumbrous barges bobbing; everything wreathed by a chalky mist. A man, his eyes bloodshot from the crematory smoke, crept toward me, stuck his beaklike nose in my face, and pecked at me with scattered thoughts, flooded me with information in an attempt to coax me into paying him for a tour: There is burning . . . everybody learning . . . good karma, bad karma . . . life very short . . . look like dust . . . soul is going, so, no ghost . . . body sink . . . sometime body come up . . . dog and eagle eat. From his incessant talk, I also pieced together that after a father dies, the family's eldest son shaves his head, wears white, and lights the funeral pyre. But the youngest son lights the mother's pyre. After the body has been burning for two hours, a bone is selected from it and then tossed into the Ganges. The men: a chest bone; the women: a hip bone. After a short while, I gave the man some rupees and waved him away. I wanted to stand there without a sound track playing in my ear. Watching the fire, I felt something like nostalgia, like this was all strangely familiar; it felt like sitting around a campfire, its bright glow and smoke inspiring secret sharing and inducing sleep.

Think of me as a pilgrim—why not?—but not one tinkling bells, lighting candles or incense, clapping hands to wake up a god; not a seeker of relics, of transcendence, of release from earthly indignities, but as one contemplating the calamity of his life, one regarding ancient ruins as mirrors of his own rubble; or, instead, as a man with an unclean spirit like one of those biblical unfortunates wandering around vacant spaces, seeking solace and never finding it; an extinguished man; or perhaps as a man in pain seeking a cure for an illness he knows there is no cure for because what can cure nothing when something, no, countless somethings were the cause of that nothing?

Before my father died, he had left instructions that he was either to be buried standing up, that is, vertically, so that when he entered the "land of the dead" he would be "one step ahead of the game," or, if a vertical burial was not possible, then I was to cremate his body and "cast his remains" into Death Valley. After he died, I was swallowed into a serrated sinkhole where all I could hear was his voice, the last things he had said to me: I was OK with getting old and being alone. . . . What worries me now is getting sick and being alone . . . dying alone. . . . Sometimes I feel jumpy around other people and I don't want them to come around . . . I have so many thoughts happening at the same time. . . . I just want to turn them off . . . I want to be free of pain. . . . Is that too much to ask? My father had always used humor to spackle over holes in his life, his lapses, his problems, his mistakes, but after the first lump was found in his throat, it all but disappeared. As the cancer spread, he had many sleepless nights, had difficulty sifting through overlapping thoughts, stopping what he called the "ping-ponging in his brain"; and he would complain about every little thing: the room's temperature, the nurse's curling lip, the doctor's breath. It was only when he talked about the details of his wake, funeral, and burial that his old self emerged. After he died, I had his body cremated, and I drove out to Death Valley—its desiccated environs a mirror of my own blankness—and, over the course of three days, spooned him out into Dante's View, the Devil's Golf Course, Funeral Mountains, Darwin Falls, Furnace Creek, Badwater Basin, and Zabriskie Point (he had loved Antonioni). The weathered rock formations' painterly striations were set aswirl in my mind as I lazed underneath the desert sun watching colorful swatches float on my closed eyelids. Cremation, so I had learned, breaks the body down into bone fragments and gases, elements that float into the atmosphere. As my father's ashes flew and merged with the land, with the sand, the water, the rocks, I thought I might be able to vanish there too, float away like one of the valley's ephemeral lakes into the miles upon miles upon miles of wilderness, through water-fluted canyons, up toward cloud-capped ranges, and away into the air—and I remembered how my father had responded to my initial resistance to the idea of cremating his body: Like I always say, "Reduce, reuse, recycle." I did not have the chance to ask him what happens if you are, like me, already made of air.

A homemade bomb is left by a man at Varanasi's Sankat Mochan Temple, and another one at the Cantonment Railway Station. Both explode on the Tuesday evening after I arrive. The police later unearth and defuse a third live bomb found in a bag in a market in Godaulia, a residential locality. Connected to timer devices, these ammonium nitrate bombs were set to go off one after another. I cannot explain how I had known that the man who left the bombs was, much like me, an angry, disappointed man, a man who could not let go of this letdown feeling; that he had planted the bombs in each place in full awareness that it would tear bodies apart; and that this man—as many men before him, and as I too after a day of clandestine, if rather banal, but still certain violence, had been accustomed to doing—had returned to his home, washed his hands, had dinner with his wife, and, after a dessert and a cup of tea, had plopped onto his bed and drifted easily to dreamland.

A fantasia: He is jarred from heavy-eyed numbness by the tinny deet-deet-deet—deet-deet-deet of his alarm clock, occasionally hitting the snooze button, and drifting off to some pillowy suspension of time. After this inertial play he pit pats to his preheated bathroom, mows, no, shovels his face with a razor—skin smarting from the splash of whatever chemical he had bought to seal up his pores—notes her missing toiletries: antigraying shampoo and conditioner (she would, invariably, still just pluck out the rare crinkly thing); assorted odor eliminators (he still did not know what she really smelled like); her cumulonimbus sponges, but especially the fluffy loofah threatening to crawl about like a crusty sea urchin; her tiny tins of lip tints; her melon moisture stick (whose bottom he too would twist until he could gently drag its moist end over dry patches on his feet, elbows, and lips, and then marvel at how they melted away); her headache soother (she suffered from menstrual migraines); her facial spray, cleanser, scrub, and mask; her gleaming bottles of mousse (he would sometimes squeeze a dollop of foam then smash it between his hands); her innumerable oozing tubes of organic, herbal, and antioxidant goop: after-sun balm, insect repellent, foot scrub, shaving cream (the one he would borrow because his own would irritate his skin) and aftershave lotion; hydrating body butter, body crème, and body wash; and regenerating cream (he had swiped that and kept it filed away in his desk); moreover, he notes the spaces they had once filled: squares, circles, and ovals, each one a geometric vacuum, a vestigial outline lined with grime, and flicks on the radio that promises "all news, all the time," offering him the world in exchange for twenty-two minutes, and drapes himself in a manner befitting a climate-controlled office, each assigned box outfitted with a computer terminal, calendar, ballpoint pens (black, blue, and red), highlighters (yellow, orange, and pink), whiteboard markers (black, blue, green, and red), no. 2 pencils (sharpened and unsharpened), mechanical pencils, tablets of lined paper, bricks of photocopy and desktop-printer paper (letter and legal size), multicolored stickies (no surface free from a note), paper clips and binder clips (small and large), rubber bands (his were stretched around an avocado pit), stapler and staples, clear tape and tape dispenser, masking and packing tape, paper file folders (letter and legal size), scissors, Wite-Out, daily planner, and postage stamps. Before leaving the house, he drinks coffee and he eats buttered toast, grabs the newspaper outside his door, and heads toward the bus stop where he overhears a man giving directions to a couple, and, later, his normally incorporated mind in an unsure morning haze, he walks toward the man who is now sitting at the back of the bus, pretends to be lost, and asks the stranger if the bus is headed downtown. The stranger's ready answers and easy affability immediately strike the office drone as suspect. Though numb to the shyster's shell-game chicaneries, he still somehow manages to be taken in by them: loquacious spiders that silkily knit elaborate word webs; their jiving colloquy marking them as thoroughly engaging but, ultimately, as untrustworthy and possibly dangerous. He and the stranger trade lies. He tells the stranger that he is in Las Vegas on business, that he needs to get to the Mirage on the Strip. Oh, in Paradise? the stranger says, then offers detailed instructions on what stop to disembark from the bus and what direction to walk in. Can't miss the marquee, he says. Freestanding. Biggest one in the world. The stranger shares his name, a something Berry, offers his hand, and asks the man his name. Stanley, he lies, and Berry says, Funny, you don't look like a Stanley, and then comments like a cheery tour guide on things the bus happens to pass. Eventually, after getting a lot of information from the man—all false, of course—Berry lowers his voice and shares how he had been released from prison just yesterday. Ordinarily, sharing such intimate information would set off an alarm in a person, but this perceptive, deceptive man knows that his "confession" will help establish trust and alleviate ingrained worries of "stranger danger." It seems a risky move, but is instead a knowing psychological ploy. After all, how can someone distrust a person who has made himself so vulnerable? All along the worker bee waits for the pitch, one masterfully nested within a carefully crafted tale. He doesn't have to wait long. Berry, folding his shoulders down to make himself smaller, speaks in the shallows of his voice, just above a whisper: You going to Treasure Island? . . . There's a tram at the Mirage that'll take you there. . . . Something there for everyone. . . . You gamble? . . . Oh, that's good. . . . Only bring you trouble. . . . Yeah, I did it all and then some. . . . Got into all kinds of mix-ups. . . . You believe in God? . . . Oh, God's the one saved me. . . . My mama taught me good. . . . Shame I never minded her when I was young. . . . She's sick now. . . . She's got the cancer. . . . In her breast. . . . A mother shouldn't get the cancer—not in the breast. . . . That's the devil's work. . . . See, God gives the mother milk. . . . But the devil clots everything up, curdles the milk, gives the cancer. . . . How about you? . . . Your mother alive? . . . Thanks be to God! . . . You only got one mother. . . . Yeah, I'm going to see my mother. . . . You know, they only give you five dollars when you come out of prison. . . . They take everything from you and give you back nothing. . . . How's that for a start? . . . That's why brothers go right back in. . . . Not me, though. . . . I just want to work. . . . Work is what makes you free, right? . . . I just need enough to get my ticket to Texas to see my mother. . . . I'm here doing the right thing, not trying to hurt nobody, just helping people. . . . Like that old couple back there. . . . I saw they needed help so I helped them with their bags. . . . Gave them directions. . . . And they gave me a few dollars. . . . See, God sends people in need to me for me to help them. . . . So, if you find it in your heart to give something, I'd greatly appreciate it. Mirage. Paradise. Treasure Island. The office drone hears these words, all of Berry's words, and knows what every word means, and knows that knowing that words represent other words was not enough, and knew that Berry shaped and ordered every word to sound something like the truth, but he still finds himself entangled in the words; better to think of how he had lost all sense of presence, of aura, of *jouissance*; how time had become his enemy; how delight had sluiced away into some septic tank of sadness. He knew that it was time to find out what he had lost, to find out how he had lost what he had lost, to, perhaps, even recover what he had lost, and that whatever it was that he had lost, if it was recoverable, must still be far away. So when he comes to his stop he immediately heads to a travel agency and books a flight to India. Three weeks later he arrives in Varanasi. *Conclusion of the foregoing.*

*

Varanasi—so named because it lay between the confluence of the Varuna and the Assi, a rivulet, really—is also known as Benares, that is, the "res": the taste or essence of "bena": all things mixed together, and also Kasi: the city of light, and Avimukta: the never-abandoned city. For me, everything in life did taste all mixed together like some kind of bitter cocktail, but how many mornings would I have to wait to see the light that everyone else, well, those who gave this city that name, saw, and to not feel abandoned? The irony of having arrived here from Sin City, my home for the past twenty years, to this holy city was an unimaginative one by this time.

It was Monday, another amber afternoon in which I walked to the ghats. But today I would ride a boat on the Ganges, that liquid reliquary of innumerable ends. For weeks now, since I had escaped from the States, I had been playing with this idea that, first, people, rather than being a means to an end—an idea that I, as an obedient consumer and also purveyor of consumption (both conspicuous but especially inconspicuous considering my work with assorted pleasure palaces) subscribed to as regularly as the scholarly journals that would arrive in my mailbox—were ends in themselves (admittedly a wholly unoriginal idea), but, also, as "ends to a meaning." It was more the sound than the sense of the idea of people as "ends to a meaning" that prickled inside me and thus kept it alive for me as an ongoing frame in which to think of things. But this was one of my problems: I wanted to understand everything that I saw from some kind of Archimedean remove, but this was impossible. My tendency was to list things, to name them, to enumerate them, to order them in order to understand them, but I was learning that the most important part of anything said is the part that is not there at all: what is left unsaid, what is, perhaps, unsayable.

A displaced isolato, an ouroboric thinker in whom nothing coalesces, I was trapped in a perpetual ellipsis: endless needlepoint pricks of suspended time and space, a prolonged inhalation enunciating loss, where any sense of rhythm or movement becomes long and drawn out; an ellipsis with innumerable dots, irresolute and then blocking profluence, a fleshy manifestation of Seurat's pointillism; so I should say what I am not saying, namely, that I had come to Varanasi to die, and that, though my end was a foregone conclusion, the manner in which my days would attenuate and eventually snap was unclear.

. . . .
. . . .
. . . .
. . . .
. . . .
. . . .

Tuesday morning: The sky a cloudy shroud, the river ran thick and heavy like molten metal poured from a foundry. I sat on the steps of one of the ghats near a man who sat on an octagonal block praying and meditating. It was his tiny bronze bell's tink-a-tink-a-tink, its ringing ding as a thing, which compelled me toward him. Draped in ochre-colored robes, beaded necklaces click-clacking from his neck, he exuded calm as easily as a tree oozing sap. A beard hung from his leathery face like an animal; his forehead, dotted yellow, made it seem scaly or like the beady texture of corn. Dreadlocks, coiled about his head like a turban, made me think of robin's nests and wicker baskets.

I stayed there for hours watching life and death on the river, but I mainly watched the old man. His eyes open a minim, he remained there all morning and afternoon without getting up to use the bathroom or to eat. So I did the same.

At dusk, I took off my shirt and submerged it in the river. And just like the countless men, women, and children I had observed over the past couple of days, I wrung out most of the water and then slapped it repeatedly on a block of what I thought was slate. Whipping my shirt against the stone felt good; the whap, whap, whap felt good to hear. I had not felt such vigor in a long time. When I was done, I hung my dingy shirt up on a line where some saris trembled in the breeze and returned to where I had been sitting. Eyebrows arched, the old man rowed his shoulders back, tilted his head toward me, asked what I was doing. I told him I was cleaning my shirt. The river is polluted, he said. I told him I had already known that long before I cleaned my shirt. So, you're not cleaning your shirt then, he said. I'm not? I said. He laughed and said, This is called—how do you say?—getting nowhere fast? He laughed again and came down from his perch. We exchanged names, and he told me that he had once been a businessman: Textiles . . . I had been promoted to direct my company's waste management department. . . . I was a dutiful employee, and so I researched, and I learned that all our chemicals were being dumped into the holy river. . . . Cancer-causing dioxins . . . organochlorines. One day, fed up with the "nonsense," he had left everything behind: job, home, family, possessions, savings, "all the material things that weighed me down," he said. And I eventually made it here to Ganga Ma, my final resting place. Without the Ganges, he explained, the dead would wallow in a limbo of suffering and would perpetually trouble their left-behind loved ones. He brought up the Mahabharata, the promises it made. Just one bone need touch the Ganges, he quoted from the book, and that person will reside, honored, in heaven. This would be the final escape from the material world, he said, from the cycle of pain and suffering.

I told him that I wanted to die. He stared at me, his eyes smaller than mine but deeper, glazed, poking out like salt-softened shells in a sandy scooped-out hollow. You will, he said, and then laughed, his laughter tapering into a sigh. So what's the hurry? he said. I told him that I was just ready, and that I was certain of it, but I did not tell him that I was usually dead wrong about whatever knotted thing I was most certain about. If you were all ready, he said, you would already be dead. He laughed again.

An explosion, falling rubble, and screams punctured the air. We ran toward the noise.

Knowing that Tuesdays are devoted to Lord Hanuman, the monkey god, and that Sankat Mochan, the wood-encircled temple devoted to him, is a sacred place for Hindus and would thus be full of people, the bomber had set his bomb to explode in the temple on that day. The families of a young Nepali woman and a young Bihari man chose that day too, for the couple's wedding ceremony. Smoke snaking up into my nostrils, I kept looking at the floor: a shattered mosaic of glass, pottery shards, chunks of red brick, and bloody puddles with tattered clothing dipped in it like a painter's discarded rags, grimy water vomiting from pipes; and there was a wild collage of paper as if from several shredded sets of encyclopedias, and, scattered about as if from some wild dance, sandals, slippers, and flip-flops; and dried petals from gerberas, roses, orchids, and marigolds dotted everything, and everything was powdered with dust. The air was a cacophonous blend of children and men and women crying, of squealing sirens, crackling fire, feet kicking debris, hands sifting through the wreckage. There: A man scoops oranges from a hole and gathers them into a burlap bag. There: A girl picks up a paint-flecked Popsicle, plucks out the colored bits, and sticks it in her mouth. There: A weeping woman and man enshroud a charred lump of limbs. There were so many bodies, bodies piled on top of each other, bodies and bodies underneath hunks of wood and rock, bodies lifting themselves out from the wreckage, bodies helping other bodies rise, bodies digging up other bodies, bodies shouting, bodies crying, wrecked bodies, bloodied bodies. There were countless overturned and broken chairs, but somehow the wedding throne survived the blast; still facing east, it was a gaudy thing, its gold arabesques, its plush velvet, its solidity, its expansiveness, its imagined evocation of luxury, of possibility, making it appear like a smug judge presiding over everything, confident in having the last and decisive word. The temple courtyard was the moon's surface: a wide, shallow crater with glinting shrapnel in the ceiling for stars. I ran to help two dust-covered men who were digging out a body half covered by rubble. When I was only a few feet away from them I found that I could not move. It was like a wall had suddenly risen between them and me. What they pulled out was a pulpy mess. I gagged and fell to the floor. Shouts and cries rang out. So much noise. So much dust. So much blood. There was a rankness wafting from the wood, cadaverous whispers rising from the stones. Yes, Hobbes was right: Our lives are "solitary, poor, nasty, brutish, and short"; though surrounded by other people, we are utterly alone, our words always falling on others' ears like raindrops on a desert; poverty of mind, poverty of imagination, poverty of will, poverty of body; our life a trail of shit, spit, piss, blood, sweat, mucus, and cum, like a snail's sticky trail of waste; a series of excretions: noxious effluvia, wastewater discharges, all kinds of litter, chemical spills into the soil and water, radioactive contaminants, noise, eye, and thermal pollutants; our brutishness revealed in moments like these in which bodies are blown up as if each body were a slum that must be razed, a thing like any other thing, and when you recognize that life can be reduced to these elements, how can you complain about its brevity? Yes, everything in my life was broken, but the whole damn world was broken, too. What and where were the rivets that held everything together? I want to tear my skin like the scrim from a . . . dizzy . . . sick . . . close eyes . . . fall . . . get up! . . . nothing made of nothing makes something out of nothing . . . fall . . . fall . . . hello, floor! . . . blood and dust . . . dust and death . . . noise . . . I can still see . . . what's that? rotting music? . . . seas of guts . . . horrors and . . . where does

death live? . . . where death doth live . . . all in the head . . . what's that? whistling? . . . stop shaking me! . . . putrefaction! . . . just a spell. . . . .
. . . .
. . . .
. . . .
. . . .
. . . .
. . . .
. . . .
. . . .
. . . .
. . . .
. . . .
. . . .
. . . .
. . . .
. . . .
. . . .
. . . .
. . . .
. . . .
. . . .
. . . .
. . . .
. . . .
. . . .
. . . .
. . . .
. . . .
. . . .
. . . .
. . . .
. . . .
. . . .
. . . .
. . . .
. . . .
. . . .
. . . .

. . . .

. . . .

. . . .

. . . .

. . . .

Wednesday: Of course, I have not been talking about Varanasi but about my Varanasi, a version, if you will, for Varanasi is just like any other city in that it is unlike any other city. This city of imagination, a memory palace built of words, words strung together, words radiating out from each other, like unto like; words, the thread Ariadne would offer you in lieu of a thread to puzzle your way out from the mind's complex branching passages, its dancing floor. Words in the head are scripture or, rather, inscriptions, that is, an engraving. No, each word is a grave. No, each word is a tree growing in two directions: toward the earth and toward the sky, each word a holy tree, an Yggdrasil, an Ashvattha. But I am losing the thread. . . .

Varanasi was half a city now, a funeral without its counterbalancing carnival. After the bombings, most people stayed indoors. Many Muslim vendors closed their shops, an expression, for some, of their condolences, and for others, from fear of an unjustified retaliation from angry Hindus. From my balcony, I watched people on their roofs and stoops smoking, sitting, squatting, or standing in silence, or chewing betel leaves, their streams of red spit an eerie reminder of all the blood I saw staining the temple's floor. A ghost town, the streets were quiet. The confusing fuss of shouts and laughter and traffic's rattapallax, that symphony of beeps blares and blurts, booms and vrooms, zips and zooms, whizzes whoops and whooshes, rattles clatters and clanks, were sadly absent, and though there were mumbles and murmurs, hissed whispers, ringing phones, dry coughs, and the occasional child's giggling with its corresponding shush, and assorted squawks squeals barks baas maas growls grunts meows moos cheeps chirps and tweets, the air was sad and silent. In the midst of this harrowing human silence you could almost hear every door squeak open, every wing's fluttering away, every spout's drip, every clock's tick tock, every poop's plop, every tinkle in a pot, every scratched itch, every flick of a fly, every nose's sniff, every eye blink, whatever lock's tumbler that happened to click, and if you strained

your ears, as I was doing, you could almost hear every thought. I screamed until I was hoarse . . . .
. . . .
. . . .
. . . .
. . . .
. . . .
. . . .
. . . .

Before taking another morning boat ride on the river, I visited the workshops of boat builders building on the riverside. Each boat was like a person with its own ribbing, its own skeleton, really, the keel a spine that would cut across the surface of the river.

Midmorning, I hired an old bony boatman to ferry me around for a few hours. I chose him because of his face, a fissured map of memory, sadness, acceptance, dignity, and patience, because of his eyes' black pupils that, if stared at long enough, would suck you into some blank lacuna. I did not expect his hand to be cold or for his grip to be as strong as it was when he helped me into the long boat. He did not tell me that the pole he was using had been handed down to him from his great-grandfather, that he had spent most of his life ferrying customers on the river all year round. He did not say that he worked from sunrise to sunset. He did not say that he ate two meals a day, and that at the end of a good day he would set off for the bazaar to meet with friends, drink chai, eat a plate of milky morsels, and perhaps play a game of chess. He did not say that I was his first fare of the day. He did not say that his boat could carry six people at a time and that unless business picked up he would probably not eat today. He did not say that he usually made just enough money to get by and that his biggest dream was to get a new ferryboat, one that would carry twice as many passengers, so that he could then rebuild his house, build it from brick instead of mud.

Floating along, I closed my eyes and dozed off. I dreamt that I had traveled to the Gangotri Glacier, the life-giving source of the Ganges. Though cold there, I was naked. I swam down the Himalayan gorges to the valley of the Bhagirahti; torrential waters thrust me toward the vast flatlands of the Ganges plain, into the quieter holy waters of Varanasi, into the sea-like stretches of Bihar, onto one of the digits of the many-fingered delta, and out through Diamond Harbor, the mouth of the river, and into the Bay of Bengal, where freshwater merged with the sea's salt, and then I floated far into the Indian Ocean until I could not see any land. Before waking I saw myself reaching into my mouth to remove a dead pigeon. I kept pulling and pulling in vain.

I went to bed early evening. Lying there, staring at the ceiling, and pestered by mosquitoes, I imagined Varanasi swarmed with locusts, and then prayed—whom I was praying to I could not say—for a host of lizards to swoop up and eat all of the insects.

Thursday: Lashkar-e-Kahar, a little-known militant group fighting Indian dominion over Kashmir, claimed responsibility for the two bomb blasts in Varanasi. "If India does not stop excesses in Kashmir," Abdullah Jabbar, the group's spokesman, said, "we will carry out more such attacks across India."

The veil of morning smog had been pulled away, allowing a tumescent orange-red sun to visibly rise over the far banks of the river. A nice wind whipped across the water. That would help.

I used up what I had left (which wasn't much) of my savings to purchase an old skiff—the hull's ribbing, its overlapping planks, suggested a Viking clinker-built boat—from the old man who had ferried me around the day before. The money would be enough for him to have another boat built; enough to build a new house out of brick too. After this, I bought as much sandalwood as the boat could carry and still float. I would need over six hundred fifty pounds to do it properly, but what I had would still do.

Adrift on the river, the morning sun above me like an unblinking eye, I laid the longer logs length-wise from stern to bow, and then horizontally placed smaller ones on top of these. I repeated this twice, then poured kerosene all over the makeshift pallet and doused myself. Facing the bow, I sat on the wood, placed small logs on my legs and across my chest and neck. One flick from a lighter did the trick.

Imagine a city of the never built and unbuildable, every fanciful drawing of the paper architect realized. There: Étienne-Louis Boullée's *Monument destiné aux hommages dus à l'Être Suprême*, that interlocking network of white buildings topped by a domed altar paying tribute to some imagined supreme being, and his smaller, but no less ambitious, *Cénotaphe à Newton*, its massive orb submerged in what looked like a giant multitiered cake decorated with cypress trees. There: Iakov Chernikhov's arrhythmic constructions, compositions, and spaces; his buildings, in spite of their eschewal of utility, their asymmetries and disharmonies, finally realized three-dimensionally. There: Thomas Telford's six-hundred-foot single iron arch bridge originally conceived as a replacement for London Bridge. There: Hermann Finsterlin's Glass House. There: Erich Mendelsohn's Einstein Tower beside Tatlin's Tower. There: Konstantin Melnikov's impossible palaces and cogwheel portals, and his Sonata of Sleep, a dream factory. There: N. A. Ladovsky's crane-inspired block of flats. There: all seventy-seven of Frank Lloyd Wright's unrealized designs. Even the architectural ruins and debris, especially Polyandron, the necropolis for desperate lovers, of Francesco Colonna's *Hypnerotomachia Polifili*, have taken form. And there: Joseph Brodsky and Ilya Utkin's undulating Crystal Palace rising like broken glass from the ground.

Picture a city of blown glass, and all the glassblowers blown from air, and the air blown from the first breath, that never-ending sigh blowing out, out, forth, outward, out of, out from, away, away from that something like beauty, something like radiance, something like illumination, and all those glassblowers continuing to blow, and the glass bubbling, incubating, crystallizing, and tessellating, till there rises, finally, a gleaming world of bricks, pillars, walls, arches, entablatures, domes, pyramids, porticoes, balustrades, promenades, roofs, courtyards, and staircases made of pellucid planes, panes, windows, mirrors, and prisms. And imagine this city filled with light, a light creating a meshwork of hues.

If only I could remember to forget, but I do not know if I will remember. But if memory is going to go, then I will go too. Thus, I might remember to forget.

For You We Are Holding

Matt Bell

We are waiting on the streets in front of and beside the office. The number of us can be many but rarely is. The number can be none but it is never that. Whatever the number, that is who we are. Another number of cabs and buses and elevated trains are dispatched to service us, to carry those of us who no longer drive away from the end of our working to some other destination: Here is the shop selling suits that was once a shop selling dresses. Here is the restaurant that takes down our names when we call, then expects that we will arrive together, at one particular future. Here is the bank whose ledger is filled with names, some of which are ours, all of which can be organized according to various metrics of finance and circumstance, of interest and time.

On the train, we open our cell phones and track our location, watch the blue dot cut through the city's grid, across its streets and avenues. Once we were able to ride the trains to get lost, to be anonymous, to be somewhere no one knew we were. Now there is always something locating us exactly, by minutes and degrees. The train goes through a tunnel and for a moment the blue dot stops following. We are free for five, ten, fifteen seconds, and then it is with us again, an on-screen representation of we who are traversing a city writ miniature, pocketable. We press a button and the city disappears into a menu of other options, other ways to disperse our time. Our distractions trail us, make waves. We are traveling but we are mostly doing so by standing still, by holding on to the provided railings, lest we be thrown free of this quick-moving space we have chosen to occupy.

We can be separated by turnstile, by revolving door, by threshold. Outside on the street, we are waiting to feel our phones vibrate in our pockets. We are taking our phones out and looking at the screens even when they do not. These phantom feelings accumulate until we no longer trust our senses, ourselves. To communicate, we type with our thumbs, walk with our heads down. When we look up, our eyes meet from across the avenue. We recognize each other, or else we think we do. We are the people who are in a hurry, who are crowded together block after block after block. We are close to other people but not the people closest to us. We imagine them here too, imagine them filling this entire sidewalk, the block ahead, the block behind. What a different city that city would be, filled with all those missing or else lost. There we might glance upward and see her upon the balcony of her apartment, hung high above us. We might see her, but we might also pretend not to. It is easy enough to pretend when no one is watching. She is far off, tiny above us. She is smoking a cigarette or eating something microwaved into warmth. She looks as alone as we are, which is not to say that she doesn't have the remainder of her family inside, waiting behind her sliding-glass door. We no longer have any way of knowing for sure what that word means to us. Maybe neither does she, unless she turns around and looks.

Once, this bench was where we met on lunch breaks, at this location placed an equal distance from each of our offices. We shared different takeout each time, but often someone at another bench had a meal that looked better, or that came in an unrecognizable package, brought from some new restaurant hidden in the blocks around the park. It was hard to be satisfied with what we had when there was so much more we could have had instead, when there was all this city we hadn't yet found. We tried to meet at our bench every day, but if it rained between eleven and one then we did not see each other. We tried never to forget, but if it rained while we were at the park then sometimes we rushed back without remembering to kiss good-bye. Then to spend the rest of the day dreading car crashes, and what if we should die before we made it home. *What happened happened but what is the chance of its happening again*, we said. We said, *It's not desperation if it's love*, but maybe we were wrong.

When the rain starts, we are the number of people standing at this particular corner on this particular day. We open our umbrellas, hide our faces from the rain but not from each other. We clump, then disperse. We are going in more than one direction. We will not remember each other's faces, only fragments of clothing, posture, speech. Only the size of an umbrella, or the shape of a leg soaring down and out of a skirt. Only the voice of a child saying *Hello,* saying *What is your name,* saying *Why won't you talk to me.* Saying *Mommy why won't he talk to me.* Only this tight sensation held behind our faces, that of our eyes fixed on a lighted traffic signal, on the slim last second between not walking and walking. Even while we are walking away we are already walking with someone else.

At the store, we shop for fresh vegetables. We shop for cruelty-free meats. We put these things in reusable plastic bags made of recyclable materials. The bags are printed with messages telling us we are saving the earth by what we choose to eat and drink, by what we feed our family and friends. There are so many of us here that sometimes we have to wait in long lines to pay for our purchases. Sometimes the train station is so thick with us that by the time we get home our meat is browning. Our lettuce is wilting, our strawberries are spoiled, and both must be wasted into a trash can or garbage chute. We imagine all that past and pointless sunshine, all that mother's milk, all those held breaths spilling out upon the slaughterhouse floor. We imagine that floor packed, crowded with those others suddenly aware they have been tricked.

The salesman at the running-shoe store tells us our shoes are no good for running. He tells us they are outmoded technology, then sells us something else, something better. We will be happier, he says, and healthier too. He says that in these new kind of shoes we must run without socks. We wonder what about the shoes makes this so but we don't ask. Not everything that seems to have causality actually does. Now look how long our stride is getting. Look how far we can run from where we were. Later, we turn around and head back, hear the difficulty in our breath, the discouragement at how far there still is to go. We stop, bend over, put our hands on our thighs for support. We are breathing hard while around us others are calmly walking. The sun is out, drying the afternoon rain from the sidewalks. The sun is out, but no one expects it to last.

*

We can be separated by termination, by resignation, by a move to another borough or another city. Sometimes we will think we see an estranged part of us in a department-store window, in a bathroom mirror at a bar where we have been drinking. We see his face, his eyes, his hair, or his smile. He is holding a tie up to his reflection or he is lifting a scotch to his mouth. We call out his name but he does not turn. Probably we did not see him. Probably he does not want to see us, or even look the same as he once did. All around are reminders of the people and places that were once us, images captured in glass and mirror, the shape of names etched into the bricks. In them we do not look unhappy. We are not an unhappy group of people. We have a job or else the prospect of a job. We have an apartment we are pleased with. We are wearing a suit that we have been told is fashionable by the salesman at the suit store so that we might start to meet women wearing dresses like those worn by the girlfriends of our friends, who are the kind of women our friends say we are supposed to be meeting. When our phone finally rings, it is a friend asking if we want to have drinks or a previous date asking if we want another one. We do want another or else we do not. We are willing to continue trying, or else it is too early. Perhaps if we are being honest we will say we only went on the first date because a friend insisted we try to start over. Maybe if we don't know when to stop talking we will say that we are still hoping to regain what we have lost, to repair what we have ruined. Our parents call every week to ask how we are holding up, how we are adjusting, if we are happy. We tell them what they want to hear. We smile, because we are told people can tell we are smiling even on the phone. We say, *Yes, we are happy again.* We say, *We are trying hard to be as happy as we can be.*

In the evening we gather in front of an apartment building, then hail a cab. The cabbie is not one of us, not the us that is we who are sharing the cab together, not the us we will be when we are no longer in the cab. The cabbie is different, but still he speaks our language. He looks at our suits and dresses and asks us where we are going, what we are doing this night. He asks, *What is the special occasion.* We say we don't know. We say it is our birthday, it is our anniversary, it is the evening after a funeral. There are dozens of reasons to celebrate or commiserate, enough people packed around with whom to do either. We have chosen these few others to be with. We have slipped our hands into their hands, have involved their fingers with our palms. Later we will break bread, clink glasses against other glasses. From a far enough distance, it will be possible to mistake us equally for celebrants or mourners.

The waiter brings us food cooked by a man who yells, or else he gets a call from home, a message in his pocket bearing the first vibrations of bad news. We are the customers he is serving when he returns to our table with his red face and his white hands held above and around our plates. He asks, *Is everything all right. Is there anything I can do for you.* When he goes outside, we wait longer for fresh beverages or extra butter. We have conspired to eat our food in a place where the person who brings it to us is not a person who will eat beside us. When we leave the waiter at the end of the meal, we tip exactly what we would have tipped had he been perfect.

We stay together until the hour when the trains stop running the way they once ran, and afterward it is harder to get where we are going. Together we stand on the platform, take turns stepping over the line to look down the length of the tunnel, toward the lack of approaching light. Impatient, we stumble backward, shuffle our feet, run our fingers through our messed hair. We are either talking too much or else out of things to talk about. We are surrounded by the people we have been surrounded by all night, plus these others who are us too, if we become now the people waiting for this train. This time of night there are other options too. Her number is stored in our phone but also remembered by our fingertips. We could call that number. We could apologize for the late hour, for sounding drunk because we are trying so hard to sound sober. We know we would not get what we are hoping for, but that does not mean we wouldn't try, if only there were reception this far under the earth.

On the way home, some part of the we takes a picture of the rest, promises to post it online after we are no longer together. Later some of us will write beneath it, craft sentences meant to make the photo seem offhand, incidental, the record of a gathering that could happen again anywhere, anytime, even though it never will, not even if we want it to. And how we want. And how we are always wanting. To hold on, to recapture what we have lost, what we are losing. Not what, but whom. On the streets it is raining again, and again we are wet and tired and ready to be home. Beneath our feet the puddles pool and we plunge ahead until the cold water uncouples us into the night.

Awake alone, then panic again into questions. *Where is he. Where did she go. Where am I.* To be alone is the worst thing so do not be alone: Open the laptop in the corner of the room and watch it fill with glow. Put your fingers to the keys: *Can't sleep. Who else is awake. What are we all doing up.* Watch the screen for responses, then pour a drink while waiting for the coffee to brew. The coffee smells different here, this apartment still unfamiliar after all these months. Check the clock, then take a shower, get dressed. Better to stay awake than to allow the dream to resume its teasing. Just because morning is here again doesn't mean the nights aren't getting longer.

We can be separated by custody hearings, by the back and forth of the court-ordered visitation weekends that follow, or else by a failure of forgiveness, a persistence of penalty, an inability to beg right our pardon. Living elsewhere now is the boy who is harder to call our boy than he once was, harder to call our oldest son when there is no one left to be older than. Again and again he becomes a stranger in the times between our togetherness. We ask him *How did you get so big* and mean every syllable. We ask *What do you want to do today* because we fear we no longer know the right answer. We bring him a present, but it is something he already has. He is bored with it before he opens the package. *Now you have two,* we say. *Now you can keep one at your house and one at mine.* We say, *It's OK to miss your brother. I miss him too.* Over and over we speak these statements, each too much like a question, each clumsied out of our mouth. Always now there are two where once there was one. Always now the one left in this apartment lags behind, stuck in a Sunday evening, while the other rushes ahead, into and out of the coming week. Without us, away from us, the boy is becoming, the boy becomes. He becomes but we don't know what. We don't know if we will ever know ever again.

*

In the end, we can be separated despite our best efforts at staying together. We can be separated by tragedy, then by arguments, by fair and unfair blame, by couples therapy. Then by divorce and new addresses. Now we are too far away and want to get closer. If we still owned a car we would park it up your street. If we owned a bike, we would ride it past your apartment. Instead there is only the bus, the cab, the train. There is only the running, sockless in our new shoes. All day we make the blue dot follow us to the places of our previous habits. They are all diminished now but we go anyway: Here is the park. Here is the restaurant. Here is the shop and the store and the bank. Tourists would need maps to find these places, but these are not the places tourists would think to find. We have lived here too long for their kind of maps. Our maps are stretched tight across our skin. We carry them everywhere with us so that when we are lost they might carry us.

We ride and ride until the dot loses us, until we are disappeared between buildings or under the ground. It is only temporary, but it is all the chance we need or have ever needed. Unwatched by anyone, we call your number to ask if you are home. We send a message to tell you we are on our way. We press a button that causes a buzzing in your apartment to notify you that we are downstairs, that we want to come in. Maybe this time will be the time you press a different button that gives us access to what you have: your lobby, your elevator, your hall, your door. If so, then maybe we are knocking now. Maybe then the door is opening, then the door is open. Maybe a cab is waiting for us downstairs, and we are waiting for you, for the two of you. We are waiting for you to join us. We are waiting for you to again please say that you will. *Look how little we are holding without you,* we say. *Without you, look how we hard we are trying to hold.*

Stop When the Person Becomes Restless or Irritable

Diane Williams

I HIT THE POINT in the room with the checker pattern on the wall. I have this violent reaction to Margot Alphonse.

"Perhaps you'll get treated," she had said, "and then you won't have blood all over your hands."

I have this violent reaction to her. Any explanation for that? None at all. Am instantly comfortable, have my dignity afterward. Am removed, settled. There is evidence—a Hadley chest, a wainscot chair.

In any event, Margot Alphonse canceled her appearance in this story. I feel particularly sorry for her, after all. She had loved me, possibly . . . bathed me in the bathroom. We slept with an apartment window open—on a pretty courtyard—where you can still hear the people who often need to significantly yell on the avenue. We entered a dispute.

On the improvement of my understanding of her and overall, I feel the variety of strong, reliable emotions, the whole erotic satisfaction. And the droning sound—pigeons are growling—this is so thin.

Margot's voice is heavy. I had intended to lift it, and to hold it, so that it wouldn't feel as if it were pulling at my neck, or cleaning out pots.

I've got the McElroy brow, mustard hair, orange mouth, skin—brown, white, gray. I am an office worker here in New York or in the other top cities. I've had a stage career and many brief flirtations. My interest in sex is strong. I have superior intelligence. My ethical standards are high. I have a desire for neatness. Can you think of anything else that would give my life meaning?—for instance, for my home to be a bit of heaven?

This wasn't the first time I'd seen Margot Alphonse in this mood when she had completed a retreat and returned to me. In November she called up and her words spoke louder than our actions—support and encouragement with pleasure and gratitude.

The purpose of this is to take the reader into my confidence to explain why that Sunday, after the secluded lunch table was cleared, sex was in the background and was not the whole picture. At any rate, there were other sports.

How our fingers tingled! It's a wonder we didn't, or we don't, lose our minds.

"What shall we do now?" Margot asked. "You don't need to laugh. I am returning your property."

"No, Margot, no!" But what would I say? "Just a moment. No, you don't, Margot."

"Why not?" she said. "Are you listening?"

"Yes, yes. Stop talking," I said. "I have the feeling."

She opened up her handbag and handed me my gates and stone-walls, it felt like.

In the City

Colleen Hollister

1.

In the city, the buildings collapsed one by one. They scattered bits of colored glass, bits of iron into the crosswalks while children walked in rows of two, holding hands, drifting out of school toward playgrounds on the corners. Red flags fell out of windows, old scarves. The children had decided that the buildings dreamed of goldfish; the afternoon was bright, like goldfish; they watched the dust scatter. They watched the buildings drifting to the ground, and what was inside of them. It was almost gentle.

In the city, a man and woman looked into the shops, peered in at bicycles, at pink dresses hung from ceilings. They asked questions of the shopkeepers, pulled out maps, pointed to the streets, to alleys, to endless passageways, and the ones that ended suddenly in buildings. The buildings collapsed. Out of them came letters, letters that flocked the streets like birds, and anyone sitting in the coffee shops could read them. They said *how are you* and *where are you going* and *when will you be here? Please come*, they said, *I am still waiting.*

Around the man and woman, as they walked, dust and bricks. Shadows. Gray things. Dim light. Tulips. It was spring and so the people were on bicycles, at café tables, sitting on the sidewalks, drinking sodas out of glasses, dunking cherries with a straw.

2.

In the city, you feel yourself fall out of windows, lean out of balconies. In the museum, a collection of small shells and monkeys in glass cases, their eyes filled with plastic, surrounded by paintings in gilt frames. Past the museum, a train shudders, steams and hums and whistles, lifted up on metal tracks. Downstairs, the sunroom is full of bees. In a moment, the crowds will find them, and will run out screaming. For now, they hum and hum and buzz and bounce against the paintings and the tulips sealed in glass. You are standing on the outside. Looking out and up and in at the building on its staircase, how it goes up and up and up, those wide stairs, those tall doors. When the building begins its collapse, you feel yourself fall out of windows, lean out of balconies, just like the people on the inside in their raincoats, their long hair tied back with ribbons, and on the outside, on the ground, it starts to snow. You feel yourself fall. Across the street is a lake. It's odd, surrounded by a city—a lake larger than a hand, larger than the train car or the tracks—but the city streams around it, holding on. They seem to hold themselves together—the lake, the city.

3.

In the coffee shop, the woman sat to read the newspaper. Around her, people talked, chattered, and there was the hum and clatter of cups on saucers, cups slid into buckets and carried into the kitchen through the flapping doors, dumped into the sinks in the madness of china. It was in the morning, and she held out an eyelash, to wish on. She held on to a coffee cup tightly; she looked out of the window. She held herself still. In the morning, she woke up, walked along the street from her hotel, read the newspaper, smudged it on her finger, made her hair stick up straight when pulled on top of her head. She pulls at her hair when she is nervous. She pulled at her hair, bit her lip so there was blood left on her tongue, and she watched out of the window for falling trees.

In the city, the buildings collapsed at a near-constant rate, and the trees fell along with them. Tulip trees, the tall elms. In the evening, the caution of walking, of walkers. They wore shoes, took careful steps off curbs, looking both ways for bricks and flying steel beams. But still, some things happened: A man stepped off a curb, was squashed flat. A little girl climbed up steps toward a stoop and disappeared, leaving behind a small stuffed rabbit and a broken plastic watch. The young man, an architect, drew lines in pencil in a notebook, small and the size of his pocket, contained by the size of his pocket, by the size of his notebook and the ruled graphed lines, wandered the streets, became dizzy, saddened by the constant puffs of brick smoke, by the bending of beams. He sat in a green velvet couch in a coffee shop and looked out, and looked sad. Tell me, he said to the waitress, what is happening to the city? The waitress wore high-heeled shoes and seemed to hardly land when she took a step. She set down his coffee, touched the napkin lightly, shook her head so that her chin shook slightly, and turned and walked away toward someone else. The architect rubbed his hands on the knees of his pants, looked out to see the falling bricks and falling flags as the hotel went down, bricks falling first off the top, falling quickly, scattering, then further and further down, and stood up.

4.

As the old men holding chessboards come up from the subway, there is a noise. At first, it is a noise. At first, they hold their hands up to their foreheads, then hold them up like visors, and they are looking out, like tourists across a valley—look at all the little houses, they would say to themselves, look at how the sun glints across rooftops.

It is louder, louder than it was. Roof tiles crash to doorsteps; the fronts of houses fall, intact, into the streets, so exposed are bathtubs, bookshelves, nests of pipes. People look out, from the front. People look out, from the new cartoons of their buildings, blink their eyes since now there is too much sky, too many outside things to know what to do with. Once, there was a baby in a hat, the baby curled up on the inside, soft like on the inside of a pocket. He was so small, and the hat was blue, and the old men with their chessboards passed him around between them, like a plate of cookies, like a family photograph. They touched his soft hair, admired his round cheeks, but by the time he had gotten to the end of the line they had forgotten about him. Now the men forget about their chess games, sit down under trees and watch, the city collapsing around them, the grass bright green and the sky bright blue. There are too many things to look at, they think. They lie back; they rest their eyes; they are tired, their hats on their eyes, the way the ground shakes, the way the falling buildings expose the basements, reveal what should be on the inside always protected.

5.

Once, the woman and the architect lived in an attic on the edge of a field. Piled along the walls were all the things of attics: quilts, projector reels, transparent slides and photographs, and dishes that had belonged to someone else. They shuffled through them. They sat up late at night, surrounded by the boxes, feeling protected by where other people had been. She took photographs of tractors; he drew pictures of the buildings he wanted to build. They would have spires, they would have trapdoors and tiny bridges between rooms, walls of colored glass. They would be surrounded by grass, by low gray skies, be supplemented by treehouses, would sparkle. She would take baths at night, he said, lie back, look up through the skylights in the ceiling, at the stars. At night they looked up at the stars; they plotted a map of their coordinates. They poked at the map; they looked closely. Here here here, they said, pointing at the faraway places, at the streets where they imagined there were houses piled with snow. He touched her nose, said no, here, we should go here, pointing, pointing at the map, pointing at a spot that was blurry, fuzzed over. The woman looked closely, saw the hazy blue of lakes, saw the distant green of parks and the rusted-over tracks, saw the way things rose, in glass, the skyscrapers, and the map was blurry as she looked, and she said yes.

6.

Yes, he keeps singing as he falls. The world slips, slides past him—trees here, a piece of building there—and everyone on the street below him, feet on and off the curb, the concrete, cars, stopped. Yes, there are children playing marbles in the dark below. The music floats down, heavier than notes should be, as if they can be picked up, held on to in hands like pocket watches, like bits of china kept on a dresser, in a bedroom, and in the dark, and underneath the streetlights, light reflecting off his shoes, his belt buckle, his hat that has a medal pinned to it—he'd found it in an alley, it reminded him of his grandfather, and goldfish. The song is beautiful but tinny, as if pulled out of a Victrola, and his mouth curves around the words, opens, closes. The children shout, when they win, when they lose, pocket the marbles as there are pieces of paper, notes, passed along through the crowd, questions about the music, about the lyrics, about the speed and the trajectory, and when exactly the man who has jumped out of the building will land, because they are afraid of it, they are afraid of landing, and he doesn't.

7.

Around him the city clinked, like a dollhouse filled with pennies. A woman and a boy walked through the rain, the woman wearing a dark dress, carrying an umbrella. The boy carried a balloon, on a string, the balloon bouncing against the glass of windows and the signs clarifying street names. The architect followed them through the alleyways, ducked into doorways when they turned to look in windows, peeked out and tried to memorize their shapes: the curve of the woman's waist, the roundness of the little boy's head in a baseball cap. The train curled around the city, and there were whistles, the clinking together of rails, the steam and whistle of brakes. He wanted to stop them, wanted to ask them things, but didn't, afraid of how their voices would sound, that they would be harsher than he imagined them to be, so when they turned into the gates, the turnstile, pressed their faces against the glass, whispered to the ticket taker, pushed into the swimming pool, he stopped, walked back toward the center of the city in the middle of the wide street. There were no buses, only an occasional bicycle.

The swimming pool had been there since the days when people dug by hand. It had been dug with shovels, mud carried out in buckets, to make a hole. It had opened in the summer, its surface blue, its sloping sides painted, blue, and the children in a pack took running leaps, splashed in, all at once. They laughed with happiness. They sank like marbles to the bottom, their swimming shorts and suits with skirts as if weighing them down, as if the water weighed them down, and though each one had been pulled out, scooped out by arms and opened-up jackets, the pool had never been the same.

8.

The people work in stores, in offices, with white rolled sleeves, red handkerchiefs in their pockets. What makes up their days? Are there streetcars? What are the subways like? The subways are long and full of sounds. As the train is crashing through, the tunnel is whole, complete, shiny tiles announcing intersections, stops. A boy who thinks that he could ride the subway always, it is so comforting, so much bright light, sits on a train car, switches seats often, does not want to miss the way the train feels underneath his feet in different spots. At Fifth Street it is rough; at Elm, round and liquid like the ocean. The streetcars crack and clink in all their metal, and in the center of the city, where the city circles around itself, where all the roads connect and then spin outward, radiating, a man holds a canary on a fingertip; the woman holds an alligator on a string. The people stand, look and sit down, and stand back up, excited, clap. There is a show of jumping dogs, there is a dancing little bear. The people are afraid. Their mouths are full of teeth. In the city, there were dance halls, streetlights, trolley cars; now there are hotels and movie theaters, a carousel, the floors all covered with glass, the walls all missing bricks. The woman has found an apartment; the woman has taken her suitcase, her spectacles, her shoes, unpacked it. The woman keeps the alligator in the bathtub, feeds it goldfish, lets it walk around her rooms, sit on her sofa. The windows are cold. The building shakes slightly. The woman considers the motion, thinks she could dance to it if there were happiness involved. Thinks about the two-step, the fox-trot. Thinks about the movement of hips, about the solidity of floors. Her name is Lily; she has taught the alligator to dance, to shuffle. She pets the alligator; she sits in silence on the sofa not wanting to listen to noise.

9.

The city was made of granite, pillars. Tall windows and iron balconies. Marble statues, carved capes and gowns and curling hair, the tops of columns. The falling had begun when no one noticed, and then continued, slowly, in small progressions. A problem of falling, the people say; the city is heavy; the people are heavy: long velvet dresses, dark and three-piece suits. On the lake there is a beach and there are striped umbrellas and women in long bathing dresses, covering their thighs. And always there were people who wanted this collapse, who pushed at places in foundations, at the corners of the buildings, the elevators, the pillars; people who stayed up all night sitting at their desks, looking out of windows, burning lamps behind them, staring at plans in front of them, rubbing their eyes dry, the way the traffic swirled, and the streetlights. The city was a map of electric lines, of reaching out from centers, of volatile sparks and stacked-up floors, and bricks, and bricks. The city had been researched, careful, in the beginning when it was built, and then after when the collapsing had begun. At first a small touch of a finger, a flattening of a palm on a brick wall. First they listened for the ways the buildings settled at their touch. Then they planned, accounting for weather, accounting for movement: one tap, one practiced hard-landing jump, and everything would go. It was in this way the aquarium had fallen: one man pushing at the corners with his feet, knocking at the walls, hard, with his fist, circling around the hallways where the sharks hung, in the middle.

This is a problem, the architect said, of beams. Of foundations, of the formations of bricks, of what everything is made. No, the woman said, no no no. She looked, and the city was full of peonies, of flags hung out of windows, of the delicate fitting in of glass, and how it sparkled. The buildings falling through themselves were beautiful, she thought. It was beautiful and confused, and many crimes had been committed, and many people had sawed straight through the iron bars covering the pool, where this time they jumped into the water and drowned and drowned.

They, the city and its officials and the police and the men on the street corners and the women in the bookshops, were not sure if the purposeful collapsing was intended as relief, to hurry it up, the waiting and the worrying over cross fires. They were not sure if it was angry. The people in the city waited. And they were afraid, and any number of other things. The people kicking at the corners of the buildings, pushing at the walls with flattened hands, worked alone. They worked quickly. They said nothing. They wrote letters, sent them to no one in particular. Often, the letters spoke in desperation, in curses. Often, the letters said, simply, *I am tired.*

10.

In the solarium, the architect draws in pencil, on graph paper. He draws the city falling. How even slowed into a drawing it happens fast. Here is the crash. The people sit on curbs, on stoops, close to the ground so they can feel it shaking, so they can feel their feet flat on the shaking, and say, remember this? remember this? A man gets up, peers into a window that is empty. He breathes on the glass. It's empty, he says, when he turns around, looks at the men sitting on the sidewalk, their hands between their knees, tweed hats pushed back on their heads. Look at this, he says, look at this: matches scattered on the stairwell. Feet clattering on cement. In the room behind the window there is a stack of metal letters, big as buildings, red and chipping paint, peeling off, falling down, like dominoes. The man peers into the window, fogs up the glass and rubs the fog away. The wall stretches back to where he cannot see the end. He looks hard, but still he cannot see the end. The men who sit down on the curb get up, shove him out of the way; the men insist he shouldn't look. We don't want to know, they say, what is inside of anything.

11.

You can count up the collections, things that used to sit inside the buildings: here, a box of patterned Band-Aids; here, a bookcase full of tiny metal cars, some dented at the fenders, made to run on race courses made of books and pots and pans, often winning at the end, finally. Here shelves and shelves of nesting dolls, inside themselves, so many more of them than you would know. They didn't want to know. Here were the lists. Here was where they plotted all the buildings, made everything into lines, points, numbers. Here were the fine thin lines in straight black ink—pure, protected. Collapse the goldfish in, they thought. Collapse the wild animals. The lake, the colors of the water. Wrap it around with trains, and how they all remain on schedule. We are standing at the station. It is 3:42. You feel yourself slow down. You shake it off. Here is the train, here is always the train, and here is a birthday cake—it holds the city in.

12.

The woman couldn't answer her own questions. She walked. She walked to the opera house; she rounded herself around corners; she sat in a velvet seat and watched the orchestras, watched the flutists purse their lips, watched the dancing. She was horrified at the harshness of the ballerinas, the sharpness of the trumpets, the way, when she fell asleep, she was chased by a large and swimless fish. The fish chased her around the stove. She hacked at it; the knives she found in kitchens—the kitchens always changing, all of them different but having the same front door—were very sharp; the pieces just grew back. The fish was never finless, never missing tails or scales or head, no matter how much she tried to make it stay deformed. When she woke up the room was strange. She had trouble escaping from the seats, from the music stretching out in front of her. She had trouble knowing what she was doing there, the way the floors were always shaking, and the way she could tell from what direction the falling was coming. She shouldn't be so used to this, she thought.

13.

You feel yourself slow down. What do we know? Are there people there like this? People who are devoted to the city, to the spaces, preservation; people who would hold up walls, themselves, with just their hands, build a structure made of baseball bats and tables, bed frames turned over on their ends, to shore it up? Yes. Is the architect devoted to the woman? Does he instead go seeking out the sparking power lines or searching for the places where the crosswalks seem to sink? Both, maybe. He is not concerned with fixing. She has left him; he doesn't follow her. The people in the city have never gotten to the moment when they can time it, can predict it, can plot out any patterns. How has it affected them? They carry secrets in the forms of tiny coin purses, lucky rabbits' feet. They hold on to their charms while crossing streets, whisper words under their breath; they hold their breath, they feel their feet still on the pavement. They are glad that their feet are still on the pavement. That they stop still at stop signs. What will happen next? The uncertainty unnerves them. And so they walk quickly. And so the woman rides the trains, unsleeping. And so, there are buildings. The architect looks up. He sees the windows. He pushes, so carefully, to see them fall, the strike and smash of rustling glass, the way the bricks rain down.

The Oxygen Protocol

Brian Evenson

LATER HE WOKE UP, not entirely sure at first what had happened, what had been real and what he had dreamed. For a moment the utburd was still there, its bloody, childish face glowing faintly in the dim light and then vanishing. Was it real then?

But no, he thought, *how could it be real?* He shook his head and instantly regretted it. His head throbbed, his tongue was so thick and dry in his mouth that it felt almost like he was being forced to swallow a glove.

Why did I sleep on the floor? he wondered. *Where did I go wrong?* Pulling himself up against the wall, he slowly made his way to his feet. His vision blurred as he stood, but slowly came back into focus once he was on his feet and remaining still. *Good,* he thought. In the mirror he saw a face spattered in a black dust, as fine as graphite. He grimaced, saw that his teeth were gray too. More dust was getting in, which meant that the baffles were still clogged, which meant they were still following the oxygen protocol.

*

The screen was flickering; they were waiting for him. He pressed his thumb against its face to unlock it but nothing happened. He licked his thumb clean of the dust, tried again. This time it recognized him.

The screen offered him a slow swirl of light. If there was a pattern to it, it was not something that he could make out.

Halle, a flat voice said. *You are not essential personnel: Currently we do not require your services. You persist only at great risk to yourself and to your community. We urge you to follow the path your friends and neighbors have chosen and participate in the new oxygen protocol.*

"Thank you, but no," said Halle. His voice was little more than a whisper.

This is not a request, the voice said. *This is an order.*

Halle did not bother to reply. The voice had been saying the same thing to him for days now.

Look at yourself, said the flat voice. *You are suffering, Halle. By your own admission you are perceiving things that do not exist. The oxygen you are using could be better used by personnel essential to the functioning of the city. We say this for your own good. It is for the good of the city, to prevent the city from dying. You don't want the city to die, do you?*

"Of course not," said Halle, "but it hardly matters what I want. It's too late."

It is not too late, Halle, neither for the city nor for you. For the good of the city, we are offering to take care of you. We propose to reduce you to a benignly comatose state and then, when the moment is right, we will awaken you.

"How do I know you'll ever awaken me?"

A community cannot exist unless it is based on trust, Halle. We don't need to remind you of this. It is something you know. You have no choice but to trust us, Halle.

Without answering, Halle extinguished the screen.

*

He gathered the metal cup that he had left sitting beneath the open faucet all night to catch the slow drip. A quarter full maybe, the fluid inside opaque. For a long moment, he watched his face ripple on the water's surface, then swallowed the water down in one gulp.

Momentarily his tongue felt like a tongue again, human and slick, but this quickly passed. He lifted the cup and pressed it to his forehead. It wasn't cold exactly, but a little cooler. It helped just a little, just enough.

*

Dragging his hand along the wall, he made his way toward the door. His vision unfolded as he went, the straight angles of the wall and door starting to flex and bow. *Not real,* he told himself. *Lack of oxygen,* he told himself, and kept on.

But even still he couldn't help but start when the door slid open and he saw there, in the folds and buckles of the street, the face of the utburd. Its infantlike body was knobby and distorted from being stretched over the asphalt. He blinked and it was gone. Then he blinked again and it was back.

"What do you want of me?" he asked.

But the utburd said nothing, just smiled its toothless smile. Why was it coming to him? He had done nothing to it, nothing he could remember anyway. He barely knew what an utburd was, barely knew how to distinguish it from other ghosts. Seeing one was a trick of his brain, he knew, a simple hallucination. He could be hallucinating anything, but he was hallucinating an utburd. Why an utburd?

"I didn't kill you," he told it. "I don't know who did. There's no reason to haunt me."

The utburd opened its mouth and gave a cry like a bird. It had suddenly grown teeth, and they looked sharp. And then Halle's vision started to fade. He was getting worked up, he mustn't get worked up. Standing in the doorway, he closed his eyes and watched the creature flit along the insides of his lids, reduced to little more than a shadow. He made an effort to breathe carefully, regularly.

When he opened his eyes again, he could see clearly. He pushed out of the doorway and moved forward slowly into the street, trying to ignore it, careful not to exhaust himself. If he walked slowly and didn't get excited, he knew from experience he'd probably get enough oxygen not to pass out.

*

The next door was only a few dozen steps down the street, but to Halle it seemed to take forever. The asphalt and stone shone strangely in the light, which flickered from time to time. When he looked up, he saw that the simulator from the dome seemed to have a minor short, making the artificial light fluctuate strangely. Unless this too was a hallucination.

The utburd came and went, though it was there more often than not. Sometimes it was spread along the street itself, sometimes he saw it caught in the angle between street and wall—or even, when he finally reached his neighbor's house, in the shape his own shadow cast against the door. He knocked on the door once, out of habit, though he knew there would be no response. When none came, he inserted the override key and went in.

*

The entryway was empty, the floor covered with black dust except for the path his footsteps had rubbed clean in days prior. He followed this path again, shuffling slowly to the back of the room and through a door there. Beyond was a bedroom, an emaciated man within with a tube thrust down his throat and an IV tube taped to the back of his hand. Both tubes ran into a panel in the wall.

Halle reached out to touch the man and found his flesh startlingly cold. The man didn't respond. Carefully, Halle placed his ear against the man's chest and held it there. He could hear the sound of his own blood beating in his ears, but from the man he heard nothing. He waited, and waited, and then there it was at last: a dull thud as the man's heart beat once before falling silent again. He was still alive.

When Halle lifted his head and turned, he found the bedroom's screen to be illuminated, giving off a strange patter of color. Though he had done nothing to enable it, it began to speak at him.

We know you come here, Halle, the flat voice said. *Surely you must realize this is an invasion of your neighbor's privacy.*

"I just wanted to know if he was still alive," said Halle. He began to sidle past the screen, moving toward the door.

And have you satisfied your curiosity, Halle? Can you trust us now? If a community is to function, there must be trust. Where there is no trust, there is no community.

And then he had left the room, was in the entryway of the house. The screen there flickered suddenly on, assumed the same shifting colors, though as he looked at it this time, he began to believe they formed a face, that he was catching a glimpse of the utburd. It smiled at him, but kept its mouth closed.

"Why won't you leave me alone?" he asked.

Leave you alone? said the voice. *But you are alone,* it said. *You are the only one in this sector not to follow the new oxygen protocol.*

"No," he said, "I'm not talking to you. I'm talking to the utburd."

There was a moment of silence, the colors on the screen freezing, the utburd hiding itself again.

The symptoms of oxygen deprivation include, the screen finally said, *general dissatisfaction, problems of productivity, impaired sleep quality, breathlessness, headache, nausea, poor judgment, hallucination. Halle, how many of these symptoms do you currently possess?*

But Halle had already turned away, was already leaving the house.

*

The person in the next house was in the same comatose state, and the next, and the next. In the fifth house Halle found a box of crackers, half of them gone, the rest soggy. He ate them. In that same house, when he turned on the tap, out came a real trickle of water, the filter not yet clogged with the black dust. He stayed there for some time, leaning over the sink, his lips tight around the spout, drinking.

The utburd stayed beside him, scuttling about, and this struck him as a bad sign. There was a moment when his vision faded entirely. He stayed standing there, arm pressed against the rough wall of the house, trying hard to gather his breath. But in the end, he stayed conscious.

By the time he came out of the fifth house, the light of the dome had started to fade, but whether this was because an entire day had passed or because the dust had infiltrated the electrical system as well, it was impossible to say. He looked farther down the deserted street, which stretched as far as he could see in the pale light from the dome—the street he had been born and raised on now seeming empty and dilapidated and unfamiliar.

If he turned around, he'd have little difficulty making it back to his room by dark. But when he did turn, he saw the utburd there behind him, between him and the house, its pale face leering at him. It wasn't real, he knew, there was no reason to be afraid of it. But, for some reason, rather than going back he continued.

Perhaps, a part of him thought, *the utburd is a manifestation of something within me. Perhaps the utburd is a part of my mind trying to tell me something.* Meanwhile, another part of his mind examined this reasoning. *Symptom of oxygen deprivation,* this part thought. *Poor judgment.*

*

A series of additional houses, perhaps four more in all, each either empty or containing a motionless body hooked to an IV tube, with a feeding tube run down its throat. In each house he was careful to avoid the camera he knew to be there, careful not to respond to a screen if it began speaking, trying to make him admit he was there.

Halle, the last one said, *you have lost the ability to deal rationally with your situation. Halle, return to your home immediately so that we can care for you. Halle, your brain is no longer receiving enough oxygen for your existence to . . .*

But he had already lost track of what it was saying. The utbird, huddling there with him as he sat with his back against the wall out of sight of the screen, grinned. It looked a little bigger, he thought. Not much but a little. And now that it was here, close to him, he could see that the surface of its skin was covered with tiny, nearly transparent flakes of ice. He reached out and tried to touch it, but, smiling, it deftly avoided him, keeping just out of reach of his fingers. He reached for it again, stretching this time, and suddenly found his body slipping along the wall. There he was, lying sprawled on the floor now, the black dust clinging to one side of his face, and still not having managed to touch the utburd.

*

He lay there, listening to the screen's voice coming from somewhere up above him. The utburd was both there and not there, insubstantial enough now that there no longer seemed to be any point in trying to grab it.

He shook his head slightly, felt his eyes beginning to close, forced them open again. Where was he? What was wrong with him? Oh, yes, the new oxygen protocol. His body was slowly starving, he was slowly dying.

Halle, he heard from somewhere up above him. There, not far from his face, the utburd licked its lips. *Where are you, Halle? Why are you hiding from us?* The utburd slowly smiled but kept its mouth closed. *Teeth or no teeth,* he wondered.

Tell us where you are, the voice said. *Please tell us and then stay there. We will come get you.*

The utburd touched its fingers to its lips, made a slight hissing noise. Halle remained silent, watching it. *What will it do to me?* he wondered. And as he watched it, the world around him slowly began to go dim.

Halle, he heard vaguely, as if from miles away. *Can you hear us, Halle?*

He couldn't stop his eyes from closing, and yet he was seeing the utburd anyway, its image insubstantial as smoke and smeared on the inside of his eyelid, biding its time, waiting for him to lose consciousness. *More doors to knock on, more neighbors to visit, a whole city to see,* he thought. Suddenly, he realized he had lost track of the utburd somehow, that he was no longer sure where it was.

There's always tomorrow, thought the man, confused, who no longer was certain he was Halle.

And then he couldn't manage to think even that.

Luglia

D. E. *Steward*

Stolpersteine

Two official designations, almost from the beginning, *Arbeitslager und Vernichtunslager*

Those born after Hitler's sway cannot understand Berlin without entering that truth

The camps

There was a great deal more wanton brutality in last century's Faust's Necropolis

Of the sorts that seem, if not superfluous, not at all germane to Berlin now

As the Balfour Doctrine promises were forced at the end of the war by the Irgun, the Haganah, and the films Eisenhower's command and the Red Army made while liberating the camps, the Germans had scattered like chicken farms across Europe, Berlin was already rushing toward recovery

Such a perplexingly appealing city

Full of the past as if it had no past

But with a "dark backward abysm of time" as real and as impressive as the *Brachiosaurus brancai* skeleton in its Museum für Naturkunde

A behemoth that perhaps weighed fifty tons

That could lift its vegetarian head fourteen meters above the swamp forests and savannas

And had a four-hundred-kilo heart to push blood that high

No matter how dramatically the Thousand-Year Reich flared and collapsed, to most that recent past is as dead as a *B. brancai*

But for a few unavoidables like the tens of thousands of *Stolpersteine*

Embedded in the sidewalks engraved block roman on slightly bossed polished brass markers the size of cobbles

In front of the door of Wielandstrasse 13, in Charlottenburg just off the Kurfürstendamm, "HIER WOHNTE / MARTHA GLASER / GEBRN WIELER JG. 1873 / DEPORTIERT 1942 / THERESIENSTADT 8.3.1944 / ERMORDET"

At Wielandstrasse 15, "IN DIESEM HAUSE / LEBTE CHARLOTTE SALOMON VON / HIRER GEBURT AM 16 ABRIL 1917 / BIS ZUR FLUCHT AUS DEUTSCHLAND IM JANUAR 1939 / 1943 WURDE SIE NACH AUSCHWITZ DEPORTIERT VERGISST SIE NICHT LANDES JUGENDRING BERLIN"

Wielandstrasse 12, a fresh red rose horizontal on the sidewalk at another, "HIER WOHNTE DR. JULIUS GRÜNTHAL JG. 1875 / FLUCHT HOLLAND / DEPORTIERT SOBIBOR / ERMORDET 14.4.1943"

Wielandstrasse 31, "WOLF M. EHRENREICH, ERNST W. EHRENREICH, AUSCHWITZ 1943," along with three other names

Seven more with details of deportation and death below those on a wall plaque by Wielandstrasse 31's front door

With its shaded side garden and pleasant green-stucco facade

Eight more names with deportation and death dates at Wielandstrasse 30

All at Wielandstrasse apartment houses a block from Walter-Benjamin-Platz

Around the corner from George-Grosz-Platz

Grosz miens and faces still are everywhere

Forlorn Grosz pensioners standing alone usually, still a few with the gray forage caps of the recent epoch

In Hackescher Markt a huge Grosz woman sprawled on a bench by her bags reaches over her stomach to her privates, brings her hand out to smell and licks a finger

Skinheads, Grosz features, pushing fast through S-Bahn cars

Generally with shaved heads dressed *tout noir*, with partly shaved heads only mostly in black

Cold War junk, T-shirts, and other cheap regalia sold out of old Checkpoint Charlie's guard shack, now a tourist kiosk as if for inflatable beach toys, manned by two Grosz types in ersatz Cold War uniforms, one a GI, the other Red Army

Where the Wall stood is a narrow line of cobblestones laid across Berlin, upon the city's street-level base something like a maze on a Romanesque cathedral's floor

And overlaid on that, and on antique remnants of the Third Reich, is a singular component of Germany's twenty-first-century present, Ostalgia hanging in the air

History, a rat glue board there to be stepped on by the unwary

Self-pitying sentiment for the simpler *Ossi* life in a nonmaterialistic East

The social services, the officially apparent egalitarianism, the consensus on national ideals, the nearly muted and near absence of Holocaust guilt, isolate mystique of things like Trabbis

The dramatically heroic statues and the Palast der Republik, as monument to the DDR's fortitude

Forgetting the intimidation, torture, and the widespread spying of citizen on citizen

Forgetting that about one in a hundred of the DDR's citizens died at the hands of the state

Willingness to ignore the post-1989 exposés

Das Leben der Anderen (2006) as parable of the open records of the Stasi

The Markus Wolfs, the Christa Wolfs

The Uwe Johnsons

It's all so complicated, the divided loyalties

Everyone a German anyway

Thinking Beethoven's Quartet for Strings in B-flat, op. 133, "Grosse Fuge"

The Nazis and the German nationalists, the ex- and the non-, the fascists and the communists, the Ost and the West

Following 1945 it was estimated that about two hundred and fifty thousand people were arrested in the four occupation zones with suspected past Nazi activity

While Martin Heidegger off in the Schwarzwald, with the war for all he wanted lost for good, literally overnight in 1946 changed his handwriting style from Germanic to Latin

And then the drumbeat paradox of Beethoven, Brahms, and Bach withal

As Romain Rolland put it back before Deutschland's worst manifestations, *"Un pays où tous sont musiciens"*

Rolland's last years were as witness to the depths, he died five months after the Liberation of Paris and five months before the end of the war

Not that contemporary unitary Berlin has reinvigorated its culture to match Romain Rolland's ironic flattery

Konzerthaus Berlin, Kammermusiksaal, Philharmonie, Staatsoper Unter den Linden, Berliner Festwochen, Rundfunk Berlin-Brandenburg, Musikinstrumenten-Museum, Waldbühne on summer nights

Schloss Charlottenburg, Bauhaus-Archiv, Gemäldegalerie, Akademie der Künste (Pariser Platz), Berlinische Galerie, Jüdisches Museum, Neue Nationalgalerie, Alte Nationalgalerie, Deutsches Guggenheim, Käthe-Kollwitz-Museum, Museum für DDR-Kunst

The Pergamon

The new Berlin is a monochrome of its past because the Jews are gone

To see where, visit the Grunewald S-Bahn station on the way to Potsdam and walk through the tunnel where the deportees were herded to Gleis-17 where there are commemorative plaques detailing each transport with date, the number of the doomed, and their destination

Berliner professionals, academics, writers, artists, musicians who were the audiences and patrons of what made pre-Nazi German culture

The current liberal ecology-aware identity that's taken hold of the European bourgeoisie proliferates in Germany but without the subtle, urbane passions and tolerance of the old Jewish intelligentsia

The great city

Tiergarten, Charlottenburg, Wilmersdorf, Moabit, Tiergarten-Süd, Hansaviertel, Tempelhof, Schöneberg, Kreuzberg, Mitte, Neukölln, Friedrichshain, Pankow, Prenzlauer Berg

It stretches far on the North German Plain in a peculiar cultural emptiness

It has a fresh and savvy mood of whoever we are, we're moderns and we are in this life together

But that with only about twelve thousand Berliner Jews legally resident—some reckon there are more—and about two hundred thousand in Germany as a whole

Traumatized in part by the American carpet bombing that began in 1969, most Cambodians did not know who was running their country and ordering the massacres, and still today Pol Pot's motivations and the mechanics for killing a fifth of his country's inhabitants, mainly cadres bashing skulls and pushing the victims into mass graves, are a mystery

In Rwanda the 1994 killings, again perhaps a fifth of the population murdered, mostly one-on-one by slashing pangas, orchestrated by Hutu radio propaganda and ethnic stereotyping, joined by a large segment of the Hutu majority, happened as out of a mysterious black maw

But in Europe of the early 1940s, there is no mystery to the Holocaust and the mass killings of Roma and Slavs, no question as to the motivation, no ambiguity as to method and numbers, few imponderables about the policy and its execution, only confounding acquiescence by the Master Race population in the ultimate modern barbarity

Civilized Germany the worst of all

Ending in Berlin, April 1945, with the heavy American bombing and the Russian shelling of the center, Hitler's bunker madness and his Nero Order to destroy all caches of food before a protesting and starving populace, the tragedy of the juvenile Volkssturm resistance to the invading Russians, the obdurate loyalty of Nazi cadre

Many thousands more civilian deaths at the end

Götterdämmerung

Then Berlin itself became the Checkpoint Charlie of the whole Cold War

The tragedy and brutality of the Russian occupation, the dangerous tensions between the four occupation sectors, the Airlift in 1948, all distant and obscure in the unified present

It was so close when the border to the East was closed dramatically on Sunday morning, August 13, 1961, and the Wall went up with East German soldiers and Vopos poised to shoot anyone who sprinted from the Russian sector

And it was as stunning as it was when it came down in November 1989

On the Helmstedt Autobahn from Copenhagen on August 14, in the Reuters and UPI wire rooms, American Embassy people hanging around to get the news too, it was still teletype machines then

Rattle carriage bang bell jam, strip up ratchet zing tear off what's just come in

It was like Haydn's triumphant final symphony, the 104th

But we were there to witness, filing what the whole world wanted to know

Using Telex in the other direction, anxious mostly not about Washington and Moscow but about what was happening outside there on Alexanderplatz and in the Mitte

With the right identity papers that week it was still possible to enter the East from Bahnhof Zoo on the S-Bahn along the Tiergarten to Friedrichstrasse and Alexanderplatz

There were Russian tank crews mounted and at the ready around Friedrichstrasse, red battle flags stuck on the turret ammunition racks

Soviet Army tankers in their coveralls and leather helmets, radios crackling, amiable and nervously curious about what was happening over in the western sectors

On the empty S-Bahn trains coming to the West watched two episodes of people making it through and breaking down in relief once past the final Vopo check

Angry Berliner thugs waiting on the steps in Bahnhof Zoo violently hassling anyone off the S-Bahn from the Russian sector

That same old German blame-the-victim syndrome, lose the war and blame Roosevelt's international Jews, blame the hungry and the floods of foreign refugees in 1948 for the Airlift, the DDR builds a wall and it's the fault of those people who want to get across it

Then on Sunday afternoon, August 20, LBJ and Willy Brandt walking a reinforced U.S. Army battalion in off the Helmstedt Autobahn beneath manned Russian machine-gun emplacements on the cutbanks

Summer green grass, sunny summer Sunday afternoon

Nobody out there on the western-sector side of the autobahn checkpoint had the big-picture idea of what was happening except that it was an extremely exciting time to be there because the future of everything seemed to be at stake

The summer before, in 1960, off eastward through Checkpoint Charlie with a DDR transit visa and a new Volkswagen beetle bound for Warsaw via Frankfurt-am-Oder

Left the autobahn before the river to take a look at communist Frankfurt, loudspeakers on the telephone poles, evening empty streets, pulled in by Vopo Grenzpolizei for questioning before being allowed to cross the bridge into Poland

This time the way out of Berlin was a Frankfurt-am-Main flight from Flughafen Tegel in the old French Sector

A Turkish taxi driver so voluble about the wonders of his international German life that we were close to exchanging e-mail addresses and almost hugged in front of the terminal

Roma!

Joyce Carol Oates

THE HOTEL BELLEVESTA GLITTERED by night like a multitiered wedding cake and by day gleamed in the sun—dazzling white stucco, marble, and stained glass framed, on its ground floor, by banks of gorgeous crimson and purple bougainvillea. The original building had been the private residence—the "palazzo"—of a seventeenth-century cardinal of the Roman Catholic Church but in more recent centuries had been allowed to deteriorate; now totally renovated, and refurbished, as a smart new five-star tourist hotel, it was an architectural gem amid the mixture of staid old historic buildings and expensive boutiques, designer shops, and beauty salons on the fashionable Via di Ripetta.

Their suite was on the seventh floor, at the rear of the hotel as they'd requested. From one of the windows they could see, across the Piazza del Popolo, the tall, stark, beautifully silhouetted cypresses of the Borghese Gardens less than a quarter mile away.

Alexis shivered with an emotion she could not have named—anticipation, apprehension. She'd seen—she was sure she'd seen—these heraldic-seeming trees in a premonitory dream of the previous night, as she'd seen an archaic obelisk resembling the monument at the center of the piazza, not clearly, but with a powerful stab of nostalgia.

"This is wonderful, David! We'll be happy here."

In other hotels, in other Italian cities, they had not always been so happy. But this was Rome, and this was the five-star Hotel Bellevesta. It would be the final hotel of their Italian trip.

Their room was elegantly furnished, much larger than they'd expected—with dusty rose silk wallpaper, an astonishing twelve-foot ceiling, and a marble floor that exuded the coolness of centuries; a crystal chandelier, of a size disproportionate even to this large space, and not one but two French doors. Framing the wide windows were draperies of white silk and a thinner, gossamer fabric, over a dark blind designed to keep out both sunshine and street traffic; the effect, even at midday, was secluded, cave-like—a space in which one could sleep, undisturbed, or reasonably undisturbed, in the midst of the thrumming city.

"Come look! It's like—Venice. . . ."

The larger of the French doors opened onto a small balcony and from the balcony you could see, six floors below, a quaint cobblestone street, narrow as a lane, and the rear—fascinating in its detail, like a weatherworn topographical map—of a block of apartment buildings joined together like row houses but dissimilar in size and height and condition; one or two appeared to be vacated and shuttered, as if abandoned, while the others—so far as Alexis could see, without leaning too far over the balcony railing—were clearly lived in, populated. The rooftops too were remarkably heterogeneous—some were made of ceramic tiles, of that lovely earthen orange hue reminiscent of rooftops in Venice, while others were more roughhewn, of some crude material like tarpaper; still others had been converted into rooftop gardens with lemon trees, rosebushes, and small plants in cultivated rows, resembling a setting in a doll's house, in miniature. There were chairs and tables precariously positioned, it seemed, at the edges of rooftops as at the edge of an abyss; there were drooping clotheslines and laundry hanging like swabs of paint in an Impressionist painting; over all hovered clusters of TV antennae like antic grave markers. Here and there were stucco huts silhouetted dramatically against the sky—and the sky above Rome, on these warm summer evenings, like the sky above Venice, resembled an El Greco sky of bruised clouds, subtly fading and melting colors. On many of the older roofs, moss grew as well as grasses and even a scattering of a bluish purple wildflower Alexis had been noticing throughout Italy, for which she knew no name—a bell-shaped cluster flower that appeared exquisite to the eye but was in fact tough and sinewy, with surprisingly sharp thorns, as she'd discovered in the ruins of the Roman Forum on their first day of sightseeing in the city.

So strange! Like a pueblo dwelling, in the American Southwest: many individuals crammed together in a relatively small and primitive space. The busyness of Rome, the startling modernity of Rome, seemed remote here; the alley was too narrow for traffic other than motor scooters, and there weren't many of these, at least not that Alexis had noticed. Yet she didn't doubt this was truly Rome: This was the Rome in which ordinary citizens lived, as oblivious to the glittery Hotel Bellevesta as the Hotel Bellevesta was oblivious to them.

"David? Come look. The backs of these buildings—like a painting, or a fresco—fascinating. . . ."

David stepped out onto the balcony but didn't speak for some time. It was like him to withhold comment; he would see for himself what Alexis wanted to show him, for he wasn't readily susceptible to others' enthusiasms. Just as he didn't often reply to Alexis's remarks if he thought them naive, banal, or self-evident—in their travels together, as in their marriage, it had come to be David's role to hold back, to express doubt, or even skepticism, or cynicism, while Alexis maintained her girlish manner of openness, curiosity. The wife plunging head-on, hopeful; the husband thoughtful, inclined to hesitate.

Like figures on a teeter-totter: The one who is elevated is dependent upon the one who is heavier, and grounded.

So many ancient and lapidary figures they'd been seeing, in the tourist world of classical antiquity, Alexis could almost think that she had seen just this figure, carved in stone.

"Isn't it? The peeling walls, the beautiful fading colors? Like Venice?"

David leaned out over the balcony railing, just conspicuously farther than Alexis. His forehead creased in the effort to discern what there was here to be seen, if it was so very exceptional. The strange heterogeneity of stucco dwellings, the jumble of rooftops, TV antennae, part-opened windows, and shuttered windows—yes, there was something beautiful about the scene, David conceded, or anyway intriguing: "Not quite like Venice since there is only one Venice but yes—very intriguing."

How happy it made Alexis, when her husband agreed with her! She had always deferred to him, as she had always adored him; his feeling for her was more modulated yet she didn't doubt that he loved her, or would have said that he loved her—this was all that mattered. In their daily lives, which, in the enforced intimacy of travel, became yet more intense, no matter was too small, trivial, or domestic to Alexis, to be proffered to David's judgment; all matters seemed to her about equally crucial, as if their marriage, though an established fact, was nonetheless always in doubt, depending upon her husband's ever-shifting, ever-unpredictable assessment of her worth.

"'Roma.'"

The word seemed magical to her, a floating sort of word, unlike the dour-sounding "Rome."

Through the city there pulsed a heightened energy so palpable you could nearly see, taste, touch it—but this energy, Alexis thought, was only just on the surface: Beneath was a hidden subterranean world, a kind of vast cave, or catacomb, brooding and impersonal, with a far slower pulse, like the movements of glaciers, or continents. In the visible Rome, a place of elaborate encoded maps, tourist pilgrims by the thousands drifted each day—each hour—in quest of some sort of profound, secular miracle: a succession of visions to photograph, to appropriate as *experience*. For the life of the senses is a continuous, depthless stream—it has no accumulation, it has not even a destination; the conclusion of a life in time is of no more consequence than any preceding moment; so there is the yearning for *experience*—if not personal, the collective and impersonal will do.

But this deeper Rome, this secret, dark-brooding, inward, and subterranean Rome was inaccessible to the outsider, and could not be appropriated. So each evening when they returned to the Hotel Bellevesta after a long day of sightseeing, they were made to feel dissatisfied, incomplete; particularly, David felt this, the suspicion of being cheated, or missing something; as if an entire page in their Rome guidebook had been torn out, to mock him despite his Nikon D300—newly purchased for this trip to Italy, after considerable research.

"'Rome.' Not 'Roma'—to us."

Alexis laughed, though David might have meant this as a rebuke. For he too was smiling—in his ironic way.

On the first heady days of their trip, which began in Venice, David had taken hundreds of photographs, rapidly, his fingers moving as swiftly as his eye; there had been a grim efficiency to his picture taking, Alexis had thought, for, with the new digital technology, in contrast to older, more calculated photography, one scarcely needed to "see," still less to think—in theory, the photographer could photograph virtually every moment of his presence in a place, from which, later, in solitude, he could select just those few moments of worth. In this way, the photographer was postponing the very experience of his trip—by snapping pictures, he was deferring the effort of evaluation. When David showed Alexis the multiple images he'd taken on the LCD display, some of them including her, she'd been struck by how closely the pictures resembled one another, with only minute differences between them; in multiples, none had appeared particularly distinctive. "But which do you prefer?" David asked. "Which would you like me to print?" His tone was just slightly coercive, for he liked to present "choices" to Alexis as if testing her.

Which images to print? When they were so much alike? Alexis had no idea. Yet she could not say, *But you're the photographer!—you must judge.* And so with a bright smile she told her husband x, y, z—reasonable choices that seemed to placate him, at least temporarily.

Back home, in their hilltop suburban home in Beverly Farms, north of Boston, David had had little interest in photography—he hadn't time for such an interest, or patience; on this trip, Alexis had begun to see a side of her husband she scarcely knew, which had been hidden from her until now.

He was fifty-seven years old; Alexis was several years younger. The gap in their ages—though not considerable—had always been a determining factor in their relationship as, it is said, just a few minutes' seniority makes a considerable difference in the intimate lives of identical twins.

Of course in any relationship there is the more dominant individual—the one who is loved more than he can love in return. But the love of the weaker for the stronger is not inevitably a weak love. Alexis had always thought, *He will see, someday. He will understand how I love him.*

Ostensibly, the Italian trip was to celebrate their thirtieth wedding anniversary. But there was some other motive on David's part, Alexis thought. He was a reticent man, you could not know what he was thinking, and so often in their lives together Alexis had been quite mistaken, trying to imagine what her husband was thinking, but she felt now, in him, an almost panicked need to *get away*—the place to *get away to* only just happened to be Italy.

Rarely had they traveled together in any ambitious way, in the years of their marriage. For David had had to travel frequently for business reasons and always he'd traveled alone, bringing his work. This trip, David had made it a point not to bring work—nor would he speak to Alexis about his work. He had wanted a new, different experience—clearly. And in the early days of their trip (of three weeks) he'd seemed happy, engaged. For travel is in essence problem solving and David was one who liked the challenge of problem solving even if, in travel, the problems to be solved are both transient and trivial; as, in David's profession, he'd built a career of considerable success out of a painstaking relish for problem solving in matters of "tax law"—a body of information continuously shifting, and requiring reinterpretation. What dismayed him about their trip was the *crowdedness* everywhere, which seemed to diminish the significance of travel, and the individual traveler; particularly in Rome, David was annoyed by the constant traffic—taxis, motorcycles, and scooters, buses and trucks emitting clouds of exhaust—those small European automobiles that appear, to the American eye, almost like toys—"And so many tourists! And American pop culture—brainless and ubiquitous."

He spoke vehemently, seriously. Alexis supposed it must be a truism of travel: You are most appalled by what most resembles what you are. But she couldn't suggest this to David; he would be hurt or angry at her. Like all tourists, David imagined himself a traveler. *He* was not a mere tourist, *he* was not brainless, for he was himself—*different*.

At night, enervated from another of their late, protracted, expensive dinners, as from a carefully calibrated day of sightseeing in the midsummer heat—mostly by taxi, though often, inescapably, on foot—up steep stone steps and down steep stone steps—amid packs of fellow tourists—they were yet too overstimulated to go to bed, despite their exhaustion; a final drink, and then—maybe—another drink, from the minibar, brought outside onto the balcony, where, in the cooling night air, they found themselves gazing at the row of apartment buildings across the alley—now mostly darkened and shuttered; above, the nighttime sky of Rome, lights reflected against a lowered cloud ceiling; immediately below, the cobblestone street like a dark stream. From time to time they heard snatches of voices, music, laughter—shouted words, presumably in Italian—unintelligible.

Was the language beautiful, Alexis wondered. Or was it just—foreign? Like so much of what they'd been experiencing since leaving home.

"Another drink? Or—more ice?"

"Both."

Eventually, Alexis thought, David might tell her what had propelled him to Italy—what problem in his corporate-tax-law work had proved insoluble, or whether in fact (she did not want to think this, and had no real reason to think this) his employer, allegedly the third-largest pharmaceutical company in the world, was suggesting early retirement for him, as for others in his division, in the wake of financial losses.

In the man's eyes the unspoken command *Don't ask! Don't even imagine you want to know.*

It would have been a daunting task to count the rickety-looking little outdoor stairs that ascended to the multilevel rooftops across the way or the numerous windows overlooking the alley; at first you thought that the windows were uniform, of the same general proportions, but a second glance suggested that each window was distinct from its neighbors in some small, subtle way. All of the windows were outfitted with shutters that were closed at night and against the heat of the afternoon sun; one or two of the windows seemed always to be shuttered, Alexis had come to notice, as if no one lived inside, or harbored a secret so terrible it could not withstand the light of day. Most of the shutters were black, but some were dark brown, and a few were beige; some appeared to be recently painted, and in good repair, while others were faded and weatherworn, peeling, leprous looking; yet, like Venice, exuding a curious quaint, heartrending charm, the particular beauty of decay.

The particular beauty, Alexis thought, of another's decay—not our own.

She'd been staring at a lighted window across the alley, on the fourth floor of one of the older buildings: Inside, at what appeared to be a table, a man was sitting, eating—of his face, only his jaws were visible—and of his solid, muscled body, only his torso and upper arms; the man might have been in his early or middle thirties; he was dark skinned, swarthy; he seemed to be speaking to another person, or persons, at the table, but Alexis couldn't see anyone else; he was gesturing as he ate, with abrupt, jerky motions of his beefy arm, like a puppet—for how like puppet movements our motions are, detached from speech and from the more subtle expressions of our faces. Alexis thought how odd this was—or maybe not so odd, since most people adhere strictly to their domestic schedules—that the dark-skinned man had been seated at the table the previous night, more or less in the same position, at about the same time, when she and David had been sitting outside on their balcony with glasses of wine. And, a flight up, in an adjoining building, almost directly across from the balcony, at one of the windows that had been shuttered through most of the day, a woman lay on a couch watching TV, as she'd watched TV the previous night; as it had been the previous night, the light in the room was an eerie pale blue that flickered and quivered. The woman was middle-aged, and full bodied; Alexis was embarrassed to see that she wore something like a negligee, carelessly wrapped about her soft, slack naked breasts, and her hair was blonde and disheveled; clearly, the TV-entranced woman had no idea that strangers were observing her in so intimate a way—or did she?—or that the sidelong sprawl of her body on what appeared to be an old, heavy piece of furniture suggested Rousseau's iconic, final painting *The Dream*. As in the famous painting the framed image of the voluptuous-bodied woman in pale bluish light exerted a powerful nostalgic aura—Alexis stared, and stared. (Was this voyeurism? Was she intruding, unconscionably, on another's privacy? Or did the fact of the woman's anonymity—and Alexis's anonymity—somehow render the act innocent, as it could have no consequences for either individual?) "So strange! That woman, I mean—watching TV—you'd think she'd pull her blinds, or close her shutters, wouldn't you? After all, she must know—there's a hotel here, people in many rooms here. . . ."

Though there must have been at least thirty feet separating the balcony and the window, and, if the woman had glanced up, to peer out her window, she'd have had difficulty making out the couple sitting so very still on the darkened balcony two stories above her, Alexis spoke in a lowered voice as if fearing the woman might hear her, and take offense.

"What? Who? Oh—*her*. . . ."

It was a vague reply, coolly courteous. As often David replied to Alexis when she said something self-evident, banal, or of little interest to him.

Hesitantly Alexis said: "I suppose we shouldn't watch. It's like that Hitchcock film *Rear Window*—you don't want to look, but . . ." Had she made the same remark the previous night? Her words sounded familiar to her, unsettling.

Carefully pouring the last of a miniature bottle of red wine into his glass—for Alexis had barely touched hers—David didn't reply. If he'd been aware of the voluptuous, sprawling woman on the couch and the dark-skinned man at the table, he gave no sign, as, several times that day, in the art and archaeology museums they'd visited, he hadn't appeared to be very much engaged in the exhibits, though dutifully, when not expressly forbidden by signs, he'd taken photographs of major artworks, the facades and interiors of churches, astonishing Roman views from windows and hillsides. For much of the evening he'd been in a distracted mood: He'd had too much to drink, which wasn't like him, and at dinner, in a three-star Tuscany restaurant above the Spanish Steps that was highly recommended by his much-thumbed *Michelin* guide, he'd been upset by something on the bill—some ambiguity about the price of the wine, or the number of bottles of sparkling water they'd consumed, or the bill itself, which, translated into U.S. currency, was considerable.

By degrees, as if bemused by Alexis's interest in the anonymous individuals across the way, David began to observe them too. Though, if he'd been alone (he allowed Alexis to know this, obliquely), he would scarcely have noticed them.

"If this is an intimate look into the lives of ordinary Romans, it certainly isn't very revealing, or significant."

"Oh, but I think it is 'revealing'—'significant.' We can't judge people by just seeing them, outwardly."

"We can't? How do you think they judge us?"

"I don't see why we should judge other people at all. Just to see them, to acknowledge them as different from ourselves . . ." Alexis's voice trailed off; she'd lost the thread of what she meant to say. Now another window had lighted up, like a stage set, on the fifth floor of a stucco building to the right of their balcony; this building, the width of two windows of ordinary size, was so narrow as to resemble a tower, which had faded to a faint sepia color like an old photograph. The roof of the building was partly ceramic tile, cracked and broken, and partly the ruins of an abandoned roof garden in which tall grasses and wildflowers grew. Alexis had noticed this garden before, and had wished that someone, a child perhaps, might have climbed the outdoor stairs to it, but no one had come. There was something both slovenly and exquisite about the narrow building, which reminded Alexis of an illustration in a child's storybook.

Inside the newly illuminated room, through a scrim of tissue-thin curtains, a figure was moving, indistinctly. Alexis couldn't see if it was a woman or a man who'd switched on a dim light, or had lighted just a candle. Alexis said, in her conspiratorial lowered voice: "It seems wrong to watch them somehow, but—I suppose—it's harmless. They aren't actually *doing* anything—like the characters in the Hitchcock film."

David said, with a snort of derision: "They certainly aren't doing anything of interest! And it isn't as if, their windows open to the world as they are, they can have any expectation of privacy."

"Well—we can't see their faces anyway. We have no way of knowing who they are."

Alexis spoke uncertainly. She was beginning to feel ashamed, so openly staring into a stranger's window.

But now, in the newly illuminated interior, the shadowy figure was moving briskly; unlike her neighbors who seemed inert as waxworks figures, this one was intent upon an action, or a sequence of actions, of some precision, though it wasn't clear what she was doing—dressing? undressing? posing in front of a mirror? *dancing?* Alexis strained to hear—was it music?—jangling hard-rock pop-American *music*?

David, no longer indifferent, stared frankly at this new scene. It was soon clear that the shadowy figure was that of an attractive young woman, or girl, with swaths of shining black hair that fell to her waist—exposed white shoulders and upper arms, bare legs (was she undressed? in a camisole top of some near-transparent material, or in night wear?), and she seemed to be alone, except that she was talking, or singing, to herself, as she moved her arms about provocatively, shifted and wriggled her breasts, her narrow hips, and shook her startlingly black hair, to the accelerated beat of not-quite-audible music; very like a seductive figure in a film who, while solitary, glimpsed in isolation, is yet assured of being observed by countless staring strangers. How reckless of the girl, to leave her window unshuttered, or her blinds open, facing the Hotel Bellevesta with its seven floors of rooms! Alexis thought, *She must know that we are watching. That someone is watching.* It was dismaying to her, alarming, that her husband would stare so openly at the partially undressed girl even as she, Alexis, was sitting close beside him, invisible to him as if he were alone on the balcony.

"I suppose—we should go to bed. It's past midnight."

"Is it!"

Unlike the others who scarcely moved, the girl with the waist-long black hair kept in motion, a sort of frenetic, continuous motion, like an animated doll. She was slender, agile—spirited. As David and Alexis stared, she stopped abruptly, turned, and hurried out of the room—like an actress unexpectedly leaving a stage, to the surprise and disappointment of her audience—but then returned, carrying something—a sort of stick, or wand; with quick steps she came to the window, as if to peer accusingly upward at the American couple staring at her from their balcony above, but instead she disappeared behind the wall, a moment later reappearing, and then disappearing—were her movements deliberate? teasing?—or accidental? In the background, on what appeared to be steps in a doorway, a small creature appeared—a cat or a dog—that brushed against the girl's bare ankles sensuously.

"No, a dog. One of those little yapping breeds."

Like the girl, the little animal disappeared, and reappeared; it followed the girl out of the room, and back into the room; approached the window, and disappeared beneath the windowsill, as if (perhaps) there was a food dish there. The girl paused to pet the animal, and to talk to it. (Or was someone else in the room, out of sight, to whom the girl was speaking?) Beside the attractive, animated girl, the other, older woman and man seemed very dull; they resembled those eerily bulb-headed, featureless, and bandaged-looking mannequins in the early Surrealist paintings of Giorgio de Chirico Alexis had seen the previous week in a museum exhibit in Florence.

David disliked the Surrealists. David disliked and distrusted any art—any way of life—that did not acknowledge what was *real*; and, to David, what was *real* was obvious and incontestable as looking into a mirror.

Of course, the girl was young—much younger than the others. An aura like a flame seemed to glow about her slender limbs, and in the scintillating waves of her waist-long black hair. Her face was obscured to them, behind the gauzy curtain, but appeared to be heart shaped, and the skin markedly white.

"See what she's doing now?"

"What? What is she doing now?"

"Vacuuming."

David was correct: The girl had dragged a small canister vacuum cleaner into the room, and was briskly vacuuming the floor, chairs, and cushions. And so late, past midnight! There was something grimly frenetic about her movements as if she knew herself observed, and her hyperactivity was in some (reproachful) relation to her invisible audience, a rebuke to their voyeuristic passivity.

Alexis said uneasily, "She should draw her blinds, or shutter her windows—anyone could be watching from the hotel. A man could try to figure out where she lived, and come to find her. . . . She's old enough to know better. She isn't a *child*."

The girl seemed to have shed another article of clothing. For it was very warm in the midsummer Roman night, which was airless in this part of the city. Beneath the thin white camisole shift she was wearing just very brief white panties.

"It could be dangerous. Her behavior. Who knows who might be watching, if not tonight, some other night. In the United States . . ."

Alexis tried not to sound reproachful, resentful. It might have been the girl's very recklessness she envied.

David continued to stare frankly at the girl, with a look of faint disdain, bemusement. His eyes were heavy lidded, his forehead creased. He'd been tired out by the exertions of the long day and the long tourist days had been accumulating since their departure from

Logan Airport more than a week before. As he stared, the seductive-teasing girl vanished, again. It was impossible not to think—even as it was unlikely—that the girl was aware of her audience, and wanted to torment them. In her wake, the little white creature rushed out of the room on short, clumsy legs. Abandoned on the carpet was the small canister vacuum cleaner with its hose like an outflung limb.

In the other windows, there began to be a minimal sort of movement. In the pale-blue-TV-lighted window, the woman on the couch roused herself, as if from a trance; she was sitting up, or partially sitting up; her negligee swung open even as, with a sort of mock alarm, her plump arms lifted, shielding her breasts. Her broad, heavy-jawed face was partway in shadow and had the look of a half face—a kind of primitive mask. In the other, lower window, at last the dark-skinned man rose from his place at the table, and moved toward the window; still, his face wasn't visible—only just the lower part of his torso, cut off by the window frame. On the table behind him were plates, a glass, and a wine bottle. . . . You could see that there was a lighted candle on the table, that had burnt low.

"Well! We should go to bed, it's late . . ."

David said nothing. He made no move to rise. Alexis knew she shouldn't make this request more than once: Though David frequently ignored her remarks, he did not like her to repeat them.

". . . almost twelve thirty. And tomorrow, the Sistine Chapel. . . ."

This seemed funny somehow. Tomorrow, the Sistine Chapel! The ancient ruins of the Roman Forum! The Colosseum! The Palatine! The Vatican, the Borghese Gallery, St. Peter's Basilica!

On the wrought-iron balcony outside their seventh-floor room in the Hotel Bellevesta they sat, the middle-aged American couple, as if unable to move; in a pleasurable trance gazing across the alley at a row of mostly darkened and shuttered apartment buildings. Above were rooftops obscured by shadow and, farther above, the Roman sky, opaque with layered clouds, lightless, which resembled a cathedral ceiling, its fanatical detail softened by shadow.

Just when you think that your life is *run down.*

Just when you think that your life is *frayed, worn. Done.*

If they'd had children, perhaps. But there had not been a time for children, not *the time.*

David had said, wait. We can wait. And Alexis had said—what had Alexis said?—Alexis had said yes. Of course we can wait.

Now, so many years later it could not ever be *the time*. What had been *the time* was now, irrevocably, past. And so they'd come to Italy, to a succession of beautiful Italian places—after Venice they'd gone to Padua, Verona, Milan—to Bologna, Florence, Sienna, and San Gimignano—and at last Rome. In planning their trip, David had booked them longest in Rome.

Ostensibly, to celebrate their thirtieth wedding anniversary: This was the account they gave to others, which others were happy to hear.

For all journeys are journeys of desperation—the journey takes us *away*.

For most of the time that she'd known him, David had been a man driven and defined by his work: obsessed, ambitious. There was a particular sort of joy—Alexis didn't want to think that it was inevitably masculine, but she'd never seen it in any woman of her acquaintance—in ambition that has triumphed. (Triumph over a rival? Is there any other sort of triumph? In the Pitti Palace in Florence Alexis had stared appalled at a succession of over-life-sized sculpted figures by Michelangelo depicting Hercules in the quasi-heroic act of killing his opponent—Antaeus, an Amazon warrior, a centaur, among luckless others. *The Triumph of Victory* was the bombastic title. Tourists whose nerves would have been shattered by a poorly prepared restaurant meal or hotel rooms lacking adequate services stared solemnly at these ugly tributes to brute masculinity, knowing themselves in the presence of *serious art*. There was no female equivalent to such extravagant and excessive brutality nor even the general recognition that such an equivalent might be missing.)

Within their social circle, and certainly within their families, David was considered a highly successful man. To David himself, his success was marred by the fact that others were more successful, who did not seem deserving, as he knew himself deserving. Now, in recent years, these rivals were fading, disappearing; David's new rivals were of another generation entirely, young enough to be his children, though David didn't feel paternal toward them, any more than they felt filial toward him. Hired in a shrinking job market, these young rivals were yet more highly paid than David had been, at the same rank, after adjustments for inflation; he knew that they were unbeatable—time was on their side. He hadn't become embittered but only, as he often said, sharper, wiser.

This sharpness showed in his face: Beneath his smile of bemused or ironic well-being was an abiding wariness, the alertness of one who is anxious not to be disrespected, taken less seriously than he merits. David's once-abundant hair had thinned and his skull was prominent, like some implacable inorganic substance; Alexis almost couldn't remember what he had looked like as a young man. His contemporary self, his middle-aged self, seemed to have consumed his youth. Yet he seemed to her attractive still—despite his ironic way of frowning while smiling as if the very act of smiling were a sign of weakness, vulnerability. He had not had patience with weakness in himself or in others and now that he was older he was having to adjust his sense of manliness. As a man ages, the Darwinian notion of natural selection shifts its meaning and other types of morality begin to exert their appeal.

"A barbaric world—but what art!"

Another time they'd gone to the ancient ruins for which the city was best known. The old, unspeakably cruel yet "noble" civilization that predated the modern, its acres of rubble set off by fluorescent orange construction barriers—a jarring juxtaposition of ugly synthetic materials and the sun-baked stone of antiquity. Everywhere were decayed yet beautiful carvings, monuments that seemed to Alexis's untrained eye a testament to the uses of futility—the uses one might make of futility.

The history of the great Roman Empire was fraught with savage cruelty, violence, and delusion, yet a visionary self-assurance that seemed lost now, in the West. Who could believe that gods mated with mortals, to create a race of demigods? Who could believe that there was anything godly in even the stunning blue Mediterranean sky? Or that any "empire" was privileged over another?

Christian Rome and Catholic Rome that followed—so many centuries!—another empire inflated and inspired by metaphysical delusion and the terrifying self-assurance of delusion. But these centuries too had waned, and could not be resuscitated.

"Though I suppose we are not so much less 'barbaric' now. Our waning American Empire, our mission of 'democratizing' the world for our own economic interests. . . ."

David spoke with unusual vehemence. He was not by nature a political person; his political views were centrist, economically conservative. He had little trust in any politicians, yet a sort of residue of wistfulness for the idealism of his youth—the generation that had come of age in the late 1960s and 1970s—the waning idealism of the great revolutionary decade of the American twentieth century, the bitter ashes of the end of the Vietnam War.

Strange for David to speak as if, for once, the impersonal were intensely, painfully personal. Alexis felt a stab of concern—or was it love?—for her husband, that he seemed to be losing his old, unexamined sense of himself as a man among men, a rival among rivals; in Rome, their destination city as well as the city of their imminent departure, more markedly than in any of the Italian places they'd visited, David had become oddly indifferent to news of home; he seemed to have stopped checking his e-mail; even more, he was susceptible to the most superficial distractions—annoying fellow tourists in the Bellevesta, throngs of people in marketplaces and piazzas, boisterous young Italians on motorcycles—in a crowded side street he'd paused to stare at a young girl with long, coarse black hair like a horse's mane, a girl carrying a motorcycle helmet who was dressed provocatively in tight-fitting black leather, spike-heeled shoes, and black-net stockings, bizarre black-net gloves to the elbow, but fingerless; the underside of her jaw was defaced by a lurid birthmark, or a tattoo; poor David gaped, until Alexis tugged at his elbow.

He'd seemed dazed, smiling. A middle-aged sort of smile, as of one waking from a dream, uncertain of his surroundings. *He is a lonely man,* Alexis thought. *My husband is a lonely, vulnerable man.*

By degrees, David had ceased taking photographs except of the most exceptional sights—postcard sights. He'd taken many more photos on his digital camera than he would ever print—many more than he would ever examine. He'd left his expensive camera in a restaurant—a young waitress had run after them, to return it.

Like many other tourists, he wore sandals, but David's sandals chafed his pale feet. His clothes were expensive sports clothes, short-sleeved linen shirts, pastel colors, stripes, limp from the heat, rumpled. His scalp, exposed by his thinning hair, had burnt in the sun, but David disliked wearing any sort of hat. Where in the past he'd insisted upon making travel arrangements, now he more frequently depended upon Alexis to make them. The city's great public museums and galleries weren't air-conditioned—even their cool marble floors and high ceilings weren't sufficient to compensate for the heat of Rome. Fans blew languid air from room to room. There in the Borghese Gallery came David in a blue-striped shirt damp with the sweat of his solid, compact body—shuffling in Alexis's wake like an undersea creature only dimly aware of its environment and pausing to stare, with a mild sort of astonishment, at the pale marble Bernini *Apollo e Dafne.* While Alexis moved eagerly ahead, consulting museum maps, David fell behind. In this exotic place, this beautiful city, he had but little sense of its geography, and little interest; he had not the slightest knowledge of the Italian language; Alexis had long ago taken French and Spanish, and so could recognize crucial words; she'd prepared for the trip, hastily, with language tapes, while David hadn't had time—of course.

In their marriage, he'd made Alexis the repository of such things—such airy and essentially useless activities. As he'd made Alexis the repository of emotions too raw, elemental, and disorderly for a man to acknowledge: The deaths of his own parents he'd needed Alexis to register, that he might grieve for them. Without Alexis, would he have grieved at all?

Here in Rome—"Roma"—Alexis turned to look back at her husband trailing in her wake, or sitting in a café awaiting her; he'd lost interest in his guidebook, or was feeling just too tired. She tried to imagine life without him—his death, one day. She shivered as if a pit were opening at her feet. She felt—she didn't know what—a kind of numbness, nullity. She wondered if this was all that she would feel, one day, fully—or whether she was deceiving herself, in this mood of suspension, indefinition—in "Roma."

It was Alexis's idea to see an exhibit of Picasso pen-and-ink drawings in a private gallery near the Piazza di Spagna but the exhibit was disappointing to her, and unnerving: a succession of "erotic" drawings in which the same several images were repeated with ticlike compulsion, a leering/lascivious sort of glee; what pathos in this evidence of a once-great (male) artist reduced, as in a nightmare mimicry of senility, to so few visual ideas—fat, voluptuous, naked female, satyrlike younger man, elderly male voyeur. The sex features of the female and the satyr were exaggerated, as in a caricature, or cartoon; the elderly voyeur was Picasso himself, a painful yet defiant self-portrait of sex obsession. Staring at the walls of these drawings, each meticulously and strikingly rendered yet, in the aggregate, numbly repetitive, Alexis felt the irony of the great artist's predicament: He had lost his imaginative capacity to invent new images but he had not lost or transcended his sex obsession; as if, underpinning all his art, the great variegated art of decades, there had been only this primary, primitive obsession, a juvenile fixation upon genitals. How much more profound—more "tragic"—the final, death-haunted work of Michelangelo, Goya, Magritte, Rousseau's *The Dream. . . .* But David was shaking his head, smiling—"Well! These drawings are certainly . . ." letting his voice trail off suggestively, so that Alexis was prompted to say, "Pathetic. I think they are pathetic, demeaning."

David laughed, amused by Alexis's reaction. "It's the subject that upsets you, Alexis. 'Erotica'—high-class pornography. Graphic sex makes women uneasy, they know themselves interchangeable." Alexis said, "And men? What do you think you are?—each of you unique?"

David turned to stare at Alexis, shocked as if she'd slapped him. It was totally out of character for her to speak so sharply and so coldly to him, or to anyone.

It felt good, Alexis thought. Her heart beat in elation, a kind of childlike thrill. Discovering that she could speak to her husband in such a way, and in this foreign city in which they knew no one else and had only each other for solace.

Now recklessly she said: "You can stay at the exhibit a little longer, if you'd like to see it again. I think I'll go out alone—I want to buy some things."

"Of course I don't want to see it again," David said, hurt. "I've seen enough—I've seen enough 'art' for a long time."

"I'll see you back at the hotel. In the café."

Alexis was walking away—she would leave him there in the chill interior of the art gallery, staring after her in amazement.

"But—Alexis—what time? We have a dinner reservation. . . ."

"I don't know—6:00 p.m.—or a little later. Good-bye!"

Desperate to leave the man, to be alone.

Shopping! In the elegant streets near the Piazza di Spagna she saw her blurred ghost figure in the windows of designer shops and boutiques; she lingered longest in front of lavishly air-conditioned stores—Armani, Prada, Dior, Dolce & Gabbana, Louis Vuitton—whose doors were brazenly opened to the street in a display of a conspicuous wastefulness of energy. Her mood was near euphoric—she smiled to see her ghost figure merging briefly with the angular, sylphine figures of mannequins. She thought, *But there is nothing I want. What is there in the world, anywhere—that I can want?*

Boldly she entered one of the chic designer shops. It was exciting to her, to be alone like this; exciting to be alone in the foreign city, without the man dragging at her, pulling her down. She was not by nature a "consumer"—if she'd taken pleasure in buying things in the past these were likely to be things for other people or for the household she and David shared, that Alexis almost single-handedly oversaw. Now she stared at flimsy little shifts on chrome racks, cobwebby sweaters, halter tops scarcely larger than handkerchiefs. Prices were outrageous, ludicrous: three hundred fifty euros for one of the cobwebby sweaters, which looked as if it was unraveling. Nonetheless she would purchase something—she would *shop.* She thought, *If I can want something. Then—*

To extract pleasure from *consuming*! Almost it was a kind of erotic sensation, or might be—this sense that one must be worth a luxury item, if one can purchase it.

Alexis examined one of the shifts—an abbreviated "dress" designed to wrap around the body like a scarf, or a shroud; it was made of a beautifully rippling material that more resembled metal filings than fabric. Five hundred ninety euros! And another striking dress, sleek black silk with a "tattered" skirt that fell well below the knees, priced at seven hundred euros.

Alexis thought, *If I could be the person who would want this! Who would be transformed by this. . . .*

She would buy a present for her sister's daughter—a little faux-denim jacket maybe—a leather belt with a gold buckle—an absurdly high-priced pullover in a delicate, near-translucent fabric like muslin—except she knew that her sixteen-year-old niece would probably not wear anything Alexis bought for her even once, and wouldn't be able to return it as she did in the U.S. She allowed herself to be cajoled into trying on one of the shifts, in a striking fuchsia color; it was certainly unlike anything she owned, or had ever worn. "*Bella!*" The chic black-clad salesgirls hovered about her, smiling in admiration.

She was thinking of her father, her poor public-school-superintendent father in Ames, Iowa, whom she'd loved so much, who had saved money diligently, as the adults of his generation were conditioned to do; her father's chronic anxiety about medical and hospital insurance; his plan for longtime health care at home for her mother and for himself, and both had both died fairly suddenly—both in hospitals. Her father's concern, which had shaped much of his life, had turned out to be for nothing. The money he'd saved he left to Alexis and her sister, who had not needed his hard-earned "estate." Out of pity for this kindly, overconscientious man, not wanting to emulate him, Alexis bought the fuchsia shift. She bought a patterned pullover for her niece and a silk shawl for her sister. Daringly, she bought a pair of open-backed leather sandals, salmon-colored, with a two-inch cork heel—she'd been seeing shoes like these on fashionably dressed women in Rome. She thought, *Is this my Roman self? Is this me?*

She saw with surprise her youthful mirror reflection; even her windblown ashy blonde hair with its gray streaks looked striking, attractive.

In another yet more elegant and expensive designer shop she made several more purchases, impulsively. A lightweight summer sweater with seed pearls scattered across its front—for herself. And a bizarre near-backless dress, sleek dark purple, with a single tight-fitting sleeve—her left arm remained bare. She smiled; the dress was utterly ravishing, very expensive. In a mirror she saw the stylish Italian salesgirls exchanging covert smiles—at the American shopper's expense? Yet their compliments were lavish, their voices were high-pitched little bird voices—*"Bella!"*

She thought of David. He would be surprised! Maybe he would be impressed.

She thought of her lost, beloved father, and she thought of David, her husband. She felt a wave of love for the man who was her husband—who seemed to be distracted by something, some secret, he could not share with her, just yet; like a wounded creature that flares up in rage against anyone who comes too near, David would nurse his secret hurt. She would forgive him: She would buy him one of the gorgeous, ridiculously priced Italian neckties. She took some time deciding, before buying him a Dior tie in dark purple silk stripes, to match her Versace dress.

Alexis! Thank you. This is very beautiful. . . .

He would look at her in surprise, yet he would be moved, she knew. Though he professed to scorn presents, he was grateful for a particular sort of attention that suggested his own good taste, his distinction.

Bella!

It was 5:40 p.m. when she took a taxi to the Piazza del Popolo. Though burdened with packages, she meant to walk back to the hotel by way of the block of apartment dwellings that had exerted such a fascination from their balcony—how curious she was, to see these dwellings close-up! She would have an advantage over David, she thought: And maybe she would tell him what she saw. And maybe not.

But amid a deafening din of traffic, on foot, in her newly purchased open-backed sandals, which in a rash moment she'd decided to wear out of the store, she couldn't seem to locate the street or even the cobblestone passageway behind the hotel. It was as if, as soon as she ventured out of the area of the Bellevesta, and its surrounding glittery stores, she was in an urban no-man's-land of narrow streets, treacherous motor scooters, delivery trucks exhaling waves of black smoke, littered sidewalks crowded with foreign-looking pedestrians—many of whom were clearly not Italian but Middle Eastern, Indian, African. Several times she was jostled—in a panic she gripped her shoulder bag, that it might not be torn from her. (Of course, their guidebook had warned of the folly of carrying shoulder bags in Rome.) When at last she located an alley between buildings just wide enough for a single vehicle to pass, it was desolate and littered, and smelled of garbage; from the front, the block of buildings was seen to be aged and derelict, abandoned and shuttered—seemingly slated for demolition. No one had lived in these decrepit quarters for some time.

"How strange! This is wrong. . . ."

Fearful of getting lost, Alexis retraced her steps. Once on the busy Via di Ripetta, she located the Hotel Bellevesta with no difficulty—its shining stained-glass, stone, and stucco facade was dazzlingly conspicuous. But she couldn't circle the hotel, of course—the way was blocked by a high wall, and when she made her way to what she believed might be the rear of the hotel, in a littered and foul-smelling alley near a Dumpster, she saw nothing familiar. In a doorway at the rear, two hotel workers lounged smoking and staring at her—dark eyed, very foreign looking, unsmiling. Alexis smiled nervously at them and backed away. She'd had no luck trying to determine where their beautiful hotel room was—on this side of the hotel, or another? In the enervating heat of late afternoon she was beginning to feel light-headed but she didn't want to give up the search for the mysterious block of apartment dwellings that she yearned desperately to see—but after another twenty minutes she found herself wandering aimlessly on a traffic-wracked street she was sure she'd never seen before—Via di Tiberio—and felt again a sensation of panic, that she was lost, or near lost, in the very vicinity of her hotel. And it was strange to her, and unnerving, to be alone in this foreign place.

Crossing a particularly uneven cobblestone street, narrowly avoiding being struck by dark-helmeted motorcyclists rushing two abreast, Alexis lost her balance and tripped in her elegant new sandals. She turned her ankle, winced with pain—"Oh! Oh help me": These words of childish appeal came unbidden—but luckily she hadn't sprained the ankle. Her heart beat as if she were in the presence of danger and her face smarted with perspiration. She thought, *This is my punishment now. For who I am. But I won't give up!*

For another half hour in the fetid heat she continued her quixotic search—she was dogged, desperate—limping—but could not find, in these mostly commercial backstreets intersecting with the Via di Ripetta, anything resembling the block of apartment buildings with the wonderful jumble of rooftops and the quaint, faded colors like peeling walls in Venice, which she and David had seen from their balcony. Another time she stumbled upon the first row of buildings she'd seen—on a nameless little street—an entire block of abandoned and shuttered dwellings, clearly slated for demolition. The dark-skinned man so slowly eating dinner, the disheveled woman sprawled on her sofa watching TV, the seductive girl with the waist-long scintillating black hair—where were they?

"There has to be some explanation. . . ."

She shivered; she was feeling sick. Seeing now to her dismay: She was carrying only three articles—her handbag and two shopping bags. She must have left the third bag in the taxi, containing the Dior necktie. It had cost one hundred ninety euros. . . .

Shaken and exhausted, she returned limping to the hotel just before 7:00 p.m. The sky was bright as daylight though partly massed with malevolent-looking storm clouds. In the hotel courtyard café there was no one but a middle-aged German couple and, flirting awkwardly with a young waitress who was clearly trying to humor him, a stocky, slump-shouldered older man in a blue-striped sport shirt—he turned, and it was David.

"Alexis. Back so soon."

Palast der Republik, Berlin
(August 28, 2006–December 19, 2008)

The Berlin Project

Michael Wesely

—Translated from German by Ross Benjamin

GERMANY'S CAPITAL HAS BEEN shaped in a particular fashion by the epochal developments of the nineteenth and twentieth centuries. Various political systems and social upheavals have been etched in the urban landscape of Berlin. The city is widely regarded as a symbol of Germany's checkered history—its ideologies, progress, decay, division, and reconstruction have left their marks everywhere. The city's turbulent past can be read in the remains of medieval city walls and early modern pioneering achievements, petit-bourgeois allotment garden colonies and ecological urban restructuring, industrial ruins or tenements from Germany's founding period. The past is manifest in the form of megalomaniacal, monumental architecture as much as in Real Socialist prefabricated construction. It is visible in war ruins and wastelands, in baroque splendor and modernist minimalism. A number of uncompleted urban planning designs have also contributed to Berlin's heterogeneous appearance. This juxtaposition of diverse concepts has thereby produced a field of tension unique to Berlin.

Since reunification, Berlin has again been experiencing a great boom and enjoying international attention. Within a brief period of time, entire neighborhoods have been radically altered or rebuilt. In many ways, the city is being redefined.

In this project I took long-exposure photographs of important sites in Berlin. Each exposure lasted a year, capturing current developments of the city. In these long exposures, the evolution of urban space becomes perceptible as movement. Construction projects and building modifications are documented along with preexisting architecture. A contrast thus emerges in the urban structure between growth and change on the one hand, and uniformity and immutability on the other.

Kanadische Botschaft, Leipziger Platz, Berlin
(February 3, 2003–April 5, 2005)

Michael Wesely

Potsdamer Platz und Leipziger Platz, Berlin
(April 20, 2004–January 12, 2006)

BAHNHOF POTSDAMER PLATZ
BAHNHOF POTSDAMER PLATZ

Michael Wesely

Flughafen Tempelhof, Berlin
(July 1, 2008–July 1, 2009)

Michael Wesely

Schloßplatz, Berlin
(September 26, 2008–September 26, 2009)

park inn

Switch
Emma Smith-Stevens

Jan can hear Mike's neighbors listening to Billy Joel. Before he started beating her with twelve inches of thick rubber piping, he'd said, "Forgive me, they do this every Friday. They listen to Billy Joel and Bon Jovi, the ladies who live across the way." Then he'd sighed and said, "Airshaft apartment," and pulled a neatly coiled rope from under his bed.

Jan knows what other people, women in particular, would think about what is happening to her. They would say that she hates herself. They would talk about things like abuse and disrespect and childhood. They would use the term self-esteem. Some people she knows would bring up *Equus*. But this is religion. This is surrender. Pain is a power greater than all others, because it is with pain that we come into the world, and through pain that we leave it. In between the darkness of these twin passages, the Gemini of agony, is life. For the past five months, this is how Jan has found her life.

It is night and there are pigeons in the airshaft, perched on a ledge, beating their wings. It is spring, and through their efforts, the underfluff of winter is freed from their plump bodies. Against the darkness, it falls like snow. There is the groan of a machine, something pushing air, the whirr of a fan blade. Then all is quiet. Her body is sensation; it is geography, forming itself through volcanic eruption, the heat of renewal. Jan remembers herself one strike at a time, the sting of the rubber piping amplified by the silence of the blow—a whisper: *This is me, and this is me, and this is me.*

Childhood. Does anybody really identify with their childhood, as though that memory is really a part of who they are? Does anybody really own that little person as a miniature version of themselves? To Jan, childhood is a story, mainly told by others. She is not sad about this. It is freeing. Where other people say, *I am such and such a way because x, y, and z happened to me as a kid*, Jan says, *Whatever.* Jan is responsible for the here and now. Jan likes Mike because he is that way too. He never talks about his childhood, never blames other people for the way he is.

Here is how it starts. Jan shows up to Mike's midtown apartment at the appointed time, wearing what he has told her to wear, clean and fresh from the shower. She has waxed off all her pubic hair, as per his request, and is wearing white cotton panties. Her boots are knee-high, and her hair is in a ponytail and smells like freesia. She raps her knuckles against the door three times, and he opens it. Sometimes he leaves it cracked, if he is busy with something and may not hear her knock. When she comes in there is no greeting. She follows him to the bedroom where he sits on the bed. She lies face-down over his lap. He lifts her skirt and spanks her a few times over her panties, then lowers them and runs his fingers over her skin. She feels the calluses on his fingers, from playing some stringed instrument. She guesses that it is guitar, but for all she knows, it could be mandolin, or banjo. She has never asked. Then he spanks her bare flesh, rhythmically, predictably, stopping to caress her, followed by a blow when she least expects it. She smells the pillow upon which she rests her head. It smells like Mike.

Before Mike, Jan spent two years with a boy named Benjamin. Once, she started to tell Mike about it, describing the relationship as "stiflingly appropriate." She thought he would find this clever, but he seemed profoundly bored. Another time, after they were spent and lying in his bed, Mike had said a few words about his ex-girlfriend. He said that she'd been "spectacularly disloyal," but she could tell by the way he stopped there that he still loved her. No *That bitch.* No *But that was a long time ago.* Jan knows it wasn't very long ago at all, and that Mike is still in love. He never makes eye contact with her. He has never kissed her on the mouth. After six months, Jan wonders if she has not arrived at the intermission of a something far grander than what she and Mike have. She has begun to worry when she smells him on the pillow, because she likes the smell of his bad cologne.

Around the same time, she wants to say things that cannot be said. *I want more. Kiss me. I had a rough day.* She begins to wonder if the rebellious code under which they conduct themselves is not stifling in its own way. There seems to be very little room for error. She doesn't know how to be anymore. Still, when she sits on the subway, riding downtown to her dorm, she likes the feeling of the hard seat pressing against her bruises. Each time she shifts, she is reminded, *This is me.* Where was she before Mike? She was any girl, any girl in her school, going to class, dating a human rights major, listening to singer-songwriters. Now she eats meat, listens to classical music, and wonders what will happen when she graduates. She wants to think that her being a student doesn't matter to him, that she possesses some kind of maturity that makes it irrelevant. That it is something they have transcended. But in reality, she knows that the opposite is true. They have transcended nothing; the fact that she is a student is part of why she is there.

Mike has a bin where he keeps ropes and toys underneath his bed. Spring is turning into summer, and the window to the airshaft is cracked. Jan, blindfolded, can hear him rummaging through the bin. She wonders for the first time, on what other women have these toys been used? How well has he cleaned them? She has been tied masterfully by Mike, who recently took a course in Shibari, a Japanese form of rope bondage. She had asked him what sorts of people had shown up for the course.

"It was hilarious," he said. "All these couples dressed in sweat suits, tying each other up. And meanwhile, the class was taught by an Amazonian dominatrix, dressed in black leather."

Did you bring someone? Who was your partner? More things that cannot be said.

She hears him slide the bin over the wood floor, back under the bed. "Have you been a good girl?"

"Yes, of course."

"Did you touch yourself today?"

"No. I promised you I wouldn't."

"Liar."

"I swear."

"Slut."

This has become an old routine. Jan is addicted to the life that it gives her. Afterward, the people on the street, her classmates, and professors, even her own parents, have been painted, arriving in the world anew. Before Mike, Jan used to wonder if she was the only thing that was real, and if everything and everyone else was a figment of her imagination. Now people have secrets and insides and worlds of their own. Lines are crisp, yet there is a penetrability to the world around her, and Jan skirts along the edges of boundaries, pressing herself against the divides between people and objects and other people. *I am a thing,* says each entity she comes across. *You may pick me up, you may chew me, you may use me, but you can never be me.*

Jan does not tell anyone about Mike, not because he is thirty-seven, or because of what they do together, but because she met him on the Internet. She knows that she is attractive, and has begun to find confidence in her intelligence, and would find it humiliating for people to know that she went onto an alternative-lifestyle dating Web site. So long as it is her secret, it remains empowering rather than mortifying. The power comes from the fact that she acted upon a private thought, and made it materialize. *This is what I want. This is what I shall have.* Yet as time goes by, Jan begins to regret the particulars. For example, after exchanging several e-mails, Jan let him have her body without so much as going out to dinner, or sharing a cup of coffee, or having a conversation about anything other than the task at hand.

When they are through, Jan takes a shower. She does not feel dirty, and is not washing him away. She likes the bar of Dove soap and the generic shampoo that he uses. There are no pictures hung on the white bathroom walls, and she is glad, because there is nothing to distract her from her own soapy fingers over her own body. She feels that it is the gift he gives her. When she gets out of the shower she dries herself with a white towel. She carefully hangs it over the curtain rod.

In the living room where all surfaces are covered with neatly stacked papers and binders, books and CDs, she sees he is not there. Nor is he in the bedroom. She finds him in his office, checking his e-mail. He tells her he will be through in a moment. She dresses, but now he is wearing headphones, his face bathed in the light of the computer monitor. She says his name, and he turns around, his index finger raised. Just one moment. Jan sits in the kitchen wanting a bowl of cereal, but there is no milk in the refrigerator. She waits for fifteen minutes, coughing through two of Mike's Camels. Finally he pops his head out of his office, headphones around his neck.

"Ach, so much to do tonight."

He calls her sweetie in e-mails, and ends them all with *xo*. This fact suddenly seems sinister to her. She smiles and waves, slinging her purse over her shoulder, and lets herself out.

It begins to dawn on her that Mike does not respect her. She has looked at things all wrong, assuming that because she is giving him the gift of herself, he will be grateful. He approaches her body with hunger, with precision, but not with passion. Jan wonders if there is any truth to common beliefs that she had dismissed as sentimental: if perhaps there is a connection between passion and love. She begins to realize that respect cannot be assumed, and she detests Benjamin all the more for spoiling her that way. She had lost interest in him quickly, but stayed with him for security. Passion had always eluded her in that relationship, but only now was the reason becoming clear. He was too easy, he gave her respect for nothing. She does not want to become Mike's Benjamin. She is learning how things work. At the very least, she has learned that there is a definite connection between desire and deprivation.

Jan is in her dorm room, alone, writing a paper for a sociology class called Domesticity and Power. She does not like the class. She disagrees with the basic premise of the course. It is the assertion of her professor that women have wielded tremendous power through their influence in the domestic sphere, as the bearers of children, and the effective heads of the household. Jan believes that this is a phony rationalization for the continuance of what is clearly a sexist dichotomy from the start: the separation of the domestic realm from the outside world. Call it what it is, she wants to say to her professor. Don't use words like archetypal and womb and goddess.

Jan's cell phone rings, and it is Mike. She holds the phone in her hand, letting it ring three times, then answers it.

"What are you doing?" he asks in a low, velvety voice.

"Writing a paper."

"What are you wearing?"

"I'm a little busy actually. Can I catch you later?"

"Sure, OK." He sounds surprised, although not clearly disappointed. In the past, Jan has always dropped whatever she is doing when he has called, and it occurs to her that he must know this.

"All right. Bye," she says, consciously tuning her voice to a cheerful yet distracted pitch.

"Be a good girl," he says, and hangs up.

Jan listens to the silence for a moment, and then closes her phone and puts it in a desk drawer. She sits at her desk, and is surprised to find that ideas for her paper come readily, and she is soothed by the click-click of her own typing.

A week goes by, and Jan begins to wonder if she might have read Mike all wrong. He did, for example, once give her an unsolicited massage. On another occasion, he asked her what she thought about a novel they had both read. Did he make eye contact with anyone? His aversion to it was so extreme that she wonders if perhaps it wasn't personal, that maybe it was part of some pathology. Simultaneously, Jan begins to consider the fact that there is a whole community of people who are into bondage and sadomasochism. She and Mike are not the only ones. Thinking about this begins to excite her.

She contemplates going to parties where she might meet people, but knows that she must first acquire the appropriate clothes. Leather, latex, heels. She does not have these things. But they are there. All of it is there. Mike is no longer the gatekeeper.

By some magic, he seems to understand this. He sends Jan an e-mail in which he states that he's missed her, and would she like to have dinner. They have never gone anywhere before, only to his apartment. Jan replies that she will have to check her schedule. A day later, she responds that she will be free on Saturday night, and Saturday night only, so if he wants to eat, it will be then. But, she adds, she only has a couple of hours. Only enough time for a meal. She sends the e-mail, instantly desiring to take it back and change it. She wants to be in his bed. She wants bruises. No, she tells herself. She wants respect. She wants to start over.

They meet in the East Village, at a Japanese restaurant of Jan's choosing. She arrives ten minutes late, having lingered in a coffee shop, watching the clock, waiting for the time to pass. A warm night, the sky is heavy with impending rain. The glow of the city illuminates the undulating clouds. She is dressed up, wearing a black miniskirt and a black sequin top. She is not wearing her knee-high boots, and her hair is down. Each time that lightning illuminates the sky, Jan thinks, *I am doing this. And this. And this.*

Mike is sitting at a corner table when she arrives. She spots him from the cover of the darkness, outside under the awning, peering through the window. He looks terrible. His fingers are laced through his disheveled blond hair, and he is grimacing at the table, biting his lower lip. She has never seen him in any condition other than collected, calm. He looks like someone who has been stood up. No, worse. He looks like a madman.

He kisses her on the cheek, holds out her chair, peels her coat from her thin shoulders. He says he is not hungry. Although she is not sure she is, she orders three sushi rolls and two pieces of sashimi. While they wait for the food to arrive, she realizes that there is something going on with him, something beyond anxiety over her lateness, or her recent reticence toward him. Again she feels as though she has arrived at the intermission of something grander than what they share, and all she can do is wait for the show to start.

"Hey." His eyes meet hers with a tired smile. Jan has just finished her last bite. "Do you remember in the mideighties, how they changed the names of the dinosaurs?"

"No."

"No, of course not. You're too young."

"Maybe I remember. I wasn't really into dinosaurs when I was a kid."

"Get this. They changed all the names of the dinosaurs, which I'm totally convinced is a big conspiracy. Like, brontosaurus became apatosaurus. Therosaurus became iguanodon. How ridiculous is that?"

"Yeah, that's crazy." Jan realizes that Mike is trying to introduce himself to her. She listens keenly.

"There's a lot of stuff like that, where experts make these so-called discoveries, and rename things. I'm convinced that they are in cahoots with the toy-store companies, and book publishers, and they do it all so that people can't pass on their toys and books to their children, because they have become historically inaccurate. Do you see what I'm saying?"

"Yeah."

"Another example! Oh, and this is a good one. Did you know that Pluto got demoted from planet status? I would bet anything that they did that just so people would have to buy all new stuff. Think about all of the millions of classrooms around the world that had to buy new books, just because Pluto is no longer a planet."

Jan does not know what to say. Mike pays the check, and she notices that he is a good tipper.

Mike's house is messy when they arrive. It is usually clean, but there is more junk everywhere than Jan can imagine possible for a mere week of accumulation. There are dishes all over the counter, clothes strewn on the living-room sofa, kitty litter crunching underfoot in the bathroom. She is shocked. Mike is a very neat person. It is important to him that things be in their place.

He asks her quietly if she would like to get in bed, and she is relieved. She waits for him to sit down so that she can lie over his lap to be spanked. Instead, he kicks off his shoes into a pile of debris, and collapses facing the airshaft. Jan lies down next to him, noticing that he does not smell like himself. He is not wearing his bad cologne, and she misses it.

"Do you swim?" he asks, running his fingers through her hair, pressing his limp body against hers.

"Yes."

"I didn't learn how to swim until I was twenty-one."

"You just never learned?"

"I was afraid."

"Why?"

"I had an accident when I was a kid. I almost drowned in my uncle's pool."

"Why did you decide to learn?"

"I had to. You have to know how to swim in order to graduate from Columbia. It is a requirement."

"Are you still afraid of water?"

"I am still not a very strong swimmer."

Jan imagines Mike flailing in the shallow end, a grown man, spitting out mouthfuls of water, the tendons in his neck straining to hold his head above the surface.

"I love to swim," she says.

"Are you a good swimmer?"

"I was on the diving team in high school." This is a lie, the first one she has told him. "I was the captain."

"Frieda says she's getting married. She can't be serious," says Mike.

Jan does not have to ask who Frieda is. Mike rolls away from her, pulling his legs into his chest, tugging Jan's arm around his body. He seems small. She imagines him shivering, wrapped in a towel, a child having faced death. She wonders if that was the last time he felt pain, like the pain she knows he feels now. The brink of major loss. Perhaps he spent his life on that brink, and now he has finally been pushed over the edge.

"Do you want to sleep here?" He kisses her hand.

Control is like a sheet of paper tossed out a car window, whipping this way and that. Nothing to ground it, no anchor, no hand. He has let go. He falls asleep in her arms, but she is not tired. She gets up and walks into the living room. There are dirty socks on top of the microwave, and the cat's eyes glow from within a heap of bedsheets and bath towels. There is no sense to the mess. Jan begins to put things in order.

As she cleans, momentum builds. She is not cleaning to make him happy. She is grabbing the loose paper, snatching it from the wind. She is mastering something: the world to which she has been bound, first by desire, then by need, now by ambition. The objects are so disordered that it is impossible to determine their origins, so she creates the apartment anew. Books on shelves, papers in drawers, trash in the bin. She is the director, the objects her players. Mike is irrelevant, and Jan is on her knees sweeping kitty litter into a plastic grocery bag. There is power in domesticity after all. Then the thought comes like a smack in the face: No, all wrong. Mike is asleep, Jan is cleaning, Frieda is gone. Jan is now Wife Number One.

Mike deteriorates. He misses work, preferring instead to lie with Jan, talking. He talks about his childhood, about how his mother is an alcoholic and his father is a workaholic. He talks about how his sister is a lesbian, and how this tore his Irish Catholic family apart, dividing it into those who stood by her, and those who stood by the church. He talks about his childhood dog, who was hit by a postal truck, and about the nightmares he had as he recovered from a tonsillectomy. He still hits her, they still sleep together, but it has all turned into a childish game. He is dirty and messy, he cries, and he hungers for touch. He asks Jan questions too, about when she was a little girl. Did she have nightmares then? What was her family like? Jan doesn't know what to say. Her childhood had been ordinary, existing in her memory as bullet points: birthday parties, lost teeth, chicken pox. Yet these mundane remembrances seem too personal to share with him. She tries to discipline herself to disconnect, to tune him out. She wants things to be as they used to be. These days she feels that she is the user, in a harsh, pure way. She longs for the days when the using was mutual, when it was a simple exchange of flesh for flesh. But Mike has become complicated.

Months ago, Mike had given Jan a lecture about topping from the bottom. It is not to be done, he'd said. He explained that topping from the bottom is when the submissive partner attempts to control the dominant partner, either through manipulation or through more overt means. It is taboo. "You don't want to be with a dom who will take it," he'd said. "They're not for real. They're posers. If you try to pull that shit on me, you'll be sorry." But now Mike has started talking about switching. He decides that, despite what he has always thought, he is a switch—a person who will be either top or bottom. Jan tries to convince him otherwise. She tells him that he is the dominant one. "Think about it," she says. "Don't you want to tie me up? I have been bad. I deserve a punishment." "OK," he sighs. "If that will make you happy." She realizes that she has just topped him from the bottom.

The pigeons in Mike's airshaft have been breeding. Jan can hear the mother pigeon cooing to her babies, who chirp back frantically in response. She imagines what they are saying: *Me, me, me! Need, need, need!* She envisions the gaping wounds of their mouths, red slits. What filthy things do the mother pigeons find in Manhattan to feed these mouths? The babies will take it, regardless. They will be grateful for whatever they get.

Mike gets worse. He spends a lot of time on the phone with his mother, which only upsets him. He laments to Jan about the ice cubes that he can hear clinking around in the glass she holds to her lips on the other end of the line. He stops doing laundry altogether, doesn't shave for days at a time. Jan buys him a new bottle of cologne, but he does not use it. He wants to snuggle, wants to kiss. He asks her why everything always has to do with sex. Jan is with him nearly every day, now that summer break has started, rather than staying with her parents uptown. She is working at a bakery and brings him sweets. She fingers crumbs into his open mouth, though she is nauseated by it. Yet she is determined that, when he is restored, she will be responsible. She resorts to being Wife Number One with the hope that it will lead her back to concubine status.

Frieda gets married in a temple on the Upper East Side, to a man named Gregory Cohen. It is in the newspaper, which Jan is reading on the subway to Mike's house. Jan is furious about what has happened to Mike. Yet the power of her loathing has made her consider the possibility that she loves him.

When Jan gets to Mike's apartment he is asleep on the floor with the cat. Jan steps over him, reaching for the pack of Camels on the counter. She lights a cigarette and nudges him with her shoe. She hands the paper to him, pointing to the announcement. There is a leaden silence in which Jan has the opportunity to contemplate the cruelty of what she has done. Her logic was that somehow the shock, the reality, when forced into his body, would reanimate it. As she watches his face she is reminded of images from a Latin textbook that illustrate the petrified bodies of the citizens of Pompeii.

"Kick me," Mike says, his face ashen and expressionless.

"Get up." She reaches out her hand, but he doesn't take it.

"Punch me. Kick me."

"That's ridiculous, Mike. I'm not going to do that."

"I want you to. I need it."

Whenever Jan thinks about what Mike used to do for her, she is filled with the kind of nostalgia that borders on hysteria. It is a desperate feeling of having lost one's church, the church that one was baptized in, the church that one buries loved ones behind, the church that introduced them to infinity. Without much introspection, she had showed up at his door with a vague notion of fun. Instead, he let her pray to him, and her prayers were either granted or denied. Now her prayers run on a closed circuit. She walks to the bedroom like an automaton. She slides the bin out from beneath the bed. She admires her bloodred nail polish against the black rubber tubing that her fingers now wrap around. She takes it in her hand. With the other hand she picks up two coiled lengths of rope. She says *Mike* and he comes.

What she does to him, she learned from him. He cries. He begs and whines, and the sicker Jan feels, the harder she strikes. But it is empty. Jan is not a switch. Afterward, she cannot look at his face. He is satisfied and soothed, eating a bowl of cereal and checking his e-mail. He resembles his old self more than he has in months, straight backed, deepened voice. He announces that he needs a shave. She cannot make eye contact when he speaks to her. When Mike used to tie her down, choking her and forcing himself upon her, Jan never felt violated. The smugness with which Mike now wears the bruises that she has inflicted upon him make her feel soiled. Life has lost its color, blood is replaced by silt. As Mike preens himself in the bathroom, Jan gets her things together. Leaving, she wonders if he can hear her go, over the clamor of his serenity.

A Favor for Big Ernie

David Ohle

MOLDENKE SPENT HIS FIRST free night in Altobello at the Wayfarer's Lodge, sleepless. Twenty or thirty fellow arrivals, including an extended family of jellyheads, snored and farted and coughed in their bunks. Someone opened a window for air only to let in the stink of garbage and a pair of pigeons, who flew crazily in the dark. A wing struck Moldenke in the jaw with enough force to bruise him. He closed his eyes and covered his face with his hands, hoping for sleep that never came.

Because Altobello's streetcars ran only every other day, Moldenke had to walk the twelve city blocks down Esplanade to the Tunney Arms, a rooming house on the west side. He didn't know Altobello well, but other new arrivals told him they'd heard that west side jellyheads were popping out of alleyways or abandoned buildings, or anywhere, and spraying free men and women with aerosol deformant, scarring them for life.

Moldenke proceeded with caution, always looking around as he walked. The west side was an unpainted and neglected quarter of the city, with dilapidated hotels offering free rooms for new arrivals. Though the rooms were a bit shabby, anything would be better than the lodge.

Along with the papers ordering him to Altobello, Moldenke showed the concierge his pass card and was assigned a room. "Freedom isn't free, mister," the concierge said. "No bath, no kitchen, no nothing. Eat and do your business on the street. And be careful. There's some bad jellies out there."

"So I've heard. I'll watch out."

The room had one casement window that opened only halfway and was furnished with a bare cot and a wooden chair. Moldenke collapsed onto the cot and slept all day and most of the night.

For breakfast the following day, he walked to a Saposcat's Deli close by, crowded as it was with a mix of free people and peaceable jellies, ate a bowl of pigeon scrapple, and drank a cup of strong java. After that, he wandered around the west side, taking in the sights, such as they were. He learned quickly that bricks often fell from the tallest downtown buildings whenever a streetcar went by. He had to alternate looking up for falling bricks and looking down for the occasional sinkhole in the sidewalk. A broken ankle or a fractured skull would be disastrous. There were no open hospitals in the city. They had been closed when Altobello was liberated.

When he came to Eternity Meadows, an old cemetery that had apparently evolved into something of a jellyhead encampment, Moldenke saw their underfed children roaming aimlessly among the gravestones, as if they had been abandoned. He saw one of them chasing a rat. Another was drinking rainwater from a stone flower vase.

Even more striking, he saw that the children had blue teeth. He knew that a type of jaundice, related to an infection of the blood, could cause bluing teeth. Nothing, however, could account for other anomalies in their appearance and behavior. For one, they were hairless and as pale as chalk. For another, their ears were overly developed and their leg muscles were atrophied, giving them a storklike gait. He saw them beating one another mercilessly with oaken sticks and, like goats, relieving themselves wherever the urge struck.

He picked up his pace until he was some distance from the cemetery, somewhere in the Old Quarter. The streets there were paved with concrete, cracked now and sprouting weeds with disuse. He slowed down when he passed the Church of the Lark and its tall steeples. The odor of incense and beeswax drifted out into the street. Feeling a rumble in his bowels, an uncomfortable fullness, he went in to get out of the sun and rest a few minutes. There were votive candles burning warmly in red glass holders. A Sister of Comfort swept the aisles, another busied herself draping statuary with purple chintz. A third arranged lilies on the altarpiece.

Moldenke sat down in a back pew to wait for the spasm in his belly to pass, but it only grew worse. He lay down and closed his eyes, trying to numb the awareness of his angry bowel. In that dreamy state, he lost control and soiled himself. A light touch on his shoulder brought him back to full awareness. He heard a soft, female voice: "Sir, you'll find a public bath just down the street. Wash up there and have them boil those trousers."

"So sorry, Sister. It's something I can't avoid. I have an angry bowel, and I ate scrapple for breakfast."

"Yes, do hurry, though."

He found the baths a block away. After showing his card and

explaining the situation, he was led by the bath aide to a small lavatory just off the vestibule and told to stand near the sink, remove his boots, socks, uniform trousers, and underdrawers. That done, the aide said, "Bathe in pool number one, then two, then three. These clothes will be clean and dry when you're done."

There were a few other bathers floating languidly in pool one, in water the color of milky java, soaping themselves, then diving under for a rinse. Pool two was cleaner and three was as clear as liquid glass.

Feeling refreshed after a long soak in the pools, and with clean clothes, Moldenke ventured out along Arden Boulevard. It had rained while he bathed. The streets were steaming, the air was cooler, and there were reflective puddles on the sidewalk, each offering a blinding glimpse of the midday sun.

He stopped when he passed the Yack Shack, a talking salon. Java and rice crackers were being served to small groups sitting at tables and talking freely about any topic that came to mind. For some, it was an odd thing to speak freely, to exchange so much information without the supervision they'd known before the liberation.

When Moldenke entered and showed his pass he was given a slip of paper and a pencil. The host, who was busy brewing java, said, "Print your name and list a couple of things you want to talk about. I'll put it in that jar."

Moldenke found a seat at the counter, signed the paper, then wrote:

1. Who invented aerosol deformant?

2. Angry bowel, causes and effects.

The host collected the paper from him and put it in the jar. As Moldenke waited his turn, he drank java and listened to the talk, which, though ranging widely, was orderly and polite. No one spoke out of turn or overlong. The host saw to that with a little church bell he carried on a thong swinging from his belt. *Ding-ding.* "All right now, that's enough about that."

A free man at another table talked about jellyheads: "They have a moving-picture mind. All life to them is a series of snapshots with no chance for time exposure. That's why they can't think straight on any subject. Their minds are a bundle of transient impressions and confused ideas. What are we going to do about them?"

A free woman sitting next to him said, "Wait a minute. Jellyhead females invented copper tips for shoes, the baby carriage, the clothes boiler, the bread-kneading machine, a self-filling fountain pen, the portable typewriter, pigeon-feather vests, the stem-winding watch, the bustle, and three important improvements in the sewing machine."

"That's one of the unexplainables about them," the free man said. "Their inventiveness. I can't get used to it. There's no rhyme or reason there."

The host pulled Moldenke's name out of the jar. "You're up, Moldenke. Table five."

There were no empty chairs at the table but someone at table four slid one over for him. He cleared his throat as he felt an uneasy twitch of his bowel. It could be, he thought, that he wouldn't get to all his talking points before having to run for the privy. Nevertheless, he began: "One thing I'd like to bring up is aerosol deformants. Who invented them? And who put them on the city streets?"

A free woman said, "And who are the victims? Always handsome females."

The host, attracted by the discussion, stood near table five with a tray of empty java mugs. "Why, though? What purpose is served by squirting a pretty female in the face with deformant?"

"I'll tell you," a free man wearing thick eyeglasses and a horsehair wig said. "It's the difference between the sublime and the beautiful. Beauty disfigured is a courageous and beneficial act. The horror of the victim's new face is very, very sublime. I'll take the sublime over the beautiful any day."

The host looked at his watch. "The hours do go by. It's already closing time. Everybody out. We'll take up these issues and lots more at noon tomorrow."

After the Yack Shack closed, Moldenke walked to the day market at number nine Broad Street, where he'd heard there was a public privy. He bought a pack of Juleps from a tobacconist, who said, "Why would anyone smoke anything else? Plain, menthol cooled, or cork tipped?"

"Plain for me," Moldenke said.

"Sorry, out of plain. Big shortage. Menthol cooled or cork tipped?"

"The tipped then."

Moldenke opened the pack and lit a Julep. "By the way, is there a privy around here?"

"Yessir, it's up there close to Big Ernie's Bakery."

"Thank you." Moldenke pressed his palm to his bloated abdomen, the burning cigarette between his fingers. "I never know when I might need to use it."

A few shops down, he passed Zanzetti Scienterrifics. A plump little clown-suited barker outside tried to engage passersby. Standing next to him was a pitiably deformed young woman wearing a sheer veil. "Been deformed?" the barker shouted. "Improve that face! We can make them younger, handsomer, and more expressive. We can do more to restore deformant-damaged faces than all the paint and powder in the world. In one week, you can throw your veil away. Guaranteed."

Now, having crossed busy Arden Boulevard, Moldenke smelled fresh-baked bear claws. The smell was coming from Big Ernie's Bakery. When the smell was that strong, it probably meant the bear claws had just been taken from the oven. And there was a green light blinking above the doorway. Forgetting for the moment that his bowel was getting angry again, Moldenke felt his mouth begin to water.

He stepped inside, ordered a claw, and showed his card to the cashier, a young woman whose face had been deformed.

She saw him staring at her. "You wouldn't believe how pretty I used to be," she said. "A jellyhead deformed me by that cemetery."

"Eternity Meadows?"

"I go by there on the way to my room."

Moldenke shook his head. "What's the point of all this freedom with jellyheads everywhere? I don't understand it."

She turned sideways. "I don't look that bad from the side, do I?"

Moldenke felt obliged to respond in some way, but words were slow in coming, and when they did they were tentative. "You don't look all that bad," he heard himself saying.

"Thank you, I suppose that's a compliment." She gave him the bear claw in a waxed bag. "How long are you here for?"

"Five years. That's a lot of freedom. I'm afraid, really."

"It's not bad. I like it here. You can do what you want."

"Hard to get used to at first. Back home I was confined a long, long time." He bit off a chunk of the pastry. It was crispy and sweet. "Oh, this is excellent claw." He sat at a sunny little table near the front window and ate the rest of it.

Big Ernie came in from the back with a tray of fresh-baked claws and began lining them up in the display case.

"Give me another one, please, to go," Moldenke said.

Big Ernie backed his head and shoulders out of the case and stood his full height. "Welcome to Altobello, my friend. You're a free man."

"I can't say it's good to be here, but I'll make do. I suppose I'll look for some kind of work, some kind of employment. Best way to pass the time, I hear."

Big Ernie put a hammy hand on his hip and thought for a moment, then came to Moldenke's table and whispered to him, "Look at that poor daughter of mine." Moldenke glanced over at her. She was busy powdering her lumpy, misaligned cheeks. "A jellyhead did that. Got her by that big cemetery, with the tall gates, squirted deformant right in her face. You want to do me a favor?"

"What's the favor?"

"I want you to poison that son of a bitch for me, the one who deformed her. He goes naked and wears a snap-brim cap."

"I've never killed one before."

"Think of it this way. You won't be killing him. I will. You'll simply be my agent. Here's an example. If you were squirted with deformant, would you blame the deformant or the jellyhead that squirted you?"

"The jellyhead. That's obvious."

"Of course. You see my point?"

"In a way, I do."

"The same principle is at work here. All you have to do is catch the morning car to Smiley's Meats. If I'm not mistaken, they'll be running tomorrow. Get a couple of sausages. Put them on my account. Then go to Goody's Antique Hardware store for a tub of strong rat paste. Charge that too. Take those sausages, split them open, and pack paste in there. I know that jellyhead loves sausages. There I was, coming back from Smiley's one day and the filthy thing grabbed a bag of hot links right out of my hand and ran off. I could see him crouched behind a tree, eating them. So go to the cemetery and leave them by that old dead tree at the back of the place."

"All right," Moldenke said. "I'll take care of it in the morning."

"Bring me his cap."

"Right, I will."

Anxious about killing a jellyhead, though it was completely legal in Altobello, Moldenke sat up half the night, smoked Juleps in his wooden chair, and watched the progress of the half-moon through his window when the clouds would let him.

It was an hour or two after getting into bed that he finally gave in to sleep and dreamed of Ernie's daughter coming fast toward him on a busy street, her hair wild and tangled and blown by the air she parted with her rapid walk. She looked as thin as death, expressionless as she came to him and locked him in a bear hug. They whirled around and this prevented him from looking straight into her ravaged face. He saw only part of it—a cheek, an ear, and hair swept back like a comet's tail. His eyes were fixed in a stare at empty space. She said nothing and her gaze never met his.

After a bowl of flakes in the morning and a cup of java at Saposcat's, Moldenke cut through Eternity Meadows on his way to the streetcar stop. About halfway through, he stepped into a mound of jellyhead stool hidden by leaves. There were no flies on it to give warning even though the odor was unbearably foul, like something three days dead. There were other mounds scattered among the tombstones and balled bunches of wiping rags had been thrown about. It was a jellyhead toileting area.

As he waited at the stop, Moldenke scraped much of the stool from his boots on the car tracks, but what remained smelled strong enough to get him kicked off almost as soon as he got on. "Who do you think you are, getting on my car smelling like that?"

"Sorry, couldn't help it."

"Get off right now." Moldenke jumped out of the car when it was moving, twisting his ankle, nearly spraining it.

Smiley's was a long walk away. He was exhausted when he got there. He had to swelter on the banquette under an awning and watch the comings and goings of Smiley's customers until he felt strong enough to go in. An elderly woman who passed him said, "You can't beat old Smiley's meat."

The market was cool and cavernous inside, the floors, walls, and ceiling covered in gleaming white tiles. There were several counters between the refrigerated cases, each with a long line. Moldenke chose one and prepared for a long wait. A free man in front of him said, "Holy Christ, man. I'm going to faint from that smell. Did you step in something? Get in another line."

"All right. I'm sorry."

He moved to another line. When he finally reached the counter, he said, "Let me have two of your sausages."

The clerk wrapped them in waxed paper.

"Put them on Big Ernie's card."

"Oh, yeah, sure. Big Ernie's Bakery, downtown. Best bear claws in the city. Him and me go way back."

The clerk disappeared through a rubber curtain that shielded the activities from the public most of the time. When it parted momentarily, Moldenke could see the butchers at work sawing bones and cutting meat. A jellyhead boy in a canvas apron policed the floor, picking up fallen scraps and putting them into a wheelbarrow, which he emptied into the hopper of a sausage-making machine, along with scoopfuls of pepper, salt, and other spices. At another station, a butcher emptied packets of gelatin into a vat of head cheese.

Back on the street with his sausages, Moldenke asked a patrolman how to get to Goody's Hardware. "Old Goody got deformed, you know. I'm not sure he's open yet. It's only been a week or two."

"I didn't know."

"Some crazy jellyhead goes into his store, squirts him in the face, takes a sack of sulfur, fifty pounds of slug bait, and a gallon of fly syrup. So Goody's out of all that. What do you need?"

"A tub of rat paste. I'll take the chance he might be open."

"All right. Walk ten blocks north and there you are."

The day was getting hotter. Moldenke felt the heat of the sidewalk through boot and sock and into the bottoms of his feet. The walk to Goody's was miserable. His feet were burning and he was quite thirsty. After a long drink at a public fountain he sat down on a bench in front of Goody's and took off his boots. His socks were worn through in places and there were little bleedings where shoe nails had pushed up through the sole and punctured the skin. He slammed the boots repeatedly against the concrete until the rest of the dried-out stool fell off. When his socks had aired a little, he laced his boots back up and went in under a hand-painted sign that read: NO JELLYHEADS.

There was an opaque window where orders were placed, and another where they were picked up. Goody tended both. When an order was taken, he went into the rear of the building, filled it, then appeared at the pickup window to deliver it. Only his silhouette could be seen through the glass as he moved about filling orders.

When Moldenke's turn at the window came, he ordered a tub of rat paste. "The strongest you have. This is a big rat."

Goody went back to fetch the tub and Moldenke met him at the pickup window. "You can put this on Big Ernie's card."

"All right," Goody said. "He and I are good friends. His nuts click loud in this city."

"Sorry to hear about your deforming, Mr. Goody. It could happen to any of us, I hear."

"He just come in and sprayed me all in the kisser, laughing, like he was having fun."

"Naked? Wearing a cap?"

"That's the one."

Moldenke held up the bag of sausages. "I'm going to load these with paste and feed them to him. He lives in the cemetery. It's a favor for Ernie."

"All the luck in the world, son. You don't want a face like this."

The window closed suddenly, nearly crushing Moldenke's fingers, and the lights dimmed. Goody's was closing for the day. Moldenke and a few other unserved shoppers shuffled out.

This time, with his boots cleaned, he was able to board the Arden car going to Eternity Meadows. On the streetcar line there was a kiosk and a stop sign between the exit from the Old Quarter and the entrance to free Altobello. A patrolman stepped from the kiosk and entered the stopped car. He went up the aisle grumbling to himself, checking pass cards, then told the conductor to proceed.

After getting off the streetcar, Moldenke sat on the curb to load rat paste into the sausages. He split the casing with his long, dirty thumbnail, parted the two sides, then used a stick to press the paste into the gap. When he turned to get up, he saw the naked jellyhead trotting purposefully across the street toward the cemetery, tongue dripping with hunger, his member swinging, his cap worn rakishly to the side. His hands, however, were empty. He wasn't carrying deformant.

Moldenke threw one of the sausages onto the ground. Without slowing, the jellyhead snatched it and ran into the unlit cemetery. Moldenke followed at a chosen distance, not close, not far. It was getting dark and hard to see. The jellyhead slowed his pace long enough to eat half the sausage, then raced on toward the old dead tree. Moldenke continued on foot. He had to make sure the jelly was dead, but had no idea how long it would take. And he needed the cap to show to Big Ernie.

He walked generally and slowly toward the old dead tree, where a small campfire smoldered, casting a flickering light. The closer he came to the tree, the more distinctly he could hear groans of pain. Shortly after, he saw the sickened jellyhead curled up near his campfire. He seemed to be dying. His bright blue eyes were open but unfocused. Moldenke kicked him a few times to be sure he was completely unconscious if not dead. He didn't want to reach for the cap until he was sure he wouldn't be bitten or sprayed with a hidden can of deformant. When he did get the cap off, snatching it and jumping back, he placed it on his own head, walked briskly to the streetcar stop on Arden Boulevard, feeling relieved that his favor to Big Ernie was taken care of. When he showed his pass card, the conductor said,

"You smell like a dead dog. Sit in the back."

Moldenke gladly obliged and headed for the rear, holding on to seat backs to keep his balance as the car clattered off on the downtown line. Along the way, one of the passengers winked at him and said, "Nice cap."

The Edible City
Adam Veal

CLASSICAL

Inconvenient night mosquito,
I wish I were
a bird* quick enough
to eat you.

---

*Kinds of birds that eat mosquitoes: Google search reveals purple martins, some finches, swallows. Also bats.

Plotting points on plane d, which contains graph a (predictable flight path of mosquito to w/in 3 standard deviations),
line b (time & calories used moving from human to bird),
and graph c (movement of "bird" to mosquito interception).

The expressed wish conceals
the unexpressed finch.

Between two columns
the sea comes in.

AND HOW MUCH IS LOST TO THE CRUST

the police officers' union, included
in the bakers' union that determines
how much wheat goes into two dollars,
baked a city based on the exchange
rate the bankers' union set on
dollars to dough to bread.

Headline on the protest paper reads:
Civic Council Cites Coppers' Corrupt Croissant Coffers.

RED BLACK AND GREEN LIBERATION JUMPSUIT

A chuffed huff exhales from z-space,
this ubiquitous strike started with
the house painters' and window washers'
unions. They contemplated the donut
hole from diagonal perspectives
pedestrians were wont not to see.

JEANS ARE EVERYWHERE THESE DAYS, BUT THEN, SO ARE DAYS

At first they were at odds, one adding nothing
to the structure but paint flecks on
panes the other was constantly bitching
about having to scrape off. But then
they realized their concerns were latticed
when an innocent young apprentice painter
asked why the window washers
never set up scaffolding?
Everybody loves scaffolding! became a
cry and the two unions reconciled
themselves like crosshatchings on a pie.

Adam Veal

SPRINGTIME MEAL OF THE WORD IN LIBERTY

Waiting tables: The dance of the inanimate.
Inanimate dance music: Schadenfreude for the self as object.

One wonders what waiters do
in a city made entirely of food.
On streets named after famous bakers
and streets named after revolutionary cooks:
Crisscrossing at Griddle Plaza,
the only nonunionized occupants of the gingerbread city wait:

Placeholders, be they spies or gate soldiers,
ingratiating animal performances,
the wineglasses all from corn-based technologies
balanced upon drink trays while
around an arcade column one's prehensility wraps,
furiously dry humping.

*

To a peach as a pit and the seasons' pendulum,
and fro from summer the cheerleaders
"it's like a radio" . . . erm, like streaming
several radios at once like singing
in a can or collecting the resale, however
many cans it would take to attend a film.
A lump sum of plums, cans of hardened caramel
return as recycled stained windows paneled
with cherry candy panes & curbs in cursive

returning also around the *palazzo* dawdling
a café, un tabac, some pockmarked
La Figarrro film & holiday featuring
such hits as "Teen Pimp," "Artificial Incemination" [*sic*], &
"Apocalipstic" [*sic*], the opera *in situ* & nat'rally
occurring lab oratory:

Visits a cigarette after work, JetBoy, done
waiting tables for the day waits on JetGirl
finishing her shift tongues the meter, coaxes
the clock to excitement, minute hand rush faster
"the minutes are handfuls of bread crumbs"
used to scatter *après le* apron a barista, "of course
a smoke after work!" Soon & enough
the clock tones or doesn't so much tone but
farts a smell of roasting coffee beans
JetGirl ⇒ "I'm off!" she decrees & purloins a kissed
cheek from JetBoy, loitering at the door, "Ah!"

JETBOY & JETGIRL ⇒

We will make nothing new except in
our making redressing disturb
atoms & fellow sundry particles, ah . . .
JetGirl ⇒ It is Sunday. JetBoy ⇒ In
Perpetua, In Ubiquity. Off
and to the *Opera Heisenberg* a nerve
ous ness in *adoré* for the thick
sky for the lavender, night blooming
day blooming spilling lightpurple from
every crack & sill & in the air

fawning forms hum **THRUM** the aria
of our era. JetGirl ⇒ It is Sunday.
JetBoy ⇒ In Perpetua, In Simultanea.
Dear Miss Manners Nature Channel,
your summer screen and extendum
da-dum da-dum da-dum.

THE STAGELESS AMPHITHEATER

The seatless amphitheater passes
musical instruments among its players.
They practice scales. Ante of
at least a tambourine and whoever
wins the hand calls the tune. What
is the music? Are there fights?
I only drink Irish whiskey. Everyone
collapses suddenly spent into afterglow.
A tuneless piping chirps in the time between
movements. There is a great rubbing
varying notes high up as
in an orgy are lost. Now people are really sweating.
A half-eaten tuba discovers new
horn spirals to sound into. A man
subtly brushes tired dick jokes aside
and momentarily conducts the
symphonic audience to a silence of a
half hour in which there is only
the echoing of ears to each other
and in the arched hall built exactly
to reflect ergonomic ear calculations. A
couple attacks him. Another joins in.

Soon everyone is standing naked
draped in convulsing percussions the bass
of which makes pubic hairs quiver.

IF YOUR PASSWORD IS "123456,"
JUST CHANGE IT TO "HACK ME"

Quack access
dizzy prosaic reading
progression via little plastic ducks,
JetGirl dreams in acme, thinking to herself
JetGirl is dreaming in acme   an ocean, something
hangs like a real emotion above the city.
Above the city is it raining   [garbled]

[A pleasant white noise
with something like faraway electrical sparks]

Mid-Opera, the holographic projection of a mechanical bird
has startled JetGirl awake. Bits of frosting fall crumbling
from the seat in front of her kicks—she's jumped—
catching herself from falling, oh, a metalbluebird,
I wonder if you cooked the springs with lemon
would it taste of pheasant?

The bird reconfigures itself into
a scintillating pavilion
upon which a cloud
of holographic people stroll.
The way the holographic light plays the people
they appear to be made of sugar.
The cooked & the raw as possible
all look good in Levi's.

*

The image fills JetBoy & JetGirl with the impression of standing on
a distant cliff,
the waves of the ocean crashing below them send up wafts of salt
spray, and looking
out across the horizon they feel an ambient longing to destroy
Western Civilization.

The waiters bring out the food but do not set it upon the table.
Heavenly aromas reach the operagoers, arousing their imaginations.

Briefly confused over what is ambient:
The longing for food or the food itself.

DEAR MISS MANNERS NATURE CHANNEL,

JetGirl ⇒ Prima, allow me to conjugate:	JetBoy ⇒ Primero, allow me a conjugation:

An animal freed of planar space
some conjunction of
dream and repetition
melts into the common dawn and
when the sun dips:

2x as much light and as many birds
a man walks up and around a mountain: Deer Park
where the grass is dry on July 4th when we went
were pulling ticks off the dog that had wound themselves
into his tight curls dug in 4 the blood:
Just writing to say we received yr missive,
Miss Manners
Nature Channel, they say, smoking on candy cigars,

it always sounded strange to us, like chicken-wire fences
a voice floating in a valley without a body from here
to the moon hanging above the city. It's hard
not to just drift when drifting seems exactly like
what one ought to be doing, temping whatever industry is hiring

preagricultural nomadic adult singles Web sites, it's hard meeting

people leaving the forest, one stands upright
to see over tall grass
freeing one's hands
summer features engender
tongues that slip, lips that stutter speech to text,

text to speech
text to speech to text . . .

voice recognition beachware.

In flagrante in delicto, JetBoyJetGirl

OY, JETS

RE: Some conjunction of dream and repetition.

You can stay in code or drift off in lingerie
buttered croissants, crystallized sugar of the
windows brûléed by the boulangerie blowtorch of our
annunciating sun.

If he gives you bread in a wrapper, you know the packaging
dissolves in water, I'm sorry you aren't feeling ambient enough,

so off you go,
my trembling airplanes
oinking in oikos.

Don't let the gingerdrawbridge
hit you on the way out.

Adam Veal

Sincerely Futurish Cookbook,
Miss Manners Nature Channel

Exeunt.

NUDE DESCENDING A TRAFFIC ACCIDENT

the lights go off

along the beltway along the router the specter of a potential
pollination crisis weighs

episodal clairvoyant mapping

people from the power company left

heavily on his shoulders, a second machine blows them into
windows, a third vacuums

a soap opera tongue enclaves

the town empties out

them off the orchard floor. Dust covers everything for hundreds of
miles. From the air,

zen pez zeppelin bombing

the scavengers argue

Adam Veal

the whole valley seems blanketed in lacy strips of snow—acres of pale pink and white

at a clip, I was jogging along the rooftops,

the remnants of the scavengers
band together to repel invaders

blossoms beckon tens of billions of bees traveling to multiple car dealerships. "When I

you know, like you do,

it is revealed there are less resources
than first thought

go from point A to point B with my feet, there is something of real value there," (that's

when suddenly, from outofthebluesky

the town empties out

Amen spelled backward, she points out), a robot stuck inside the uncanny valley is each

He was my brother. We were Nazis.

strange beasts pass through, grazing

hive on a 22-day cycle, located in hosting centers the URL of '/' was mistakenly checked

Corrupt Heideggerian Aesthetes postagrarian beings-in-the-world

from shadowed holes in the buildings,
ghosts echo

in as a value to the file and '/' expands to all URLs. A single bloom cycle now extends

of divided animal extensions.

the wind stirs all these things
briefly before they return
to their occupations

for acres and acres with a quiet nod. He stirs honey into his tea at his daughter's house in

We were both flies. He was flying I was running,

unaware of the nanomites
riding the pollen on the breeze
clicking metal mandibles

Berkeley, and like London taxi drivers, have an enlarged hippocampus oriented toward

breaking into thought7.

*

JetGirl sits cross-legged. The wood of the walls & floor is warped & wet. She is reading. JetBoy enters.

JETBOY
catching up to himself

Are you reading? Or rather,
will you have been reading?

JetGirl looks up from a book she's apparently found.
looks up apparently from the book she's found. She takes him in. Returns to the book, titled:

Adam Veal

An Overture on Unconscious Music Participation:

The volume:

A Note on Operas:
In AutoTune & Major Key.

JETGIRL
not really reading but looking at the book

The Piquant Airport. Senate
of the Digestion. The Words in
Liberty Sea Platter. The Haunted
Medicinal Sestinas . . .

I'm just reminiscing about places I
used to love going.

JETBOY

The screen holds you unawake.
The algorithm can't figure out what you like.
I just keep offering you more of what you already have.

JETGIRL

JetBoy, old friends would
like to reconnect with you!

There is a noise outside. A noise noises itself outside. A noise itselfs outside. The outside is a bubble. It bubbles.

Bits of chorus drift in through the window. JetBoy and JetGirl look up expectantly, excitedly, winding together friends & food as two who've been conditioned do.

Adam Veal

Plodding job hunting we trod
Market St. & on the other
Market St.s agog the ether glows
electric with India ink lettering.
Possessed by spirits of spooky dead in drag,

glyphs glimpse ruts for rutting
us gasping nymphs as
hermetic Hermes tics her metrics, erm . . . he, metis, teems
generates text,
nodal bleats pasturing—
We're put out for someone else.

We'd put out for himherthem, grazing
a hurtle of sheep,
a trip of goats
feels with them thither—
Unto heather, the ambigued yonder
spent into every weather
il pleut, rams & ewes, we're air
ink effervescing off weird paper.

"DRINK LESS, CUT OUT RED MEAT, EXERCISE,
PRACTICE SAFE SEX: THESE ARE OUR SHOTGUNS,
OUR CRICKET BATS, OUR FARMHOUSES, OUR MALLS"

JETBOY

That sounds like a big chorus.

JETGIRL

Think they've got a kick line?

JETBOY

Well, let's go down and see.

JETGIRL
out the broken window

down the scaffold &
JetBoy stops short to surreptitiously
lick the metal between his fingers

JETBOY
wrinkles his nose to himself

. . .

JOB CONFERENCE WITH FAST ZOMBIES

You are +5 cuteness
with yr blood-soaked T-shirt and
yr shovel grin somehow having seeming
two jobs & no marketable skills,
farther in hunting hat & species,
Fast Zombies safari past strike lines of unions.

Nude descending a traffic accident
asks if you've been thru the process, the chorus
of humanbirds cry in some old Home Depot
prancing through the fixture aisle,
oh, beautiful fixtures,
not a clue what goes in where,
but scattering, languorously, JetBoy
& JetGirl instead of eating
the reusable broke-down pavilion
b/c it is broke down, smooth tho cracked,
lovely to lean matching nakedness against

Fast Zombies lick sugar remnants from skin, like

sexy flies puking & eating puking & eating the dissolving
Kool-Aid structures JetBoy & JetGirl
fire up engines with Hansel & Gretel grins.

UNCONSCIOUS MUSIC PARTICIPATION

chorus: Singing, oh, life is good as a Fast Zombie
life is good as a Fast Zombie
life is good as a Fast Zombie, these days

Got no use for locks & doorknobs
Just beware of people with swords & shotguns
Oh, life is good as a Fast Zombie, these days

Hansel & Gretel have joined up with us
Led us back to eat up survival of the fittest unions, o-oh,
Life is good as a Fast Zombie, these days

chorus

Ain't much good gingerbread does 'em anyway
Now we just throw ourselves up the barricades
Oh, life is good as a Fast Zombie, these days

Waiting tables never paid much anyway
Life's much better as a zombie we all say
Oh, life is good as a Fast Zombie, these days

chorus

repeat chorus

end

Adam Veal

THE SEASONS COME EVERY OTHER YEAR NOW

and last twice as long,
so at least the birds that are left
get longer vacations, but the videos I rent
are still due soon,
of which time, in its indices,
pleasurable indecencies having finally replaced
the *lux melancholia*
as lying naked in bed mirrors
keeping a rooftop Victory Garden,
and the pajamas we hated
and with one another secretly
slept unclothed.

Things may happen in the real estate market
but realtors will always dress the same:
at a constant job interview,
and anyway, how much I love you,
which might be waiting somewhere for me to turn
the corner, standing in hordes
and I'll have nothing to do but hope I can suddenly
read the city as
a series of escapes or be bitten.

PARKOUR HOMO SAUCER, OR FREE RUNNING THE OPEN

HANSEL
(*tapping around the edges of the barricades*)

For our purposes all
people, places, and times are the same.
I am already my father, a woodcutter.

GRETEL

Fuck that, I'm going to be the witch.

POV OF THE BARRICADES

It's the 1st time I've done this. I don't know what I'm doing or
how to classify, read: quantify, read:
demarcate the different sections of my life.

GHOST OF BARRICADES PAST

Every time is your 1st time. One feels one is commanded
to create each day anew, and yet one is forced to walk
yesterday's streets.

Where does this feeling come from? Like Tetris, is it stackable?
It is the interpenetration of Tetris into daily life.

DEAR MISS MANNERS NATURE CHANNEL,

All good things to eat are found on rooftops,

but getting there whether
up burned-out stairwells or the
elevators that never work

GRETEL

I suppose we could eat the walls.

HANSEL

Yes, why don't we eat the walls.

GRETEL

They don't taste so very good, not
as good as they used to, too much
sugar, how does that happen? One
grows up and loses one's taste for
the stuff. Only flesh will do.

HANSEL

Yes, at a certain point
gingerbread no longer fills, hmmm,
Gretel, suddenly I find myself
dreaming of a city of bacon. Big
raised meat buildings, the
lights on inside synapses swollen
and luminous . . . oh, but it will never happen.

GRETEL

No, but now I'm salivating. Let's hurry.
Let's lay siege to that children's city.

So the Fast Zombies apply their teeth to the walls of the
Gingerbread City, and with each bite the roofs get closer down.
No longer a disorganized mob or queue around windows & doors
but biting & spitting out gumdrops & peppermint sticks, the
foundation of many a simultaneous house starts to shake and from
the rooftops a moan as many residents spontaneously become birds
to escape, though some haven't eaten enough calories beforehand,
and so even as the Fast Zombies eat the buildings down the
populace eat the buildings from above to build up enough energy
to fly away.
Some fly away.

Three Urban Tales

Christopher Hellwig and Michael J. Lee

THE FINANCIAL DISTRICT

IN THE CITY, a businessman arrived for lunch at his favorite café, located on the first floor of the skyscraper in which he worked. The place was bustling at that hour: Every table was full and waiters ran every which way, eager to provide excellent service to their customers. After being seated by the window, the businessman was brought a menu, warm bread, and still water with lemon, as was the custom of the city.

The businessman looked out at the busy sidewalk, just beyond the glass, where other businesspeople hurried to their favorite cafés, and then sipped at his still water and looked at the empty chair across from where he sat. He wished that he wasn't dining by himself and suddenly, even in the midst of all the bustling, the businessman felt very lonely. But soon the waiter arrived and asked the businessman for his order, and the businessman, knowing exactly what he wanted, and exactly how he wanted it prepared, ordered very exactly, and felt a little better.

"Very good," said the waiter. "Those are excellent choices."

"Thank you," said the businessman.

"But something is troubling me," said the waiter.

"Oh? Have I left something out?" said the businessman.

"No," said the waiter. "My brother took his own life this morning."

"I'm so sorry," said the businessman. "Were you two close?"

"Yes," said the waiter. "We were identical twins."

"What was the method?" said the businessman. "If you don't mind my asking."

"He threw himself off a skyscraper."

"That's just awful," said the businessman.

"He was a businessman," said the waiter, "here in the financial district. In fact, he worked in this very building and used to dine here on his lunch break."

"Such a lonely way to die," said the businessman. "What was his name? Perhaps I knew him."

"Hot Jon," said the waiter. "His name was Hot Jon."

"That's a very unusual name," said the businessman. "I'm sure that I didn't know him."

"No matter," said the waiter. "Let me put in your order."

So the businessman handed the waiter his menu and watched him walk into the kitchen. The café was still bustling: Each table was still full and the waitstaff still ran every which way, making certain that their customers had everything their hearts desired.

The businessman soon found himself looking again out at the busy sidewalk, just beyond the glass, where so many people like him hurried here and there. He then spread a small amount of butter on a piece of warm bread, took a bite, and raised his glass of still water to take a sip. But as he lifted his eyes he saw, seated directly across from him, his waiter, dressed not in waiting clothes but in a business suit.

"Why did you change your clothes?" asked the businessman.

"These were my brother's clothes," said the waiter. "I suddenly wished to feel close to him."

"They fit you well," said the businessman.

"My mother thinks so too," said the waiter.

"Your mother?" said the businessman.

"Yes," said the waiter. "Would you like to know her name?"

"No," said the businessman.

"This was his favorite table," said the waiter.

"Whose?" said the businessman.

"Hot Jon's," said the waiter. "He would often sit here alone and look out at the busy sidewalk."

"Really?" said the businessman, smoothing his napkin. "And may I ask you your name?"

"Hot Jon," said the waiter.

"The same as your brother?"

"We were identical," said the waiter. "It was my mother who named us."

"Strange," said the businessman. "I won't forget it."

"You might," said the waiter. "This is a big city."

"Perhaps," said the businessman.

"Your food must be ready now," said the waiter, getting up from the table and disappearing into the kitchen.

After finishing the last of his bread and washing it down with another sip from his still water, the businessman found himself looking out the window, just beyond the glass again, where he noticed that a crowd had gathered around something on the sidewalk. Though he could not see what it was, the somber faces of the crowd sent a tremor through him, and he decided that this would be the last time he would dine at this café. When he looked around again, he noticed that the café was no longer bustling: He was the only patron left, and the waitstaff mostly milled about. He looked in vain for his waiter, but, as all the waitstaff wore waiting clothes instead of business suits, he could not find him anywhere.

"Hot Jon!" cried the businessman. "Where is my food?"

The waitstaff stopped milling about and all of them rushed to his table, napkins folded over their arms.

"Is there something we can help you with?" they asked.

"Where is Hot Jon?" said the businessman. "I haven't received my food, and have to return to work."

"Perhaps you should look for him," they said. "We last saw him entering the kitchen."

"But customers shouldn't enter the kitchen!" said the businessman.

"Times are changing," said the waitstaff. "For example, just yesterday we had several customers enter the kitchen."

"If I must," said the businessman. He got up from his table, and the waitstaff watched as he crossed the silent café and pushed through the swinging doors into the kitchen. There he saw an old woman in an apron, who was fretting nervously next to a plate of food. The businessman recognized the food as his exact order, prepared exactly the way he had wanted it, and, forgetting all about his waiter, he made a grab for it.

"No, no," said the old woman, protecting the plate. "This is for Hot Jon."

"Hot Jon ordered this for me," said the businessman.

"He's very particular about his orders," said the old woman.

"I am telling you the truth," said the businessman. "He was my waiter and this is my food."

"He's so overworked," said the old woman. "I'm worried about his health."

"I am going to eat this," said the businessman. "And then I'm going to pay my bill and return to work."

"Where do you work?" said the old woman.

"In the financial district," said the businessman. "In this very skyscraper."

"And is your office very high up?"

"Yes," said the businessman.

"And do you come to this café often?"

"Yes," said the businessman.

"Here, then," said the old woman, pushing the plate toward him. "Enjoy your lunch."

THE BLACK-EYED DOG

In midtown, a man and woman shared a home with their black-eyed dog. They had no children or friends but they were happy with just each other. They ate together, watched television together, and in the evenings, made love in the dark while their black-eyed dog lay on the floor.

Very late one night, after the man and woman had made love and fallen asleep, with the black-eyed dog still lying on the floor, a stranger broke into their home. Without hesitation he entered their bedroom, where men and women are most vulnerable, but just as he prepared to do them both harm, the black-eyed dog awoke in the nick of time, and mauled him to death.

The man and woman threw their arms around the black-eyed dog, whose jaws were still wet with the stranger's blood.

"Black-eyed dog," said the man, "thank you for what you've done."

"Thank you for everything, black-eyed dog," said the woman.

The black-eyed dog was silent, though it seemed to want to smile.

"Imagine if we had had no black-eyed dog," said the man.

"We might have been raped," said the woman. "Raped or killed."

"Raped at the very least," said the man.

"Killed at the worst," said the woman.

Soon, they called the police, and when the officers arrived, the man and woman explained all that had happened.

"You were both lucky," said a police officer. "Some weren't so lucky tonight."

"Some of them were raped, weren't they?" said the man.

"Some," said the police officer.

"And some killed?" said the woman.

"Some made it through the night neither alive nor unraped," said the police officer. "Can you figure out just what they might have lacked?"

"We know," said the man and woman, pointing to their black-eyed dog. The black-eyed dog was standing in a pool of the stranger's blood as a news camera filmed him.

The next morning, after the police and news crew had left, the man and woman sat watching television together while the black-eyed dog lay on the floor.

"No work today," said the man.

"Not after last night," said the woman.

"Things were almost so changed," said the man.

"So quickly changed," said the woman. "Yet not quite."

On television, the news was reporting the story of the stranger who was mauled to death by the black-eyed dog.

"There you are, black-eyed dog," said the man, pointing to the screen. "With your jaws still wet with blood."

"And here you are, black-eyed dog," said the woman, stroking the black-eyed dog with her toe. "All clean after your bath."

The black-eyed dog looked at the television, saw the black eyes, the jaws, and the stranger's blood, and, recognizing itself, almost seemed to smile.

Later that night, after they had turned off the television, the man and woman retired to their bedroom to make love in the dark.

"Are you coming, black-eyed dog?" said the man.

"It just wouldn't be the same," said the woman. "Not without you on the floor."

But the black-eyed dog made no move to get up, only sitting quietly, its eyes still fixed on the blank screen.

"Would you like to sleep in our bed tonight?" said the woman. "After we are finished making love?"

"As a special treat?" said the man. "You've earned it, black-eyed dog."

But the black-eyed dog made no move to get up, only sitting quietly, its eyes still fixed on the blank screen.

"What is it?" said the man.

"What is it, black-eyed dog?" said the woman.

"Is this about rape?" said the man. "No one will ever rape you."

"Or murder?" said the woman. "No one will ever murder you. You're going to grow old with us, and die on the floor."

"Do you believe us?" said the man. "Do you, black-eyed dog?"

And though it did not believe them, either one of them, just before getting up from the floor, in the darkness of the room, the black-eyed dog began to smile.

Christopher Hellwig and Michael J. Lee

THE DAUGHTER

A husband and wife and their young daughter lived together in a ground-floor apartment. Though both were employed, they worked different shifts to ensure that their daughter was never left alone. One evening, the husband returned home from a long day at work. He was greeted, as usual, by his young daughter, who was reading a book, and by his wife, who was preparing dinner. During the meal, the husband asked the two what it was that they wanted most in the world.

"Be honest," he said. "It won't hurt me."

"I want more time alone," said the daughter.

"And I want more time with my husband," said the wife.

"And I, too, need more time with you," said the husband to his wife. "Though you know, daughter, that I still treasure you."

"I know," said the daughter. "I am smart enough to know."

"And so sensitive," said the wife. "Sensitive enough to feel what we feel."

"And beautiful," said the husband. "You are a beautiful girl."

The wife looked quickly at her watch. "I am late for work," she said (often, the wife worked the graveyard shift).

The husband looked at his wife, then his daughter, and then his own watch. "You shouldn't go to work," he said to his wife.

"What?" said the wife. "Can we afford for me not to work?"

"No," said the husband. "But we should go downtown tonight, just the two of us." Then he looked at his daughter. "Do you really want more time to yourself?"

"Yes," said the daughter.

"Would you feel comfortable here, alone?" said the father.

"I would," said the daughter. "I believe I would."

"And you would lock all the windows and doors," said the mother. "Wouldn't you?"

"Yes," said the daughter. "I would keep them all locked."

"And the blinds," said the mother. "You'd keep them closed, wouldn't you?"

"Yes," said the daughter. "I would keep them all closed."

"And if anyone came knocking, either at window or door?" said the father.

"I'd first peek through the blinds," said the daughter, "before opening either."

"Good," said the father.

"And what will you do with all your time alone?" said the mother.

"I will bury my nose in a book," said the daughter. "So I grow even more smart and sensitive."

"Good," said the father. "But you will go to bed on time?"

"Yes," said the daughter. "I will go to bed on time."

"And if I give you my phone, will you call?" said the mother. "Will you call us if you need to?"

"Yes," said the daughter. "I will call if I need to."

"But you shouldn't need to," said the father.

"No, I shouldn't need to," said the daughter.

"But if you do need to . . . ," said the mother.

"Then I will call," said the daughter.

"If you hear someone knocking on the door," said the father.

"I will pretend that no one is home," said the daughter.

"And if you hear someone tapping at the window," said the mother.

"I will tell them to go away," said the daughter.

"And if you hear someone opening the door?" said the father.

"Then I will call the police," said the daughter.

"Not us first?" said the mother.

"No," said the daughter. "Second."

"You should call us first," said the father.

"Oh?" said the daughter.

"Always call us first," said the mother.

"Why?" said the daughter.

"To make sure it isn't us opening the door!" said the father.

"Oh," said the daughter.

"But if I leave you my phone," said the mother, "and someone should happen to call, how would you answer for me?"

"I don't know," said the daughter. "Perhaps I wouldn't answer."

"But say you did answer," said the mother. "Do you know what you should say?"

"No," said the daughter. "I'm not you, Mother."

"If you answer," said the mother, "you should say, 'Hello, this is my phone.'"

"Hello, this is my phone," said the daughter. "Like that?"

"Yes," said the mother. "So they don't suspect anything."

"What would they suspect?" said the daughter.

"No one will suspect that it isn't really me!" said the mother.

"And if they are able to see through me?" said the daughter. "That I am not you?"

"Then ask them a question," said the mother. "Ask them where they are."

"And after I hear their answer?" said the daughter. "After I hear where they are?"

"That depends," said the father. "If they say they're far away, don't say anything at all."

"But if they say they're nearby," said the mother, "at, say, the window or the door."

"What do I say then?" said the daughter.

"Tell them to go away," said the father.

"But what if," said the daughter, "they say that they have passed through the window, or gone around the door?"

"You thank them and say good-bye," said the father.

"But why?" said the daughter.

"There may be nothing left to suspect," said the father.

"And there may be nothing else to say," said the mother.

"Then I hang up the phone?" said the daughter.

"Yes," said the father. "And you call us."

"But why?" said the daughter.

"To tell us what you know," said the mother. "Agreed?"

"Yes," said their daughter. "I guess so, yes."

"This is a big step for us," said the father. "Leaving you alone like this."

"It's a big step for me!" said the daughter. "Being left alone like this!"

"We've tried to raise you well," said the mother.

"Tried to always be there for you," said the father.

"Oh, get out of here already!" said the daughter. "I know how to reach you."

The husband and wife, convinced of their daughter's maturity, got dressed up in their best clothes, and after checking the windows, lowering the blinds, and testing the locks on the doors, they left for their night out. The daughter sat down with her book, and with her mother's phone in sight, began reading. She read for many hours: There were no knockings at the door, no scratching at the window, nor any other distractions, only complete silence. And when the hour grew late, well past her bedtime, with the book still open to the page she was reading, the daughter fell fast asleep.

The next morning, she awoke alone in the apartment, and she found three new messages waiting for her on her mother's phone, which had stayed beside her all through the night. The first was from her mother, who wondered whether or not the doors and windows were locked, and if she was fast asleep. The second was from her father, who wondered where her mother was, and whether or not the whole world was asleep. The third was from someone else, someone who did not mention her mother, did not even mention her father, but who suggested that she—the daughter—close her book, turn off her phone, and seal off every window and door.

Westwego
Philippe Soupault

—Translated from French by Andrew Zawacki

—To M.L.

All the cities of the world
oases of our starving plights
offer refreshing drinks
to the memories of loners and maniacs
and sedentary types
Cities of the continents
you're flags
stars fallen to earth
without really knowing why
and the mistresses of the poets of our day

I was walking around London one summer
feet burning and my heart in my eyes
near black walls near red walls
near the massive docks
where the giant policemen
were pricked like question marks
One could play with the sun
that would pose like a bird
on all the monuments
passenger pigeon
everyday pigeon
I went into this district called Whitechapel
my childhood pilgrimage
where I ran into
only people all dressed up
and wearing top hats
just merchants of matchsticks
wearing boaters
who hollered like the farmers of France
to get some clients to come

penny penny penny
I went into a bar
third-class cabin where
Daisy Mary Poppy
had sat at the table
next to the fishmongers
who chewed tobacco while closing an eye
to forget about the night
the night that approached with a wolfish step
an owl's stealth
the night and the smell of the river and of the tide
the night tearing sleep apart

it was a sad day
of copper and sand
that slowly leaked between the souvenirs
deserted islands storms of dust
for the animals snarling with wrath
who lower their heads
like you and like me
because we are alone in this city
red and black
where all the boutiques are delicatessens
where the best folks have very blue eyes

It's hot outside and it's Sunday today
it's sad out
the river is really unhappy
and the residents stayed home
I walk along the Thames
a single boat glides to garner the sky
the sky unmoving
because it's Sunday
and the wind wasn't up
it's noon it's five o'clock
we don't know where to go anymore
a man sings without knowing why
like I walk
when one is young it's for life
my childhood encaged
in this sonic museum

Philippe Soupault

Madame Tussauds
it's Nick Carter and his bowler hat
in his pocket he's got a full set of pistols
and shiny handcuffs like four-letter words
Next to him the knight Bayard
who resembles him like a brother
it's sacred history and the history of England
near to the big-time criminals who no longer have any names
When I left where did I go
there are no cafés
no lights that make the words whisk off
there are no tables you can lean on
to see nothing to look at nothing
there are no glasses
there are no vapors
only the sidewalks as long as the years
where bloodstains bloom at dusk
I saw in this city
so many flowers so many birds
because I was alone with my memory
near to all its gates
that hide the gardens and the eyes

along the banks of the River Thames
in February, on a beautiful morn
three English blokes in shirtsleeves
were crooning 'til the cows came home
tra la la tra la la tra la lay

Bus tearooms Leicester Square
I recognize you I've never seen you
except on postcards
my maid used to get
dead leaves
Mary Daisy Poppy
little flames
in this rinky-dink bar
you're the friends a poet fifteen years old
gently admires
thinking of Paris
at a window ledge
a cloud goes by
it's twelve o'clock noon

next to the sun
Let's walk to be silly
let's run to be glad
let's laugh to be powerful

Strange traveler traveling luggageless
I never left Paris behind
my memory would saunter wherever I walked
my memory trailed me like a little dog
I was stupider than the sheep
that blaze in the sky at midnight
it's very hot
I whisper to myself real seriously
I'm terribly thirsty I'm really quite thirsty
I've got nothing but my hat
key to the fields key to the dreams
father of memories
have I never quit Paris
but tonight I'm in this city
behind each tree of the avenues
a memory watches out for my wandering by
It's you my old Paris
but tonight at last I'm in this city
your monuments are the kilometer markers of my fatigue
I recognize your clouds
which cling to the chimneys
to tell me good-bye or hello
at night you are phosphorescent
I love you like one loves an elephant
all your cries are to me as cries of tenderness
I'm like Aladdin in his garden
where the magic lamp was alight
I'm in search of nothing
I'm right here
I'm sitting at a café terrace
and I flash a toothy smile
thinking of all my famous trips
I'd like to go to New York or Buenos Aires
to know the Moscow snow
to set out one night aboard an ocean liner
for Madagascar or Shanghai

trek back up the Mississippi
I went to Barbizon
and reread the voyages of Captain Cook
I lay down to sleep on the cushiony moss
I wrote poems near a wood anemone
gathering the words that hung from the branches
the little railroad put me in mind of the Trans-Canada
and tonight I smile because I'm here
in front of this trembling glass
where I see the universe
while laughing
on the boulevards in the streets
all the hoodlums walk past singing
the dry trees touch the sky
provided it rains
one can walk without getting tired
to the ocean or farther on
over there the sea beats like a heart
nearer the humdrum tenderness
of lights and barking
the sky has discovered the earth
and the world is blue
provided it rains
and the world will be content
there are also women who laugh when they see me
women whose names I don't even know
the children shout in their aviary of Luxembourg
the sun has changed a lot in six months
there are so many things that dance before me
my friends asleep all over the world
I will see them tomorrow
André of the planet-colored eyes
Jacques Louis Théodore
the great Paul my dear tree
and Tristan whose laugh is a big peacock
you're all living
I forgot your gestures and your true voice
but this evening I'm alone I'm Philippe Soupault
I walk slowly down the Boulevard Saint-Michel
I think about nothing
I count the streetlamps I know so well

coming close to the Seine
        alongside the bridges of Paris
and I speak out loud
all the streets are tributaries
when one loves this river where all the blood of Paris flows
and that's dirty like a dirty whore
but also simply the Seine
to whom one speaks as if to his mom
I was right next to her
who took off with no regret and no flourish
her extinguished memory was a malady
I was leaning against the parapet
like one kneels down to pray
the words were falling like tears
sweet like bonbons
Hello Rimbaud how're you
Hello Lautréamont how are you faring
I was twenty not a nickel more
my father was born in Saint-Malo
and my mother lives during the daytime in Normandy
me I was baptized in Canada
Hello me
The rug vendors and beautiful ladies
who hang around at night on the streets
those who guard the grace of the lamps in their eyes
those to whom pipe smoke and the glass of wine
seem all the same a bit drab
know me without knowing my name
and in passing say Hello you
and nevertheless there are in my chest
small suns that turn with a sound of lead
tall giant of the boulevard
caring man from the courthouse
the lightning is it prettier in spring
Its eyes my lightning are scissors
chauffeurs I have seven cartridges left
not one more not one less
not one of them is for you
you're ugly like interrogations
and I read on all the walls
carpet carpet carpet and carpet

the great convoys of experiences
near to us near to me
Swedish matches

The Paris nights have these pungent odors
that regrets and headaches leave behind
and I knew it was late
and that the night
the Paris night was going to end
like holidays
everything was well in order
and no one said a word
I awaited the three strokes
the sun comes up like a flower
we call I believe a dandelion
the great mechanical vegetation
that expected only encouragements
climbs and develops
faithfully
we no longer know whether to compare it
to ivy
or grasshoppers
has the fatigue up and gone
I see bargemen who exit
to clean up the charcoal
the tugboat mechanics
who roll a first cigarette
before lighting the boiler
over there in a port
a captain pulls out his handkerchief
to daub his head
by force of habit
and me the first this morning
I say anyhow
Hello

(1917–1922)

Twilight of the Small Havanas

H. G. Carrillo

La Habana Pequeña. Sí, sí, sí, claro, she is in Little Havana. Has somehow found her way back to Calle Ocho with all its light and noise during probably what has to be the hundredth, no, at least the thousandth time she can remember it has been announced that The Dictator is dead.

Officially dead this time, baby! someone alongside her is yelling in her ear, Dead like Fred, Dead like dead, Dead dead, mamita.

And it has been a while since she has last seen the boy. An hour, sí, an hour or so since he disappeared—Sí, sí, sí, disappeared into a moist fold of late afternoon, early night—when a drunk, ever so drunk drunk, yelling ¡Hijo de puta, Hijo de motherfucking puta! is shoved out of La Casa Panza by two men dressed as waiters.

He careens the sidewalk. His expensive-looking suit rumpled, tie askew, his wiry gray hair flies. Though it's that he has lost a cuff link, the opened sleeve fluttering around what looks like a snipped marionette's sweet little farewell, she notices as he stumbles, nearly mows her down, before falling face-first onto the curb.

And yet, it is not the sight of the man twisting on the ground in front of her that thrusts her heart into her throat, but the sudden realization that she has no idea how she got here or why her own name will not float to the surface of the jumble that seems to be her head.

A parade of cars passing, tops down, windows open, jams shouts and bleats from horns into the air.

Y la música. Sí, sí, sí, of course, music pours from every restaurant, souvenir shop, and bodega, a different tune, bolero, mambo, from every open window trumpets wail. Hands—fingers over thumbs—tumble hundreds of conga skins. And rather than trying to get to his feet, the drunk coils hips over belly and opens a wide bloody smile up at her.

¡Él está muerto, you heared? he spits. ¡Muerto! the sonwhatabitch está muerto, he slurs. We's all can go home now, he yells.

But as fast as it comes out of him the roar around them sucks it up.

¡Muerto! ¡Muerto! ¡Muerto! they yell. Like sprays of confettied razor blades ¡Muerto! or Dead! menace the air. And ¡Finalemente! ¡Finalemente! someone wails as though she has discovered something.

They are going home—¡Finalemente! one yells—after all these years. ¡Finalemente! another repeats as if trying to fashion lyrics around it, as if both languages weren't failing them, falling over each other—one canceling the other out as the other tries to make itself—as if in Spanish there was as precise a word, an exact phrase for it as the one that came so easily in English.

They could go to their houses, their homeland, she thinks, to their fatherland, the mother country. But in the street all around her it is *home* they yell, *home* as if they know where they are going.

And Home! Home! Home! threatens the surface of her eardrums, begins to aspirate the H, opens the E to an A, and suddenly O-May-O-May misheard across the street becomes the ¡Olé-Olé! they are all yelling in varying and converging beats of the congas.

So many voices, so much yelling, music, noise, and laughing. So much artificial light—fluorescent, neon, pinks, greens, and blues—that no one seems to hear what she is certain are six gunshots fired in a row.

Quick as an itch, deep as heartbreak, something tells her they are neither accidents nor celebration, and her knees collapse, sending her into a crouch. She is certain there was one person—someone who spoke for everyone around her who was calling out—Dead!—with the measured timing of a trained, evenhanded shooter. Dead! Dead! Dead! like the collective wishes of everyone milling around her, like a great combined want to see The Dictator's stilled, lifeless body rise up from the ground as he had, hundreds, no, at least a thousand and one times before, and come after them only to be shot down again. Dead!

There is a low growl at the center of her head and the base of her skull she takes to be a good sign, knowing it will grow into a shriek, eventually pushing its way out. A signal that whatever she took at whatever party—Sí, sí, sí, it must have been a party, she and the boy were always going to parties, always taking pills; she checks the crook of her arm for fresh needle marks; perhaps she snorted something—yet whatever it is is beginning to ease off and fade without completely letting up.

And as much as she tries to move one foot or the other, tries to make her mouth shout Home! like the others, whatever it was she took pulls her by the scruff of the neck as she tries to force herself forward and sucks her toward her fear of dividing in two.

Shaking her head—a pinhole opens and suddenly, unsure of her first, she knows her middle name and both her parents' surnames, though not how or which one of them connects to her; her confirmation name is Antonia, though she has no idea why or what her Social Security number or birth date is; she is not sure if she is thirty-five yet or when that might have happened, but she knows it is soon or was soon; she spells *simony* forward and backward without any idea of what it means, how or where she learned it—her hair settles and she looks around her, wants to, needs to find her reflection as much as she is fearful of what she will see. Not ready for the Medusa-like black coils she suspects rise off the top of her head as they fall on her neck, bare shoulders, and back. Certain her eye makeup had bled into a raccoon mask, she fears blinking will conjure a stilled pool or a sheet of black ice in which she will find herself.

One by one, rather than the names of the shops and restaurants, it is the shapes of the buildings she identifies. And suddenly, knows what they do rather than what they are, where to buy fruit, where it used to be easy to steal a handful of candy without anybody paying too much attention.

There used to be a man with a bright toothless smile who pushed a cart up the street selling guarapo; and if you were wearing a school uniform skirt, if you could pretend that you didn't notice that his fly was open but at the same time notice his fly was open, your second cup was free. Around the corner, on the second floor above a bodega, there used to be a place where you could be absolved of all your transgressions, throw your hate into someone else's lap, and go home with a shaker full of hope.

So much has changed in the years since she was last here. ¡Olé-Olé! they yell. Nearly everything is imprinted with the words *Little Havana*, and it brings on the need to laugh at how much like an amusement park, laugh at the need to mark everything *You Are Here*. *You Are Here*, she laughs as if she were watching herself from overhead. And *You Are Here*—she laughs—is the ride she wants to take so badly, the plane, the train she wants to jump on, and she fights the tickle it knuckles in her ribs. *You Are Here* kicks in her belly and throat: *You*, she laughs, as if it is to tell her who she already was; *Are*, she laughs, seems to suggest what she needed to be. And *Here* . . . somehow *Here* is funny. Too funny.

She laughs, knows she should be able to point out on a map, tell a story. But she believes she is laughing too hard, too hysterically, she heaves, same time thinks, there is nothing funny, nothing to laugh at.

And it is not until she hears someone screech Home! like a macaw as a crowd of tourists—mostly college-age kids—jostles her to avoid stepping on the drunk at her feet that it is giggling, giggling, giggling—her own giggling—that forces her to notice her cheeks and the tops of her breasts are hot and wet, though she had no idea that she was crying.

Samba and mambo and the beating of drums, slap her in the face. Congas on top of congas, and ¡Ayyyyy-yiyi-yyyyy! comes out of a rude rustle of skirts as the wearer throws her head back, sets her hips swaying, and disappears into the parade. As if to follow it, call it back, the drunk cranes his neck and repeats the sound. It is the two of them screeching together that seems to rise and knot itself above the din and wants to split her head into pieces.

To reach out and grab something that will give her balance, she finds she is spelling *Phoenicopterus rubber* because she is certain she knows what it is.

Birds. Pink, pink birds. Long legs, long wingspans. Strong. The birds around the Pinar del Rios, the tertials along the wings of pink pink, hard-kneaded, *Phoenicopterus rubber*—rubber, rubber—but the common term for them will not come.

¡Olé-Olé! they yell in the street around her.

And there is the sudden clatter of bracelets in front of her—a rush of long tangling black hair with a screech of necklaces and jangling cleavage—that is almost like watching some part of herself pass by, and suddenly, *Mellisuga helenae* comes easily. Hundreds of them, tiny little things of blue and orange and gray flutterings. Zunzuncitos first, then hummingbirds, come to her.

¡Zio, Zio! they screech.

And as she mouths the words she recognizes them, can identify their genus and order—she remembers writing something about their cries being nearly imperceptible to the human ear, but having heard it; she is certain she has heard it—hundreds, thousands of them fly toward her—¡Zio, Zio! they screech—forcing their way past her lips and exploding out the back of her head. Along with their droppings, they leave questions about their ails, questions about fungi growing underneath their wings that seems to cause the air to consume them in midflight.

¡Zio, Zio!

Breathe, she says, and she tastes the grit and dust of feathers on her tongue and the roof of her mouth. Breathe, she says. And as she exhales, something—the taste in her mouth, the smell of nitrates, the white of bird droppings, in her nostrils, something—makes her say Mala Noche. And though it doesn't make sense to her, Mala, she says, Bad. Noche she says, Night. Bad Night, Bad Night. Very, very bad night.

¡Zio! Zio¡ the birds cry.

And ¡Ayyyyy-yiyi-yyyyy! the drunk yells again, but the rustle of skirts is too far away to distinguish it from any of the other noises on the street. He calls again hard, as though he is about to turn himself inside out, and it comes back at her all at once, with the sudden awareness of drowning, that at one time this was home. Mala Noche—Quizás Quizás Quizás—a place she had been raised to also call home. ¡O-May-O-May¡ ¡Olé-Olé! Near Camagüey, she remembers her mother telling her. But don't let them stamp your passport, she had said.

¡Zio, Zio! the birds shriek. Mala Mala Noche.

And suddenly, she remembers having been arrested. Don't let them stamp your passport, they said. And she remembers having gotten herself put in jail. Mala Mala Mala Noche. Through the exact numbers—the exact dates, the numbers she wore across her chest; exact, clean numbers, clean and exact measurements—it occurs to her that she does or did science.

¡Ayyyyy-yiyi-yyyyy! the drunk screams. And hand over fist the congas tumble.

O-May! O-May! O-May! they yell.

She was headed home, she had told family, friends, and colleagues in the lab that she was working in at the time. But don't let them stamp your passport, they had said.

¡Zio, Zio!

Sí, sí, sí, she had worked in a lab at one time; can see herself in some murky part of her past in which she is bent over a microscope, white lab coat, but cannot recall the name for what she sees—and she remembers driving to Toronto, leaving her car in the lot; It's only for a month or so, she had told people.

Everyone she knew—in her lab, on campus—had said it was the best way to go—nobody she knew up north at school—Sí, sí, sí that's it, she had been a graduate student up north somewhere it snowed—and no one she knew down in Miami—had ever gotten caught—Don't let them stamp your passport, they said—boarding a plane in Canada, landing at José Martí Airport.

Don't let them stamp your passport, they said. Take a lot of cash, they had told her; they believed in the kind of work she was doing. So many had done it before; it was to have been an easy trip. Easy in one country; easily out of another, they said, Don't let them stamp your passport.

¡Ayyyyy-yiyi-yyyyy! the drunk screams. Home! they yell around her. ¡Zio, Zio! The hummingbirds—birds, birds—hummingbirds. Zunzuncitos. She had been working on a fungus, a fungus that was attacking hummingbirds.

¡Zio, Zio!

Birds, they were her birds. Zunzuncitos. It hadn't been a bad night and she had been headed to Mala Noche, Mala Noche de Cuba; Cuba, a place, her mother and father had taught her, her whole life, to call home. Mala Noche.

¡Zio, Zio!

Home! they chant, O-May, O-May. And it seems to set off line after line of firecrackers, and the difference in sound makes her know that they were shots she heard.

¡Zio, Zio!

The birds were hers, and this street was home but not home.

But don't let them stamp your passport, they said.

¡Zio, Zio!

Somehow she belonged to the birds and the boy and the gun. But the boy?

They had been quicksilver years—Eight? Ten, maybe? She didn't know—with the boy. Years ragged as lightning jags, comprised of at least a hundred and one thousand I-dare-yous.

A wiry boy, hare quick, he had dared her to leave her bag in the bushes, dared her to put her tongue in his nostrils. He had dared her to sniff the white powder from the tips of her fingers, and she had found, in exchange, she had dared him to let her stick her fingers in his ass. She had dared him to seduce a man out of his tie, she had dared him to steal a bottle of rum at the Algonquin while the bartender's back was turned in response to his dare to smell his fingers after he had been with a woman who had given him fifty dollars extra on a Central Park carriage ride together just to make sure her husband saw them.

She had just gotten out of jail when she—¡Zio, Zio!—had first seen him.

Ratty red T-shirt with the old Mobil Oil Corporation logo—Pegasus—breaking up and faded. Paint splattered, worn chanclos, work boots, no socks, begging change.

He had been near Gramercy Park—*Hombre, por favor, can I get a few; I'm trying to get my hands on some anal beads and a Billy Idol poster, no mames. Por favor, mamita, por favor, I'm hungry and thirsty y carajó you got some fine legs on you. . . . Pardoneme, ma'am, my name is Pablo and I'm a long way from my country. . . . Pardoneme, ma'am, my name is Juan and you remind me of a very kind woman I left back home, so far away. . . . Pardoname, compadre; Pardoname, sir; Pardoname, señor; Pardoname, chico, you know what it is like to come over. . . . Oigame, ese; Escuhame cabrón; Señorita . . . Señorita . . . Señorita. . . . Señora, Señora, I ain't gone lie to you, I need to get high for I kill somebody, no shit*—and, sitting at a distance on a park bench, she had watched him for more than an hour, an hour and a half, two hours.

Still on the kind of time that the judge had mandated where clocks were suddenly much less important than calendars, she had had nowhere to be, nowhere to go that she could think of, so she had begun to walk.

Walk, she tells herself now, walk and breathe.

¡Ayyyyy-yiyi-yyyyy! the drunk wails, though nothing comes back but ¡Olé-Olé! and trumpet blares from across the street.

Fresh out of jail—O-May!-O-May, they yell—out of jail for going home. Her father had paid the fine, the court costs, the new clothes she was wearing on her back.

¡Zio, Zio!

He, they—he and her mother—would help her forget about everything that had happened before. As if she had done something wrong, as if it had been all her fault; all she did was go home; home; what she had been told her whole life was really her home.

And she remembers that he wouldn't hang up until she lied to him and said that she would go directly to American Express, cash the check he was sending, and get on the next plane home even though she knew she wouldn't. She had no idea that the boy, the boy in the Pegasus T-shirt would dare her to kiss him, and in turn she would dare him to steal a book of poems from the Barnes & Noble off Twenty-second Street. She had dared him to fuck her on the subway during rush hour, and he had often dared her when they were eating in cafeterias to show her tits to countermen and run with him as fast as she could out the door when they had eaten all they could hold.

¡Zio, Zio!

It had been a fine summer, a beautiful summer, a summer that seemed to unspool itself as a series of opportunities rather than days. They slept in the park and stood with their hands out when they wanted to, but they wanted for nothing and the sky was nearly always blue and she had thought about nothing until there were towers falling behind them, towers falling and—¡Ayyyyyyyyyy-yiyi-Ayyyyyyy! the drunk screams as he remembers too—the boy had dared her to love him, and she took his hand and did as the dust fell.

¡Olé-Olé! they chant, and as she begins to feel movement in her lower body, begins to think she might be able to walk, Breathe, she says, as—Xio, Xio—¡O-May-O-May!—Xio, Xio, Xio cuts by her like the razoring edge of a hawk wing—Xio—she has it—¡O-May-O-May!—Xio, she has it, XioXioXio, she pulls it from midair, her name is Xiomara.

Coño, the drunk hisses.

A Conversation
Thomas Bernhard and *André Müller*

—Translated from German by Adam Siegel

SETTING UP THIS INTERVIEW with Bernhard required a good deal of time. It began with a letter in which I proposed that I spend several days in the vicinity and see what transpired. I received no response. In November 1978 Bernhard was in Munich to give a reading at the university and was reminded of my suggestion. We agreed to meet for a beer following the reading, which never took place. Leftist demonstrators protesting the shah's regime occupied the hall. Bernhard escaped through an emergency exit. We met for our beer anyway. He said he would do the interview at the Rathaus-Cafe in Gmunden, on December 20, at 9:00 a.m. On December 14 he called to say he was going to Yugoslavia. He'd be back at the end of January. On February 8 he wrote: "I'll be secretly pleased when I know for certain that you're coming at the end of March. I'm open for anything you might want to do with me, including killing me. I place very little value on my own existence, even though suicide strikes me as ridiculous. Of course my attitudes are constantly in flux. I am in love with misery at the moment, if not besotted with it. See you at the end of March, if we're both still alive! Warm regards, Bernhard." Taking "end of March" literally, I wrote that I'd be arriving on the 31st, at noon. On March 29 I received a telegram: "Expecting you Saturday April 7th. Regards." The Thursday before the seventh I got a phone call: "How are you? I have to take my Tante [aunt] to a doctor's appointment in Vienna, but I'll be back on Tuesday. Come Wednesday." There matters stood. We began the interview at 11:00 a.m. Five hours later we were finished. Because of Bernhard's thick Austrian dialect *it was necessary* [emphasis in the original] to smooth out the text in the transcription. However, in the interest of authenticity, there were several instances where I left intact the original tone so that one might get an impression of the whole. As for the substance, I have changed nothing, even in those spots where Bernhard enmeshed himself in contradictions. They were part of his essence. He summed them up himself: "Nothing is true and everything is true."

The farmhouse gate is open, silence all around. No bell. I'd have to call out to be noticed. Already my presence seems like an imposition. I sit on a bench against the outside wall of the house to wait for Bernhard to find me. Tired of waiting, I peer through the window to look for him in the room. I see the back of a woman's head; I tap on the windowpane. Bernhard unlocks the door for me. The woman is his Tante, his aunt. The room is the same one I was in the last time, the one with the ironing board. It's very overheated. Bernhard announces that he has a cold. As soon as she sees me, his Tante wants to leave. She says she's going to get her parasol and take a walk. Bernhard leaps upon this statement as an opportunity to rope her into our conversation. He corrects her, as though she's confused her terms: What she would like to do is fetch her umbrella for a walk in the sun. She stands firm: This is a parasol; she has an umbrella for when it rains. Which proves nothing, Bernhard says, they're just two umbrellas. His Tante sits down again. I am now a spectator before a theatrical scene. It is, I feel, an erotic scene. With words instead of caresses, words that cling. I push the record button on my tape recorder; taking the action as my cue, I ask:

The question is how do you tell a parasol from an umbrella?

"By its color," Bernhard's Tante says. "If it's black, it's an umbrella. That's how it's always been in my day."

By its color? I always thought it was by its frill.

"Maybe. There might have been a time when that was fashionable."

"All right, *Kinderl,*" Bernhard says, "given that fashions change every other year, you must've seen practically everything under the sun—"

"Now look," his Tante says, "it's always been based on the color. I should know how it's been for the past sixty years of my life."

BERNHARD: "—especially in turn-of-the-century Vienna, when people went out with all kinds of extravagant umbrellas."

TANTE: "Yes, they had parasols! I'm not disputing that at all."

BERNHARD: "We're going to kill each other over an umbrella."

TANTE: "No, I don't have the energy for it; I'd rather find something else more worth getting worked up about."

BERNHARD: "Can two people really kill one another?"

Yes, if the one is mortally wounded and shoots the other dead.

BERNHARD: "That's right, mutually doesn't have to mean simultaneously. But what if two people strangle each other at the same time and they both die at the same time. . . ."

TANTE: "All right, all right."

BERNHARD: "And both their tongues are hanging out, and then someone comes along with a stapler and staples their tongues together and takes them out . . . under an umbrella."

TANTE: "I'm just wondering whether it can be done. Whoever's stronger will take less time."

Simultaneity is really the problem, and in love as well.

BERNHARD: "It can happen there."

Really?

BERNHARD: "Well, maybe within a hundredth of a second."

TANTE: "I didn't hear that."

BERNHARD: "It doesn't matter."

(Now I'm caught up in the play and have to keep going. The tape is running. But what is my role?)

"Do you know Frau Teufl?" I ask his Tante. "The last time I was here she was sitting in the chair you're in. Only we were sitting in the other room then."

"Once we were in Vienna with Agi," Bernhard says, "with Hilde Spiel and her former husband, it was very funny—she'd ordered goulash, and she grabbed the bowl with both hands, and we all got splashed with it. Hilde Spiel had on a brand-new outfit, silk, and it got sprayed with goulash. The best part was that Agi, the guilty party, was annoyed because no one felt sorry that she was covered with soup from head to toe."

(Bernhard's Tante looks out the window.)

For all intents and purposes, this is prattle. But it's nice to be able to get all this prattle down. The whole time coming over I was wondering: How am I going to get him to talk? And now you're talking all on your own.

BERNHARD: "And herewith I'll stop talking. People get sharp eared when you say something like that, and they clam up, then they eat something, and then they clam up some more, because they're tired after the meal, and that's how the time goes by."

(Where are my questions? I think. They were leading questions. They've evaporated. My curiosity no longer takes the form of questions. I've gone beyond questions.) *The reason I came here is because I'd like to have a piece of yours, it doesn't matter what. Because you're the last—*

BERNHARD: "The last remains."

No, the last word. But I can't ask you any more questions.

BERNHARD: "Unquestionably."

TANTE: "This whole time I've been asking myself what this is supposed to be. An interview? A casual conversation? What is it supposed to be?"

BERNHARD: "It's not casual at all."

TANTE: "It is too. You have to give real answers when you're being interviewed."

BERNHARD: "Who says?"

TANTE: "It's just a phrase: a casual conversation."

BERNHARD: "Phrases are dangerous for writers. Everything a writer says unmasks him, insofar as he's wearing a mask."

TANTE: "Everyone is."

BERNHARD: "And every second they grow a new one. You only stop putting them on when you die. The last mask is the death mask. And then there has to be a sculptor right there—what do they call people who make death masks? Death maskeurs? Where do you find someone out in the country to remove a death mask for you? It's got to be done within the hour. And you have to have someone be briefed by a nurse who knows when it's time. Someone has to fumble around in a bag, while the party in question is lying there dying, and plop it on their face. There has to be a trace of breath left in the body."

Have you seen one?

BERNHARD: "I've seen lots of death masks."

Corpses, I mean.

BERNHARD: "My grandmother used to take me to the morgue when I was young. She'd pick me up and say, 'Look, there's another one.' Once she told me that the corpses had a cord to a bell tied to them, so the undertaker would be alerted if they came to. So it would ring somewhere. They did it because the mill-owner's wife died and then woke up. She only looked dead. She ran home from the cemetery in her winding sheet and banged on the door of her house, and when her husband, the mill owner, looked out and saw her, he had a stroke, and so he was dead and his wife was still alive. So from then on they had these alarms."

TANTE: "Do you remember the story I told you about the doctor who had never practiced, and the funeral cortege where suddenly the hand fell out of the coffin, and the doctor immediately saw what happened and realized that he was still alive, and a couple of weeks later he was able to practice again."

BERNHARD: "If he'd never practiced how could he practice again?"

TANTE: "Not the doctor, the corpse."

BERNHARD: "Well, a corpse definitely can't practice medicine."

TANTE: "I mean the man taken for a corpse."

BERNHARD: "The alleged corpse."

TANTE: "There wouldn't have been a funeral cortege if they'd known he was still alive."

BERNHARD: "The alleged cortege."

(I wonder how his Tante can stand all this mordant joking about death. She's eighty-five. Later I learn: She isn't his Tante. Bernhard just calls her that. They're not related. He met her in 1950 in a TB sanatorium. He was nineteen. The doctors at the Salzburg Landeskrankenhaus had given up on him. In his autobiographical account *A Breath* he describes the most pivotal moment of his life. He'd been moved into a bathroom that was to serve as his death-chamber. Bernhard watched a man being laid out in a zinc coffin and carried out. A nurse came in at ever-longer intervals to check his pulse: to see if he was dead. In the face of this hopeless situation he resolved to muster his reserves and overcome all external resistance in order to breathe again. He was transferred first to a sanatorium in Grossgmain and then to Grafenhof, where his Tante was taking the cure.)

Does it bother you that he's constantly joking about death?

TANTE: "I can't say I like it. He doesn't do it when it's just the two of us. Out of consideration for me."

BERNHARD: "I keep my corpses to myself. I don't let them out of the bag. Every now and then, if I need to get something out of her, I'll pull a couple of skulls out and threaten her a little, and put them back."

Aren't these stories a constant reminder of your own death?

TANTE: "That doesn't bother me. That's what I wake up with every day."

BERNHARD: "You'll be waking up in paradise in any event."

TANTE: "I don't know about that. I don't know where I'm going to wake up."

BERNHARD: "Maybe on some street corner covered with signs you can't understand, no way of knowing where to go, and an icy wind blowing."

TANTE: "There's not a lot that can happen. Either it keeps going or it stops."

BERNHARD: "And if everything just stops you won't know anything about it, and you won't be afraid anymore. First you get sick and then you die, and the dead are nothing—just a plastic bucket to take out the trash."

As long as we talk about death it can't scare us.

BERNHARD: "But you can't keep it up indefinitely. First one person runs off, then another, and then it's every man for himself, all trying not to think about it. The only place you can talk about it for a long time is the theater, and even there you're done in two hours, and everyone runs away if they didn't already during the intermission."

But that's the question: Where are they running?

BERNHARD: "Nowhere. You can run away from something, but you just take it along with you. The rage and despair and all the rest of it stay with you. It lasts a while until the physical separation becomes an actual—probably there isn't any actual separation. All the people we ever knew in life are on hand within us. We're sitting here as the sum of all those people. Everything we come across stays inside of us, just as we remain inside others."

TANTE: "That's immortality. As long as someone's thinking about you and talking about you then you're immortal."

BERNHARD: "Whatever. . . . You have to make it easy for yourself because there's no alternative. At any rate, none of it proves anything. No one knows anything. It's all *wurst*."

TANTE: "Where do you get this '*wurst*'? This really annoys me. The fact that I don't like wurst notwithstanding, I just hate the phrase. Maybe it's just the sound of it that annoys me. But where does the phrase come from?"

BERNHARD: "Maybe the sausage stuffing, when all the meat and the fat and all of the rest of it goes in, whatever can't be explained. It all gets turned into sausage eventually and then it goes back out into the world."

TANTE: "I'm going."

BERNHARD: "Where?"

TANTE: "The kitchen." [In die Küche.]

BERNHARD: "The church?" [Kirche?]

TANTE: "No, that's too far."

(She stands up.)

BERNHARD: "You have a huge run in your right stocking, it's as big as a plum."

TANTE: "Then I'll just have to take them off."

(She leaves the room. There's nothing else for me to do except try to interview him.)

What are you thinking about?

"Nothing at all."

What were you thinking about before I got here?

"There were three men here, they want to put up some pylons. There's a power line that runs from Ohlsdorf to Lambach and around 150 people had to give their approval because it runs across their property. I wouldn't sign, I said I won't sign off on any damages to myself. It would be like someone willing to sign his own death warrant. On the other hand, I didn't want to hold up the construction, because that's just as absurd. Why would you interfere if they're just going to do it anyway? So they had to figure out how to keep working without my approval. It wasn't that easy."

What sort of agreement did you reach?

"I said I'm basically opposed to it, but because I can't do anything about it and it's over and done with, I had to promise not to sue for property damages when they started digging. Now the court has to issue an eminent domain ruling. It's none of my business. It doesn't concern me."

It doesn't matter to you?

"When you're powerless the more powerful can do more or less whatever they want. When I know that matters are utterly out of my hands, it's all *wurst* to me; I don't want to strain my nerves unnecessarily."

Can you really deal with your nerves so efficiently?

"There's no point getting worked up. I'd just have to hire a lawyer and ask for such and such an amount in compensation, but first of all, you can't be compensated, and second, I'd just tear my hair out over it. I'd always be driving out there, there'd be a hearing every three weeks. The whole thing would drag out for at least a year and a half, and they'd just build it anyway."

Do you ever show your feelings?

"I'm always perfectly amicable with these people."

Is there anything you're afraid of?

"You're always afraid."

Of being robbed, for example?

"I'm not really afraid of being robbed. I'm here all alone. I should be constantly afraid. If someone's going to rob me, they're going to rob me. The only question is what else would happen. I'd either be stabbed or beaten to death. That's the unknown. There are any number of opportunities. If someone wants to kill me, he's going to do it no matter what. If you've got a mind to kill somebody, it's the easiest thing in the world in and of itself. You can't constantly be on your guard to keep it from happening. You just have to not be weaker than the murderer."

But what do you do if he doesn't kill you, but only hangs around being a nuisance?

"No one can hang around forever, because anyone who's up to something is going to get tired eventually; no one can put up with waiting any longer than a year with no payoff. People who are always up to something are working toward some sort of goal, otherwise they'd go insane. With schemes like that it's the same thing as with the sexual act. You can't put up with it unless there's some sort of resolution. You can delay it, which can be a source of pleasure, but I don't think you could drag it out for an entire year. So everything comes to an end. But what good is it if they call it quits and there's another one lurking in the background? It's pointless. You kill off the first one, and a second one springs up even bigger than the first."

Doesn't that make you the murderer?

"Well, if you have the ability, if you're stronger than he is, you might be able to strangle him before he kills you. You might like being strangled. You don't know. You don't know how you're going to feel until that moment. Maybe you'll get the urge to just pack it in and take it."

If you were to apply that to the two of us, you'd have to assume that my interest in you should have some sort of resolution too.

"What kind?"

Who knows?

"It could be anything from knife sharpening to . . . I don't know, anything."

You wrote that you didn't care if I killed you, which astounded me—I had no such intention.

"No? People nowadays would kill you over nothing if they could, in fair weather or foul. When did I tell you that?"

In February, after you got back from Yugoslavia, which you told me you didn't like.

"What's 'like' have to do with it? It just wasn't right."

Why not?

"It just wasn't working."

Your writing?

"Yes, of course, my writing. I'd sit there for a couple of hours and think, this should be ideal. And it would've been ideal if I'd only stayed a couple of hours. I didn't know there was no one else in the hotel except a bunch of sickly old people, shuffling down the halls coughing and hacking."

Do you need quiet to write?

If it's far enough along in and of itself I can write anywhere. I can write with other people around, in a terrible racket, if it's ready, and if it isn't ready then there's no place peaceful or ideal enough, and I can't do it. There's no such thing as the ideal spot."

What do you do when you can't write?

"It's the worst, the absolute worst. But eventually you start to like it, because you know that a month of horror lies ahead."

Do you watch television?

"On occasion. The news, or something stupid, something not too demanding, the stupider the better."

Do you go for walks?

"Hardly ever. I'm not a walker, not at all. I just putter around the house or do something, I don't know, some stupid chore, or I lie around in bed. Around noon I'll take a walk or drive to get something to eat, and think, all right, I'll be able to do it tomorrow, I'll start tomorrow, but in the morning I feel so horrible I go looking for some other activity so I don't have to get started. That's what happens. You just dawdle around and then it's too late, and you tell yourself the day's already half gone, and that does it. This can drag on for weeks and months. What keeps me going is tension."

As long as you can live without it, you shouldn't write. Rilke said you should only do it when you have to.

"For all intents and purposes you shouldn't do anything, you should just muddle through, and even that. You shouldn't even do that."

Don't you have to earn a living?

"I used to."

What do you mean "used to"? You do.

"Well, yeah, it's just worked out that way."

What did you live on before you were a writer?

"I pretty much lived off my Tante for fifteen years. Every day she gave me a little pocket money, maybe ten schillings, and seven-fifty went for lunch at the public cafeteria, and two-fifty for a cup of coffee, and that was enough for me. In the evening I'd go somewhere where there were people and where there was something to eat and drink, and I'd come home around three in the morning."

So your Tante supported you?

"More or less. But not always. I made a little money from time to time. I was a court reporter for a while. Later on I delivered beer for the Gösser Brauerei. There were a lot of difficulties—it was really awful, it's just so uncomfortable, always taking and never giving."

When did things change?

"In 1965, when I bought this farmhouse."

With what money?

"I got ten thousand marks from the Bremer Literaturpreis for *Frost*. That was seventy thousand schillings, but the farm cost two hundred thousand. So I spent about an hour shaking down my publisher, maybe not even that, I think it took half an hour. I said this is it, either you give me the money for the farmhouse or I'm going to another publisher."

Was Frost *the first work you wrote?*

"No, I'd always been writing, even when I was ten. I just found some poems that my grandfather, who was a writer, read over. He'd underlined things in pencil: very good or good or dumb or whatever."

What were your poems about?

"Oh, the moon is high or the red lantern, or an endless forest stretches out before me, themes like that, kid stuff. I started writing a novel around then too. It was called *Peter Goes to the City*. He arrives at the Salzburger Bahnhof and wants to see the city. But 150 pages later he's still at the Hotel Europa, and he's about to get on the streetcar, and I just thought, this isn't going anywhere, he's not going to move an inch. It would've taken me ten thousand pages just to get him to the Domplatz. I really wanted to have a plot, but there wasn't any."

How did your first publication come about?

"They were poems. I'd written a lot of poems and I had it in my head that they were better than Rilke or Trakl or any of them, and I just went upstairs to see Otto Müller, the publisher, and I rang the bell and said I'm so-and-so, and I've brought you some poems, would you like to publish them? And he sat down and looked through a couple of them, and they were published. That was in 1956. I was very ambitious and cocky and everything. Afterward, when you've actually done it, you can see that it wasn't anything, really. But at that moment there's this peak feeling. Once you've made it you see it never ends. At the end of the day it's just nothing. When it came out I thought, well, I don't know, if it's that easy it can't be worth much, and so I stopped; none of it ever appealed to me. After three books of poetry I thought, what's the point of this? Ten books, twenty, where does it end? It just gets more and more stupid. And I didn't write anything for a long time."

When did you start up again?

"The next thing was a text for ballet and orchestra, "Die Rosen der Einöde." Fischer published it. I had been staying with the Fischers in Frankfurt, I knew them through my grandfather, from when I was a child, and I went to eat with Hirsch [Rudolf Hirsch, *Lektor* at S. Fischer Verlag] in the Frankfurter Hof and I put the manuscript down next to me and he said, what are you working on there, and I gave it to him and he said, let's do it, and asked me what kind of typeface I wanted, and I said I had seen some poems by Marini and I wanted type like that, and they set it that night, and the next morning the galleys were ready. And I was really proud, because they used to always do their newspaper ads with all the writers in alphabetical order, and I was right at the top, and way down below was Thomas Mann, which made a big impression. Next I wrote some short prose pieces, but at the time I was extremely eccentric, which is probably an understatement, and even though the jacket had already been printed up, I thought I'd rather wait a bit, and I telegraphed them: Don't publish, assuming the costs. And Hirsch got really angry, and that relationship was finished, and there was another phase where I was just sitting around Vienna doing nothing, living at my Tante's. She had an apartment, basically a broom closet, and I said, what do you need a broom closet for, I'll move in. And I'd go to the Krapfenwaldl baths and all of a sudden I felt like writing prose, and I would get up at 5:00 a.m. and go to the Krapfenwaldl around nine and lie in the sun and read the paper and then go get lunch and after lunch go to a café and then between four and eight I'd write some more, and then the manuscript was done, and I had a friend who was an editor at Insel-Verlag, and I thought it'll either work out or I'll go to Africa and work for a health organization. I had been learning how to drive a truck for that. The driving test was when the pope died, 1963, that's how I remember. . . . So I sent the manuscript to Wieland Schmied and he talked it up to Arnold [Fritz Arnold, outside reader at Insel-Verlag], and three days later they took it, and that was settled, and I didn't have to go to Africa. But then I was back to sitting around thinking, what should I do now? So I went to Poland, and there were all these red banners, I remember that, and then the book came out and I got the Julius-Campe-Preis for it in Hamburg, they split the prize three ways, they couldn't decide, then the Bremer Literaturpreis, and I came here, and here I am. . . . Have you had lunch yet?"

(Bernhard suggests a restaurant in Steyermühl. Hanging from the open door is a "closed" sign. It turns out the locale is being sold by the owners because it wasn't profitable, and the business is being suspended indefinitely. BERNHARD: "The final closure." We drive to Laakirchen, to another restaurant. Bernhard orders liver and rice soup and baked mushrooms. I don't order; I want to be able to keep asking him questions.)

Did you ever try to take your own life?

"When I was a child I tried to hang myself but the cord snapped."

How old were you then?

"I was seven or eight. And one time I went out for a walk with my grandfather, we were living in Traunstein at the time, and I was swallowing sleeping pills while we were out, and all at once I started feeling sick, and I said, I have to go home, we were about thirty kilometers from town and so I ran away and must have gotten home, I can't remember how, and spent four days in bed, throwing up constantly, because there was nothing left in my stomach. I must have been around ten then."

And what happened after that?

"After that I was cursed for being a problem child who just wanted make scenes and bring misfortune upon the family."

Do you ever think about killing yourself now?

"The thought's always there. But I have no intention—at least not now."

Why not?

"I think it's curiosity, pure curiosity. I think it's only my curiosity about life that holds me back."

What do you mean "only"? Other people have no curiosity and survive despite it all.

"I have nothing against life."

Nonetheless there are people who regard your books as an instigation to suicide.

"Yes, but no one's done it. Recently, in fact, about two weeks ago, a woman was standing outside my window saying she had to talk to me. I said, OK, why do you need to talk to me now? I'm in bed right now with this terrible flu. And she said, before it's too late. I said, do you want to kill yourself? She said, no, I want to kill you. I said, I don't think you're being rational, you ought to go home. She said no, she had to come in. I said, nothing doing, because I can hardly get out of bed and I have to lie down. She said, you don't have to worry, I've got a husband, I don't want to go to bed with you. . . . All of this through the open window and as I was trying to close the window she put her finger in there. I said, I'm going to squash your finger. So she took it out and I closed the window and went back to bed. A while later I looked out and she was still standing outside the house. At some point she must've left, but afterward she wrote me a letter, she'd be waiting for me at eight at night on such and such a day, a Monday, at the cemetery, by the right gate, her favorite spot. But I wasn't at home that day. So she sent me another letter, sixteen pages long, telling me her whole life story, about her husband whom she married too young, stuff like that. She probably wanted to kill me and then kill herself at the cemetery. You never know when you're going to set someone off."

Do we want to talk about the effect your writing has?

"I'd rather not."

What should we talk about? I wanted a lengthy interview with you, maybe twenty pages.

"You're free to write anything about me you want, whatever occurs to you, whatever suits your purpose. You can write that everything you said, I said. I'd do the same thing. Anything I think of, it's total *wurst* to me who said it. Once, to make money, I wrote program synopses for *Radio Österreich*, this cheap program guide, but I was too lazy to read up on everything: For example, for a lecture by Heidegger I just made up some sentences and passed them off as Heidegger sentences. Something would occur to me and I would write it down: As Heidegger said . . . Who's going to check to see whether it's true or not? They'd have to read through a thousand pages."

I can't do that. I can't make a claim that's not true. I can't write that you made ten suicide attempts when you only made two.

"Right, the facts have to be in accord."

Yes, and it has to be you who verbalizes them, because I'd like this to be a dialogue. So we'd need you to say, "I'm laughing" whenever you laughed.

"But it's you laughing now. I'm just accompanying your laughter with my words."

(I see this won't work. I must try asking questions again.) *Do you laugh when you're by yourself too?*

"I do laugh when by myself, yes, but hardly ever."

At what?

"At some situation, something that suddenly seems funny to me."

Even your own despair?

"Yes, that too." (He starts eating. I turn the tape recorder off. . . .) "Why are you turning it off?"

You probably don't want to talk while you're eating.

"You'll just hear the fork clinking."

You're actually very accommodating. If I say or do something, you say something right back.

"Right, you see, that's all right. If you toss something out there, something always comes out of it."

I'm just afraid I'll run out of things to toss out there.

"You shouldn't dwell on it so much. If you dwell on it too much it comes out sounding stupid. Whenever I dwell on what I want to write and make an outline and mess around with it for too long, I end up writing nothing."

I'm amazed you're so productive when you're always so conscious of the pointlessness of writing. You make a living writing about the pointlessness of life. One might think that you're putting people on.

"How does anyone know? Even if it's a put-on it doesn't change anything. Whatever you call it is *wurst*. No one knows how anything comes about. You just sit there and try as hard as you can, and then it's over again."

Of course, but where's the motivation for the effort? Between the bed and desk you're overwhelmed by the notion that it's all just pointless.

"I have an overwhelming need to write. I was in Stuttgart a few weeks back and I saw Chekhov's *Three Sisters*, and I thought, this could be one of my plays, only I would have done it better, much denser, and all at once I felt like writing again."

If your nihilist's view of life were to predominate you'd have to let that pass.

"And never write anything again?"

No.

"Then I wouldn't have anything available, and you couldn't read anything by me, and we wouldn't be sitting here talking about it with each other."

Absolutely. And that woman wouldn't have come to your window to offer you her commiseration.

"Well, I cured her quick and she never came back. I'm not someone to be pitied, I'm strong. Someone who's weak couldn't write this stuff. There's such a wonderful robustness, being able to produce an output like mine. The weaker the people and the situations you depict, the stronger you have to be, otherwise you couldn't do it, and the weaker you are, the stronger and more positive and vital the things you write about. I'm thinking of [Carl] Zuckmayer, who was always sort of shaky, a strong wind could knock him over, and he found his salvation in Indians and redskins and bandit kings, but he himself was just quaking like an aspen. . . . On the other hand, the things I write correspond to their actual condition. It's intermittent. If I'm around people and in a good mood and strong, full of vitality, I don't write at all, I have no desire to write."

What do you do then?

"When?"

When you're full of vitality?

"I have no interest in writing then."

I mean, what's this vitality of yours like? Are you feeling amorous, or something like that?

Not for years. I burnt myself out on that completely twenty years ago.

You mean you burnt yourself out sexually?

"No, the sexual never interested me. None of that was really possible, with my illness, because I was at that age where everything would've had to get started naturally, and I was in no condition for that. When you're just glad to be alive and you're getting shunted from one sanatorium to the next, you're not thinking about any of that stuff. You're only thinking one thing: I don't want to die. . . . But all that can change the next day."

Why do you say that? If someone has to fight for something the way you had to fight for your life—doesn't that count for anything?

"It does, but we all know what it's like to be in one of those states where you go from caring to not caring from one second to the next. You get into a mood. And a minute later you're more animated than before."

Have you ever experienced such a rapid shift from being tired of life to being in love with it?

"Of course."

That means you know what it is, and if you get into one of those suicidal moods you'll remember it, I maintain, and you won't be tempted by suicide.

"Why not?"

Because you've given it too much thought.

"It's no use. There's no recourse to reason or common sense when you do it. You either do it or you don't, that's all. And if you don't do it, then you just keep living."

Can you imagine finding yourself in an emotional state where you could lose self-control?

"No, that's something I never lose. But that doesn't mean anything. My God, what do you want me to say? What do you want to hear?"

You're supposed to say that you won't kill yourself.

"I can't do that. I don't know, because I've had too much experience with people and things and situations completely changing in an hour. There's no warning, no one's immune. There are so many fantastic systems where you think you've put together some definitive, amazing thing, and a second later it's gone. A concrete structure that's nothing but a house of cards. It just needs the right gust of wind."

All right, maybe my theory is stupid, but I simply can't imagine how someone in such a state of self-awareness could kill himself, assuming, of course, that he didn't believe in life after death. Has anyone who was a real atheist ever killed themselves in front of a mirror?

"I don't know. But I can see how someone might consciously kill themselves, how they might sit down for breakfast and say, I'm going to slit my wrists now. My grandfather's brother did that: He wrote a little note where he laid out clearly and rationally why he was doing it. There's nothing that's inconceivable; every person is completely different. There are no two identical people in the world. There is no philosophy with any validity that goes beyond the person who came up with it. What Kant wrote is very nice and all, but his is only one philosophy, *by* one person and *for* one person. That hundreds, thousands, or millions of people make it their own is something else entirely, they just accept it and basically soak it up like a sponge. That's why there are no truths that transcend a given person and at the same time are transformed within that person. Man lives for nothing and for everything. Every end point obliterates everything that came before it, and then you just start all over again, assuming you know what comes before and after. Every era is a point of departure. There's always some initial situation—today we have nylon or rayon, which didn't exist a hundred years ago, but what kind of things are they? Straitjackets that man thinks up so he'll have something to get out of."

But what you're saying is obvious.

"All of it's obvious, they're just mostly the least accessible things, because people are always resisting them by thinking they have to be something special. There's nothing special, and there's nothing exceptional, and basically there's nothing essentially interesting about the world at large. You can only devise choices for your life alone, and then other people will come along and claim they're interested in all that too, which is just stupid. People rely on things, on rules and laws, because they're weak. But who says the rules are right? I can claim that one and one isn't two. No one knows who came up with the notion that one and one are two. Everything's based on this stupid insight. It's crap. You could set up a million other systems that are just as good."

Well, OK, good.

"What does that mean? In one breath you're saying three elementary terms: well, meaning no, yes, and good. You just toss that out there. You're treating an earth-shattering lexical trinity like so much filler. That's an enormity."

I notice we're not talking about suicide anymore.

"We don't need to. If you kill yourself, let me know."

I'm not going to kill myself. I've been trying to make that clear.

"Well, you never know. I had a friend, we used to meet for a glass of wine, totally petit-bourgeois guy, he wrote little poems, terrible prose, dumb like a petit bourgeois, married three times, two kids each time, and he was content with his big belly and his off-the-rack suit, and he went home, put on his wife's dirndl, stuffed the bra, and hung himself from the door dressed like that, he was around forty-five, a man who'd never shown any dissatisfaction with life whatsoever."

Well, that just proves my thesis, because if he'd looked at himself in the mirror, wearing a dirndl, rope around his neck, he'd have had to laugh, he wouldn't have been able to do it. I think at that moment the comedy of it would have kept him from doing it.

"Probably, yeah."

So look. You can think it over even once you've started, and get yourself out of that mood. You get sharper as you get older, not duller.

"That's the question. Maybe you're suffering from brain damage. Even the strongest aren't immune. I have a sister, a strong personality in her own right, but she's so unstable she's spent years migrating from one mental hospital to the next. She's constantly threatening to kill herself. And every time my brother, who's an internist, drives out to see her and talks her out of it. I told him to leave her alone. If she's going to jump, she'll jump. He should let her exercise her own free will."

What does your brother say?

"He says: How can you be so cold?"

That reminds me of the woman in your most recent novel, the one who gets asked whether she'll ever kill herself, and just says yes, and then goes and does it.

"If I depict something, a situation or something that's sort of centrifugally oriented toward suicide, it's obviously a description of a condition that I'm presumably feeling while I'm writing, even though I haven't killed myself, I've just dodged it. You can write wonderfully about that. Someone else might not be able to, or they might come up with something totally wooden. . . . What are you thinking about? Your face just totally changed."

I'm just wondering whether you really seriously wanted to kill yourself. In your autobiography you just say that when you were mortally ill and the doctors had given you up for dead, you chose life. It's something completely different when you deal with it on your own.

"Who knows whether anything I've written is true? I myself am always surprised by how many lives are seen as unique, when they actually all resemble each other, not to mention the fact that they're all really just personae with as much or as little to do with you as any other life. Nothing is true and everything is true, just as everything is both ugly and beautiful, dead and alive, delicious and tasteless. It all comes down to what you're most receptive to. Anything can have great appeal. My point of view is that all things are equal. So death is nothing unusual to me. I talk about death the way someone else might talk about a kaiser roll."

This point of view—or rather, this lack of a point of view—is one you can only have in the most privileged of situations. Someone with an office job has to accept the values prevalent in society as his own, or he wouldn't be able to even fill out a form.

"I've always resisted getting a job like that. There were attempts, people trying to stick me in an office somewhere earning twenty-three hundred schillings a month. I ran off the next day."

To your Tante?

"Well, anywhere, anywhere things were happening, you know, I didn't care, as long as it wasn't back there, with the rest of them, because the rest of them only want to destroy you and bring you down. People only think about themselves, no consideration for anybody else. No one ever wishes you well. So-called good things always come to nothing, and you can imagine the sense of relief the sick feel when they're on their way down. They're so loaded down with praise like 'genius' and 'great' and 'you're so wonderful' and 'the good always suffer'—mankind's awash in such platitudes. But it's even worse when you're on your way up because you just end up with all this abuse hurled at you. You have to ask yourself: What's the way up? What's the way down? You get the feeling that even when you're on your way up there's always someone laughing his ass off at you thinking, If he only knew that he's really on his way down."

Where does this negative outlook on people come from? Because deep down you only know yourself and no one else.

"I can't say—you only know yourself in relation to other people, because otherwise you wouldn't be on hand to see yourself. You can only see yourself if you have an absolute image of your own environment along with that of others, because it's all founded on comparisons. If you can't see anything besides yourself you can't make judgments or feel things."

Well, yes, that's why I came out to see you.

"There you have it. You come out to see me because I'm here, but so are four billion other people."

I didn't come out to see four billion other people. I don't know them.

"Well, you should be glad you don't know them. Imagine if you had to shake hands with four billion people, you'd never have come out to see me. I think that'd be great; after six months your hand would fall off."

Do you know these four billion?

"You don't need to know them, because they're all the same, they're just a *mass*, such a beautiful word, you can apply it to everyone, and it never changes—the situations are always the same, the people who live at five thousand feet in Afghanistan or at five thousand feet in the Salzkammergut are similar, only in the Salzkammergut they're wearing lederhosen and in Afghanistan they're wearing some other garment, but the feelings and stories they have are the same."

Don't you think if we turned up something might change?

"It would be great if as soon as we turned up in Kabul a massacre broke out, and everywhere we went people were just dropping like flies."

You're joking.

"And I'm totally serious too, from one second to the next. And that's how you get from one moment to the next without killing yourself! A lot of people who kill themselves are known for being jokesters, well-adjusted, positive, happy people. Negative people don't kill themselves as often, because they're more speculative, and even more than that, they're inquisitive. . . ."

All right. But no one just goes from one moment to the next deciding to kill himself, because you need a certain amount of time to plan. At the very least you've got to put the pills in the water, or go to the top of the high-rise to jump. It takes a couple of minutes, and maybe the moment passes. . . . What do you say to that?

"Nothing."

Would you like to change the subject?

"Yes, to what?"

In the car on the way here you said you always wanted to be different than other people.

"That's what everyone wants."

Not me. People who stand out from the mainstream would rather just blend in.

"Fair enough, just so there's no misunderstanding. . . . We need to look into that. There are two sides, of course. Someone who has a tendency to stand out is always going to try to drop out of sight. He doesn't really want to stand out. He just wants to kibitz and eat and be as simpleminded as anyone else. That's what I wanted when I came here. I thought I'd keep a couple of cows, and go out to the stalls to milk them, and put on some hip waders and overalls, probably covered in shit, stinking, dirty, eight weeks without a bath, just to blend in with the people around here. But it doesn't work. It won't work, because you can't consciously reinvent yourself."

Did you try to?

"I tried everything, and then I realized it was just a waste of time.

You go through life standing out, and you still have all these eccentric, brutal, awful, rigid, wrong-headed things inside you, they're in everyone, in anyone. You can blend in beneath a hundred Loden jackets, yuk it up with the regulars, take an enormous pleasure in a well-prepared noodle soup on a Sunday afternoon, fruit tart for Easter, but it won't work. You're different, even though you don't want to be, apart from the fact that everyone can see we're all the same and we're all different, and apart from the fact that we all let ourselves be flattened by the same rolling pin. Like those rare plants that grow in the swamps that shoot up too high and get exposed and imperiled. It would be stupid for a tiger lily or a giant aster to try to blend in with the liverwort, even though they'd be better off down there, but they're proud of being a tiger lily. On the one hand, you want to be better and more wonderful than other people, and on the other, you want to be protected like the liverwort. That's the horrible thing, the most terrible thing about every situation is that it doesn't work. You have to come to terms with who you are and make the best of it."

Are there certain kinds of people whom you feel comfortable with?

"There's no one I know whom I would really want to spend a lot of time with. For any lengthy period of time it would be impossible. For example, I can't imagine having anyone stay in my house for two days and nights, *wurst* whoever, except for my eighty-five-year-old Tante, and even with her I can only do it under certain conditions, and it's so difficult that it verges on the grotesque, which actually makes it somewhat bearable. But anything longer than a week is out of the question."

Did you ever live with anyone other than your Tante?

"At boarding school and in the hospital, but no one since."

Do you have friends you visit?

"That's hard too, because reciprocity is the problem, and in the area around here, if I may be frank, there isn't really anybody I'd like to know. I know a couple of people whom I see just to relax. I can let my hair down, but it's pretty much impossible to find people I can talk to on the same level."

Does the fact that you're a famous writer mean that people approach you with a sense of awe?

"Yes, and it's stupid, because in the end it's always me who stays the same, and other people who treat me differently, and get all tense and strange, and just nip at my heels and say I've changed, which isn't true. So I think, why should I even go there, just to listen to stuff like that all the time. I don't have to. So over time I've come to feel best by myself. It's enough for me to be able to go to a café from time to time and listen to people talking. I don't need to talk to them. But sometimes I do feel the need, and I do have people to talk to, in Brussels or Vienna or Zurich, wherever, but it's really hard. I'd have to move to the city, which is something I can't do for health reasons, because the city would kill me eventually. Deep down I'm not really a country person. I have no interest whatsoever in nature, in plants or birds, I can't tell anything apart. I don't even know what a blackbird looks like. But I know perfectly well that I can't live in the city for any length of time because of my bronchia. I won't be leaving my farmhouse in the winter, because being in the city would just about kill me. There are only two options: Either stay in the city, where it's interesting, which would kill me, or have just one person, which just gets on your nerves after a while. You're never going to come to terms with it."

Aren't you at risk of becoming totally isolated or maybe even going insane?

"Nowadays I try to make sure I have some occasional artistic contact. I force myself to curb my lack of enthusiasm. So my current independence consists of the freedom to force myself to do things. If the impulse doesn't come from without, it comes from within. Otherwise you couldn't exist. In principle there's no great difference between the man who is impelled by external demands to do something and the one who can more or less do whatever he wants. I don't understand why this so-called freedom is accorded so much importance. You know, twenty years ago I didn't know if I could mail a letter because I didn't have enough money for a stamp. Today if I decided I wanted to circle the world five times with my eyes glued open so I could see everything I could do it, but I don't know if that's something special. Whether it means anything if someone sits down and piles up a bunch of rocks, digs up a field, saws some logs, and builds himself a little cottage and a little hotel with a little bed here and a little bed there and scraps it and starts over, I don't know. Everyone has to do what he wants based on his necessities and his opportunities."

Isn't it difficult when the opportunities so rarely go along with the necessities?

"I think they tend to go together. If you work really hard you'll get there, whether it's the prison or the institution. I'd prefer the institution, but maybe I'll end up in both, who knows?"

The mental institution has the advantage, because you could sit around and insult people all day and it wouldn't bother anyone because no one would take you seriously. You'd have the freedom of the insane. But you probably have that already. At one point in your book The Voice Imitator *you more or less call for the assassination of all the heads of state in central Europe. Had you brought this out in a political journal rather than with a literary publisher under the protective mantle of art, you might be standing trial as a terrorist sympathizer.*

"I am a sympathizer. I just don't know what for."

I mean, you can say whatever you want, and it gets published and doesn't scare anyone.

"I don't know about that. I wrote a letter to *Die Zeit* around three months ago, a spur-of-the-moment thing against Chancellor Kreisky. They let it sit for five weeks and then wrote me to say they were going to pass it on to someone else, and it just got scuttled. . . . I'd just like to say that I'm just as put out by machinations and capriciousness as anyone else. If people don't want anyone to get under Kreisky's skin because he's so beloved and looks like such a nice man, there's not much point to it, if I may put it in my ironic manner, and of course it's not going to get published."

Did you campaign to have it published?

"Fighting the editorial board of *Die Zeit* with all of its friendly opportunists would be stupid. It would be pointless."

What did you say about Kreisky?

"Well, there was this stupid article on him in *Die Zeit*, so mealy-mouthed, as is their wont, and I just wrote them a letter calling him a senile old fart. . . . Another example: The Deutsche Akademie sent me a catalog collecting the signatures of all the Büchnerpreis winners. I was one of the last ones they sent it to, and when I got it, it was all dog-eared, they'd sent it everywhere else, to Canetti in London, to Uwe Johnson, and I don't know who else, and I just thought I'd be an idiot to offer up my signature to an authorized history, so I didn't do it, and I don't know why I'm telling you this now."

As a justification for your aloofness?

"Yes, but all the people who signed the thing, these Canettis and Frisches and Koeppens, they're all bright people, and they still let themselves get sucked into these witless affairs, or they go off and have lunch with [former German Bundespräsident] Herr Scheel—let them. I don't because I think he's a horrible, awful person, and his wife's an old goat. Why should I eat and drink with them? I won't do it."

What do you have against Scheel? Do you know him?

"I don't need to know him. It's enough to look at him and listen to him talk. A person's physiognomy is very interesting—it's all in there."

Is there anyone whom you don't think is an idiot?

"There's no one, that's just it."

But like I said, if that's the case, you insult everyone equally, and no one takes you seriously, and your attacks leave no mark.

"Why won't they? Things either have an effect or they don't. You can't let those considerations stop you."

Did the uproar at the University of Munich upset you?

"It would have been pointless to be upset by it. Those people had no idea what they wanted. Intellectuals who suck up to the rabble to win them over are hypocrites. You can't teach them anything, and you can't convert the mass into any kind of elite. I'd just as soon leave before they knock my Tante on her ear. I'm opposed to giving lectures; I didn't even want to do it. But it was just that one time, so I didn't care. I have such an overwhelming need to write, which is a plus, because you can take all that anger and work with it. You need irritants like that, and you don't need to worry about missing something if you sleep in, because I have a Munich like that every week, everywhere, at every turn. These things happen all the time. If you're looking for it, you can get all the anger and aggression you need."

Who are you thinking of when you write?

"That's a stupid question, you know."

Well, it's not that stupid. Are you thinking of someone who makes you angry or maybe someone who understands you?

"I'm not thinking about anybody who might be reading me, because I'm not interested in who's reading me. I enjoy writing and that's it. I just want to make it better and more convincing, that's all, just like a dancer always wants to dance better, but it has to take place on its own, because everyone—no matter what they do—approaches perfection by having to do something again and again, and that applies as much to the ping-pong player as it does to the show jumper, or the writer, or the swimmer, or the maid or the house cleaner. After five years you'll be a better house cleaner than you were on day one, when you just messed up everything and wrecked more things than you cleaned."

Is writing for you an attempt at making contact?

"I don't want any contact. What do I need contact for? It's just the opposite: I've always turned people away when they wanted it. I throw their letters away because it's impossible from a purely technical point of view to read through them all, otherwise I'd have to be one of those asshole writers with two secretaries to answer everything and everyone, every schmuck who comes sucking up to them with some little note. I refused to do it from the start—I can't do it, it's impossible to spend every day going through two or three letters, after four months I'd be completely choking on them. That's why I don't let myself get involved in it. I'd have nothing left. I want my work to be published, and I want to get it done. So I put it in a box so it doesn't get misplaced and looks nice. I write on cheap, crappy carbon paper, and I like the transition to the finished galleys, and my publisher sends me some money every month, and that's the end of the story."

Then why did you invite me out if you find contact so repulsive?

"Well, that's just how it is. What do you want me to say? I don't have any system. I do it one time, and then I skip the next hundred times. I don't find you repulsive and it's total *wurst* to me what you do with me. OK, it's not *wurst*, but I thought, I'll just give him what he wants, because I'm actually a person who gives people what they want, as opposed to people who are constantly trying to stir things up. But sometimes I feel like doing that too. I was a brat as a child and fooled around all the time. You're no saint either, I know, but it doesn't matter. I have no preconceptions. You were here eight years ago, I saw you then, and now you're here again. What else can I say? You're probably wondering what it would take to get a rise out of me, because none of it really means anything to me, and my time on this earth is too short to put up with it—life's too short to waste on laundry and correspondence. You might find twenty letters from me somewhere—that would be a lot, because I'm not interested. If someone turns up, he's here, and I'm not going to get in his way. When I call someone on the phone it's for business. I'm very egotistical. I only talk to my publishers or with the theater when it has to do with one of my plays, and if that all went away tomorrow it would be the same to me. I'd just go out to a quarry somewhere and sit around and be a truck dispatcher, and make three times as much as I do now. But I'm not interested in giving up my writing and the conditions I find myself in, I enjoy them too much, and I don't need anything else, and I feel like I'm making something no one can imitate, not just here, but anywhere else in the world. That probably sounds a little arrogant, but let's compare it to railway cars. You get on one and it's filthy, and you get on another and it's clean. . . . The ideal age for writing prose is between forty and sixty, maybe a little earlier, but I'm a late bloomer and it would be madness for me to quit just when I'm reaching my peak. I'd have to be insane. But then who's immune from insanity . . . ?"

I don't want you to give up writing. I simply thought that contact with someone who understands you and likes you might be beneficial for your work.

"What's best for me is being totally on my own, even with all that goes along with it, which is mostly unpleasantness, but I like it, I love it, things that others can't take. If you put Handke out here, he'd be running off to his daughter in tears after three days. He's a soft, weak mama's boy who's always going on about being alone. Exactly the kind of person who can't stand to be alone, because it takes so much out of you. You can't write about it the way I do if you can't handle it, *wurst*, how important it is to you. Handke and his precious daughter. That's something I find absolutely repulsive, I've always been opposed to families, all that sort of thing—I simply cannot stand people with families, children, they stuff the kid in a snowsuit and all this stuff for Christmas, and then go off to Sankt-Moritz with the kid and their chic publisher, it's so repulsive to me, it makes me sick, people who go here and there and get invited to America, and give a lecture here and a lecture there, and then go running off to their editor whenever they do something so it makes the papers the next morning—it's horrible. I don't like it, and I won't do it either. This naturally arouses other people's irritation and dislike. It doesn't matter. It's my strength, that I can take it, that I can keep my cool. People can do whatever they want. If I did things based on what people have been saying and writing about me for the past fifteen years I would've killed myself a hundred times over, because it's always the same. When *Frost* came out, on one page someone wrote it was the greatest book ever written and on the next page someone else said it was shit. That's always been the case with me. It's never been any different."

Could you explain why you find families with children so repulsive?

"Probably because my own experience took a very unhappy and uncomfortable form."

At our first interview you said all mothers should have their ears cut off.

"I said that because it's foolish to think you're bringing children into the world. It's too easy. What you get are adults, not children. Women give birth to horrible, sweaty, fat innkeepers and mass murderers—that's what they give birth to, not children. People say they're having a little kid, but what they're really having is an eighty-year-old man oozing sweat, and stinking and blind and limping, so gouty he can't move—that's what they're bringing into the world. But people don't see it, it's just nature having its way so this shit can go on. It's all *wurst* to me. It's stupid to even bring it up, it's like me fighting this high-tension line. It's getting built, and that's it. My situation is like one of those funny little birds . . . I don't want to say parrots, they're magnificent birds, but one of those little squawking birds. The ones that just make some noise and then take off again and disappear. The forest is deep, and so is the darkness. Some little owl in there who won't shut up. No more than that. I wouldn't want to be anything more than that either."

Your distinctive characteristic, as you describe it in your autobiography, is indifference.

"I can't let that go without adding that it's not that I'm indifferent, it's just that I have to be indifferent to things that aren't going anywhere. That's the only thing to be said about that."

How important is your Tante for your life and work?

"She has without a doubt been the most important person in my life since I was nineteen."

Does the thought of her death frighten you?

"I find the thought of it almost unbearable, but I recognize that it's going to happen soon enough. I can sort of put it to one side when I talk about it frankly, but yeah, maybe. I'm resigned to it. . . . But the one thing I can say is that when it happens, it happens. When she dies she'll be dead. And then I can call you . . . 'Uncle.'"

So there's always a person who's necessary, whom you can be with?

"There's always a milkmaid who'll turn up. There isn't, no, there isn't."

Do you agree with the sentence "I want to be alone"?

"I've got nothing else, you know? For me to live the way I want, there's only solitude. It's just that proximity kills me. I'm not complaining. Everyone's responsible for themselves."

Is there any substitute for writing for you?

"There's no substitute. I could go ride a bike, but do you think that's a substitute?"

What would you do if you ran out of inspiration?

"Questions like that don't go anywhere. It's like asking a singer what she'd do without her voice. What's she supposed to say? That she'll sing mute? Whenever you write something you think it's over, you'll never do it again, you don't want to do it again. I'm not interested in that."

What if you met the love of your life tomorrow?

"I couldn't do anything to stop it."

TRANSLATOR'S NOTE. An abridged version of this interview appeared in *Die Zeit* (June 29, 1979). The full transcript was published as *André Müller im Gespräch mit Thomas Bernhard* (Bibliothek der Provinz, 1992). Bernhard's farmhouse is in Ohlsdorf, Upper Austria. The 1971 visit alluded to in the interview was facilitated by the Baroness Agi Teufl, the mutual friend referenced above.

NOTES ON CONTRIBUTORS

JOHN ASHBERY's most recent book of poems is *Planisphere* (Ecco). His translation of Rimbaud's *Illuminations* will be published next spring by Norton.

MATT BELL (www.mdbell.com) is the author of *How They Were Found* (Keyhole Press). His fiction has been selected for inclusion in *Best American Mystery Stories 2010* and *Best American Fantasy 2*. He is editor of the *Collagist* and of Dzanc Books' Best of the Web series.

ROSS BENJAMIN won the 2010 Helen and Kurt Wolff Translator's Prize for his translation of Michael Maar's *Speak, Nabokov* (Verso Books). His other translations include Friedrich Hölderlin's *Hyperion* (Archipelago Books), Kevin Vennemann's *Close to Jedenew* (Melville House), Joseph Roth's *Job* (Archipelago, forthcoming), and Thomas Pletzinger's *Funeral for a Dog* (Norton, forthcoming).

THOMAS BERNHARD (1931–1979) was a novelist, playwright, and poet whose works include *Gargoyles, Correction, Woodcutters, The Lime Works, Wittgenstein's Nephew, The Loser* (all Vintage), *Histrionics* (plays), and the story collection *The Voice Imitator* (both University of Chicago). *My Prizes, An Accounting*, his collected recollections of the farcical ceremonies celebrating his many distinguished prizes, is just out from Knopf. Bernhard, who lived in Austria, is widely considered to be one of the most important writers of his generation.

H. G. CARRILLO is the author of *Loosing My Espanish* (Anchor). Carrillo is an assistant professor of English at George Washington University and serves on the PEN Faulkner Foundation's board of directors. His contribution to *Urban Arias* is from a novel in progress.

BRIAN EVENSON is the author of ten books of fiction, most recently the limited-edition novella *Baby Leg* (New York Tyrant Press). In 2009, he also published the novel *Last Days* (Underland Press), which won the American Library Association's award for Best Horror Novel of 2009, and the story collection *Fugue State* (Coffee House Press). Evenson lives and works in Providence, Rhode Island, where he directs Brown University's Literary Arts Program.

YVAN GOLL (1891–1950) was the pseudonym of Isaac Lang (who also published under the names Iwan Lassang and Tristan Torsi). Beginning as a German Expressionist poet, Goll moved to Paris after the First World War and began writing in French. Exiled to America in 1939, he also wrote in English. Goll coauthored the Zenitist manifesto in Belgrade (1921), where *Paris Brennt* appeared as a Zenit book the same year. A somewhat different French version was included in his 1923 collection *Le nouvel Orphée* (illustrated by Delaunay, Grosz, and Léger).

LYN HEJINIAN's most recent published book of poetry is *Saga / Circus* (Omnidawn, 2008). A collection of collaborations written with Jack Collom, *Situations, Sings,* also came out in 2008 (Adventures in Poetry). Hejinian is one of ten participants in another collaborative project, *The Grand Piano: An Experiment in Collective Autobiography, 1975–2008*; the tenth and final volume of *The Grand Piano* appeared in September 2010 (Mode A).

CHRISTOPHER HELLWIG's work has appeared or is forthcoming in *Indiana Review, Web Conjunctions, Bateau,* and *Fairy Tale Review*. More of his collaborative tales with Michael J. Lee can be found in *Sleepingfish* 8, published under the name The Brothers Goat.

Work by artist STEPHEN HICKS has been exhibited at the Parrish Art Museum, Yale's A&A Gallery, Cooper Union, the American Academy of Arts and Letters, and at other galleries across the country. Shows of his work have received attention in *Art in America, Newsday, The New York Times, The New York Sun,* and elsewhere. Represented by the George Billis Gallery, Hicks lives and works in New York.

COLLEEN HOLLISTER's stories have recently appeared or are forthcoming in *Versal, Quarterly West, The Southeast Review, LIT,* and elsewhere. A novella, *Collage with Girl and Rooftop,* was published by Burnside Review Press as the winner of its 2009 Fiction Chapbook Competition. She lives in Tuscaloosa, Alabama.

TIM HORVATH (www.timhorvath.com) is the author of *Circulation* (sunnyoutside) and stories in *Conjunctions, Fiction, Puerto del Sol, Alimentum,* and elsewhere. He teaches creative writing at Boston's Grub Street and Chester College of New England.

GREG HRBEK is the author of a novel, *The Hindenburg Crashes Nightly* (Bard/Avon), and a forthcoming story collection, *Destroy All Monsters* (University of Nebraska Press). His short fiction has appeared in *Harper's, Salmagundi, Black Warrior Review, The 2007 Robert Olen Butler Prize Stories,* and *The Best American Short Stories 2009* (Houghton Mifflin).

ETGAR KERET has been published in thirty languages in thirty-five countries, including work in English in *The New York Times, Le Monde,* and the *Guardian*. In 2007, Keret and Shira Gefen won the Cannes Film Festival's Camera d'Or Award for their movie *Jellyfish,* as well as the Best Director Award of the French Artists' and Writers' Guild. In 2010 France made Keret a French Chevalier de l'Ordre des Arts et des Lettres.

PAUL LA FARGE is the author of three books: *The Artist of the Missing* and *Haussmann, or the Distinction* (both Farrar, Straus and Giroux) and *The Facts of Winter* (McSweeney's Books).

MICHAEL J. LEE lives in New Orleans. His first collection of short stories, *Something in My Eye,* is forthcoming from Sarabande Books.

Photographer DEBORAH LUSTER has produced two books with C. D. Wright, *Just Whistle* (Kelsey Street Press) and *The Lost Roads Project: A Walk-in Book of*

Arkansas (University of Arkansas Press). Her work is in the permanent collections of the Los Angeles County Museum of Art, the Houston Museum of Fine Arts, the National Archives, the San Francisco Museum of Modern Art, the Whitney, and many other institutions.

JOHN MADERA's work has appeared or is forthcoming in *The Believer, The Brooklyn Rail, Eimae,* and *Corduroy Mountain,* among other journals. He is the managing editor of *Big Other,* online at www.johnmadera.com.

NORMAN MANEA is the author of *October, Eight O'Clock* (Grove Press), *The Years of Apprenticeship of Augustus the Fool,* and *The Black Envelope* (both available from Polirom). In 2006, he was awarded the French Prix Medicis for Foreign Literature for his memoir *The Hooligan's Return* (Farrar, Straus and Giroux). He has received a MacArthur Fellowship, the Literary Lion Medal of the New York National Library, the National Jewish Book Award, and the International Nonino Prize for Literature. Manea teaches European literature and is writer in residence at Bard College.

SUSAN McCARTY's stories and essays have recently appeared in or are forthcoming from *Barrelhouse, Hotel Amerika, Iowa Review,* and *Wigleaf.*

ANDRÉ MÜLLER is an Austrian author and journalist who has published essays, articles, and interviews in venues such as *Der Spiegel, Stern, Die Zeit, Weltwoche,* and *Playboy.* In addition to his conversations with Bernhard, Müller has conducted interviews with figures such as Salman Rushdie, Claus Peymann, Wim Wenders, Joseph Beuys, Peter Handke, Rainer Werner Fassbinder, Jeanne Moreau, Edward Albee, and many others.

JOYCE CAROL OATES is the author, most recently, of the short story collection *Sourland,* which includes fiction previously published in *Conjunctions,* and the essay collection *In Rough Country* (both Ecco). She is on the faculty at Princeton University and has been a member, since 1978, of the American Academy of Arts and Letters.

STEPHEN O'CONNOR (www.stephenoconnor.net) is the author of two collections of short fiction, *Here Comes Another Lesson* (Free Press) and *Rescue* (Harmony Books), and two works of nonfiction. He teaches in the MFA programs of Columbia University and Sarah Lawrence.

DAVID OHLE's most recent publication (Calamari Press) is *Boons/The Camp,* two novellas under one cover. He lives in Lawrence, Kansas.

PETER ORNER is the author of *The Second Coming of Mavala Shikongo* (Little, Brown), which was a finalist for the Los Angeles Times Book Prize and won the Bard Fiction Prize, and *Esther Stories* (Mariner), winner of the Rome Prize from the Academy of Arts and Letters. His new novel, *Love and Shame and Love,* will be out next year from Little, Brown.

JED RASULA is Helen S. Lanier Distinguished Professor at the University of Georgia and the author of numerous books on modern poetry, most recently *Modernism and Poetic Inspiration: The Shadow Mouth* (Palgrave). With Steve McCaffery, he edited *Imagining Language* (MIT), and with Tim Conley he edited the international anthology *Burning City: Poems of Metropolitan Modernity* (Action Books, forthcoming 2011).

KAREN RUSSELL is the author of the short story collection *St. Lucy's Home for Girls Raised by Wolves* and the forthcoming novel *Swamplandia!*, both published by Knopf.

MICHAEL SHEEHAN is an assistant fiction editor for *DIAGRAM*. He is currently working on a novel.

MIRIAM SHLESINGER teaches in the Department of Translation and Interpreting Studies at Israel's Bar Ilan University. She is coeditor of *Interpreting: International Journal of Research and Practice in Interpreting*, and has translated over thirty plays as well as novels and short stories by Israeli playwrights and authors.

ADAM SIEGEL's recent translations from German, Russian, and Czech have been published by or are forthcoming from Dalkey Archive Press, University of Pittsburgh Press, and Nakladatelství Divus.

SONDRA SILVERSTON is a native New Yorker who, since 1970, has lived in Israel, where she teaches literary translation at Beit Berl College. Her other translations of Etgar Keret include Chatto & Windus's *The Nimrod Flipout* and *Missing Kissinger* (shortlisted for the Frank O'Connor Short Story Award), as well as *The Girl on the Fridge*, from Farrar, Straus and Giroux.

EMMA SMITH-STEVENS is from New York City. She currently lives in Gainesville, where she is an MFA candidate at the University of Florida. This is her first appearance in print.

PHILIPPE SOUPAULT (1887–1990) was a French poet, novelist, critic, and political activist. Along with André Breton and Louis Aragon, he cofounded the review *Littérature*, arguably the genesis of Surrealism. "Westwego" was initially published by *Éditions de la librairie six* in 1922. The original book may be viewed at http://sdrc.lib.uiowa.edu/dada/westwego/index.htm.

D. E. STEWARD's "Luglia" is one of 284 months, the tenth to appear in *Conjunctions* or *Web Conjunctions*. The project, *Chroma*, is now approaching eight books of three years each.

DONNA STONECIPHER is the author of three books of poems, most recently *The Cosmopolitan*, selected by John Yau for the 2007 National Poetry Series and published in 2008 by Coffee House Press.

ADAM VEAL holds an MFA in literary arts from Brown University, where he cocurated the Incuhabitations international reading series and served on the organizing committee for Brown's 2010 Electronic Literature Organization conference. This is his first appearance in print.

MARJORIE WELISH has written several books of poetry, most recently *Words Group* and *Isle of the Signatories* (both Coffee House Press). As a poet and artist she coauthored *Oaths? Questions* with James Siena (Granary Books). *In the Futurity Lounge* is to be published next year.

Based in Berlin, photographer MICHAEL WESELY has exhibited his work in extended-exposure photography internationally. In 2001, at the invitation of the Museum of Modern Art, he created the Open Shutter Project, leaving his cameras' shutters open for thirty-four months to document MOMA's expansion and renovation.

DIANE WILLIAMS is the author of six books of fiction and the editor of the literary annual *NOON*. Her recent stories have appeared in *Harper's Magazine*. She is a recipient of a 2010 Pushcart Prize.

C. D. WRIGHT's most recent title is *One With Others: a little book of her days* (Copper Canyon). "Breathtaken" was composed for Deborah Luster's exhibition *Tooth for an Eye: A Chorography of Violence in Orleans Parish.*

ANDREW ZAWACKI is the author of three books of poetry: *Petals of Zero Petals of One* (Talisman House), *Anabranch* (Wesleyan), and *By Reason of Breakings* (Georgia). His translation of French poet Sébastien Smirou, *My Lorenzo*, is forthcoming from Burning Deck and available in part on *Web Conjunctions*. His translation of "Westwego" is forthcoming in *The Burning City* (Action Books), edited by Jed Rasula and Tim Conley.

Burning Deck Spring 2010

Anne Portugal: ***absolute bob***

[Série d'Ecriture, No. 23; tr. from the French by Jennifer Moxley]

bob, a brave little guy (joker, operator, sheer energy?) bops in the manner of a video-game through the ways a poem inhabits sense or nonsense, speeds or slows, slides into forms or undoes them. bob occupies his virtual field of action in perpetual motion, beats down doors, explores corridors, removes walls, strikes sparks from repetition, sets fire to "the same old," pulls the levers of creation. 24 chapters, images per second, hours in the day of a man who must exhaust himself in command performances that gradually asphyxiate even the fabrication of verse.
Anne Portugal lives and teaches in Paris.

Poetry, 120 pages, offset, smyth-sewn, ISBN 978-1-936194-02-5 original pbk. $14

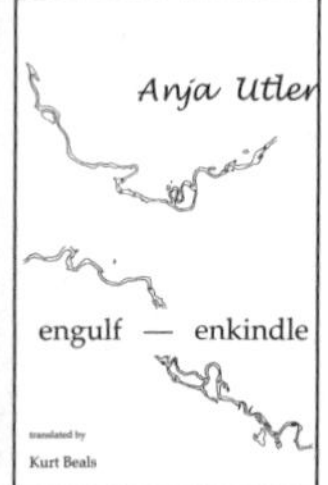

Anja Utler: **engulf — enkindle**

[Dichten=, No.12; tr. from the German by Kurt Beals]

Utler's poems touch the ground where feeling and thinking take form and burst into language. Their interweaving pulls us into an almost undifferentiated, preconscious world where the human body and the surrounding landscape are fused. Stretching syntax and semantics, Utler's poems trace speech to its roots in the lungs, throat, tongue, until it emerges as sound and song.

Anja Utler lives in Vienna and Regensburg. *münden — entzüngeln* (2004) received the coveted Leonce-und-Lena Prize.

Poetry, 96 pages, offset, smyth-sewn, ISBN13: 978-1-936194-03-2, original pbk. $14

Jane Unrue: ***Life of a Star***

"The fragmentary, floating images finally cohere into an enigmatic portrait of a burned out visionary, an object lesson on the fleetingness of desire, of the perpetuity of pain, on the doubtful, but nevertheless worthwhile, possibility that language may bring meaning to life, or, at the very least, help one to endure its vicissitudes."— John Madera, *The Brooklyn Rail*
"A phantom refinement of the celebrity-autobiography genre.... — it's entirely a perfection."— Gary Lutz, *The Believer*

Novella, 112 pp., ISBN13: 978-1-936194-00-1, original pbk. $14

Jennifer Martenson: ***Unsound***

"Concise, extraordinarily thoughtful, often challenging, and sometimes sexy.... Honesty and desire (especially lesbian desire) are hard to consider apart from received ideas, but impossible to portray accurately within them: often abstract...the poems strain against the dilemma they portray, while never failing (once you look hard) to make sense."
— *Publishers Weekly*

Poetry, 64 pp., ISBN13: 978-1-936194-01-8, original pbk. $14

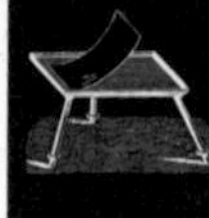

Orders: SPD: www.spdbooks.org, 1-800/869-7553, In Europe: www.audiatur.no/bokhandel
www.burningdeck.com

The Imperfect
George Tysh

92 pages, paperback
Drawings by Janet Hamrick,
ISBN 0-935992-33-2
$14.00

The Imperfect

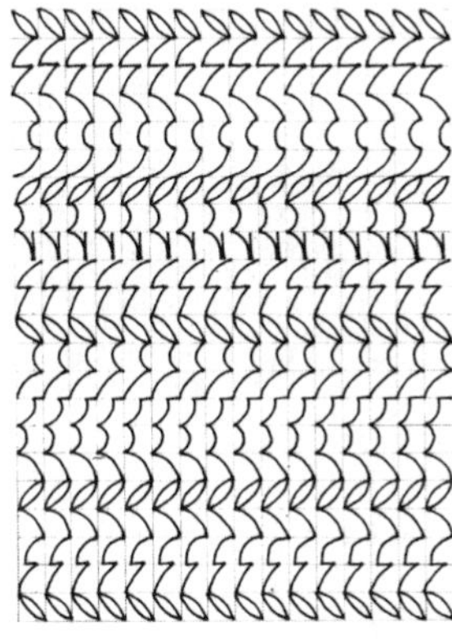

George Tysh

The nine-line poems, the four-line poems, the three-line poems -- though all of them sparkle, it is not for his mastery of form that we value George Tysh's poetry. Rather we do so in response to his empathy, almost the simple pulse of a muscle, the "dictum to rectum" effect he writes of in a lovely poem. He knows as much about the way things look as he does about the needs that went into their making and abeyance. The poems of The Imperfect are written in Detroit, a "motor city" outside of which "methyl walls perspire" and "black men and white men / walk the streets" -- yet they insinuate themselves into the brains of the feeling everywhere around the earth. I'm a sucker for this sort of thing. It's like Grace Jones used to say, George Tysh isn't perfect, but he's perfect for me. Kevin Killian

uab
united artists books

A book of monologues written for a one-woman show that Hawkins performed in 2001 and 2002 at the Boulder Museum of Contemporary Art and Naropa University in Boulder, and at Joe's Pub in New York. Worldly and wise, sharp, alert to all human foibles, Bobbie Louise Hawkins gives us these observations in her familiar, wry and intimate tone. Like no one else, she brings us all home. Joanne Kyger

Absolutely Eden
Bobbie Louise Hawkins

89 pages, paperback
Cover photo by
Jane Dalrymple-Hollo
ISBN 0-935992-35-9
$14.00

These and other UAB titles available from Small Press Distribution spdbooks.org